THE SECRETS WE KEEP

MIA HAYES

FINNSTAR

This book is a work of fiction. Any references to historical events, real people, or real places are used fictitiously. Other names, characters, places, and events are products of the author's imagination, and any resemblance to actual events, locales, or persons, living or dead, is entirely coincidental.

ISBN 978-0-692-11352-3 (pbk)
ISBN 978-1-386-15780-9 (ebook)

Front cover Design: RBA Designs

❀ Created with Vellum

For the ones who get me through.

BEFORE

SURVIVING THE SUBURBS

H ere's a fact: *In my suburb, everything you see — the perfection, the picket fences, the perky boobs – is fake.*

Another fact: *Popularity matters here. It's the key to everything.*

Last fact: *My husband and kids love this place, so I'm toughing it out because the schools are excellent, the lawns are pristine, and my kids can bike to the local pool. Really, if I were a kid, I would think I lived in Nirvana, too.*

As for me, I'm making the best of it. Or so I tell myself. I have "friends," I go to parties, I have lunches. But real friends? Ha! This is the suburbs. You don't have friends. You have people you hang out and get drunk with.

I have plenty of those.

So who do I get drunk with? Who spills their guts to me? That's easy. Everyone. But you're not interested in the ordinary folks. No, what you want to hear about is the Bitch Brigade aka the Plastics, The Barbies, The Heathers. Whatever you want to call them, they're still bitches. Sweet to your face, knife in the back. And ruthless to each other.

The head bitch in charge is Karen Newbold. It's widely known that there are three women who run Waterford, and she's the one who runs them all. These women chair every committee and seem lost when Karen isn't around to tell them what to do.

Which brings me to Alexis Frond. According to Karen, she has a drinking problem. Carries a tall Starbucks tumbler of vodka with her wherever she goes and has an obvious eating disorder in that she never eats. Poor thing lives on secret cigarettes and booze. Her three kids are monsters, and her husband is on the golf course all the time, which may be why she drinks so much.

Karen and Alexis both wish they looked like Veronica White. She of the glowing skin and flowing butter-blond locks. There are rumors her husband has been cheating on her. In fact, while drunk one night, Karen strongly hinted he's cheating with someone in the community — but no one knows with whom. I'm not sure the rumors are true, but I've met him, and he's charming as sin. So maybe.

And then there's me. Your anonymous, snarky narrator. I collect secrets - marital, financial, sexual. The dark ones people can barely admit to themselves. And I file them away here. Aren't I sweet?

Welcome to Waterford, bitches!

Piles of gray snow blocked the path to my car, and slush stuck to my Uggs, but I kept my eyes trained on my phone as I walked. The familiar face – brown eyes and stylish chestnut hair and too-wide smile – staring back at me made my heart pound, and I inhaled deeply before exhaling for a seven-count, something my therapist assured me was the fastest way to fight anxiety.

"Elizabeth!"

I jerked my head up, lost my balance, and collided into the car next to me while sliding to the ground and sprawling flat on my back. My giant handbag landed on my head, and my Coke slammed into the car before splashing back out all over me.

"Oh my gosh! Are you okay?" Sarah Cole peered down at me. "Elizabeth?"

I shoved my bag aside and blinked up at her as stars sparked behind my eyes. "I think I'm okay."

"Can you get up? I'd help you and all, but if you have a neck injury...well Kyle says it isn't a good idea to move people who've fallen." Kyle had a reputation for being a dick, so I wasn't surprised he'd tell Sarah not to help people when they were down.

"I'm fine," I said as I attempted to roll over in the dirty, Coke-stained slush and onto my side. I was so going to hurt the next day. "How are you?"

Sarah squatted next to me and picked up my phone. She glanced at the screen before handing it to me. "A friend from Portland?"

"Yes." I shoved the phone into my bag. "I was just catching up on Facebook."

Sarah flashed a white smile before lending me her gloved hand, which I gladly accepted. "Did you see the blog? The one about Karen?"

Thankfully, that's what she wanted to talk about. "I did. It's pretty bad, isn't it?"

I expected Sarah to jump to Karen and her friends' defense – that's what I would have done - but Sarah giggled. "Yeah, but it's kind of funny, isn't it? I mean, everyone knows Alexis keeps vodka in that water bottle of hers. And Pete is totally cheating on Veronica."

"Allegedly," I answered. "No one has proof about that."

"Who do you think wrote it?"

"I don't know. Maybe one of their husbands?" It was so ridiculous it almost made sense.

Sarah shrugged. "Anyway, I just ran into Karen. She likes my new gloves."

There was no concern about how Karen felt about the blog – and I'm positive she gave Sarah an earful. No, there was just delight over the fact Karen had noticed her gloves. They were a deep berry color, but other than that look like normal leather gloves.

"They're pretty," I said.

"Kyle picked them out for me as a thank-you gift for holding down the fort." Sarah admired the gloves. "He's been super busy at work, so we don't see him much, but it's okay. Letitia and I have the kids on a tight schedule." I didn't know who Letitia was, but I assumed Sarah meant her nanny. Most women - even the stay at home moms - had one.

Wet snow clung to my jeans and seeped through the fabric and onto my skin. When I adjusted my hat, it was sticky from the Coke splattering into it. Wonderful. I hated everything icy and cold. Like winter. I was from the West Coast, land of...well, I was from Portland, land of rain and fog. But still, we rarely had snow.

"You know what? Let's have lunch soon, okay?" Sarah said. It was like my fall never happened, and I wasn't standing in the cold with soda dripping off my hat. She whipped out her iPhone. "Do you like a good, greasy burger? I do, but Kyle gets upset if he catches me eating one. The man doesn't understand that I can't help myself. I'm a Southern girl. I'm not allowed to say no to food...especially dessert."

We had never interacted much beyond the occasional party. She'd be there, I'd be there, and we'd both say 'hi' and make the necessary small talk. Sarah and I were Facebook friends and social acquaintances, but that's all.

So, her asking me to lunch was a huge deal. Huge. Like we were on our way to being friends huge. And pathetic, shadow of herself me was desperate for a friend.

"I love burgers," I said while trying not to sound over eager. "The greasier, the better."

"How does this Wednesday look? We could go to a new place out in Lodi where no one will catch us." She wiggled her eyebrows. "Because if it isn't a salad, it isn't Waterford approved."

"I'm pretty sure I'm free," I said as I fished my phone from the cavernous depths of my bag. When I found it, I clicked open the calendar for show. If I wasn't with Karen, I was always free – and I had no plans with Karen.

Sarah smiled brightly. "Perfect! I'll pick you up, okay?"

"That'll be great. I really hate driving in the snow."

"Oh, Elizabeth. You're going to have to get used to it at some point." Sarah air kissed my cheeks before hurrying into the warmth of Panera and leaving me alone in the parking lot with wet jeans and a bruised backside.

I gathered my things and tossed them onto the passenger seat. When Jason bought me this car, I thought the seat warmers were a funny novelty, but I quickly learned they're essential. Especially when your pants were drenched.

My house was only a few blocks from the Town Center, but it was enough time to ruminate. How awkward was I? Did Sarah think I was socially inept? Had I air kissed the right way?

But mostly I wondered if I had done enough that day. Had I really? I hung-out alone at Panera eating food I shouldn't and spoke with Sarah while dirty dishes sat in the sink and clean laundry waited — not in the basket, but on the counter — to be folded. The boys hadn't done their chores the night before, which made me look bad, but if I got through those, maybe Jason would give me a gold star instead of the usual high-five.

Jason.

Sometimes...

No. I needed to take that thought and push it aside. We were trying, and that's what mattered.

I pressed my hand against my bag and could feel the outline of my phone. Part of me wanted to smash it so I'd never have to see it again, but what good would that do?

It wouldn't change things. Nothing would.

Nothing ever could.

2

BETTER LATE THAN NEVER

Jason was late. As usual. I had fed the kids and gotten them ready for bed, and he still hadn't arrived. He wasn't answering his phone either which drove my mind to the absolute worst places. He knew not being able to reach him was one of my triggers, and yet it seemed to be happening more and more.

I clenched my phone before pulling up Facebook on the web browser. Just to be safe, because Jason liked to check up on me, I cleared the search history and closed my secret account before setting the phone on the counter.

My stomach grumbled, and I rewarded it with leftover chicken fingers from the boys' dinner. Nothing like cold, processed chicken parts to make me feel better about the shit way I ate.

After I finished inhaling my dinner, I tried Jason again. On the third ring, the garage door opened, and I hung up.

"Hey," I said as Jason walked in the door. His tie was loosened and his hair disheveled, but I tried not to think about what it may mean. What it could mean. "I've been calling you."

He placed a peck on my forehead. "Sorry. My phone ran out of juice in the tunnel. I had to make most of the ride with nothing to read. And of course, the Red Line was on fire again."

"That sucks." I waited for Jason to notice that my hair was curled, and my lips were a plummy-berry color. I waited for the compliment on my fitted LBD and stiletto heels. I thought maybe we could salvage the evening.

I waited, but he said nothing, so I swept past him, disappointed, and into the kitchen. Maybe his mind was too distracted from the ride home? Even with the metro, Jason's commute was hell. The traffic around DC made it impossible to get anywhere easily. We only lived twenty-five miles away, but it took an hour and a half some days for Jason to make the trip. "Since it's too late to go out, do you want me to heat up some leftovers?"

Jason dropped his bag on the ground near the counter. His hand brushed my phone, but he didn't pick it up. "Go out? What are you talking about? We never go out on weeknights."

"You said - when we talked this afternoon – that you'd be home early, and we could go out to dinner if I fed the kids first. Just you and me." I stopped fussing in the fridge, turned around, and gestured to my outfit. "Don't you remember?"

My husband scrunched up his face. He had such an expressive face and could never hide his thoughts. "I wouldn't have. I had a meeting at six, so why would I say I'd come home early?"

It was so typically Jason. Nothing was ever his fault. "I don't know. Maybe because you forgot about your meeting?"

"Elizabeth, don't. I think you misunderstood me. Don't go getting mad."

"I'm not mad. I'm frustrated. I clearly remember this conversation, and you're telling me it didn't happen. I even dressed up for it."

Jason wrapped his arms around me and pulled me into a suffocating hug. His biceps were solid and thick, the result of gym time that came at the expense of 'us' time. "Sweetheart, maybe you need your meds adjusted again. You've really been struggling with your memory lately."

I leaned back and looked up at Jason. "No, I..."

The wall clock ticked steadily, and seconds slid into minutes. My shoulders heaved as I tried to make sense of what was happening.

Was Jason right? Did I invent the whole conversation? Had I imagined running into Sarah today, too? My sore ass said no, but my brain wasn't so sure.

When Jason released me, I turned toward the double oven, and my reflection stole my breath. My hair was pulled back, and I had lipstick on. I was pulled together, but it was there in my eyes. The panic and the confusion.

Breathe, Elizabeth, breathe. It's going to be okay.

"Hey," Jason said. "Where are you going in that brain of yours?"

Did I wear my thoughts like he did his? "We really didn't talk about this?"

"We really didn't."

I wandered into the family room and curled up on my favorite arm chair. Weight pressed down on my shoulders, and I hung my head while blinking back the sting of tears. "Do you think I'm starting an episode?"

"Hey, don't cry. There's no reason." Jason held my hands between his and kissed them. "Call Dr. Carter. Get in and be seen before things get worse."

He was right. Dr. Carter always knew what to do. "I'll call her in the morning."

Jason brushed my cheek with his fingertips, and I put on my brave smile. The one that told him I would be fine and was moving forward. "Good," he said. "Now what about those leftovers?"

"Oh, shit, I forgot about that. You're starving, aren't you?"

"Very." Jason plopped down on the couch and kicked his feet up on the cement coffee table.

"If you were one of the boys, I'd smack your feet down."

"You better not." Jason narrowed his eyes and gave the kind of laugh you have when you're about to make a half-serious joke. "Now, if you were a good wife, you'd fetch me a beer."

"Of course," I replied, making sure to keep my voice light. Little things, like getting Jason a beer, made him happy, and I needed to keep him happy. If I didn't...well, we'd been down that road once already. I couldn't do it again. "Do you want parm on your noodles?"

"You know I do."

I grated cheese on Jason's pasta, grabbed a beer from the drink fridge, and presented it all to him as he sat on the couch. He didn't bother to thank me, just took the plate and fixed his attention back on the television.

"Funny thing happened today," I said as I battled for my husband's attention. I'd gotten better over the course of the year of not reading into every little thing Jason did, but some days it was tougher than others.

"Yeah? Let me guess, Karen got her hair highlighted?" Jason shoveled pasta into his mouth. His honey brown eyes didn't leave the TV. He was watching CNN like he did every night because working in DC with politicians didn't fill his political news fix.

"No," I answered. "Someone started a blog called *Surviving the Suburbs*. They wrote some bitchy stuff about Karen Newbold, Veronica, and Alexis, and Stacey McLeod posted it on the Women of Waterford Facebook page."

"Wait, what?" Jason turned away from the TV. "Someone did what?"

"Wrote an unflattering blog post about Karen and her friends."

Jason chuckled. "Good. It's about time someone brought those women down a notch. Who's writing it?"

I shrugged. "That's the thing. It's anonymous."

"Awesome. Looks like the Women of Waterford will have more to gossip about now."

"I guess." I positioned myself at the other end of the couch and tucked my feet beneath me. "I mean, I hope I don't show up on there."

"It's not that hard, Elizabeth. Just don't do anything stupid."

"I don't plan on it." Jason's faith in me was less than zero. Sometimes, it felt like I was expected to do all the work on our marriage while he unfairly reaped the benefits.

As I sat on the couch, watching my husband watch television, a niggling thought assaulted me. Did I really make up the conversation with Jason? Was that possible? Was my medicine so strong that it caused me to hallucinate?

Curious, I retrieved my phone from the kitchen and googled my medicine side-effects for the hundredth time and began reading.

"What are you doing?"

"Research," I answered. "I'm so confused over our non-conversation today."

Jason held out his hand. "Let me see."

I paused. I wasn't always a doormat, but now, now I did everything I was told. Unlike Jason who needed a password on his phone for work security reasons, I had none. My life — who I spoke to, where I went, and what I searched – was exposed to anyone who cared to look. And Jason looked often. He read the screen before tapping on a few things, and I held my breath.

"No browser history? Elizabeth, you can't keep doing this to yourself. You need to let it go. Nothing will get better if you keep torturing yourself."

The disappointment in his voice tore at me, but I shook my head. "No. I fell in the Panera parking lot, and I think I accidentally deleted things."

Jason studied me closely. "Jesus, Elizabeth. Are you okay?"

"Sore, but I'll be fine. Just an embarrassing accident."

He handed back my phone and spread out on the couch. "Anyone notice?"

His words felt like a test. Like something I needed to pass. "Just Sarah Cole. But she asked me to lunch on Wednesday, so I must not be a total freak."

My husband flinched.

"What?"

He glanced at me before focusing back on Anderson Cooper. "I hate her husband."

"I know, but I'm not having lunch with him."

"Fair point."

"Anyway, she asked me to lunch, and we're going out on Wednesday. Should be fun. I really like Sarah. She seems different from the other women in Waterford."

A yawn roared out of Jason's mouth, and he stretched with his arms and legs going in every direction. Sometimes, I could still see the young man I married underneath the middle-aged veneer. "I guess. They all seem the same to me: White bleach blond hair, big boobs, and pea brained."

"Except Sarah," I said grabbing his toes and yanking off his obnoxiously patterned socks. "She has ash blond hair. Brains to be determined."

Jason scooted over on the couch. "Lay down. I want to cuddle with you."

I dropped the socks to the ground and placed my phone on the coffee table before molding into Jason's side. Tension rippled through me, and I braced for Jason's commentary, but he simply rubbed my back.

"It's going to be okay, Elizabeth. We're going to get through this."

I wanted to believe it was possible, but nothing was working. Therapy, drugs, talking...none of it seemed to fix anything. At least not in a significant way. For the better part of a year, I had struggled to get through most days without crying or beating myself up. Jason was right, I couldn't keep torturing myself. The past was the past and unchangeable.

But the future — that I could control.

I needed to.

3

THESE BITCHES ARE JUST LIKE ME

L et's play two truths and a lie. Ready?

Statement One: I write the things you wish you could say

Statement Two: I only write what's true and verified.

Statement Three: We're going to have so much fun together!

If you guessed true to all three, you're the winner!

And now, for your reading pleasure, I'll introduce Sarah Cole, a Periphery Girl who is always just on the outside of the inner group. Karen and the others don't really pay her much attention because they think she's a little forgettable and plain. But I know she has more edge than they give her credit for.

Take, for example, this little goodie: Southern, conservative, religious Sarah told a mutual friend she once arranged a three-way in France for her husband's thirty-fifth birthday.

But that's not the scandal. Oh no. She also confided she would leave her husband if it wouldn't destroy her father. She hates him. Her husband, not her father. She said that if he cheated, she'd have a reason to go, and she'd take it. She also said if he died she wouldn't be too terribly sad.

So, picture-perfect Sarah wants an out, but she doesn't want to be the one to initiate that out.

How's that for a little gossip? Good, right? Told you we'd have fun!

"You need to eat more, honey. You'll be nothing but bones if you don't." Sarah pushed the half-full tray of fries toward me and tossed a couple packets of ketchup after them. "Eat."

It was like she didn't see today's blog post, but I knew that wasn't the case. Everyone had seen it. At six A.M., Karen was blowing up my phone with, "OMG!!!" and "I'm dying!!!" and I had to turn my phone off once she looped me into a chat between her, Alexis, and Veronica because my phone was dinging incessantly, and Jason was about to kill me.

When I didn't make a move toward the fries, Sarah tightened her lips. "You know, I'm the one who shouldn't have an appetite after that blog post this morning."

"You saw it?"

Sarah blinked, looked away, and blinked again. My hand rested on my bag, ready to grab a tissue if needed. "Hey, Sarah. It's okay. The posts are stupid. Everyone says so. Take that post about that Kelly woman grocery shopping. Who cares if she wasn't buying organic food?"

"She's a personal trainer, Elizabeth. Practice what you preach and all that."

"But still, it was stupid and probably made up."

Sarah flipped her phone over and stared at it as if waiting for answers to spring forth from the screen. "Why me?"

"I don't know. Is anyone upset with you?"

"Not that I know of, and only a handful of people knew that story. I kept it close — or I thought I did. Maybe Kyle told some of the guys, and they told their wives?"

"Guys like to brag, and women like to gossip. Or at least whoever is writing that blog does." I dragged a fry through ketchup, but didn't bring it to my lips. There were probably fifteen hundred calories worth of fries sitting between Sarah and me, and if I wasn't careful, I'd eat them all.

"Oh, Elizabeth. Everyone likes gossip. Don't trust anyone who says they don't." Sarah wagged her finger before taking a long draw on her Diet Coke. "Besides, it isn't all bad."

"It isn't?" Sarah was too calm.

"Well, you know what they say, all publicity is good publicity."

"So, you're not upset?" I didn't understand her lack of tears or outrage. "Aren't you worried about what Kyle is going to say?"

"If he gets mad then according to the blog, I may get my wish." Sarah giggled. "Anyway, if anything, this just moved me up the social ladder. I'm edgy now, didn't you hear? Karen even called this morning to make sure I was okay."

Everything clicked. The salacious post had somehow raised Sarah's social standing. The workings of Waterford made me want to vomit.

I groaned and shoved my burger aside. "These things are huge!"

The grease-scented air clung to everything like cigarette smoke and threatened to give away my dirty secret to Jason. As soon as he kissed my forehead, he'd smell cheeseburger all over me, and he'd know I've been cheating on my diet again.

The buttoned-up lunch crowd rolled in around us, and Sarah and I had a prime, people-watching high-top near the windows. Sarah kept eating her burger as if nothing was wrong. The way she had embraced the sex scandal amazed me. Was it really not that big of a deal?

"Am I going to have to eat your burger for you? Am I?" she teased as she shoved my half-eaten burger back toward me.

"Pry it from my hands first," I said, and Sarah laughed as I took an exaggerated bite of greasy deliciousness. Everything flowed easily with Sarah. I wasn't constantly stressed about saying the wrong thing or talking to the wrong person. She was, as far as I could tell, authentic. What I saw was what I got.

"So, what made y'all move here? Waterford isn't exactly on most people's radar."

My heart stopped. That was the one question I had hoped to avoid because if I told her the truth, I risked ruining everything Jason and I were working so hard to leave behind. I wanted to be honest, and I would have loved to have someone to talk to when things weren't going well, but that wasn't not an option. I didn't know her well enough.

"After London, I wanted something different and my college friend, Amanda, put me in touch with Pete White – an old classmate of ours. Pete said this was *the* place to raise kids in the DC metro area, so we decided to go for it. Jason found a job, we found a house, and we packed up our life and moved here."

"I didn't know Pete was an old friend. Does that mean you knew Veronica, too?"

I shrugged. "He was more of an acquaintance," I said. "By the time he met Veronica, Jason and I were already on the West Coast, and Pete was off my radar."

I lied again. Only this was a deeper lie. One I have never admitted aloud to anyone. Not even Amanda.

"Elizabeth, is something wrong?" Sarah leaned across the table and worry filled the slight crinkles around her deep, brown eyes. "You've gone sheet white."

"It's just Pete," I blurted. "We kind of secretly dated in college."

Sarah's mouth dropped open. "You what?"

Oh my God. I hadn't wanted to say that. I hadn't. "It was nothing. Just a quick fling." I blinked and shook my head. "Please don't mention it to anyone." Desperation seeped into my voice. "Please. If Jason found out, I don't know what he'd do."

"Honey, that's an awfully big secret to be hiding from your spouse. Especially when the person in question is his friend."

I bit my lip. I needed to do some serious clean-up. "I know. That's way you can't say anything. Please. Jason wouldn't understand."

The restaurant buzzed around us, and the din of diners made hearing difficult, so I leaned into Sarah. She patted my hand. "I won't tell anyone. Your secret is safe with me." She locked her lips with a pretend key. "I promise."

Some of the panic oozing from my heart eased, but then it raced again because if my secret ended up going public, Jason would lose it. "The blog..."

"I'm taking this one to the grave."

"Thank you," I said.

"That's what friends do. We watch out for each other."

Friends. I had trusted one of my biggest secrets to a woman I was just getting to know, but something told me I could trust Sarah. Maybe it was her earnestness, or just the calming way she has about her, but I believed her. More importantly, I believed she was my friend.

I could trust her.

"The burger is awesome, but I. Am. Full." I was obviously changing subjects.

Sarah pivoted the conversation with me and grinned. "Don't tell me you're going to turn into one of those stick figure bobble heads with fake boobs and a tummy tuck."

I laughed. "My boobs are large enough. And perky." I pushed out my chest. Sarah and I had also bonded over our breast reductions. Neither of us had implants unlike 95% of the women at our country club, and we kind of gloated about it. "But I won't rule out a tummy tuck."

"Oh, me too. I want to wear a bikini again. Three kids and a love of burgers haven't done me any favors." Sarah wasn't the thinnest woman, but she looked average to me. Like a normal middle-aged woman with jiggly bits and stretch marks.

I solemnly nodded my head. "I wear a bikini, but probably shouldn't. I don't have much to strut these days."

Sarah raised her eyebrows. "You are tiny. Please don't tell me you have body image issues because I think you look amazing."

"You should have seen me when we lived in London. I was a size 0 or 2."

She gave me a funny look.

"What?" I asked.

"Honey, I've been all over your Facebook, and you did not look better. You looked emaciated."

Her tone wasn't harsh, but the words were.

"Really?"

Sarah dipped a french fry in ketchup. "You and Jason were so cute in Portland with all your friends and parties, but something was missing in London. You looked...sad. More like you do now." She swallowed a bite of fry. "Do you miss Portland?"

Why had it never occurred to me to remove all the old pictures? I didn't want to remember, so why leave them up where anyone can see?

"Wow," I said, pointing at the line snaking out the door. "We got here just in time."

"I told you this place had a growing reputation. It's good, isn't it? And we haven't even had the famous milkshake yet."

"God help us." I lined up three French fries so that their ends were even before biting into them. The fries were crunchy on the outside and potatoe-y on the inside. Sheer perfection. "I'm going to need a shower, breath mints, and new clothes after eating here."

Two men with trays full of food cast dirty looks in our direction. True, Sarah and I had been taking a long time, but we were still eating. They needed to calm down and stop eyeing us.

One of them, the taller one, drew his brows tightly together and frowned at me.

"Sugar, pay them no mind. They'll find a seat. Besides, we're ladies, and everyone knows a lady gets to sit. And if they don't, they have no manners."

Sarah's no nonsense, black-and-white view of everything was so different from my West Coast perspective. I guess that made us an odd couple, but whatever. We liked each other. Or at least I thought we did. Making friends was like dating. You go out a lot until you feel ready to introduce them to your family — or in this case, your husband.

The men stopped staring and turned their backs to us. Sarah was right.

"Do you ever wonder what it would be like to be single again?" She said out of the blue. "Like if you were back on the market with three kids, would you talk to one of those guys? Do you think anyone would be interested in dating someone like us?"

17

I pursed my lips. This is something I'd considered frequently over the past year. I sometimes still did. At times, divorce or death seemed like the only two options out of the misery called my life. "Sometimes." I paused. "My boys are older than your girls, so I think it may be easier in my case. But you never know." I sipped my Diet Coke. "Why?"

Sarah rested her chin on her hand. "Well, the blog told the truth. I wouldn't be too terribly sad if Kyle died. Don't get me wrong, I don't want the girls lose their father, but I wish I had a second chance at love."

"Do you love Kyle?" I blurted and immediately regretted it. "I'm sorry, that was insensitive."

Sarah shrugged. "I wish he gave me a reason to leave. I mean, if he ever cheated on me, that would be the end of our marriage."

Her bluntness shouldn't have surprised me, but it did and I sat back heavily in my chair. "Really?"

"Absolutely. I have self-respect." She tilted her head. "Wouldn't you leave if you found out Jason was cheating?"

Panic welled inside me. "I...I don't know."

"Of course, you would," she said. "Because staying means you're okay with it, and you're too strong of a woman to condone such behavior."

Was I strong? It didn't feel like it most days. In fact, I often felt the opposite of strong. My feelings must have been all over my face because Sarah changed the topic. "What are you doing Friday night? I'm having a small cocktail party. Melissa Foster will be there. Have you met her? Cute little blond that lives on Mountain Pass?"

I smiled, relived to leave the cheating conversation. "You just described a third of Waterford."

Sarah rolled her eyes. "I guess so, but if you come over Friday night and bring a red, you can meet her. She's lovely, but Kyle hates her. He thinks she's into me." Sarah winks. "In *that* way."

If that blog post were true, Kyle should be happy about Melissa's crush given his taste for three-ways. Or maybe he felt threatened by this Melissa Foster. Who knew?

"Are you sure she isn't?"

"Oh honey, she and her husband used to swing, but that was eons ago. Melissa is straight-edge now."

"Sounds like fun. What time?"

"After my girls go to bed, so eight?"

"I have a thing at Karen Newbold's starting at six, but I can swing by after I do my official duties."

Sarah smiled tightly. "Oh. I didn't know Karen was having a party."

"It's just a small thing."

"No party of Karen's is small. She invites everyone." She stared at me for a second like she was trying to figure something out.

"What?"

"Don't you have to ask Jason? I mean, doesn't he get a say in where you two go?"

She was right. Jason hated when I planned things without checking in with him first. Plus, with his work schedule, I never knew when he'd be home. "Can I get back to you tonight?"

"Of course! There's no hurry." Sarah played with her straw. "I understand how it is. Kyle is the man of our home, too. Everything, and I mean everything, has to run through him."

I nodded. Since I had become sick, Jason had become more protective of me, and I no longer ran the household like I once had. In fact, I did very little beyond showing up and breathing.

"So, call me and let me know, okay?"

"Of course!" I answer.

Sarah's grin stretched wide. "Good! I can't wait to introduce you to everyone. It's a whole different group than the Bitch Brigade."

If Sarah's friends were anything like her, the night would be fun. And maybe, just maybe, I'd find my tribe. "Hey," I said as I swiped crumbs into my hand and dumped them in a bag. "Why don't we head over to the Club before the kids get out of school and detox this grease from our system in the sauna?"

Sarah's mouth dropped slightly open, and she glanced away

before smiling at me. "Honey, you know, we've already discussed that right? About five minutes ago? We're getting milkshakes to-go."

Heat flashed across my cheeks. I had no memory of that conversation. None. "Right," I said. "I'm just eager to go."

Sarah beamed. "Well, in that case, let's get our Rocky Road and hit the road."

I kept a smile on my lips but my brain was screaming, not again. Not again. Not again. To lose my memory with Jason was one thing; to lose it with a near stranger was another.

What was wrong with me?

4

HAPPINESS IS A WINE BOTTLE AWAY

eople, we're on high alert.

Word on the street is that Karen Newbold is not too happy with Sarah Cole. Apparently, Sarah hosted a cocktail party that directly competed with Karen's happy hour get-together. She even managed to pull a few Periphery Girls who didn't get invites to Karen's – like Melissa Foster. The big coupe though was that Elizabeth Mavery (who you will totally meet later, I swear!) left Karen's party early to go to Sarah's.

Apparently, this is causing Karen to rethink Sarah's newly found status on the social ladder because she should have cancelled her party since it was a conflict — even though she wasn't invited.

It's totally ridiculous, but like everything Karen does, it's dramatic. She could have just let it go. That would have been the easy solution, right? However, Karen doesn't do easy. She does mean.

And what is her mean? Mocking Sarah's weight to everyone at her party and posting pictures on Facebook with captions like, "Wish you were here!" and "Best Party EVAH!"

According to my source, Sarah was devastated and proceeded to drown herself in a few bottles of wine. Things spiraled downward until Sarah was a sobbing mess. Everyone left shortly after, or should I say stumbled out, because after that shit show, everyone needed a strong drink.

Ah, Waterford mean girls at their finest. Gotta love it.

Wind whipped across the field and blew my jacket hood off my head. Poor Will stood out on the turf in only performance gear and a uniform. As the goalie, he didn't run around like the other boys, and the likelihood of him getting frostbite was high. Hell, I had on my clothes, a polar fleece, a jacket, a ski cap, a hood, a scarf, and gloves, and I was frozen solid. Plus, my head throbbed from last night's drinking, and the wind only made my nausea worse.

"That's it, Will! Nice save!" Jason yelled. When I didn't say anything, he nudged me with his elbow. "I know you're hungover, but you could at least try."

"I am. I'm out here, aren't I? I could be in the car with Ollie and Henry, or at home in bed, but I'm here freezing my ass off because I love my son."

Spring lacrosse always sucked. It had since Will started playing as an eight-year-old. The beginning of the season usually had him playing in snow and frigid air, and the end of the season the temperature rose to ninety.

"Go check on the little two in the car," Jason ordered. "It'll give you something to do."

"I'm watching Will. That's what I'm doing." And obsessively checking my phone. Since the last blog post, in which I was named, I'd been waiting to hear from Karen or Sarah. So far, radio silence — which worried me.

Jason kept his gaze on the field. "Did you have fun last night? Seems like you did. You know, up until it became drama hour."

I drank too much. Again. And it messed with my medication. Again. But Sarah encouraged me, and Jason kept refilling my glass, and here I was, massively hungover. "Sarah and Melissa are great. I really like them. But I'm worried about Sarah. She was a mess, and Karen was vicious."

"I'd be more worried about you." My husband pressed his lips together, and I braced for his wrath. Instead, he said, "I'm happy you had a good time, but I've heard things about Melissa. I'm not sure you want to associate with her. Plus, Karen doesn't seem to like her."

"You mean you don't know if you want me around her because it may impact your reputation."

"Something like that." The crowd around us groaned. The other team had scored, and Will banged the cage with his stick. Thank God this was almost over. Will's team was losing by three, and I couldn't wait to get back into the relative warmth of the car. Or to lay down in my bed and swallow a bottle of Advil.

"Sarah's okay, though? Our friendship won't tarnish your reputation?"

"Do you actually like her?" Jason turned his head so that he was looking directly at me. His jawline was square, strong, manly and covered with just enough scruff to be weekend sexy.

"She's the first woman in Waterford I feel completely comfortable around."

The corners of Jason's mouth turned down briefly before he reached for my gloved hand. "That's good. You need friends, but her husband's a douche, so don't expect couple's dates and crap."

The horn signaled the end of the game. Thank God. "I'll wait for Will." Jason tossed the keys to me. "Go to the car. I know you're dying to get out of here."

"Thanks." I scurried down the frozen path toward the parking lot, and my head pounded with each step. Drinking had become my social crutch, and yet I couldn't stop. Not even when it left me wanting to vomit everywhere. Especially not when Jason repeatedly told me I was more fun when I was drinking.

My other two boys didn't hear me approach because they were so engrossed in their phones. I slipped into the passenger seat and tugged off my ski cap, gloves, and scarf. Getting out of the wind made me feel ten degrees warmer. "Hey," I said. "How are you two?"

Ollie took one of his earbuds out. "It's cold. Can we go?"

"Just waiting on Dad and Will."

"Can we get lunch? I'm starving." Henry, my nine-year-old, leaned forward in his seat, but didn't remove his earphones, so I pulled them out.

"We'll see."

The absolute last thing I wanted in that moment was food. Bed. I wanted bed. And Advil. Lots and lots of Advil. And maybe a chilled eye mask. That wasn't too much to ask, was it?

A blast of arctic air rushed over Henry, Ollie, and me when Jason opened the back of the car, and I slid down in my seat to block it. There was the thump of Will dropping his gear in the trunk followed by the door closing. He didn't say a word when he climbed into the backseat.

"Everything okay, sweetheart?" I asked.

Jason gave me the look. The one I knew meant, stop now. "Will doesn't want to talk about it. He's upset about how he played."

I furrowed my brow. I had watched enough games over the last seven years to know he played well. The defense wasn't there, and the offense couldn't score. "Don't beat yourself up, buddy." I faced him. "Do you want to grab lunch?"

"Sure." Will flung his red and white cleats to the floor and turf pelts flew everywhere.

"Hey! Be careful," I said. "Or you're going to have to vacuum up the car when we get home."

"Sorry. I didn't mean to make a mess."

"It's fine. Don't worry about it." When Will was in a bad mood, I usually went easy on him, if only because I knew what it was like to have someone try to badger your bad moods away.

Jason huffed as he shoved the key into the ignition. I never knew what that meant. Was he annoyed? Did I let Will off too easily? Was I too strict? Sometimes, I wanted to yell out, 'What the hell are you trying to say?' but I never did.

I never did.

"What do you want to eat?" Jason rattled off a list of places. Once everyone agreed, which was a rare occurrence, he drove out to the street.

"Feeling better?" he asked me. "Because you're still green."

24

"I feel green."

He laugh-snorted. "Serves you right. You drank like a fish."

"Gee, thanks."

Jason turned up the music, it was something poppy with pulsing beat that matched the throbbing in my brain, and I rested my head against the cool window. Those were the moments I loved. When everything was normal, and boring, and just life. There were no big ups or downs, no flatness. Just me loving my family.

And I would have taken that with a nasty hangover any day.

Jason wrapped a fuzzy blanket around me and tucked it under my legs. Since the game, I hadn't been able to get warm. I'd taken a hot shower, put on extra layers, and huddled under my duvet. Nothing worked.

"Who are you texting?" Jason asked.

"Karen."

"Really?" He made it sound like talking to Karen was a violation of some sort.

"Yes, really." I pressed send and lowered my phone.

"Let me see." He stood next to me, waiting, as if he didn't believe me.

I held my phone screen side out toward Jason. This suspicion had to stop, it suffocated me. I had done nothing wrong. "I'm trying to play peace keeper. Sarah's upset, and Karen acted like a bitch, but Sarah wants to be her friend — which I don't understand – so I'm trying to smooth things out."

My husband studied the screen before rolling his eyes. "Let Sarah fight her own battles. You don't need to get involved."

"She's my friend, and for some reason, Karen likes me."

Jason folded his arms. "Doesn't it bother you that your friends' business keeps showing up on that blog? Someone you know is writing it, and they're already writing about you."

I had told him about my innocent appearance on the blog, and he'd seemed disinterested at the time, so his mentioning it was strange. "What are you saying?"

"That I think it's weird they started blogging about you when you started hanging out with Sarah."

"So?" I repeated. "What are you saying?"

"Just watch your back with those two. One of them likes to gossip."

I placed my phone on the iron bedside table with a dull thud. "Why would they write unflattering things about themselves?"

"You're kidding, right?" When I shook my head, he continued. "You're a bunch of bored housewives. Isn't that what you always say when you're bitching?" He didn't wait for me to answer. "This blog puts some excitement in your lives. Something to gossip about. It's like their very own reality show where they're the stars."

He had a point. The blog had become something that everyone checked first thing in the morning and last thing at night. It created gossip not just about the subjects, but speculation over the author. Basically, it was the center of Waterford's social life, and getting into the blog somehow made people feel important. Like Sarah had when her semi-sex scandal broke.

"Get in bed with me?" I pleaded. It was the best way I knew to end what could escalate into an argument. "I need cuddles."

Jason flipped his wrist over and glanced at his oversized watch. "I can't. I promised some of the guys I'd met them up at the club for drinks, remember?"

I knitted my brows together. "No, I don't remember, and I wish you wouldn't go. I feel horrible, and the boys-"

"Elizabeth, don't. We talked about this. It's my night out. I can't help it if you drank too much and feel like shit because of it."

We had never talked about this. I was positive. Or was I? Everything from the past twenty-four hours was a bit of a mess, and it was possible he told me while I was puking. Or wanting to die. Either or.

"I put your pills on the side table," Jason said. "There's water too, so you don't even need to get up." He stood near his closet door and pulled on his shoes. "Just lay there. I'll order pizza for the boys."

He checked himself in the floor mirror before coming to my side, and my heart trembled. Why was he wearing his good shoes to go out with the guys? Why not tennis shoes? Who was he trying to impress? "You look nice," I said. "Unlike me."

"You just need some rest. You'll feel better in the morning." Jason leaned down and kissed my forehead. "Sleep. I don't know when I'll be home. You know how the guys are."

The guys. Lately, when Jason wasn't at work, he was with the guys, building his Waterford reputation as an ace golfer and drinking while I sat at home with the kids — that is when it wasn't my night to go out with Karen and her friends. These girl and guys' nights out were new to us, and I was on the fence as to whether I liked them.

"Hey," Jason said as if reading my mind. "We're good, right?"

Such a loaded question. One I knew better than to answer truthfully. "Of course."

"Good, I wouldn't want to leave you here alone if we weren't." Jason didn't sound sincere as he skirted around the bed. "I'll see you in the morning."

My chest constricted when he disappeared through the doorway. I reached for my pills — all six of them – and swallowed them as a whole.

Maybe, I thought, maybe this will give me peace.

But it didn't.

It never did.

5

MAGIC MEDICINE

D r. Carter had this way about her. The best I can describe it is "floaty." She was light and airy, and sometimes I feared she may drift away, but Jason swore she was helping me, so I kept going to her in search of the magic elixir that would catapult my brain out of the hell it was trapped in.

"You're upset that he went out with his friends?" Dr. Carter said. "You do know that having friendships outside the marriage is healthy and to be encouraged, don't you?"

I'd spent the past twenty-five minutes going over my feelings about Jason's guys' night out. The panic I experienced. The desire to drive to the Club and verify his story. The sense that something wasn't right.

"Elizabeth?"

"Yes?"

"If your marriage is going to work, you need to trust Jason again. It's the only way."

"I know." And I did. That's why I hadn't driven to the Club or called his friends. It's why I allowed myself to fall asleep and hadn't badgered him about rolling in at two in the morning. I was trying to trust.

"You seem distracted, Elizabeth. Is everything okay?"

"You know, it only took one hour in your office, a family history, and Jason's testimony to give me a life sentence of bipolar disorder."

Dr. Carter frowned. "Your brain is sick, Elizabeth. You understand that, don't you? Someone who was healthy, wouldn't do the things you do."

She was wrong. "No. I've read up on this. The message boards said it's normal to-"

"We've discussed you visiting the message boards. It's not healthy to constantly read about affairs. You need to move beyond if you truly want to heal yourself and your family."

My jaw ached from clenching it. For nearly a year, I'd sat in Dr. Carter's office and shared my fears and concerns. I'd done everything she had suggested, and yet, my progress was questionable. I knew this was true, because if I were getting better, why would I stalk the other woman? Why would I have to know everything about her? She lived hundreds of miles away, and Jason no longer had contact with her, so why wasn't I recovering?

"I spoke with Jason the other day," Dr. Carter said. "He claims you've been drinking heavily again, and you've had some misunderstood conversations. You've also deleted your browser history."

Damn him. I scowled. When I first started treatment, I signed papers allowing Jason to have access to my files. I believed it was the right thing to do since I couldn't advocate for myself. Now, it was just annoying.

"There was one conversation...well, two, actually." I left out the one with Sarah. "One he says I imagined and one he says I forgot. But I recall..."

"What do you recall?" Dr. Carter shifted in her armchair and held her pen at the ready.

"He promised he'd be home early, and we could have dinner out. Just the two of us. We haven't done that in ages, so I was excited. I got dressed up and everything." Anger bubbled inside me. "I know what he said."

Dr. Carter stopped scribbling. "I know this is difficult for you, but it's not uncommon to have a foggy memory while taking your particular cocktail of medicine. And if you're combining everything with alcohol, the pills aren't going to be effective. Not to mention, you could possibly overdose."

I knew every word she said was true, but I still wanted to scream. This wasn't fair. Why was I suffering like this? What did I do to deserve a broken brain — one that can't keep fact and fiction straight?

"Have you been having any signs of hypomania other than drinking? Any excessive spending? Desire to have sex with others?"

Why was this always about me? Why couldn't someone place part of the blame on Jason? It was always me and my mental illness. "Sex with someone else? After what Jason has put us through?"

"I'll take that as a no." Dr. Carter wrote quickly. "Any racing or obsessive thoughts?"

I paused, not wanting to say the truth, but knowing I must. "I've been stalking Jason's girlfriend again, and that's why there's no browser history. I deleted it."

"And how do you stalk her?"

"On Facebook and Instagram. And on her work account." I twist a piece of hair around my middle finger. "She got a promotion. She's a director now."

"How does that make you feel?"

"Like shit? Like her life is unicorns and sunshine while mine is filled with depression and misery."

The corners of Dr. Carter's mouth turned down. "I see." She made another note. "You do know that people only show what they want seen on social media? What you're seeing is probably her attempt to prove to the world that she is fine."

"I don't care if she's fine."

"But you do."

I did. More than anything, I wanted her to hurt. I didn't want her getting a promotion or taking a vacation to Hawaii. I wanted her to feel my pain.

And she never would.

It was unfair.

"I think, in light of everything, I need to put you back on lithium for the time being. It will make the thoughts stop, and you'll feel better quickly."

I bristled. Lithium dulled me worse than the other drugs. "No, I'm fine. It's getting better. Really. In fact, I was hoping we could start a step-down process with my pills. My goal is to be drug-free."

"I know it is, Elizabeth, but I just don't see how that's possible. You will need medication and psychiatric care for the rest of your life. You need to be realistic about it."

I tossed my hands up. "And what if I don't have bipolar disorder? What if I was simply a depressed woman whose husband had an affair? What if the "hypomanic" phases you and Jason so readily identified in my past where just my normal and not hypomania at all? What if this is all a result of the drugs and not my brain?"

Dr. Carter placed the notepad on her desk and folded her hands in her lap. "I've been doing this for twenty years. No one wants a diagnosis of mental illness, but the most successful patients are those who accept it and work within the system we set up as a team."

I jumped to my feet and grabbed my handbag. "Just give me the prescription. I'm sure Jason will force me to take it since he's probably going to call you to check up on me anyway."

"We just want what's best for you, Elizabeth."

"And what's best for me is keeping me drugged up?"

"Don't think of it like that. We're trying to properly balance the chemicals in your brain." Dr. Carter handed me the prescription. "It's going to be okay. You have a great support system in Jason."

Wonderful. My cheating husband who drove me to madness was the only thing keeping me sane.

6

DINNER FOR FOUR

I n Waterford, who you dine with is almost, if not more, important than who you day-drink with. Some people are daytime only friends, while other make their way into the higher strata of nighttime friends. These higher beings are, supposedly, your real friends.

What does this mean? That you really get to know each other? No. It means you now have someone to hang-out with and get drunk with on a Saturday night while avoiding your spouse.

But let's get back to dining. It's a big deal. Like Facebook big. Every night out must be chronicled and meticulously posted to as many feeds as possible – Facebook, Instagram, Twitter. Not only to prove how cool you are, but also to stroke the Fear of Missing Out (FoMo) in others.

Veronica didn't get invited to dinner with Karen and Alexis. Poor thing's going to know all about it because Karen and Alexis have posted the requisite photos about how much fun they had and that they "love this girl!" The husbands, of course, are mere scenery, useful only to pay the bill, take pictures, and drive home slightly buzzed.

It's a sad, sad world when adult life feels more like college with responsibilities. Get drunk, hang-out with friends, and pay the mortgage. And that's what they're doing. Drinking and friending their way through the tedious monotony of their lives.

Funny how the people who look the happiest often have the most to hide.

"Do you want to use the bathroom?" Veronica lifted her monogrammed Louis Vuitton bag off the back of her chair and slung it over her arm.

I had guzzled my third glass of water and was waiting for the waiter to refill me. My new lithium dosage made me constantly parched, and apparently, Veronica noticed. Or maybe this was just one of those woman things where everyone has to go to the bathroom in a group. "Sure."

As we left Jason and Pete at the table, Veronica put her head so close to mine that the scent of fruity shampoo filled my nose. "I swear, the two of them will never shut up. It's golf this and politics that."

"I don't mind." And really, I didn't. This dinner was the closest thing to our old life that Jason and I had done since moving to Waterford, and I was enjoying myself.

Veronica side-eyed me. "Oh. I didn't mean that it bothers me, just that there are way more interesting things to talk about."

Oh. I was supposed to complain about Jason just like all the other wives complained about their husbands. I should have said something funny about Jason, but I could never speak ill of him — especially now that the blog liked to post everyone's dirty laundry.

Veronica slowed down as we turned a corner. "How did you and Jason meet? I mean, you two are the cutest, so it must be a great story."

It had been a great story once upon a time before Jason blew up our life. Now, it was full of painful memories, but I begin my recitation anyway.

"We interned together for a US Senator." Veronica and I had reached the bar area, and I paused. "I knew the day I met him we were going to get married, and we did, a year later."

"That was fast!"

What I didn't say is that I was still getting over Pete and whatever it was we had. Jason was supposed to be my rebound guy, but something about me captivated him, and after six weeks of dating, he asked me to marry him.

"We were young and stupid and didn't know any better."

"But look at you now! You two have it all."

No, we didn't. We had nothing. But we were trying and that's what mattered. Still, keeping up appearances was exhausting and sometimes, I couldn't remember what was true and what parts were our cover story.

"I'm blessed." I really didn't want to talk about my marriage, or anything else about me. In addition to the water, I'd had two glasses of wine, and my tongue was probably looser than it should be. "How about you and Pete?" I asked. "How'd you meet?"

Veronica launched into her story, but honestly, I wasn't paying attention. We got along fine, but it was Karen who I knew better. With Veronica, I struggled to find common ground. She always wanted to talk about her girls, being a mom, and how hard it was to balance her family and social life. I enjoyed talking about real life, politics, and books. Unlike Sarah and me, Veronica and I weren't exactly BFF material, but I guess we didn't need to be.

"And when Pete told me you were moving to Waterford, he was so excited! He couldn't wait to introduce us."

"What?" Clearly, I missed a part of her story.

"Pete told me all about you. I can't believe this is the first time we're really hanging out." My heart dropped. Pete and I had never discussed how much Veronica knew about our past history, but I guessed from her enthusiasm she knew nothing. Which was fine by me.

I twirled a lock of hair around my index finger. "I hope he didn't say anything awful. I was kind of a drunken mess in college."

"No! Of course not! Do you think I'd be friends with you if he had?" And there it was. The proof that she had no clue I had slept with her husband.

And had she just said we're friends? Really? We'd barely ever spoken at length before tonight except at various social functions where Karen drove the conversation. I'd lived in Waterford for a year and this was the first time all four of us have been to dinner together despite Pete and Jason being good friends.

Basically, Veronica and I were not night time friends.

"Do you like this place?" Veronica asked as we paused before a wall of wine bottles. "Karen, Alexis, and I come here for lunch once a month. They have the best wine flights that get you just buzzed enough to still be able to drive home."

"Hmmm...That sounds fun." I didn't know what else to say that didn't come off as too eager to join in or too rude.

Veronica whipped out her phone. "Pictures? The light here is fab." She pressed her shoulder against mine. "Smile."

I didn't have time to prepare before she fired off a ton of shots. "I'm going to look awful," I mumbled.

She scrolled through the pictures, deleting as she went. "I'm sure I have something usable. Ah!" She flipped the phone toward me. "This is cute." The two of us were smiling broadly with light streaming in from the left and softly lighting our faces. "I won't have to filter it too much."

While Veronica fiddled with her phone, my mind churned. In the picture, I looked like every other woman in Waterford: drapey top, statement necklace, diamond studs, polished hair, and lipstick. It was like the me I knew — the city-dwelling, urban chic me – had morphed into a suburbanite. I wasn't sure I liked it.

"Is it okay?" Veronica asked. "I won't tag you if you don't approve."

I plastered on my best fake smile. "It's fine. We look good."

"Awesome!" She dropped her phone back into her bag. "Bathroom?"

"Right. I need to go badly." All those drinks had caught up with me.

Veronica held the door for me. "I don't have to go, I just needed to get away from Pete and Jason for a minute."

I wished I was still at the table. Jason and Pete's conversation had been interesting. All about the last presidential election and the rami-fications that were still being felt. I wanted to join in, but like every conversation I had ever had with her, Veronica wanted to discuss her last Sephora haul and where to get the best mani-pedi.

When I finished using the bathroom, I stepped up to the counter to wash my hands. "It's so great that you and Pete were here already," I said. "Jason would be lost without Pete – he's not exactly Mister Outgoing."

Veronica checked her reflection and smoothed her long, buttery blond hair. "All these years, Pete would tell me about his college days, and I've only met his fraternity brothers, so it's great to finally meet someone who saw a different side of him."

"My friend Amanda could probably tell you more salacious stories about Pete."

"Like what?" She gave me a conspiratorial grin.

That was a good question. What can I say without declaring, 'Hey, I slept with your husband,'? "I think I'll leave that to Amanda." I winked. "Those two..."

Veronica laughed. "He's told me about Amanda, but I wonder why he never mentioned you until you decided to move here."

There was no accusation in her voice, but it felt that way. Probably because of my own guilt. And I did feel guilty. I was keeping secrets from Jason, and Pete was doing the same from his wife. Obviously, whatever we had needed to stay buried in the past.

"I'm easily forgettable."

Veronica smashed her lips together and popped her eyes wide open. "Hardly. You've had such a fascinating life. London, Portland. All the places you've traveled. I mean, Cambodia sounds amazing!"

"But doesn't Pete's job take you all over the world? I thought that was a perk of being a State Department wife."

Veronica grinned. "The European tours are the best. My kids have spent more time living abroad than here, and honestly, I'm fine with that."

"Oh?"

"It just...well, you know. You've lived in other places."

I glided my lipstick over my lips. "You're not happy here?"

"Name one person who is."

"Jason."

Veronica ran her fingers through her hair, focusing on the ends. "He'll get over it. It's only been a year. Give it one more, and he'll be begging to get out of Waterford. I mean, it really is the same old stuff with the same old people all the time."

This was the longest, most honest conversation we'd ever had. I didn't think Veronica had it in her to be real.

Veronica's reflection smiled at me. "Don't take this the wrong way, but you're a little bit odd." I fought the blush spreading across my cheeks. "You don't really fit in, do you?"

"No, I guess not, but I'm okay with that."

"Well, Karen likes you, so I wouldn't worry about it."

Her words stung even though I didn't want to be a Woman of Waterford. I didn't want to be sucked into the bottomless pit of suburbia where you're never sure who your friends are and who is going to stab you in the back. I didn't want Saturday dinners with a large group because I was too afraid to spend alone time with my spouse. And I didn't want to feel like I was putting on a performance every time I left my house. But mostly, I wanted Jason to look at me the way he used to and not like a broken thing that needed to be fixed.

I blotted my burnt orange lipstick with my finger and wiped the excess on a paper towel. "Ready?"

"Sure. We shouldn't leave them alone for too long. Who knows what they'll do."

What would they do? Run away? Stiff us with the bill? I mean, really, what horrible things could Pete and Jason get into in ten minutes? They were grown men, not toddlers.

The answer: Jason and Pete had ordered more drinks — wine for the ladies, whiskey for them. Jason already smelled repulsive.

"Babe, I got your favorite: Cakebread chardonnay," Jason said as I arranged myself in my chair. So much for worrying about how much I drank.

"Thank you." I patted his arm. "That's sweet." One pour of Cakebread was like fifteen dollars or something ridiculous, so either he was buzzed or he was being generous. Either way, I got a yummy drink.

"I know what my girl likes," he said before leaning over and kissing my cheek. Everything clicked. This was all a show. For some reason, Jason felt he had to put up a façade with Veronica and Pete. Interesting.

"Excuse me?" Veronica said to our waiter. "Can you take a group photo?"

"Of course."

She handed him the phone and motioned for me to move closer to her. After I did, the guys arranged themselves behind us.

"One, two, three."

The waiter clicked a few before handing the camera back. Veronica thumbed through the shots. "These are great. Thanks!"

"Can I see?" I asked.

She handed me the phone, and I bit my tongue. The picture she'd chosen looked like a generic "look at me" Waterford photo. The guys loomed over us, hands on our chairs, and all of us had gigantic fake smiles.

"This one's a framer," I said. "Definitely Facebook worthy." Since arriving, Veronica had taken photos of everything — our drinks, the appetizers, us, the wine bottle. It was like she was trying to prove she was here or something. Or with us. It was a little unsettling to have her constantly telling me to smile or hold a plate at an angle. I couldn't get past the feeling that she'd have a mental breakdown if she lost her phone.

"Veronica is picture obsessed," Pete said. "I don't get it, but the Women of Waterford do. Right, honey?"

"I want to remember every minute."

Pete swigged from his whiskey glass. "Try living in it."

Ouch.

Pete glanced at me from the corner of his eyes like he was looking for my approval. I said nothing, but he had a point.

Jason and Pete resumed their conversation, and since Veronica was on her phone doing whatever it is she did, I grabbed mine. I opened Facebook, and sure enough, the first thing I saw were pictures of us and our meal. And lots and lots of comments about how amazing it all looked. Veronica had even captioned the public photo of the two of us by the bathroom, "Love this girl!"

Sigh.

It was all so fake. And I hated it all.

"Elizabeth, remember that time in Brazil when..." I zoned out. All I wanted was to get out of there. But I needed to sit and smile. I needed to try. For Jason. For us.

The country club bar was empty except for Sarah and me and the bartender who I think only ever washed glasses. I wished there were more people around – I hated being in this large room when no one else was there to fill it up with energy.

Sarah had called me last minute to see if I wanted to grab a midday drink and snacks. Of course, I did. If she hadn't given me a reason to leave the house, I would have still been in PJs and lounging in front of the TV while eating left-overs.

"Why didn't you tell me you were having dinner with Veronica and Pete?" She sounded hurt. Like I'd intentionally done something to upset her.

"Jason and Pete arranged it. I literally found out around four," I said, digging into a piece of cheesecake the size of my head. We were supposed to be sharing, but Sarah hadn't had a bite. Which was strange for her. "Not hungry?"

"Distracted."

"By what?"

"I've lived here for twelve years and have never, not once, been invited out to dinner with any of them." By them she meant Alexis, Veronica, and Karen. "I've known those girls a lot longer than you, and just once, I wish someone would think of me — other than to make fun of my weight."

There was a wistfulness to the sadness in her voice, and it made me feel terrible. Even though I knew Jason found Kyle annoying, I said, "Sarah, dinner was all Jason and Pete's idea. The next time, I'll see if you and Kyle can come."

"Or you could invite us yourself."

I could. "I'll do that. Maybe I'll have everyone over to my place?"

What was I saying? The thought of hosting a get together for Karen and all plus Sarah at my home made my heart seize. I hadn't entertained since before the affair, and just the thought of it exhausted me. And what if I did it wrong? Then what? Would Karen exile me?

"That would be so fun!"

It so wouldn't.

"Call Jason now, and see if it's okay." Sarah had nearly jumped out of her chair. She picked up her fork and cut off a large bite of cheesecake.

"He's in meetings today." I opened my phone. "I think we're free in two weeks. I'll double check with Jason and ask Karen and the girls and get back to you."

Sarah nodded as she chewed and stared into the distance. "That works for me. Kyle and I have that Saturday open, but I'll verify with Kyle and get back to you."

"Great! I'll get it all going once I get the okay from Jason."

A ball of dread formed in my stomach. I so didn't want to do this, but I knew it would make Sarah happy. And that's what friends do — make each other happy.

7

HAPPY HOUR

Word on the street is that Elizabeth Mavery had a Bitch Brigade get-together at her home. Just her and her closest drinking buddies - I mean friends – Karen, Alexis, Veronica...and Sarah.

Oh! Wait! You don't really know Elizabeth yet, do you? That's because she's sneaky, always prowling around the perimeter of the Bitch Brigade. Not exactly all-the-way in, but definitely not out. She's a transplant from Portland who Karen has taken under her wing, much to the dismay of a bevy of Periphery Girls.

It wouldn't be so looked down upon if she'd only follow the rules of Waterford: smile, make friends with the Periphery Girls, and slowly gain the notice of the Bitch Brigade. Elizabeth, however, doesn't care about how things are supposed to be done. And that's going to bite her in the ass.

For example, this Happy Hour party she threw? She made mistake number one by inviting Sarah Cole along. Apparently those two are BFFs now or something because they're ALWAYS together. But seriously, what the hell was Elizabeth thinking? Has no one explained the rules to her? Sarah doesn't get to come unless Karen says so. I mean, really, you're not in Portland anymore, honey. You can't do whatever you want.

As for Sarah, I heard she lived on a juice diet for two weeks so that she'd look a little more svelte. I mean, she is curvy. And tall. And nothing like the *rest of them. But starving herself so she'll fit in more...well, maybe it worked because she was there and the rest of us weren't – LOL.*

And then there were the husbands. Of course, Jason and Pete got on well, but Sarah's husband spent the night lurking around the edges and making inappropriate comments to Alexis. Or so a sweet, little gossip told me.

Elizabeth, bless her heart, is looking more and more like a social climber. Without the Bitch Brigade, she's a throw away, someone who appears interesting at first glance, but quickly fades out once you speak to her. Honestly, I have no idea why any of these women are her friend.

It's not like Waterford is lacking in entertainment or anything.

I'd read the blog post a hundred times. Maybe a hundred and one. I'd lost count. The blog post was bitchy, but right. I was forgettable.

I threw my phone on to the nearby club chair and huffed.

"It's not as bad as Susan Belogi's," Sarah said. "They didn't call you a limp, socially awkward eel."

"They said, 'Bless her heart.' That's almost as bad," I answered. "Maybe even worse. I'm a branded social climber."

Sarah shrugged. "Who isn't? Besides people know who you are now." She was spread out on my couch and had kicked the pale yellow throw blanket to the floor while shoving a decorative pillow behind her head.

"What if I want to keep a low profile?"

Sarah laughed. "Too late for that. Besides, think of it like this: you matter. To someone out there you matter."

"Fantastic."

"Subject change, Miss Grumpy." Sarah pushed up onto her elbow. "I can't believe Alexis actually said she'd rather go without Botox than ever sleep with her husband again!"

"She says stuff like that all the time."

"Really?" Sarah squealed.

"Really." I poured red wine into our glasses and handed Sarah hers. Machine gun fire erupted from the basement where the boys were playing video games. I had banished them down there while Sarah and I post-mortemed our weekend. "She's only with him for the money."

"You're the second person who's told me that." Sarah sat up to drink.

"Let me guess, Melissa?"

"Of course, Honey. It's not like Alexis would ever tell me something like that. And Karen," Sarah said. "She has to be using some sort of drug to stay that thin while eating and drinking so much."

I tucked my feet beneath me. "I take it you had fun?"

"The best night in ages." She grinned so broadly I could see her molars.

Sarah was easily entertained. I had spent the evening running around, making sure Jason and Pete didn't gang-up on Kyle and doing all my hostess duties. We were only supposed to be at my house for an hour before going to dinner, but an hour stretched to two then three, and by the time our Übers rolled into Uncle Julio's, our entire party was smashed.

I swirled my wine glass. "They're really not all that great if you think about it."

"What do you mean? They control Waterford's social scene. Don't you think it would be fun to sit at their table during the Holiday Party or watch the Fourth of July fireworks from Alexis's front yard?"

I didn't have the heart to tell her that I've already done these things.

"Oh, hey," Sarah said. "Not to change the subject again, but would you be able to babysit my girls next Thursday night? Kyle is out of town, and my nanny is refusing to work overtime."

"Sure. I could send Will over to watch them after his practice, if that's okay. He could use the money."

"Perfect. How about five? I'm going to get caught in that horrible D.C. traffic and need to be downtown by seven."

"What's the occasion?" The wine smelled heavenly, and I breathed it all in before taking another sip.

Sarah gave a little shake of her head. "Just dinner and drinks with an old friend. Nothing fancy."

"I wish my friends would come visit me." I didn't bother to hide the sadness in my voice.

"Why don't they?"

I shrugged even though I knew the answer — that no one wanted to be around crazy Elizabeth and cheating Jason. "Since moving to here, no one, not even our families, have visited. We used to be the hub of holiday entertaining. Now, it was just us, and it's rather depressing."

"Well, you do have Pete and Veronica, right? And Karen." Sarah pounded the bottom of her red wine and refilled.

"Actually, I don't think we'll be doing the holidays with them."

Sarah scrunched up her face. "Why not? They're your friends."

"I wouldn't call them friends, Sarah. More like good acquaintances." I held my hand at mouth level. "They're here." I jumped my hand up to my eyes. "And you're here on the friend scale."

"That's sweet of you." Sarah tilted her head. "But I thought you and Pete were old friends from way back. You used to date."

My heart fluttered. "Not exactly."

"That's not what it seemed like." Her sweet drawl was lovely, but her words, not so much. "With the way the two of were laughing and carrying on about 'The Good Ole Days,' I thought you were once besties or something."

I bristled. "What? We were doing what?"

"Giggling off in the corner. You don't remember?"

I wracked my brain and turned up nothing. Just a black crater where the night should have been. "That's really weird. Jason hasn't mentioned it, and I don't remember."

"Oh." She gave me a strange look.

"What?" I asked.

"Uh oh. Someone had too much to drink."

"My hangover the next day would agree with that statement."

The sound of the garage door opening rumbled through the

house, and Sarah looked over her shoulder toward the mudroom. "Jason?"

"Yes. And he's going to kill me because I've been gabbing with you and haven't started dinner."

Sarah waved her hand dismissively. "Let me handle him."

I paused. What a strange thing for her to offer, but maybe she could work some magic on him. Jason slammed the mudroom door and stumbled into the kitchen holding flowers and his work bag. "Hey, Babe," he said. "I got these for you."

Sarah stiffened before jumping up. "Oh!" she said. "They're so pretty! Kyle never gets me flowers."

"Sarah?" Surprise flitted across Jason's face. "Why are you here?"

"She's my guest," I answered. "I was lonely and called her over." I laid the flowers on the counter. "Thank you," I said before kissing Jason's cheek. "They're lovely."

"Gorgeous, Jason. Really." Sarah stood behind me. "And don't worry about dinner. I'm buying pizza for all of us. Unless you want Chinese?"

My husband looked dumbfounded. Like he couldn't make sense of what he's seeing.

"Jason?" I said. "Are you okay?"

"Yeah. I'm just..." He stared at Sarah. "Where's your car?"

"I walked over. Needed the exercise." She whipped out her phone. "Now, do you want pizza or Chinese?"

Jason gave me The Look. The one that told me to get Sarah out of there and that he wanted to be alone. When I didn't do anything, he ran his hand through his hair. "Sarah, I've got a raging headache. I'm going up to bed. Maybe some other time."

Sarah pouted. "Okay. But I'm holding you to that."

My husband tossed me another look. "We should raincheck that pizza for another day," I said. "I've got to take care of the boys and all that."

"All right, but I'm not going to let you forget." Sarah scooped up her things and air kissed my cheek. "See you tomorrow?"

"Sure." I escorted her to the front door. "I'll come by around eight for our walk."

"Perfect!"

After I shut the door, I turned around slowly. Jason waited on the top of the stairs looking down at me. His set jaw gave him the air of a very angry man, and I braced myself.

He stormed down the steps. "Next time, give me a heads up if you're having a girls' happy hour."

"I'm sorry. She was supposed to leave earlier, but we started talking and--"

"All I wanted was a freakin' warm dinner," Jason snapped. "Not to walk in on you and Sarah gossiping and doing nothing."

I braced myself against his verbal attack. I had known he was going to be upset, but I wasn't prepared for just how angry he was. "Jason, I'll have something ready in twenty minutes. It's no big deal."

He pointed to the wine glasses on the coffee table and frowned. "Drinking again, Elizabeth? Seriously?"

"It was only one glass. I'm perfectly sober." I dug around the pantry and produced a box of pasta and a jar of sauce. "How's this?"

Jason rolled his eyes. "You know what? Pizza sounds awesome, especially since you seem incapable of cooking anymore."

I stiffened. It hadn't been my best week in terms of managing the household, but I tried. I helped with homework, ran errands, and made sure Jason's beer fridge was stocked. His words however, planted doubt in my mind. Was I doing everything I could? Because if I was failing at being a good wife, was I also failing at being a sane, stable mom?

"I'll order it," I said, hoping to take some of the heat out of the conversation. "What do you want? I'll get cheese for the kids, but something fancier for you?"

"Cheese actually sounds great." Jason popped off the cap and flipped it into the sink. He knew I hated when he did that. He knew it, but did it anyway. Asshole. "Do you like your flowers?"

"I do. What's the occasion?" I kept my voice nice and level as I scrolled through my email to see if I had any pizza coupons. No reason to show how upset I was.

"I wanted to say thank you in advance of me being gone next week."

He no longer sounded angry, and I stared up at my husband. I may have been the one with diagnosed mental illness, but his moods were sometimes all over the place. "It's your job," I said. "I get it. I don't always like it, but I understand."

"Maybe Veronica can come over one night?" Jason encircled my waist with his muscular arms as his beer breath fanned over my face. I didn't shrink away even though I wanted to.

"Most likely I'll just have Sarah over. Except on Thursday. She's going out in DC, and Will is babysitting for her. He loves sitting for her because she overpays him in my opinion."

Jason twitched. It was subtle, but I felt it.

"What?"

"You two spend a lot of time together lately. I'd love to see you hang out more with Veronica or Karen or even Alexis. Sarah seems a little needy, if you ask me, and there's no reason to limit yourself to just one person."

I pulled back slightly. "With those other women, I'm always worried about saying or doing the wrong thing. With Sarah, everything comes easier."

"Babe." Jason planted a kiss on my forehead, a sign he'd moved on from being angry. "Just be you. They all like you. They do. Don't worry about trying to fit in. You already do."

"Veronica called me odd."

"What? Why would she do that?" My husband ran his fingertips down my back, and I melted a little. So much for our argument.

"Because I am." I closed my eyes and pressed my head against his chest. I loved when he touched me like this. He hadn't done it enough lately. "I get nervous around them. Like if they find out the truth, they'll think less of me."

"And you're not like that with Sarah?"

"No, and I haven't told her about the affair, if that's a concern."

Jason patted my back. "Our agreement is this is a start-over. A new chance. I don't think we need to mess it up by giving Waterford something to gossip about."

"I agree," I said, placing my hands on his broad chest. "Now, let me order dinner, and we can be classy and eat pizza on paper plates while drinking the rest of the wine Sarah and I just opened from the bottle."

My husband's hearty laugh filled my ears. "I like that plan."

"I do too."

8

PARTING WAYS

L adies and gentlemen, for today's reading pleasure, I present *The Men of Waterford*. Normally, I wouldn't blog about them because all they're good for is drinking, working, and golfing, but today's development is too good to pass up.

You see, once upon a time, there were two friends named Pete and Jason. Pete is Veronica White's husband, and Jason is Elizabeth Mavery's. The two of them drink and golf together at least twice a week.

Until today.

Funny, isn't it, the way someone reacts when they don't want to see someone else? Take Jason for example. When his good buddy Pete walked into the Club, Jason pretended he'd never seen Pete before, but his eyes never strayed from Pete's retreating figure.

And Pete? He passed by the bar where Jason stood without even saying hello.

Strange, right?

What's even stranger is the knowing smile Pete gave Elizabeth. Jason immediately stomped over, whispered in his wife's ear as she became visibly upset, and dragged her out of the Club.

So, what do you say friends? Do we finally know who Pete's been having an affair with?

"I don't understand," I cried. "Pete's your best friend, and you've done nothing but encourage me to be friends with Veronica." I paused. "*He's* the reason we chose *Waterford* and not something closer to DC."

Jason paced the room like a wild animal, and I cowered on the bed as if it could prevent his words from striking me. "I can't get into specifics, but he's not the man I thought he was."

Did he know? Had he found us out? I steadied myself before snapping, "You're not one to judge."

Jason whirled around. "Don't start on me. What I did is in the past. Let it go."

"You've heard the rumors, haven't you? About Pete's affair. Or assumed affair? The one every woman in Waterford gossips about but no one has any leads on."

My husband crossed his arms. "Yeah. That. That's exactly why I don't want you around him. You two already have a reputation for being too cozy, and I don't want people thinking you're his mistress. For God's sake, it's all over that damn blog!"

It had been a day since Jason pulled me out of the Club. A whole day and we were just talking about what had happened. When he whispered in my ear that we needed to go, he said Will had texted that something had happened to Ollie. But when we got home, the boys were fine. Jason had lied, but he wouldn't admit it. He claimed I was making things up again.

My heart banged against my ribs. "You know it's not true."

"Some of the guys have given me shit about it."

"And you believe them?" The words sputtered from my lips.

"I'm serious, Elizabeth. I want you to stay away from Pete." Jason set his jaw hard, and when he crossed his arms, I knew he was getting the final say on this. Still, I couldn't help but push it.

"How can you judge him when his affair is alleged unlike yours?" Nothing made sense to me. Ever since he came back from his firm's Partners Retreat, Jason had been acting strangely, and this anti-Pete crusade was just one piece of it. "What's really going on?"

"He's not a good guy, Elizabeth. I know you think you know him, but you don't. Trust me on this one and stay away from him."

I bit the inside of my cheek. How could I possibly defend Pete without giving up our past? "Does that mean staying away from Veronica, too? Because that means good-bye social life. If I can't be around Veronica, then Karen and Alexis are off-limits which leaves me with only Sarah."

Jason remained silent for a long while. The rise and fall of his heaving chest matched the way he clenched and unclenched his fists. "No. You're right. It would look weird if you suddenly stopped talking to Veronica."

"And you cutting off ties with Pete isn't strange?" The week before, we were planning a trip to Europe with the Whites, and Veronica and I told Karen about it. Now, Jason wanted me to stay away from one-half of the White equation. The one-half that knew me better than ninety-nine percent of the people who live here. The half I actually liked.

"It's a falling out. People will forget about in no time." Jason's deep voice was rough, like he'd been smoking. He stripped off his shirt and tossed it onto the hamper. "I'm taking a shower."

I sat upright and held my arms out to him. When he didn't come to me, I dropped them. "I know it was a long week for you at work, but you're acting strangely. Did something happen the retreat? Is there something you need to tell me?"

He didn't immediately answer, and my heart sank while a cold sweat beaded along my hairline. It was too reminiscent of how he behaved during his affair. The sudden decisions, the cutting off ties with friends, the sense that I'd done something wrong.

"Don't go there, Elizabeth. Don't. I can't deal with you retreating into your brain right now." He pressed his lips together. "If anything, think of the boys. Another one of your episodes isn't good for them."

"I'm not retreating," I said. "I'm concerned, and I had hoped having drinks at the Club with our friends would relax you after your long week."

"Yeah. It *was* a long week." Jason had stayed Wednesday and

Thursday in the city since his events didn't wrap up until after eleven and the metro had stopped running. When he had called to say good-night, he had sounded exhausted and said how much he hated this time of year. I held my tongue, not letting him know that his sleeping away from home bothered me. But it did, and I couldn't say anything — even if it did give me horrible flashbacks - because he was doing his job.

"You know what," I said. "It's only eight. What if you take a shower while I call Sarah and Kyle and see if they want to come over for drinks?"

Jason blanched. "No. I really don't want to deal with that idiot. Kyle. Not Sarah."

"Okay, then. What do you propose? Will's home, so he can watch the little ones if you want to go out for drinks just the two of us."

Jason pushed me down on the bed. "Or I could just have my way with you."

I forced a laugh. The last thing I wanted in that moment was sex, but I also wanted to be a good wife so I circled my arms around his neck and kissed him softly. Jason sighed. At least I could still do something right.

Sarah chuckled in her sexy, raspy way. "Jason's actually worried people will think you're having an affair with Pete White? You? You're — and bless your heart for this — so straight-laced. I can't imagine you being seduced by Pete – no matter how charming or good-looking he is. And I think we can both agree, he's very easy on the eyes."

We'd been dissecting this for the last twenty minutes and kept coming to the same conclusion: Jason had lost his mind. Or at least I had come to that conclusion. Sarah thought Jason was right on this one. At least that's what she said before changing her mind and saying he was ridiculous. But then, she'd say, there's that blog, so maybe I should watch myself.

I honestly couldn't keep up.

"Elizabeth, are you still there?"

"I am. Just thinking that's all. I really don't understand what would make Jason one-eighty like this."

Sarah cleared her throat. "You sure, honey, that you've never done *anything* to give Jason suspicion you and Pete may have something going on?" Her voice glided through the phone. "After all, you have your college romance, and I did hear the two of you have been seen at the Club a few times together. And there was the night we all went out. The two of you were lost in your own little world."

"Really?" I said, annoyed. "If I were going to have an affair with Pete White, I certainly wouldn't be seen with him in a public spot. We'd go out of the way. Somewhere where no one knew us. And I'd probably remember it."

"You've given this thought?" Sarah sounded accusatory.

Thought. Yes. I'd given it much. Ever since finding out about Jason's affair, I had done nothing but think about how cheater's get away with stuff. Jason had it easy. His mistress lived in New York, and he would fly there a few times a month, and when he wasn't flying to New York City to see her, they were jetting off on business trips to Europe and Asia. But what if she had lived closer? Like in Portland? Would I have found out sooner? Would I have known?

I didn't know. I really didn't, and I never would. Thinking about it made me crazy.

"I would never see someone so close to home," I answer. "Why shit where you eat?"

"Don't be crass."

"I'm just saying. Pete and I are friends. And yes, on a few occasions, when I've been up at the Club having lunch alone, he's noticed and joined me. Nothing scandalous there."

"Oh, honey," Sarah said. "Don't you know the unwritten Waterford rule? Thou shall not dine with another woman's husband unless she is present? It's right up there with 'don't ever socialize with a man for more than a few minutes without his wife knowing about it.'"

Things hadn't been complicated in Portland. Men and women

intermingled and talked at parties. Not like here where there was a pink bubble for the women and a blue one for the men. As soon as you walked into a party, the women were whisked off to the kitchen and the men to the entertainment room where the flat screen blasted sports. To venture into the space of the opposite sex was daring, to say the least. Basically, when we went to parties, I spent no time with Jason.

I hated it, but he seemed okay with it.

"Speaking of socializing, how was your dinner with your friend the other night?" I asked. Will got home well after one which was incredibly late for a school night. If I had known Sarah was going to stay out until then, I wouldn't have let him sit for her.

She breathed heavily into the phone. "Dinner was lovely. We had drinks and dessert, too. I'm sorry I was out so late. We lost track of time."

"I'm a little jealous you got away from Waterford for the night," I said. "Jason likes to remain in the Waterford 'bubble,' so we don't get out much beyond a ten-mile radius."

Laughter poured out of the phone. "You're too funny!"

I didn't feel funny. I felt lost and alone.

"I have to run," I said. "I have a ton of errands to do before Henry gets home from school."

"We should do Costco on Monday," Sarah said. "I need to restock on basics."

I hated Costco and its mammoth warehouse. Even with three boys, I didn't need six dozen rolls of toilet paper or giant boxes of Bagel Bites, but going was a form of female bonding in Waterford. "Sure. What time?"

"Nine-thirty?"

"Since you have the Suburban, can you pick me up?" I asked. A Suburban was just another over-sized thing you needed to drag all your over-sized things back to your over-sized home.

"Of course! I have so much to buy, I doubt it will fit in your little SUV."

"Great! See you then."

I clicked off before Sarah could drag me into more gossip. I adored her, but that day I wasn't in the mood for socializing. My conversation with Jason the night before had left me awake well past midnight. I laid in bed, listening to my husband's soft breathing and wondering if it was like this when he slept next to *Her*. Did his hand reach out to hers in the middle of the night like he was trying to anchor himself to her? Did he roll over and throw his arm around her the way he does me? Did they sleep at all?

And what would life have been like if he had left? Or I left? Would my kids be traumatized? Would I be okay on my own even with my bipolar disorder? If I was honest with myself, I didn't want to know. Jason had threatened, more than once, to take the boys from me, and he was probably right. At times, I wasn't a capable parent on my own. Hell, I could barely shower and leave the house some days.

My brain was about to crash into what-if land if I didn't force it to abandon mission. I stretched out on the couch and closed my eyes, practicing what Dr. Carter taught me: take the negative thoughts and push them aside. Breath in and push negativity out.

When I found out about the affair, Jason came back to me without hesitation. He'd given up his mistress and cut off all contact. He did all the right things: spent time with the boys, made sure I took my meds, and busted his ass at work.

So why did everything feel so wrong?

9

THE PERFECT KIDS

You're only as good as your children in Waterford. They are, after all, mini-reflections of your awesomeness. Like if Johnny is a baseball stand-out, somehow that means you're a successful parent. Likewise, no one admits their kid's a fuck-up. It just isn't talked about.

But holy hell, are the kids here terrors. Take, for example, dinner last night. I decided to bring my kids to the Club for a special burger and wings night since my spouse was working late. About a third of the membership was there, and kids were running wild. Like literally running. Standing on chairs. Acting like spoiled brats. And I'm not talking about toddlers. More like eight, nine, ten, eleven, twelve, and thirteen-year-olds.

And the parents? Too busy socializing and drinking to reprimand them. Too busy bragging about what a great parent they are because their child made a travel team. Or a dance camp. Or mathletes. I could go on, but you get the picture.

Everyone's kid is a special snowflake that can't be told 'no.'

Seriously, if I have another conversation that consists solely of Junior's accomplishments or my beverage of choice, I may pull out my already thinning hair.

Heaven help me if my children ever behaved like that.

Actually, Heaven help them.

"Mom?" Will stuck his head into my massive bedroom.

"I'm over here, on the couch, honey." I'd spent the entire day laying around, ignoring phone calls and texts, and wishing the outside world away. I'd tried everything from meditation to screaming at myself, but even the thought of moving to take a shower paralyzed me.

My unbrushed hair and PJs testified to my inability to do life. It was just one more thing proving how unfit I was, and the reason why I always tried to make myself semi-presentable before Jason came home. I needed to make an effort.

Will lopped in, all arms and legs and the awkwardness that comes with being fifteen. An over-sized boy trying out an adult body. It was rather amusing.

"How are you?" he asked. My children, Will especially, had learned over the past year years to approach me gently, as if I were a fragile butterfly too delicate to hold. It wasn't like that before we moved. They used to rough and tumble all over the place, and my house had been a constant whirl of action and noise.

They learned from watching Jason.

"I've been better," I said. "Tell me about your day." I closed my laptop and set it aside so Will had my undivided attention. No matter how horrible I felt, I made a point to always be available to my boys.

Will hung his head and stared up at me with sad eyes. "You forgot it was your day to volunteer." I'd waited months for my turn to volunteer at the school store. It was, among the Women of Waterford, a plum volunteer opportunity at the high school. And we were all about volunteering.

"What?" I sat upright and let the blanket slide off my lap.

"Yeah. I put the note on the fridge last week, and now it's gone. I thought you'd seen it?" Disappointment peppered his words. "I went in to tell you something, but you weren't there. Mrs. Newbold said she'd texted you a few times, but you never responded."

I didn't remember seeing a note. Was it possible I read it and tossed it? It didn't seem like me, but then again, with my memory issues, who knows?

"Will, honey, I'm so sorry." I fought back my tears. I couldn't let my son see me as more of an emotional wreck than I was. "What did you come to tell me?"

Will puffed out his chest. "I have a Spring Dance date."

I inhaled sharply and smiled. "And who is that?"

"Bella Jones."

I had no idea who Bella Jones was, but pride radiated off Will, so I had to congratulate him. I could force myself to be upbeat if that meant pleasing my son. "That's great! Were you nervous?"

He tried to look nonchalant. "A little, but I heard she liked me, so I was thinking she'd say yes?" His voice did that weird up-tick teens do — the one I'd given up correcting.

"When's the dance?"

"March 25th."

"Let me put it in the calendar." I flipped open my daily journal and wrote it down in big, sloping letters. "Do you know what you want to wear?"

"Slacks. Nothing fancy, but I don't know what shirt."

"You have some time."

"I thought we could do a shopping trip?" His voice rose, and he ducked his head. Out of my three boys, Will was the most like me. Since his birth, we'd had a special connection, and thankfully still had it despite being in the thick of the teenage years.

"Dad has a few bow ties that you could borrow." I pointed at Jason's closet. "You could raid it, and I'll find you the perfect shirt. Unless you want to come with me?"

"Can I?" Youthful optimism and concern crossed his face.

"Of course. It's your dance and your outfit."

Will folded himself up pretzel-style and sat on the ground near the end of the couch. "Mom?"

"What, honey?"

"Are you sure you're okay? You seem sad."

I closed my eyes and sighed. "I'm tired, Will. That's all."

"It's more than that though, isn't it? You get tired a lot."

Truth from the mouth of babes. I tried so hard to hide my illness from the boys, but on days like that, I realized it's impossible. At least from Will. Ollie and Henry never seemed to notice. Or it had become ordinary to them.

I fluttered my eyes open. "Honey, I'm okay. I swear."

Will shook his head. "After you had your thyroid surgery, I read up on the side effects. Maybe you need to call the doctor? Excessive tiredness is a symptom of hypothyroidism."

His earnestness broke my heart. "You really have read up on this, haven't you?"

"Uh huh. Before the surgery, you did everything — the house stuff, volunteering at school, and you had your business. You were never this tired. If it's not your thyroid, what is it?"

I balled my fists into the cushion. I hated lying to him, but Jason and I had decided it's for the best. The boys were all too young to understand bipolar disorder, and we didn't want to scare them. "Things are different here. People are different. Life is extremely different."

"Do you miss Portland?"

"Yes, but that's not why I'm tired." I softened my face and opened my eyes a bit wider. "I just don't sleep well. That's all."

Will studied me and sighed. He opened his mouth, shut it, then opened it again, but no sound came out.

"What?" I asked.

"What's for dinner?"

"Stuffed shells if I can get myself together."

He stood and extended an arm to me. "C'mon. I'll help you. We can do it together like we used to."

His simple offer brought tears to my eyes, and the flat, gray hanging over me lifted a little. "I miss that."

"I miss it, too."

"Will?"

"What?"

"I love you."

With Will's help, I finished making dinner just as Jason walked in through the garage door. My husband took one look at me, the food, and Will, and a smile lit up his face. "This is the best thing I've seen all day."

He meant seeing me interact with the boys. What he didn't understand is that I tried. I wanted to be present. But my medicine made me flat. If it worked properly, I didn't deviate too much in either direction, just plain, in-the-middle gray flatness. Of course, I couldn't say that. No one wanted to acknowledge that maybe 'normal' wasn't best for me.

"What brought this on?" he asked me.

He reached for my shoulders and massaged gently, but instead of relaxing, I tensed. "Guilt," I said. "I forgot my volunteer session at Will's school today."

Jason stepped away from me and peered into my eyed. "You okay?"

"I'm fine," I lied. "But I don't remember seeing the note Will said he put on the fridge, and I had nothing written in my planner."

Jason nodded. "You showed me the note. Talked about how excited you were, so I assumed you took it down because you didn't need it anymore."

"I did?" My mind whirled as I tried to remember seeing the note, but I turned up nothing. No note. No mention of it from Jason or Will. No nothing.

Jason eyed me carefully. "You okay?"

"I think you're going to have to help me out a little more while I adjust to the new medicine dosages."

My husband patted my shoulder. "That's why I'm here. I'm your support."

I wanted him to be my husband. My rock. The guy I trusted more than anyone else. Not just a support propping me up because I was a mess.

"What did you make?" Jason asked Will.

"We have stuffed shells, an orange salad, and sautéed spinach and arugula."

A spark grew in Jason's eyes. "I can't wait to try it."

"Daddy!" Henry, the living missile, launched himself across the room and into Jason's legs. Jason ruffled our youngest son's hair.

"Oliver! Dinner!" I yelled.

There was a beat before my middle son poked his head out of office doorway. "I'm not hungry."

"Just come join us then." I wasn't in the mood for fighting or cajoling.

"Can I finish my game?"

"All you do is play that game." Jason drummed his fingers against the counter and raised his voice. "Your mother said come to dinner, so you better come to dinner."

No...No. No. No. I stepped back, retreating from the conflict, and my pulse raced. "Please, Ollie. Come to dinner."

Panic flit across my son's face. "I'm sorry. I'm coming. Let me sign-off."

My fingers clenched the spoon I held before dropping it to the floor. All I wanted was a peaceful family dinner. I wanted everything to be like life was before. I didn't want raised voices or bargaining. I didn't want memories of our last months in Portland when Jason was always yelling, that is if he were home.

Life was once so easy.

Then Jason had an affair.

Tangled sheets. Sweaty bodies. Wine-stained kisses.

The intrusive thoughts bombarded me. I couldn't help it. I couldn't let go. The pictures that didn't belong to me, played on an endless loop in my brain. Even though I had never met her, I had read the emails and the letters she scanned and sent me. I knew the pet names, the dates, the lies he told me. I saw the pictures hidden on his phone, and I begged Jason for every detail. Demanded answers to things I wish I could take back. Now, I knew everything...and it was destroying me.

How could it have gone on for nine months, and I never

suspected? I kept making excuses to myself and his family for his aloofness. I blamed everyone and everything except him.

Wasn't it funny how he cheated, and I was the collateral damage?

My palms grew clammy, and I grasped the edge of the counter so that I didn't tip over.

"Elizabeth? Are you okay?"

No. I would never be okay again. My perfect image of my family had been shattered. The dreams I once held of Jason and me sitting on our front porch watching our grandchildren play had vanished. I had been in this marriage for forever. But now? Now, I considered it a victory to get through a day.

Maybe I *should* pursue Pete. He seemed easy enough. And he was handsome and sweet. It would serve Jason right.

I swallowed the lump forming in my throat. How could I even think that after what I've been through? How could I do that to Veronica? It would destroy her. It would destroy any woman.

"Elizabeth?"

"I'm going to go upstairs. I need some time alone."

Will picked the spoon up off the floor and threw it across the room at Oliver's head. "Way to go, Ollie."

"Stop it!" I yelled. The tension in the room was too much. Much too much. I had to escape, or I would drown in it. "Just stop," I whispered. "All I wanted was one dinner together. Why can't I have that?"

"I didn't mean it, Mom." Tears rolled down Ollie's cheeks. "Don't go."

But I had to. The urgency to run overwhelmed me until fighting it was futile. I stumbled toward the stairs. "Just for a few minutes. Just give me a few minutes. I'll be back."

"Boys, sit down and start eating." Jason ordered as he stood behind me on the stairs. His hands pressed against the small of my back. "I've got you, sweetheart. I've got you."

I spun around and the sight of my children eating alone, again, enraged me. "Don't tell me you've got me. You didn't have me for the nine months you were having your affair."

"Elizabeth, don't." Jason prodded me like he's trying to get me up the stairs as quickly as possible. When I didn't budge, he leaned into me and whispered, "Elizabeth, you want to go upstairs. Trust me. Don't make this an issue."

"An issue?" I hissed. "Like you having an affair isn't an issue?" I ran my hand over the side of my face. "Why is this my fault, again? What exactly did I do wrong?"

"Go upstairs, Elizabeth." Jason pushed me slightly, and I fell onto the stairs.

"Stop it," I said, glaring at him over my shoulder.

Jason smirked. "Stop what? Wanting you to behave in front of the boys?"

"Don't." My gaze fell on the table. All three boys had their heads down and were eating methodically. Jason's affair wasn't a secret. Not from them, at least. They knew the basics. Our therapist felt it was important for them to know since he treated them so badly for so many months. Plus, we wanted them to know Jason's cruel behavior had a reason...and that reason was his affair. But my bipolar disorder...no, they didn't know about that.

"You need me. You don't realize it, but you do. Without me, you'd never see the boys. Not with your condition." Jason's warm breath fanned across the side of my face. "So be a good girl and get upstairs. I'll get your medicine, and everything will be fine."

I shuddered as I bit my lip. Jason was right, no judge would let me have custody of the boys. Not with my history. I'd realized that right after my diagnosis — around the same time Dr. Carter urged me to take my time before making any decisions regarding my marriage. She never said it, but she was clear: leaving Jason meant leaving my boys.

10

ALL ABOUT KAREN NEWBOLD

Three things you need to know about Karen Newbold:

    1.She runs Waterford, and everyone has a healthy dose of fear of her.

    2.She is invited to every party and attends them all.

    3.She's always complaining about how stretched thin she is.

Where do I start with Karen? Maybe the time she informed Stacey McLeod that she was too fat to be seen in pictures with her? But then she changed her mind and told Stacey to stand right next to her because it would make her appear thinner. Stacey, of course, did it.

I kid you not.

She stood there next to tall, thin Karen with her cheeks and gut sucked in, trying not to breathe. There's a copy of the picture on Facebook somewhere. You really should find it.

This is all a long way of saying that Karen has a way of fucking with people's minds, and she takes pleasure in it.

But at least most of us don't have to drug our kids with Benadryl to get them to sleep. And I can take mine out in public without worrying if they're going to act like idiots — something that apparently frightens Karen because she's never, not ever, seen with her kids outside of sporting events.

Anyway, Karen. Yeah, people do what she says. Including me. If you're on her bad side, no more social invitations for you. Which means you have no life in Waterford. Which means you should probably move. Or die. Or both.

My vote: Just do what she says.

Like everything else she did, Karen Newbold swished into the restaurant like an heiress on *Dynasty*. When I was a little girl, my mother had watched that show religiously, and I was allowed to stay up late to watch the antics of Alexis Carrington. We'd laugh and gasp and cry our way through each episode, and I believed it was all real even though my mom explained that no one actually lived like that. That real woman didn't wear necklaces encrusted with diamonds to simply go to the grocery store. I pointed out that no one on *Dynasty* did their own shopping, and my mom sighed. That would be the life, she had said.

Little did I know I'd end up living a real-life version of it where other people raised your kids, maids cleaned your house, lawn men kept the grass green, and there were even people who would come in and do your laundry.

I'd fallen into *Dynasty,* and I couldn't get out.

"Elizabeth," Karen squealed even though we saw each other just the other day. I stood so we could air kiss, but Karen grabbed me by the shoulders and eyed me over. I held my breath waiting for her judgement. "You look thin. Are you eating enough?"

With my best plastered smile, I answered, "1200 calories a day, one hour of running and another of yoga will do that."

"Well, you look wonderful!" Did I look thin and wonderful? Or just wonderful? Or maybe just thin? It was hard to know with Karen. She was one of those women whose compliments were often backhanded insults that you didn't get until hours later when you'd begin to doubt everything about your encounter with her. Karen was vicious — especially toward those she didn't like. Or worse, toward those she believed were moving up the social ladder too quickly. She made the rules. She decided who was in and who was out. And she always, always got her way.

"Thank you," I said. And with those words sealed my fate of eating only a plain salad with dressing on the side despite having had nothing for breakfast. Not that Karen would care if I were starving. No, she'd probably view it as a threat and up her game by only nibbling on a single piece of lettuce.

I really hated our meal time games.

"Did you hear?" Karen tossed her long, balayage brown locks over her shoulder and leaned closer to me. "It's everywhere!"

My eyes grew to the appropriate size as I shook my head. I read the blog, of course — who hadn't – but I doubted Karen was too scandalized by it. Okay, maybe the Benadryl part had upset her, but the rest of it was like an ode to Karen Newbold and the image she promoted.

"No, what's going on?"

Karen inhaled and exhaled loudly like she was about to deliver the saddest news ever when I knew for a fact she couldn't wait to tell me. "The list? You really haven't seen it?"

It took me a minute to understand what she was talking about. "The Ashley Madison thing?"

The night before, around bedtime, Jason had mentioned that someone in the community had posted the names and personal information of everyone on Ashley Madison – a site for married people looking to cheat — on our community list serve. I didn't care, and I didn't want to know.

But apparently, other people did.

"And," I said, trying to act interested when really the whole thing made me sick to my stomach. "Anything good?"

Karen tried to cover her glee with downcast eyes and a sad shaking of the head, she wouldn't be Karen Newbold if she wasn't secretly thrilled with whatever piece of gossip she had. "Pete was all over it."

"Pete White?"

"The very one."

I pursed my lips, but that didn't stop my insides from sliding down into my toes. "How is Veronica taking it?"

"She's a wreck, of course. Embarrassed. Angry. Everything you can assume."

Poor Veronica. Here she was going about her everyday life, brushing off the rumors of Pete's affair, until, finally, hard evidence was shared in a very public way. She was now one of *those women*, the ones too blind and stupid to know what their husbands had been doing. Instead of sharing the gossip, Veronica was going to be the woman everyone would stare at with pity, and every time she would walk into a room, lively discussions would drop to whispers. It was a club no woman should find herself in.

"Should I call her?"

"Give her some space," Karen said. "She's not seeing anyone right now. I mean, do you blame her? It was easy for her to blow off the gossip, but we all suspected, right? There's evidence, now. She has to throw him out or else she looks bad. Don't you agree?"

I nodded. I got it. I did. I wished I didn't, but I had earned my affair card. If she let him stay, some of the blame would fall on her, and no woman wants that. She'd be seen as a pushover and pathetic. No doubt Veronica had already had several people — like Karen – chime in on what she should do in her private marriage. Things like 'throw that bastard out' and 'once a cheater, always a cheater.'

It was five in the morning when Jason's phone buzzed, vibrating the bed. Normally, he turned off vibrate before going to sleep but on that day, he hadn't, so I crawled out from warmth of the duvet, retrieved his phone, and tried to turn it off. But I couldn't do it in the dark, so I took the incessantly vibrating phone into the bathroom. For some reason, my hands shook as I typed in his password. And there it all was. Email after email from his girlfriend.

"Jason," I said as my lungs seized. "Is he?"

Karen waved her hand as if to banish my negative thoughts. "No worries there. He's as faithful as can be."

Sheets tangled up. The taste of wine on lips. Promises whispered that will never be kept.

Faithful, my husband was not.

Once the grind of the garage door closing ceased, I rested my head on the steering wheel and let the tears fall. My lunch with Karen had been a disaster. Not that she could tell, but it had left me exhausted mentally and emotionally.

Tears dampened my eyes as I gently hit my head against the wheel. Why couldn't I let this go? Jason wasn't on that list. He had changed, and I needed to focus on that.

When I finally dragged myself from the car and upstairs to my bathroom, I glanced in the mirror. My eyes were rimmed red, and my skin was splotchy. Strawberry blond hair stuck out at all angles from my head.

I looked deranged.

The drawer holding my pills was directly in front of my hips, and I ran my fingers over the lip. Inside was a small pharmacy of drugs. Some to take me up, some to take me down, but all to make me level.

Elizabeth, don't.

I scrunched my eyes shut, and images of my children finding my lifeless body sprawled on the pristine white tiled floor filled my mind. No, they couldn't see me like that. No one could see me like that.

And yet, it appealed to me, the thought of just being done. Of lying on the cold, hard floor and being done. Game over. End of the line. Whatever you want to call it. Done.

I touched the thin, white lines crossing my forearm. Those scars were nothing compared to the ones on my heart. Those were thick and rope-like, and they hurt more, too.

That's my girl Jason had said to me before leaving this morning when I got out of bed without nudging. I hated when he said that. Those words. I hated it.

I tapped the drawer holding my pills. Not on this day. It didn't feel right, but then again, nothing felt right at the moment.

Before I could change my mind and swallow a zillion pills, I pushed away from the vanity to put space between myself and the drawer.

There are so many good things about this day. I needed to focus my thoughts on those. Not on pills and blades and pain.

I would get through this, and I would do my best to be happy, because the last thing I wanted is for all of Waterford to know I was a basket case.

But then I grabbed my phone and looked. Searched out the thing that brought me the most pain — pictures of *Her*. I delicately tapped through her Facebook page so I didn't accidentally like any of the photos and questioned why she selected the pictures she did to be public. Was it to prove something to me? Was it for Jason? Or was she really happy and had moved on while I stayed stuck?

Would I ever know?

My phone buzzed causing my heart to sputter out for a moment when Jason's face appeared on the screen.

"Hello?" I prayed I sounded normal.

"Hey. Just wanted to see how your lunch went."

"It went okay," I lied.

"Just okay?"

"We had a long talk about Ashley Madison. Pete was on it."

Jason was silent. Like he had literally run out of words or had put the phone down and walked away.

"Hello?"

"I'm here. I'm just...Well, I told you he wasn't the man you thought he was."

This isn't about Pete. It's about Jason. It's about how for a moment, I was braced to hear the worst — that he was on that list.

"Are you still feeling down?" Jason asked. "Should we call Dr. Carter?"

"No, I'm fine. I'm just tired from being with Karen."

Jason let out a short chuckle. "Why do you do this to yourself? You don't like those women. I mean, you kind of liked Veronica, but you called her boring, so I don't get it."

"I know, but..."

"But what?"

"I'm doing it for us. To make our lives happier. Isn't that what you wanted when we decided to move here?" Really, what I wanted was to fit in. I wanted to belong. I wanted to be one of the cool girls.

"I want you stable."

"What time will you be home?" I already knew the answer: late.

"Normal time. Around seven-thirty."

I forced some perkiness into my voice. "Okay. We'll see you then."

"I love you, Elizabeth."

I wished it were true. I wanted it to be true. "Thank you."

I tapped off my phone before Jason said anything else. Anything bordering on sentimental.

With my eyes closed, I leaned against the wall. A tangle of sheets, sweaty bodies, and wine-stained kisses. That's what filled my mind most of the day. Memories that didn't belong to me.

11

ARE YOU EFFING KIDDING ME?

ttention. Attention.

The Bitch Brigade is at it again, only this time they're organizing a lavish birthday party for Alexis. She's turning forty, but the amount of Botox in her head makes her look stuck somewhere between thirty-five and thirty-eight — which is a miracle due to the amount of vodka she consumes. Like all day, every day drinking.

Between that and the secret, not-so-secret smoking, she should look like a shriveled prune. Instead, she looks like undercooked piece of fruit leather dressed up in a gaudy Tory Burch tunic.

There's a reason I am not invited to the party.

Which is totally fine. I barely know her beyond what I've seen out and about. Still it's a party of about fifty people, and somehow, I didn't make the cut.

I'll be honest, it kinda sucks to be on the outside.

Sarah Cole, however, is invited, something she's thrilled about. I overheard her say she's waited three years for this kind of invite. I can't imagine waiting years for a bunch of catty bitches to notice you, but she has.

Anyway, Alexis has asked for an all-expense paid vacation to the Dominican Republic. I can't make this shit up. She wants her friends to pay not only their own airfare and accommodations, but also hers. And people are doing it!

What the hell? What ever happened to drinks at a bar, a bunch of "over the hill" balloons, and a nasty hangover the next morning?

Clearly, I'm doing life wrong or something.

I stared at my ringing phone before tossing it aside. It wasn't Jason or the kids' schools, so why bother? It rang again, but this time it was a different number. Karen.

"Hey, Sweetie," she purred. "Did you get my Evite this morning?"

I hadn't done much except lie in bed while surfing the internet and feel bad for myself. That's how most of my mornings had been going. "I haven't checked my email yet, why?"

"Well, it's time sensitive. About Alexis's birthday party. Can you and Jay make it?" I hated the way she called Jason, Jay. He was a Jason just like I was an Elizabeth.

I pulled up my email and opened the evite. "I thought you were going to the Dominican?"

"Change of plans. It's Key West now, and it's going to be major. So, can you guys come?"

I scrolled through the invitation. The party was a little over a month away. "Let me talk to Jason. We'll have to find someone to watch the kids."

"Oh, you have plenty of time to do that." Karen took on her general bossy tone. One that told me I must agree or else.

Words poured out of my mouth. "I'm sure it will be fine. My parents can come."

"Yay! I knew you'd say yes!" I had a visual of Karen jumping up and down while her fake boobs stayed perfectly in place. "Okay, girl-friend, I have to run. Love ya!"

I sat still. What had I just agreed to? Had I even agreed? More importantly, was Jason going to kill me? He hated when I made social plans without consulting him.

My phone rang again, and thinking it was Karen calling back, I answered without checking the number.

"Forget something?" I teased. I needed to keep the tone light so Karen didn't pick up on how annoyed I was.

"Elizabeth." That deep voice. The one that made me question everything I've been fighting for. "I need to talk to you."

"I can't. Jason...he said I can't talk to you."

"Don't hang up," Pete said.

I closed my eyes and gathered all my strength. "It's better this way, Pete."

"Elizabeth, please, listen to me. There are things you need to know."

My lungs burned, and each breath was like hot ashes being poured down my throat. "You should be worrying about your marriage right now, not bothering me."

I hung up without giving him a chance to explain, because I didn't want to know what Pete knew. I didn't want to listen. I just wanted everything to go back how it was before Jason and I moved here.

No, I wanted it to go back to how it was before Jason decided our life together wasn't good enough for him. Why, why had he done this to us?

Salty tears stung the corners of my eyes, and my heart skipped. Once, twice, three times before breaking into a gallop. What if Pete had called to tell me he loved me? That all those years ago, we made a mistake.

What would I do? Would I meet with him? Would I have an affair of my own? Would I leave Jason for Pete?

No. I wouldn't do any of those things. I'm not that woman, so I needed to stop before I made myself crazy. Plus, Pete didn't think of me like that.

At least, I didn't think he did.

The urge to call Pete back struggled with my desire to do the right thing. After a few minutes of hesitation, I blocked Pete's number and called Jason. My heart lodged in my throat and when my husband answered, I sobbed.

"Elizabeth, sweetheart. Are you okay?"

"No."

"Do you need me to come home?"

"I don't want you to get fired." My voice cracked, and I sniffed.

"What can I do? What do you need me to do? Did something happen?"

I couldn't tell him about Pete. He'd accuse me of leading Pete on or something. "No," I lied. "Just come home, okay?"

There was a pause as Jason clicked away on his keyboard. "I cancelled my afternoon meeting. I'll be home in an hour. Can you wait that long?"

"Yes."

"Okay. Please don't do anything to yourself. Hang in there."

"I will. I'll try."

"Do more than try. This is important. You've got to promise me you won't hurt yourself."

Snot bubbled in my nose. How could he require such a thing from me? "I promise."

"Okay. I'm coming home. I love you."

"I know." Images I couldn't control raced through my mind. Jason and *Her* laughing over drinks. Them lounging in bed doing cross-word puzzles. Him holding *Her* hand while walking along a beach in Hong Kong. It all melded together until I couldn't separate fact from fiction, and I was a sobbing mess.

The siren call of my pills was too much to overcome, and I stumbled toward the bathroom.

I had wasted endless hours looking up drug interactions, sometimes out of fear of overdosing and other times because I wanted to overdose.

This day had veered into one of the overdose days.

I lined my pills up neatly in a row and count them out. Sixty-three pills of varying shapes and sizes. If I did this right, and maybe drank a little wine, I'd pass out and never wake up.

Everyone would be better off without me. Jason could find someone more stable; the boys would no longer have to worry about my mood swings; and I wouldn't be a burden anymore. I'd be free of this endless cycle of depression and blandness I was trapped in.

Sixty-three pills and a bottle of red. That's all it would take.

I wandered back to my bed. It would be the perfect day to die. Jason, not the boys, would find me. Plus, it was gloomy out. Sad and gray the way I felt. Dying on a sunny day was wrong. Why ruin a day like that?

But did I really want to die?

I didn't know.

I tapped the track pad on my laptop and re-read Alexis's birthday evite. Three days in Key West, and everyone was expected to make a fifty-dollar donation to Alexis's birthday travel fund. Because she's so thoughtful, Karen had set up a PayPal account where we could forward our donations.

It all felt...like I'm paying to have friends.

What was it Sarah had told me? That she didn't associate with people outside of the Club. I ran my finger over the invitee list, leaving a streak on my computer screen. To my utter lack of surprise, all Club members. Jason and I included. It dawned on me that living in Waterford was like living in a frat house. We only socialized with "our kind" for the most part.

Jason and I had done many questionable things since moving to Waterford, but joining the Club had to be the worst. My husband loved golf, and the kids and I played tennis, so it seemed like a good idea. I mean, what else do you do in suburbia other than drive insane distances for sports practices and shop at Costco?

Turn into Alexis Frond and day drink the time away?

I gently closed my laptop and moved it over to Jason's side of the bed. With my knees pulled into my chest, I fought to draw a burning breath. I didn't want to go to Key West. I didn't want to be part of whatever this, all around me, was.

The pills were there waiting, and I needed to make a decision soon — before Jason got home and called 911.

I wanted out of this picture-perfect life.

That was a lie. I simply told myself lies about everything. They made me feel better.

Of course, I wanted to go to Key West. I wanted to be accepted. I wanted friends, not acquaintances, but I didn't know if it's possible with this group of women. At least, not while still remaining true to myself.

Maybe I should have gone out more. There were people beyond the Club. I could have busted out of the bubble, but then what? Would Jason approve? Would we be exiled socially by everyone who matters? And why did they matter, anyway?

With great effort, I rolled over and lifted my bullet journal from the table next the bed. Each date had a tidy list written below it. It gave me comfort knowing my day was planned and organized. The list for that day? Shower and go to the gym. That was it. Just two things, and I doubted I'd do either. Jason used to tell me to celebrate the tiny wins, but I couldn't help but feel loserly while looking at my list.

The deep gray of depression hovered over me. I had never experienced that before we moved to Waterford. Actually, I never felt like this until Jason had his affair. In London, despite what we told people, I was a mess.

But once, I was happy. Insanely, happy.

That day, the day I found out about Jason's affair, snapped my world into two: Elizabeth Before and Elizabeth After. As hard as I tried, I was stuck in the after and couldn't make sense of it. I was trapped in something greater than sadness — it was an overwhelming fog that caused extreme apathy toward everyone and thing. I couldn't even feel love toward my boys.

I wanted out. But first, I had to explain. To Jason and to the kids. I tore a piece of paper from my bullet journal and lifted the pen, but my hand wouldn't form letters. The words, they were all in my mind, but for some reason, I couldn't put them down on paper.

I simply wrote:

I'm sorry. I love you all, and I'm very sorry, but I can't do this anymore. My brain hurts too much. I love you.

I folded the paper and placed it on the bedside table. It looked naked, inconspicuous, laying there. What if Jason never found it? What if he just threw it in the trash thinking it was scrap paper?

With a hurried hand, I scrawled his name across the front. Now, he'd know. He'd have something to show the boys. Evidence that I loved them.

The pills called out to me again, and I didn't resist. I started with the green ones – 1 mg of Klonopin each — before moving onto the white oval ones. Then the larger white, round ones. Finally, the Trazadone.

I'd swallowed half the pills before I stopped.

I really didn't want to do this. Not on that day. So instead, I climbed back into my bed and tucked myself into a ball.

What had I done?

Overhead, the ceiling fan circled, and I slipped into a daze watching it. The fan whirled and whirled. My eyes grew heavy, and I closed them while fighting off a slightly sick feeling.

"Elizabeth!" Jason's voice was fuzzy, distant. "Where are you?"

I tried to speak, but couldn't. The pills had me. I belonged to them.

I didn't want this. I didn't.

Jason stumbled into our bedroom while calling my name. He dropped to his knees next to the bed, and his strong hand grasped mine. He squeezed it tightly. "Jesus, Elizabeth, what did you do?"

My tongue, my mouth, it was all stuck together, and I couldn't answer him.

"You took pills, didn't you?" I lolled my head side-to-side, and he grabbed me by the shoulders. "What did you take? How much?"

He released me and ran into the bathroom. My eyes fluttered closed again. Everything felt heavy. My chest, my arms, my brain.

"Stay with me, Elizabeth. Stay awake. The ambulance is on its way."

My eyes glued shut. It was much nicer that way. Peaceful.

"Oh, God, what did I do to you? Forgive me, please. Forgive me."

The boys and their friends ran from the waves as Jason and I sat up on the beach near the seagrass. It was New Year's Eve day and unusually warm for Portland. No rain, just a beautiful sixty-degree day with a light breeze.

"We should talk about the summer," I said. "We promised Will a trip to Europe, and I want to get it on the books. Plus, we need to nail down our Michigan dates for my parents and summer camps." Summers were always busy for us, and I liked to have everything set by the end of January. Planning gave me a sense of moving forward and productivity. Plus, with our busy lives, a schedule and plan were a necessity.

Jason stared at the horizon. Since getting to the beach, he'd been ignoring me and focused on playing with the kids. Actually, he'd been acting distant and avoiding me for weeks — since he returned from Asia - so the fact that I'd finally gotten him to sit with me was a mini-miracle.

"Hello? Are you listening?" I said, waving my phone in his face. "We need to calendar."

"I can't do this." Jason didn't change his gaze, but his body tensed.

"Do what? Summer?" I asked. "Why can't you do summer?"

Jason turned slowly until our eyes met. "No. Make plans with you when I don't see a future for us."

The roar of the ocean — or was it the roar of blood rushing to my brain – overwhelmed me. "What do you mean, you don't see a future for us?" Jason tried to take my hand, but I yanked it away. "Tell me what you mean."

"Just give me six weeks, Elizabeth. I need to sort some things – myself, I need to sort myself out."

I didn't want to hear this. I didn't want to know what he needed to sort out. I jumped to my feet. "Have you lost your mind?"

"Elizabeth, wait!"

But I didn't want to hear his answer, and ran up the sea grass and sand dune path toward the parking lot. About half-way there, I stopped and climb a hill and found a safe place surrounded by shrubs. Tears, so many tears, ran down my face. What was happening? Where was this coming from? Yes, Jason had changed over the past few weeks, but we'd always had a strong marriage. An enviable one. Not being able to make plans? Six weeks? Time? What the hell was happening?

Was I going to be thirty-seven years old and a single mother of three little boys? Would Jason do that to me?

When he didn't come find me, it seemed unreal.

When he didn't say a word to me on the ride home, it seemed possible.

When he didn't comfort me as I sobbed on our bed, it seemed inevitable.

1 2

EVERYTHING IS GRAY

When you go to a psychiatric hospital, your outside identity vanishes. You're no longer a wife, a mother, a friend. You're a patient. A cutter. A suicide risk.

After I was stabilized and my stomach pumped, the ER transferred me to the ward. Here I was strip searched and had all my belongings taken from me, which in this case meant my clothes. I was issued hospital wear, assigned a room, and loaded up on meds to level off my mood.

It's ironic, isn't it? I took too many pills, the doctors pumped them out of me, and the psychiatrists filled me back up.

Jason sat across the table from me. Dark circles rimmed his bloodshot eyes, and his stubble was longer than normal. I guess I would look awful too if my spouse had tried to kill himself.

He reached for my hand, and I let him hold it. Having him with me was the best part of my day. "Tell me how to fix this. Tell me what I need to do."

"I don't know." My voice creaked because my throat still ached from the tube being pushed down it. I didn't want to die in that moment. But I had a few days earlier. How do I explain that to someone who's never been in my head?

He shut his eyes as if trying to find the patience to deal with me. "I told the neighbors you had a seizure. That we don't know what caused it, and you are under observation until we resolve the issue."

"Nice cover story. How long did it take to think that one up?"

"Elizabeth, don't. I had to explain the ambulance somehow. Plus, the boys..."

"Are they okay?" My insides quivered. My poor, poor babies. What kind of hell did I put them through?

Jason reached under the table and pulled up his work bag. He laid some pieces of paper on the table. "They made you these. They're get well cards."

My fingers crept toward the cards, but I couldn't make them go all the way. "Read them to me."

"It's that bad?"

I nodded. "It's the drugs. They make me flat."

Jason's brows knitted together in disappointment. "What does that mean, Elizabeth? Flat. You always say that, but what does that mean? That you have no feelings? That you don't care that our boys are freaking out about your health?"

He flung his words carelessly at me, and each one punched a tiny hole in my heart. "It means I can't. I'm selfish, or whatever you want to call it. But I can't." I stood up. "I'm tired. All this medicine makes me drowsy."

"I want the best for you. I wish we could beat this once and for all. I'd give anything for that."

"I have bipolar disorder brought on by a traumatic life event. That's a life sentence."

Jason walked around the table and hugged me tightly. "It doesn't have to be life like this. It really doesn't."

Until that moment, Jason had ignored everything I'd had to say on the matter. How Dr. Carter thought we need to move somewhere more vibrant. Back to the city. Any city. Somewhere where my creative juices could flow, and I could feed off the busy energy. Life out here, she had said, was dulling me. And she was right. I was surrounded by highly-educated, bored housewives. Was it any wonder they thrived on drama and gossip?

"Let me love you," he said. "I can't love you if you don't let me."

I lifted my arms and stiffly hugged him back. Since his affair there were three things I never did: tell Jason I loved him, kiss him first, and hug him. Even when we had sex I stayed distant. The possibility of our relationship getting better kept me going, but it had been a year, and the struggle hadn't improved.

"I want a divorce."

Jason exhaled. "Not this again. Not now. You need to rest and repair your mind."

He was right. He was always right. I didn't want a divorce because despite everything, losing my boys would devastate me. And I'd lose the boys. According to Jason, the state of Virginia gave a lot of weight to a parent's mental health. With my possibly-maybe suicide attempt, it was even more likely I'd lose them. No, divorcing Jason wouldn't make anything better.

It wouldn't lift the gray, and I would be alone and without custody of my boys.

Only going off my meds made me feel alive, and that higher place was one where I wasn't supposed to visit. Hypomania was strictly off-limits.

"Okay," I said. "I'll push that thought away."

"That's my girl." He laced his finger through mine and guided me toward the hallway. "Let me see your room."

"It's awful."

"This isn't an all-expenses paid vacation, Elizabeth."

"Maybe we can do one of those once I'm out of here. It would be good for the boys, too, don't you think?"

"I'll look into it."

We stopped outside my door. My roommate was gone, probably at group or something, so I let Jason step inside. "That's my bed." I pointed at the hospital bed where I spent all my non-meals and non-therapy hours. "It's actually comfortable."

"Let's get you out of here." Jason tugged me toward the door. "Let's get you home. I don't want to see your hospital bed or hear about you being pumped full of more drugs. I want you home with me and the boys."

Part of me wanted to scream 'yes,' but the other part was terrified. What if I went home, and I did this again? What if I wasn't ready for the outside world?

"Do you think I can? I mean, my psychiatrist here would need to approve it since I'm not voluntary, and--"

"You've been here a week. That's above and beyond the mandatory hold period. Are you afraid to come home?"

"No, of course not." I said the words he wanted to hear because I needed him to believe me. Plus, I wanted him to see me as strong, confident, and able to fight this beast that haunted me. I needed him to believe in me because most days, I didn't believe in myself.

"Why don't you wait here while I talk to discharge? Let's get the ball rolling and get you out of here." For the first time since he'd walked in, Jason seemed himself. He had a purpose and mission, and that was getting me out of the psych ward.

"Okay." I sat on my bed. "I'll wait here."

"Good. I'll be back in a few."

The psych ward was a horrible place, but I felt safe. Someone told me what to do and when to do it. I made no decisions. My tasteless food was prepared for me. My clothes were like everyone else's. I only had to deal with the outside world when it walked through the door in the form of Jason.

But it was time. Jason and I both knew it. I couldn't keep hiding.

I needed to go home.

Home felt wonderful, but scary, and I wasn't sure I was ready to answer the questions people will throw at me with the lies Jason concocted. But those lies were better than the truth. Or at least they seemed to be. After all, who wanted to be friends with the woman who swallowed a few dozen pills to try to end her suffering?

No one. That's who.

Before he went downstairs, I asked Jason to hide my pills. It was better that way. I didn't trust myself with them, and despite the lies I feed my psychiatrist, I wasn't really ready to be out. Not at all.

But I had to be. My boys needed me.

And that's the selfish part, isn't it? They needed me, and I almost took myself from them. I couldn't see beyond my own never-ending pain to envision what living without me would be like for them.

I was a horrible mother. I had more than proven that.

The boys were still at school, and Jason was making us some sort of lunch, which would prove interesting since ordering out was his specialty. Still I appreciated the effort.

I closed my eyes and listened for a little bit to him banging around the kitchen. The old me, the Before Elizabeth, would go down and take over. The After Elizabeth wanted nothing more than to avoid doing anything.

Depression had made me lazy, and I hated it.

"This is the best I could do." Jason stood at the end of the bed holding two plates. "Panini pressed peanut butter and banana sandwiches."

"My favorite."

He handed me a plate. "I know."

And that was the thing, wasn't it? He knew me inside and out. Just like I thought I knew him. My Jason would never cheat. We were happy. We had everything. And yet he did cheat. He found comfort in someone else. He left me emotionally adrift for months telling me he loved me, but wasn't in love with me. That he wanted good things for me, but wanted to move to New York for two weeks a month and leave the boys and me behind.

I was still wrapping my brain around the whys and the questions he had no answer for.

"Henry will be home in about twenty minutes," I said. "I can't wait to see him. All the boys. I can't wait to see all of them." I take a big bite of the gooey sandwich. It tasted amazing — especially after the hospital food I'd been forced to consume for the past week.

"Every night, he asks when you're coming home and if he can visit you. This will be a surprise for him. We all missed you."

"I missed all of you, too." I rested my head back on my pillow and stared at the ceiling. "Did any of my friends ask about me?"

Jason glanced toward the bank of windows lining the far wall. "Sarah wanted to visit, but I told her the hospital was only allowing family. She had some meals sent."

"That was sweet." Of course, I could count on Sarah to help care for my family. "Did anyone call you?"

Jason frowned. "I ran into Karen. She said to give you her love."

"I see."

"They were all probably busy."

Or not. They just didn't care about anyone out of sight except to gossip about them. And, if Jason's cover was believed, there wasn't much to gossip about here.

Peanut butter stuck to the roof of my mouth, and I pressed my tongue against it to loosen it up. "This is going to sound awful, but I'm worried about getting overwhelmed. I don't want to shut down in front of the boys."

Jason took my empty plate and stacked it with his. "I'll do my best to be vigilant. If you start going into distress, you need to let me know. I'm not a brain reader."

"Okay."

My husband frowned.

"What?"

"I didn't want to discuss this now, but part of your release requires a social worker visit. Or visits."

A sinking feeling filled my heart, and I leaned back in the bed. "Why?"

"Elizabeth, we need to prove you can parent. You triggered the system, and for now — until we're told otherwise – you don't have parental rights."

"What?" I cried. "What do you mean?"

Jason held my hand. "Sweetheart, it's for the best. You can't parent and get healthy at the same time."

"You had my parental rights terminated?"

He shook his head. "No. It's standard procedure after a suicide attempt. All it means is that you can't be alone with the boys for more than a few hours." He dropped my hand. "Didn't I tell you something like this would happen?"

I burrowed into my duvet and let my head rock side-to-side as I sobbed. I'd taken a bad situation and made it worse. Much worse. And now my boys were the ones to pay.

How could I have been so selfish?

13

BREAKING HEARTS AND BREAKING RULES

Meredith Baine is not to be messed with. She doesn't run with the Bitch Brigade, and she's not a Periphery Girl like Sarah. With the exception of Elizabeth Mavery, Meredith has her own group of friends that doesn't overlap at all with the Bitch Brigade. This is one of the reasons I adore her. The other is her bluntness.

The Ashley Madison leak has her livid. No, her husband wasn't on it, but several of her friends' husbands were. And to her that gives her permission to lay into them.

It all started at her ridiculously huge house party. The DJ (yes, an actual DJ) had the make-shift dance floor full, and everyone was drinking liberally — except Meredith. She abstains which I find admirable because ninety-nine percent of the neighborhood are drunks. There was a break in the music, and without warning, she turned to the guy next to her and started yelling about what a disgusting pig he was. At first, no one said anything and the guy – Bentley or something — just laughed. He took a long swig from his drink, and made the crazy sign next to his head. But everyone knew what Meredith was talking about, and his wife started crying. So, Meredith screamed at her to grow a pair and leave the dick.

No one knew what to do. Two women tried to comfort the wife, but everyone else just backed away, creating an empty space around Bentley *and his distraught wife. Picture it: here was a sobbing woman, and only two people out of one hundred stepped forward to comfort her. Not exactly the picture of solidarity.*

Even better: not one person said a word to Meredith.

All-in-all, one of my more entertaining nights out in Waterford.

There seems to be an unwritten rule that no one openly discusses cheating. No one wants to know. Except Meredith. She wants to know, and she wants you to know she knows. While the Bitch Brigade is a vice parade, Meredith is a one-woman morality crew, passing judgment as she sees fit.

Anyway, Bentley and his wife gathered their things and bolted. Part of me wonders if Meredith invited them just to make a scene. Granted I don't know her well, but it doesn't seem like her style to humiliate her friends without cause.

I'm happy to report that I wasn't carried out by my hands and feet like Janet Tildy who passed out in the kitchen. I think she hit her head, but no one seemed to care too much. They just loaded her into a wheelbarrow and dumped her out on her front lawn.

God, the people here are fucked up.

All my new pills stared up at me. They were going to stay on the counter, too, because there was no way I was swallowing them. Not in my current state of drunkenness. We had been the last to leave Meredith's party, and the amount of alcohol I had consumed showed it. While most people may have had one, maybe two or three glasses of wine, I thought I had had five. Maybe. And a shot of fireball to finish off the night.

"You have to take these. You'll be a mess if you don't." Jason scooped up the pills and waggled his hand, but I didn't reach out for them. Since I'd come home, he'd been all over me about taking my pills, and for the past week, I'd been good about doing as I was told.

The room spun around me — a reminder that I'd, once again, had too much to drink.

"I'll set my alarm and take them at four." The words slurred off my tongue.

"I can't let you do that. We have a social services meeting tomorrow. You need to be stable."

That sobered me up. "What? Why didn't you tell me?"

Jason shook his head. "I did. Yesterday. And tonight, when you were pounding back your second drink, and after the third. Oh, and before the Fireball. I told you a hundred times, and you didn't seem to care."

"You're lying," I said, panicking. "I would remember."

"Well, I'm telling you again." He held out the pills. "Now take them."

"Why do you let me drink so much?" I asked. "You refilled my glass. I remember that."

"Funny how your memory works." My husband clenched his jaw. "Really, funny."

I held out my hand. He dropped the multi-colored pills into it and gave me a bottle of water. "You don't understand. When I take them mixed with booze, it makes everything worse. I get sicker. And drunker. And--"

"Meaner."

The word hung in the air waiting for one of us to acknowledge it.

"I'm not mean," I slurred. "I don't want to die of an overdose."

"But I thought you did want to die. Isn't that what you're always saying?" He'd progressed from caring to vicious.

I stripped off my clothes and crawled beneath the covers. "Fuck you. For someone so concerned about my well-being, you certainly are being a dick."

"So that's a 'no' to dying today." Jason sat on the bottom edge of the bed and grabbed my foot from under the blankets. He massaged me as he spoke. "Elizabeth. It's just I don't know what to do. You're self-destructing, and I feel powerless to help you. We have this meeting at eleven tomorrow, and I don't know if you're going to be functioning."

"I know." And I did. He tried, but the only person who could fix me was me. Dr. Carter liked to tell me that I was resilient and strong, and for having been through so much, it was amazing I functioned at all.

But that's the thing: Was I functioning? No. Not really.

I popped the pills in my mouth and chased them with water. "When I'm sick as hell, it's your fault for not listening to me. I'm going to say 'told you so' because I'm going to be better off if I didn't take them."

Jason rolled his eyes. "I'll hold your hair back when you puke."

"Gee, thanks," I said. "But what are we going to do about the meeting?"

Jason's lip twitched. "We'll say you have the flu, if we have to."

I sighed. This wasn't going to end well.

Dr. Carter stared at me. Once again, I'd left the seemingly unshockable shocked. Her lips formed a tight, thin line. "You need to stop your destructive behavior. No amount of medicine will help if you don't make an effort. Drinking isn't going to cure anything. Haven't you learned that from your hospitalization?"

"It's not destructive, it's therapeutic. A glass of Merlot helps me fit in and takes the edge off my anxiety."

"Maybe so. However, if you learned anything from your recent hospital stay, isn't it that you need to practice better self-care?"

"Yes."

"Are you still having thoughts of driving into a tree?" She was searching for suicidal tendencies, and my favorite scenario was a one-car accident where no one else gets hurt. Just me and a tree.

"No." And it was the truth. I'd moved on to less violent things. Like overdosing.

"What else has been going on?"

I sank lower on the microfiber couch. "We had a home visit the other day."

"Oh? How did that go?"

"Weird." I shrugged. "I don't know. I didn't know we had the meeting until the night before when Jason sprung it on me after I'd been drinking."

"Did you get through the visit successfully?"

I ran my hand over the silky-soft couch. "I think so. We have another meeting next week. I wrote this one in my journal so I wouldn't forget. But really, Jason shouldn't have put me in that position, and he should have cut me off after one glass."

Dr. Carter's gaze pierced me. She was a lovely woman, and I really did think she was helping me get better, but I was frustrated by how many set-backs I'd had. After a year, shouldn't I have been past Jason's affair? And if so, why did it haunt me? "You're a grown woman, Elizabeth. You should cut yourself off or, even better, not start at all. Don't blame Jason."

She had a point. She always did, but it stung none-the-less.

"His concern for me only happens when it's convenient," I said. Until the words left my mouth, I hadn't considered this feeling. I didn't even know where it came from.

"That sounds hard."

"Sometimes." I tapped my high-heeled shoe against the shag carpet.

"You seem anxious."

The clock over the door ticked, ticked, ticked. I only had fifteen minutes to go. I could get through this. "It's nothing. Just social anxiety."

"It doesn't have to do with Social Services visiting?"

"I don't think so," I lied. The visit went okay despite my hangover. Jason and I presented a united front, and I didn't say anything incriminating. Despite all that, it was going to be at least six months before I could stay overnight with my children unsupervised.

"Well, then. Social anxiety. Are you still friends with Karen and her group?"

"They've swallowed me whole."

"How does that make you feel?"

Hmmm. "I'm not sure. Good, I guess. I mean, I have friends and having friends is a good thing."

"Do you enjoy their company?"

"I guess so. Endless hours of gossip and all that." I shifted. "I'm closest to Sarah, though."

"That's what you've said. Does she like you?"

That was a good question. I thought she did, but sometimes, I got the feeling she was jealous of me and my friendships with the other women. "Yes."

Dr. Carter's face was a mask I couldn't read. "Is there anything else you'd like to discuss?"

I tapped my head softly against the back of the couch. "Did you see the stuff about Ashley Madison?"

"I did. Was Jason on it?"

"No. For once he didn't fuck up and kept his dick in his pants."

"You're angry."

"Not really."

Dr. Carter scribbled something on her note pad. I would have given anything to know what was written there. Probably things like: compulsive liar, nut job, and self-destructive.

"Then why are you bringing it up?" she asked.

I ran my tongue over the raw spot on my lip where I've bitten off the skin. It tasted faintly metallic and bloody. "It's awful, isn't it? The way people will cheat."

"Some people find monogamy difficult. But that's not what you're saying is it?" Behind her words came a steady stream of white noise. It was supposed to soothe her patients — especially anxious ones like me – but sometimes I got lost in the sound. The whoosh, whoosh, whoosh.

"What?"

"I think there's something more to what you're asking."

My teeth worked on another spot of my lip, tugging and pulling at the skin. "It's premeditated cheating, isn't it? It's somehow worse, isn't it?"

"Depends on how you view it." More writing. More judgement about Elizabeth's mental well-being. Or lack thereof.

"Right. I guess a one-night stand rates the best, followed by getting involved with a co-worker, then probably being involved with your spouse's friend, and the worst has to be Ashley Madison."

"You've thought about this?" Scribble, scribble, scribble.

"Not really. It's just, so many people in my neighborhood were on that list — all guys – and no one, well one person, is acknowledging it. It's like these men weren't, aren't, cheaters."

"What would you like done?" she asked. "They've already been publicly outed. Their friends and family know, and people are choosing to look the other way."

"Isn't that wrong?" I said. "The way life simply gets back to normal for these guys?"

"Would you like it splashed all over Facebook the way it was with Jason and you?"

A sigh formed at the back of my throat and escaped through my nose. "I just feel like, maybe their wives..."

"You stayed, Elizabeth."

"But for how much longer?"

Dr. Carter peered at me over her glasses. "What do you mean? Do you want a divorce?"

Hearing her say it out loud made my insides churn, and I wanted to puke. "Sometimes," I admitted. "Sometimes, I worry I'm the only one doing anything to save this marriage."

"Jason wouldn't be jumping through Social Services hoops to protect you if he wanted out. Being married to a person with mental illness is a difficult decision — especially one who attempted suicide."

And there it was: because he was in my business, Jason was a good guy. It showed he was working on the marriage. But was he? My brain said he was checking off every box, but my gut told me something wasn't right.

14

MEMBERS ONLY

Do you remember being at a high school dance and worrying no one would want to dance with you? That's me, right now, at the Club's Members Night. Familiar faces are all around me, but no one takes a minute to say 'hi'. It's like I'm not here. And maybe I shouldn't be – I'm not exactly fond of these people.

I'm trapped in a sea of blingy tunics, leggings, and hookerish over-the-knee boots. The email invite said dressy casual, but I should have known what Waterford dressy casual meant versus real world dressy casual.

None of that matters, now, because I've escaped to the shadows of the Club's veranda and am typing furiously on my phone. It's North Pole cold, and my fingertips may be turning blue, but I'm not alone. I'll give you one guess who's out here with me besides the smokers. Did you say Elizabeth Mavery? Then you are correct! And guess what? Like me, she's off in the corner. She's wrapped up in a fur coat and looks like she's trying to disappear. Earlier, she was just standing in the Pub as if waiting for someone to talk to her. Since the Bitch Brigade hadn't arrived en masse yet, I assume she felt a little lost. But now she's out here alone which makes me wonder if she's had a falling out with the Karen and all.

Anyway, I'm the quiet one in the corner, watching and taking notes. Well, at least I am when I'm not out on the veranda freezing. I really should *go inside. Unlike Elizabeth, my absence has probably gone unnoticed. Like I said, it's like being at a dance where no one is interested in you. So, I'm hanging out, watching the cool kids make asses of themselves. Or at least I hope that's what happens. It makes nights like this so much more enter-taining.*

I know you want more gossip, but I don't have anything yet because everyone is behaving just as expected – like drunk toddlers.

All right, time to suck it up and head back inside the looney bin. I have a feeling tonight is going to prove interesting.

Stifling, booze-scented air enveloped me when I re-entered the Club. Karen and Veronica stood shoulder-to-shoulder, huddled up with a bunch of Periphery Girls near the fireplace looking at their phones.

Karen ran over to me and nearly knocked me over. "Who was out there with you? Did you see anyone?"

"No."

"Well, the writer of that blog is here, and they saw you outside. So, who was there with you?"

I looked over my shoulder, back towards the door. "I didn't see anyone except for a few guys smoking cigars."

"Think, Elizabeth. Who did you see?" Irritation seeps into Karen's words. I was failing her, and that wasn't acceptable.

Veronica had stayed with the other women, and when she caught my eye, she turned her head as if my mere presence was offensive. It had been like that ever since Jason told me to stay away from Pete. She must have gotten the same memo because we had had zero contact.

"Elizabeth, who was there?" Karen demanded. "I know you know. We can end this all tonight, if you just think."

The room hummed with noise, and people stared at us. Here I was, in a fur coat, in the middle of the ballroom, with Karen demanding to know who was with me. "I don't know," I snapped. "I have to use the bathroom."

95

"Go." Karen dismissed me before swinging back into her adoring gaggle. "I'll figure it out myself."

Around me, the crowd laughed and sipped cocktails, but their never-ending whispers made me nervous. As I wound my way through the room, away from Karen, I caught snippets of my name, but I didn't look to see who was talking about me. Instead, I kept my head down and tried to still my heart.

Near the sliding hall doors, Jason held an amber-colored drink while talking to some guys I didn't know. I snuck up behind him and dragged my arm across his lower back. Just a little something to let him know I was there. Despite what I told Dr. Carter, out of everyone in the room, I chose him.

Noise bombarded me from every side, so when he greeted me, his voice was lost.

"What?" I asked, leaning into him.

Jason's lips touched my ear, and the stubble of his slightly graying scruff scratched my face. His warm, liquored breath hit me hard. "Are you doing okay?"

For a second, I considered telling him that everyone was talking about us, but he looked like he was having fun, so I tuned out the whispers and smiled. "I'm great. Who are your friends?"

"Just some guys." The Scotch in his hand swayed, but didn't spill. Jason would never spill. It wasn't in his DNA to make mistakes. He was perfect. We were perfect. Everyone look away. No warts to see here. "Why don't you find Karen? She was looking for you."

"She's with Veronica." I waited for a reaction, but Jason coolly sipped from his glass. "Maybe I should avoid that whole group tonight?"

He shrugged. "Do whatever you want. I'm not going to force you to be friends with anyone."

I didn't understand how one minute he questioned my wanting to be friends with Karen and her friends, and the next, he's encouraging me to hang out with them. "I wish Sarah was here."

Jason made a gun sign at his temple.

"What?"

"You're always with Sarah. Try something new. Try being friends with people that actually matter."

Unlike me, Jason had gotten more and more comfortable running with the "popular" crew. Which meant, if I crushed his social climbing by being weird, he'd kill me.

"Maybe you're right," I said as I wrapped myself tighter into my fur coat. Jason didn't acknowledge that my cheeks were flushed from the frigid night air or that I was still dressed for outside. He, for the first time in ages, didn't notice me. He spoke to me, but he didn't really see me.

Maybe it was the Scotch. Or maybe it was that for one night, he was done caring. Done asking. Done worrying about me.

I was invisible.

The crowd churned around us, and we shuffled closer to the bar. The weight of the throng pressed heavily against my chest. It crept along my nerve endings and threatened to send me into an anxiety attack.

Breathe, Elizabeth, breathe. Count to four and breathe.

But it was no use. I needed to get out of there. Away from the noise and people and drinks. I needed somewhere warm to hide and regroup.

Against the backdrop of bedazzled women, my fur coat stood out, so I tossed it over the full coatrack behind me. It hung there like a mangled, dead animal.

A flash of dirty blond hair caught my eye, and my pulse quickened. I didn't want to turn my head, but he was there, watching me from near the windows. I trembled slightly. Since his falling out with Jason, Pete had kept his distance with the exception of the phone call.

Why hadn't I spoken with him? What was I afraid of?

The whispers around me intensify.

Jason clamped his hand down on mine. "Hey, are you sure you're okay. You're shaking and seem rattled."

Pete had vanished. Like an apparition stalking me in my nightmares.

"It's nothing. Just medicine side effects. I took Klonopin before we left." That was the beauty of taking so many drugs...they were easy to blame for weird behavior. Like suddenly having shaking hands.

"Isn't that supposed to calm you?"

"Guess I need more."

Jason went into caring husband mode and squeezed my hands tighter. "You're freezing. Are you sure you're okay?"

"I'm fine. Just a little cold from being outside." I brushed my lips over Jason's whiskered cheek. "I'm going to find Karen and the girls."

He didn't say anything, just focused his attention back to the guys. Oh. So that was how it was. I was discarded.

I didn't blame him. I'd throw me back, too.

All around me, people laughed and drank and shouted to be heard over the din. Usually, I like the anonymity of crowds, but not that night. Instead, it suffocated me, and I had to get out.

I bumped my way past unknown people before finally making it to what was once a grand hallway. Small worn spots dotted the patterned carpet, and faint stains covered the wing-chairs near the bathrooms. It was shabby, and not in a chic way. More in an every-thing needed an overhaul way, but no one cared anymore. It was one of those things where if you see it enough you stop noticing.

Half-way down the stairs toward the locker rooms, I paused on the wood-paneled landing. The whispers were gone, and it was less noisy even though the crowd above roared. I pressed against the wall as I inhaled for a four count, held my breath, and exhaled for eight. In and out. In and out. Three times, just like Dr. Carter taught me. Sure enough, my anxiety nibbled away at me a little less, and my speeding heart slowed.

Maybe I don't need medicine after all?

"Elizabeth?" I snapped my eyes open. Pete stood at the railing above me. His dirty blond hair was perfectly mussed and the top two buttons of his dress shirt were open. He looked dressy casual, and frankly, gorgeous. "Are you okay? What are you doing down there?"

He had balls going out in public after the Ashley Madison thing. Or maybe, like the blog post said, no one but Meredith cared. I didn't try to understand anymore.

"I'm fine. The room was getting a bit too crowded for me, so I left." I smiled politely.

"Yeah. I don't think they expected this kind of turnout."

"Why are you out here?" I asked. My heart raced erratically because Pete was the last person I wanted seeing me have an anxiety attack. Well, after Karen that is. The less he knew, the better. "Shouldn't you be inside enjoying a beer and talking golf?"

"Shouldn't you be with the girls discussing...I don't know...handbags or something?" His clear blue eyes skimmed over me, and a vulnerability I thought long gone resurfaced. He walked down the staircase until we were standing about a foot apart. A safe, respectable space.

I was a safe, respectable woman.

Sarah's words and warning resurfaced. He was cheating on Veronica, but with whom? If anyone saw us together, would that make the blog post more believable? Would I be cast as the woman trying to destroy Pete and Veronica's marriage?

"You should go in. Jason is going to come looking for me soon and -"

"Seeing us together will piss him off?" Pete's hand trailed over my bare arm sending shocks to my frozen heart. I thawed a little.

"You shouldn't touch me, it's not appropriate," I said even though I very much wanted him to touch me. How awful is that? I liked that a married man was touching me. "Go find Veronica."

His shoulders rolled forward. "Are you sure?"

A tiny bit of resolve latched onto my brain and drove my actions forward. "It's for the best."

He rubbed my forearm before turning away. When he reached the top of the stairs, he spun around. "Jason doesn't deserve you."

"And Veronica doesn't deserve you."

He flashed a toothy, white, chicklet grin. "Maybe we deserve each other?"

"Probably not."

A deep laugh roared out of him. "You're probably right."

When Pete's blond head disappeared around the corner, I slumped to the floor.

Sarah once asked if those men at the burger joint would be interested in dating someone like us. If Pete knew I spent time in a mental hospital, popped pills daily, and needed therapy on a weekly basis, would he still flirt with me?

Would anyone?

15

SECRETS AND LIES

A *lert! Alert! Alert! I've got something juicy for you!*
Karen Newbold took a three-week vacation to Brazil and has come back looking a little fresher than normal. I mean, the chick is forty-four and has three kids under the age of eighteen. She should have a little sag to her boobs, wiggle to her middle, and cellulite. Instead, she's perky all over, her lips are plump, her wrinkles are gone, and her stomach is as flat as a board. She claims she spent two weeks at a yoga retreat practicing for hours each day, and that's what has given her such a newly young appearance.

Interestingly, she hasn't said what she did during the other week, but I'd wager it involved Vicodin, ice packs, and plenty of downtime.

Everyone is calling bullshit, but no one will say it to her newly taut face. So, she, Karen Newbold, the woman who supposedly runs Waterford, is the current hot topic and the one everyone laughs at behind their hands.

But seriously, how do you get your lips so plump without a little filler? Did she do too many downward facing dogs, and all the blood went to her lips?

Okay, I may be a tiny bit jealous, or maybe this place is getting to me, but I really want my stomach done. I want the washboard abs everyone else seems to have, and I doubt my husband would tell me no – I've caught him staring at Karen and her friends more than once.

Anyway, that's all I've got. The perfect woman got a perfect reboot.

And hey, she looks good, so there's that.

My soaked mat reeked, so I rubbed a towel over it before rolling it up. I'd clean it with a vinegar solution at home, but at that moment, I needed to hurry; my friends were waiting to chat. Desperate to not be left out, I rushed from the ninety-five-degree room.

"That was sooo good!" I said, dropping my mat onto a black, wooden bench. "I feel amazing." It's one of the things you're supposed to say after a particularly hot and sweaty yoga class. I wasn't sure why, but it was. And lately, I was all about doing what I was supposed to.

"Me too! I'm ready for my run. It's my first one since getting back from Brazil." Karen slipped on her tennis shoes. These women were dedicated to keeping themselves in great shape. Something, I struggled with. Granted, I suspected a lot of it had to do with surgeons and scalpels, but they still looked amazing. Especially, Karen. Whatever she'd done in Brazil suited her.

"Are you feeling better?" Alexis asked me in her annoying, nasal voice. "We haven't seen you in a while."

She wasn't the friendliest toward me, so I wasn't sure how to take her question. "What do you mean? I saw you at the Member Party."

"From your seizure? Isn't that why you haven't been to class"

"Oh, right." No one, except Sarah, had brought up my hospital stay, but they must have talked about it with each other, which meant I better remember the cover story. "The doctors think it was a one-time thing."

"How scary," Karen said as she shoved her foot into her shoe. "You're so lucky Jason came home early to surprise you. It could have been so much worse."

"I know." If he hadn't come home when he did, I'd be dead. But I called him before swallowing the pills. Before making that decision, so surely, I hadn't really wanted to die. At least that's what I worked out in the hospital. I shifted my weight from left to right and back again. "My hamstrings are letting me know this is my first class back."

"Take it easy for a while," Karen said. "I know you're Miss Six Days a Week and sometimes don't you do a double on Sundays?"

"Yes." A nervous laugh lodged in my throat, but the other women were too busy getting ready to notice me. I was ripping apart at the seams, and I had my arms wrapped around myself, trying to squeeze all the bits of me together so I wouldn't spill out onto the floor.

"Just be careful." Alexis tugged on a windbreaker. "We wouldn't want to lose you. Yoga will always be here." She pointed at my bare feet. "You should probably put on your shoes."

"Right." Even though I hated my post-yoga runs, if I wanted to stay slim – Waterford slim — it was a necessary evil. "Are you running today?"

Karen answered. "We are. Farmington trail. Have you been?"

"No, but I heard it's nice." I immediately wanted to shove it back in. Did I sound too desperate? Too 'invite me, too'? My brain latched on to that idea and replayed it over and over. Over and over. Over and over.

"You should go. It's the best." Karen finished tying her shoes and stood. Neither she nor Alexis invited me. She just told me I should go. Sigh. I would have loved to be invited. Just once.

"Maybe tomorrow." I didn't have the guts to say I'm strictly a treadmill runner when on my own. The thought of running outside alone, where I couldn't quit whenever I wanted, terrified me.

Actually, most things those days terrified me.

My yoga gear lay in a disorganized pile. I hadn't made any real effort to get ready. It was like I was moving through thick, humid air, and it was trapped in my lungs, forcing me to struggle with shallow breaths.

"Class is over, Elizabeth. You don't need to practice breathing out here," Alexis joked.

I forced a high, funny laugh from my prison of a body.

Karen lifted her purse from the wall hook. "Ping you later?"

"Okay!" God, was I annoyingly perky or what?

After they left, I collapsed onto the bench and studied the shoe in my left hand. My fingers fumbled with the tight laces. The damn thing wouldn't loosen, and frustration welled inside me.

I dropped the shoe to the ground.

"Everything okay?" the teacher asked.

"It's fine. I just double knotted my shoe too tightly." No amount of breathing was going to bring me back from the edge I was sliding off, and there was no one for me to grasp onto.

Lisa, the teacher, sat next to me. "Do you want help?"

"No, it's okay. I'll just go barefoot. It's fine." I scooped up my shoes and scampered out the door and into the cold. When I got to my car, I threw everything in the pristine backseat.

My first few months here, I couldn't go anywhere unless Jason drove me, so my day was pretty much walking my boys to the bus stop and picking them up again. And I baked. A lot. I was isolated and completely dependent on Jason. I couldn't even volunteer at school.

In a way, I wished we could go back to that. Now, Jason worked twelve-hour days while I went to lunches, practiced yoga, ran, and hustled the kids around. Oh, and spent a week locked up in the psych ward where I got unlimited therapy and had to wear stupid teal, grippy socks while freezing to death in flimsy clothes.

Jason had posted updates of my seizure recovery on my Facebook account, and people had sent their best wishes and prayers over the internet, but not in person. My family freaked out, but Jason convinced them it was best if they stayed away for now.

This is how we lived. I disintegrated, and he covered for me.

It wasn't my life. It couldn't be my life.

Tears stung my eyes as I kicked my SUV into reverse. If I didn't get to the gym soon, I'd never get a run in. And I needed to get a run in. I needed a twenty-six-inch waist, nineteen-and-a-half inch thighs, and a perky ass.

Seventy-five minutes of yoga wasn't going to do it. I needed that extra five miles.

Dr. Carter said my exercise obsession wasn't healthy. She was probably right, but I couldn't let her know. I kept insisting that it's a mental thing. That gaining weight from my medication made me depressed.

She patiently explained over and over that Jason wouldn't leave me if I put on a few pounds.

How could I explain that all I wanted to was disappear?

Forty minutes in, twenty to go. I had this. It was now more mental than physical because endorphins pumped hard through my body, and if I could get my brain under control, I could probably go even longer.

Maybe I would.

My feet pounded the treadmill belt over and over again, and I lifted my wrist to check my Fitbit. Nearly four hundred calories burned. That's on top of the 213 I racked up in yoga. If I stuck to my 1200 calorie intake, I'd be negative calories for the day.

I could sneak a McDonald's cheeseburger. No one would have to know...well, I'd tell Sarah because she'd laugh about it, but no one else.

Music played through my earphones, and my stride matched the beat. God, it felt good. Why did I fight it? I actually enjoyed running. Indoors, at least. I still wasn't ready for the great outdoors.

There weren't any mirrors on this side of the gym, just a glass wall overlooking the indoor pool, so when Melissa slipped up next to me and waved, I startled.

"Hey. What's going on?" I hung my headphones around my neck while keeping pace. We hadn't seen each other since that night at Sarah's house when I got plastered. Melissa didn't run with my normal crowd, and Sarah hadn't invited us both out again, so I thought Melissa was off the radar.

"I'm taking the noon yoga class and wondered if you wanted to join us?" Melissa wore a cute little bra top and tight yoga shorts. Next to her, I looked like a nun in my cropped leggings and loose top.

"Oh. Thanks for asking, but I actually just came from my class."

"Where do you go?"

I kept running. Can't let my pace slip or I wouldn't beat my time. "Yoga One."

"I heard that's a great studio. I keep meaning to check it out."

"You should. It's fun and so, so good," I huffed.

Melissa motioned toward the treadmill. "I'll let you get back to it. Didn't mean to interrupt your workout."

"It's fine," I lied. I kind of hated being interrupted, but it was rude to ignore her. "Have a good time in class, and if you ever want to try Yoga One, let me know."

She perked up. "Really?"

"Of course. I think you'd love it." Slap. Slap. Slap. My feet pounded harder on the treadmill as I turned the speed up. I had to beat my best time of forty-three twenty.

"Tomorrow?"

"Sure. 9:30."

"Great! See you then!"

Melissa moved out of my peripheral vision, and I pulled my headphones back on. Jason would be so proud of me because, you know, inviting someone to a public place is so outgoing and all — even if it was Melissa Foster.

Still, it was a start. I was branching out and trying. Maybe I had this making friends thing down after all.

My eyes studied the screen before me. Five miles done in forty-two fifty. A smile snaked across my face. A personal best, and I still had it in me to go longer.

Six or seven miles never hurt no one.

16

BEND IT LIKE A PRETZEL

It's been a while since we've discussed Elizabeth, and it's not because she's been boring, but rather I was trying to be sensitive. I may be a gossip, but I'm not a bitch.

However, we have a problem, and it's called the truth. Something I think Elizabeth and her husband aren't well acquainted with.

You see, a few weeks back, she supposedly had a nasty seizure and had to be hospitalized for a week. Her husband posted updates to her Facebook feed, and the Women of Waterford half-heartedly rallied around him. All would have been fine, but...

There's a small problem. A little birdie is a nurse at the hospital, and someone wanted to send Elizabeth flowers, so the nurse said she'd get Elizabeth's room number.

Elizabeth wasn't a patient. She never checked in, and she never checked out.

So, if she wasn't at the hospital, where was she?

My money is on this having to do with Pete White. Why? Well, let's just say, while they haven't been having cozy lunches lately, there's definitely something going on between them. Why else would he have followed her out of the Member's Party?

What do you think? Did Jason throw her out over an indiscretion? And if so, why didn't he run to Veronica with what he knows?

"Honey, you shouldn't do so much yoga. It can't be healthy." Sarah sat on the edge of my couch and watched as I tried to stretch out my wrists. I had done too many arm balances, and my body was screaming at me. "I know the blog posts have upset you, but still."

The blog posts. My secrets — or parts of them – were being splashed all over the blog, and they weren't exactly flattering. "Yoga is good for my mental health. Some people do crosswords, I do yoga." I folded over and placed my hands under my feet, palm side up. The stretch radiated up my arms. "Takes my mind off things."

"And running?" She laughed. "Don't get me started on your running. You're going to need a hip, knee, and wrist replacement by forty if you keep this up."

I reverse swan dived up to a standing position. "Are you trying to make me fat?" I teased. "Because I'm about as chubby as I'm ever going to be."

A slow smile spread across Sarah's face. "I bet I could seduce you with a slice of my famous peanut butter pie."

Oh, God. Did this woman know my weaknesses or what? "With or without whipped cream?"

"Please," Sarah said. "Is there any way but with whipped cream?"

"Wine?" I asked. It was only eleven-thirty in the morning, but the kids were at school which gave us some time to get buzzed before having to adult again.

Sarah followed me into the kitchen. "What do you have?"

"Reds and whites. And champagne." I raised my eyebrows twice. "Always champagne."

"If we put strawberries in it, we could pretend it's a smoothie."

My laugh couldn't be contained. I doubled over and puffed out my cheeks until I gasped for breath. "I can't. I just can't even..."

"Oh, come on. You know Karen and the Bitch Brigade would call that a food group." Sarah took the bottle from my hands and popped it open while I grabbed two flutes from the cabinet. "Let's chat. I feel like I haven't seen you in ages. How's your health? Feeling any better?"

Since coming home from the hospital, I hadn't exactly avoided Sarah, but I hadn't sought her out. She didn't go to Member's Night and wasn't invited to Meredith's, and we hadn't been hanging out as much. I guess I was unconsciously avoiding her. She was too easy to talk to, and I feared I would expose myself in ways I didn't want. I had promised Jason I'd keep all of our secrets in the past, and that's what I planned on doing. Plus, Sarah knew about Pete and me, and with the blog posts about us, it was best if I downplayed our past as much as possible. Right now, I had shaky deniability, and Karen had already called me out on it. She wanted to know if I'd been with Pete on the veranda, but when I pointed out the blog said I'd been alone, she dropped it.

Or at least, I'd hoped she had.

Funny how the blog was an authority on me, but the post about her were one-hundred percent false. At least according to Karen. The rest of us had our suspicions.

"I'm doing well," I said. "The doctors say I was lucky. I guess if Jason hadn't found me when he did, I wouldn't be here." It was the truth, and it rolled easily off my tongue.

Sarah lowered her eyes slightly, just for one brief minute, and a strange look flashed across her face. "Did they say if you'll have another seizure?"

Heat flushed my cheeks. I was such a bad liar. "No one can tell."

"Poor Jason. I bet he was terrified, coming home and finding you like that." Sarah's thick Southern accent drew out her speech and had a soothing effect on me. "I can't imagine. Do you remember anything?"

The heaviness of being. The fading in and out of darkness. The strong pull of sleep. "Not really, but I'm told that is normal."

"Huh." Sarah sipped her champagne. "Well, honey, I'm glad you're here today."

I followed her lead and drank. "I am too."

"Just promise me that next time, you'll do it when other people are around, okay?"

"Sarah, I can't control seizures." What was I saying? I was bending the truth and believing my own BS. What would she think of me if she knew I tried to overdose? Would she be sitting her talking to me about peanut butter pie and champagne smoothies? Would she be here at all?

No. She wouldn't. I was damaged goods. I had a faulty brain and couldn't keep my husband happy. Not exactly winner material.

"I saw Melissa at the gym this morning. She's going to come to yoga with me tomorrow. You should come, too."

Sarah snorted. "I am not a bendy pretzel like you."

"I'm not that bendy anymore." I held out my aching arms. "My wrists are killing."

"Well, you and Melissa have fun. I'll be here waiting for you with a pie to tempt you over to the dark side when you're finished."

"You're evil."

Sarah tilted her head back and stared at the ceiling for a moment. "Hey! Have you ever thought about repainting your front room a medium gray? It would look so pretty with your furniture." Sarah pointed toward the room. "And maybe rearrange the furniture so that it creates more of a conversation area."

"That room has troubled me since we moved in." Decorating wasn't my strong suit. I liked a clean aesthetic, but once you got into colors and all that, I was lost. "I can't figure out what to do with it. First, we wanted it to be a library with room for the boys to read and lounge; then I went more formal; now, it's just a hodge podge of things."

"It can be saved. Trust me, I've seen worse." She bit off a piece of strawberry and swallowed. "You just need a focus."

"What do you think?"

"Well, since you asked." Sarah walked to the room, and I followed. "I'd start by clearing everything out." She went on for a few more minutes, and I took mental notes. But mostly, I was thankful to not be lonely during the day and to have my friendship with Sarah.

———

"Sarah was here? Today?" Jason set his bag down on the floor near the mess of shoes littering the front door area. I kept meaning to buy a shoe basket, but every time I went to Target, I forgot to pick one up. "What did she want?"

"Nothing really. We had a drink or two and discussed what to do with the front room."

"Drinks again?" Jason raised his eyebrows. "Is that a good idea?"

I waved dismissively. "It was fine. One glass of champagne doesn't even get me buzzed. Besides, it was practically a smoothie — we put strawberries in it." Jason didn't crack a smile at what I thought was a funny joke. "Really, I'm fine."

Dark circles rimmed Jason's eyes. The commute seemed to be taking longer and longer every day, and rolling in past eight was the new normal. The boys had had dinner, homework was done, and everyone had gone off to their rooms to wind down. "All this drinking, Elizabeth, it's not good."

"Can we move past that, please? I want to tell you about the ideas Sarah and I came up with."

To my surprise, Jason let it slide. "What did you two decide?"

I launched into all of the ideas Sarah and I brainstormed. Maybe it was in my voice, or perhaps in my demeanor, but Jason grabbed me by the arms and stopped me from moving.

"What?"

"Did you take your meds today? I left them on the counter, but you're bouncing off the walls, and I can't understand a word you say."

I drew my brows together. "Yes? I mean, I think I took my morning Lithium. I really can't remember."

Jason stormed past me to the stairs. When he returned, his hand was in a fist. "These were still on the counter."

All my pills glared up at me. Yesterday, I hid them in my drawer because I hate the after-effects. Which means I hadn't taken them in two days. At least, I think I hadn't taken them in two days.

I had a fuzzy recollection of taking them, but if Jason was holding them, did I?

"Am I going to have to feed them to you?" Jason dropped the pills on the counter before embracing me. "And then you had drinks? Elizabeth, you can't. Don't you remember how awful you felt after Meredith's party. You can't do shit like this. Especially not if you want to be deemed a fit parent."

His words slid off me. "But Sarah was here, and it was so nice to have someone to talk to, and she has such good ideas, Jason. Like really, really good. I know you said no couple's dates because Kyle is a douche, but maybe one? I think if you really got to know Sarah, you'd love her."

Jason released me. "Are you done?"

"Yes."

"Call Sarah."

"What? Why?"

Jason took my hand and lead me into the kitchen. An empty bottle of champagne and an empty bottle of white sat on the counter. "I want to know how much of this you drank."

Did I...I didn't remember drinking that much. We'd opened the bottle of champagne, and each had a glass, but the white? I pointed at the bottle. "We didn't drink that. We each had a glass, and then Sarah drove us to the paint store and we bought some samples for the front room. Look."

I ran into the front room. Several mini-cans of gray paint sat on the floor. "We went shopping."

"Call her."

I took my phone from my pocket and hit Sarah's number.

"Hey, you!" Sarah's voice floated over the air. "Feeling better? I hated leaving you like that, but I had to get home to help the girls with their homework."

"Sarah, how much did we drink?" I asked. I needed to hear it from her.

She blew into the phone. "I had a glass, but you finished off the rest of the bottle and started on the white. Remember?"

None of this made sense. How could I have drunk that much and not feel sick? Was I that much of an alcoholic?

I stared at the paint cans. "But we went to the paint store. I remember picking out the colors with you. You liked the dove gray the best."

Sarah was quiet for a long time. "That didn't happen. I left you passed out on the couch."

"You what?"

"Left you passed out. You really don't remember?" She pauses. "Is this a side effect of bipolar disorder? I know you said it sometimes-"

"How do you know about that?" I demand. I couldn't get my heart under control. It was banging against my ribcage, threatening to break free. "How?"

"Sugar, you told me over champagne this afternoon. You explained it all to me. Your shame over Jason's affair, your diagnosis. All of it. You just about broke my heart."

Oh my God. Oh my God. Why would I have done that? "I have to go."

I didn't wait for her good-bye before facing Jason. He stepped away from me like I was toxic or uncontrollable. "What is it?"

"Am I manic? Is that what's happening?" I pulled on my hair and tried to get my breath under control. I'd never had a manic episode, I had bipolar II which meant I shouldn't be experiencing mania. "I remember buying the paint with Sarah, but she says it never happened, so how did it get here?" I cried.

"I'm calling Dr. Carter." Jason shoved me onto the couch. "Do not move." His fingers tapped the phone's screen. "Something isn't right, and if we want to keep you out of the hospital, we need to get you seen tonight."

It was so late. So, freaking late. I was going to have to go to the hospital, and there would be a Social Services setback. Unless...

"Jason?"

"What?"

"What if I took my pills now?" I was reaching, searching for anything to keep me out of the hospital. "I could take double, and I'll level out. I'll be fine. I'll even go up to bed."

"But will you sleep?"

"I'll try. I'll take my sleeping pill."

Jason pressed his lips tightly together and sat beside me. "Good thing I love you. This up and down shit is exhausting."

"I know. I'm sorry." I folded into his arms and nuzzled into his chest. "I don't want to be like this. I don't understand what's happening."

"Don't apologize." Jason massaged the back of my head. "Don't you know? I'd do anything for you? You are my life."

My frozen heart melted a little. There was a lot of thawing to do, but it was progress.

"Thank you."

17

ALL THAT SHIMMERS

Oh Lord. There's a big – HUGE – jewelry party at Karen's tonight. Should provide some mild entertainment. After all, it'll be the first time since the Member Party that Elizabeth will see the Bitch Brigade in its entirety...and guess what? Some (read: Veronica) aren't exactly thrilled with her. Do you think it has something to do with my last post – LOL.

Anyway, word on the street is Karen Newbold is calling for my head. Again. But really, what is she going to do to me? She revels in the gossip too much to actually shut me down. And for fuck's sake, I'm not going to stop because she's threatened me. I'm not that kind of blogger.

I mean really, where would the fun be in that?

So, I'll keep blogging. I'll keep spilling secrets. And I'll keep giving the Women of Waterford something to gossip about.

Too bad they'll never figure it out who I am - they're really not smart enough.

I was running late, and I hated it. Normally, I was that annoying guest who turned up right when the party started. But not tonight. Tonight, I was late.

A bottle of red wine was tucked into my bag. Let me correct that statement. It was tucked into my green Louis Vuitton epi leather Neverfull – the one Jason surprised me with after my bad spell the week before. It was a $2,400 bag...My mind couldn't wrap around that. I mean, in Portland and London, I had nice things. Polished things. I never had to have big brand names. In fact, I searched out lesser known designers, because it was more my style.

But Jason said he liked giving me nice things. And nice things equaled expensive in his mind. Sometimes, it felt like he was trying to buy me off and turn me into a Waterford Wife.

Regardless, I now owned a very expensive handbag.

The party was at Karen's, and every acceptable woman in Waterford would be there. The Bitch Brigade. The Periphery Girls. The Randoms. All the people that blog liked to gossip about. All of us under one roof. Oh, and Sarah, who'd I'd been avoiding out of embarrassment. What if she was afraid of me now that she knew I was the crazy bipolar woman with a cheating husband?

There was only one way to find out.

Cars lined the street in front of Karen's house, so I parked around the corner and walked half-a-block. I checked my Fitbit to make sure it was recording my steps. Every little thing counted when trying to lose weight.

As I came closer to Karen's house, anxiety raced through my body, causing me to shake. Sarah knew all my secrets. I had to trust that she'd keep them secret and not hold them against me. But how to do that without bringing it all up and scaring her away? After all, who wants to be friends with the mentally unstable wife of a cheater? Not very many people, that's who.

Light seeped through the crack of Karen's ajar door, and my heartbeat played crescendo in my chest. They were all inside. Everyone. And I had to make conversation with them.

I had to talk to Sarah.

The door swung open, and there she was all backlight and glowing.

"Elizabeth!" Sarah said. "I thought that was you standing out there. What are you doing? Get inside." She rushed forward to greet me like nothing had changed. And maybe it hadn't. Maybe it was all in my head like everything else was. "You're the last to arrive." Her hand was on my elbow, guiding me toward Karen's ultra-modern farmhouse kitchen. "You can leave your wine here." She lifted it from my bag and set it on the counter with five other bottles. "By the way, I love your bag. Whoever got it for you has great taste." She winked. "I have the pink one."

Of course, she did.

Tension formed a knot at the base of my neck, and I worked my fingers into it. Going to a party shouldn't be stressful. Especially when I knew most of the invitees.

But the painful, tightening of my chest reminded me I was not one of them. I'd never be perfect, or even present the image of perfection. No, I was damaged goods, and now Sarah knew.

"This is Jennifer," Sarah chirped. "She's not a club member, but have you met?"

"No. We haven't. At least I don't think so." My cloudy brain jumbled up names and faces all the time, making social interactions even more awkward.

Jennifer smiled tightly. "Actually, we did. Right after you moved here. You're from Portland, right?"

"Oh. I'm so, so sorry. That's right," I said to the pretty blond. I wasn't sure how I was going to keep her straight from the twenty-nine other pretty blonds with perfect bodies in the room. "We met at the pool. You have kids, don't you? Little ones?"

"Girls. Two of them. In fourth and fifth now. So not so little anymore." She rolled a wine glass between her fingertips. "And you?"

"Three boys. Newly fifteen, eleven, and eight." I darted my gaze over Jennifer's shoulder and zeroed in on the Karen and Alexis, who, as expected, were surrounded by fawning women. To my surprise, Melissa was with them.

I hated small talk. "My son's in in fifth. Maybe they know each other?"

"What's his name?" Jennifer asked.

"Oliver – Ollie – Mavery."

Jennifer shook her head. "It's a big school. I'll have to ask."

Karen waved to me, a signal to join her. "Excuse me, the hostess is calling."

I was about half-way across the room when I pulled up short. I don't know how I didn't notice her before, but Veronica stood just to the left of Karen. I smiled confidently and put my left foot in front of my right. Our relationship had been non-existent since Jason broke off contact with Pete which made situations like this uncomfortable. Neither Veronica nor I seem to know what to do. As evidenced at the Member Party.

"Hi, Love!" Karen air kissed me three times. "I thought you ditched."

"I would never do that. I promised I'd come, and I always keep my promises." My shallow breathing was going to give away my anxiety. *Steady breaths, Elizabeth. Steady breaths.* "Hey, Alexis! How are you?"

She held up her wine glass. "Empty."

We laughed some more because you were supposed to. "I brought a nice Malbec," I said. "It's on the counter."

Veronica grimaced. "Oh yummy. Pete loves Malbec, and he's always trying to get me to drink it. But I love my Cabs too much."

"Jason picked it out. He's the wine guy," I said. "If it's bad, I blame him."

My attempt at lightheartedness fell flat, and a weird silence settled over the group. Did they know? Had Sarah said something?

"Karen says you're coming on my birthday trip." Alexis tipped into me and for a moment, I thought I was going to have to catch her. "It's going to be great."

"Turning forty is a huge deal," I kept my hand on Alexis's arm. "You should have a big bash."

Alexis scanned me head-to-toe. "When do you turn forty?"

"In two years. I'm thirty-eight." The extra weight of Alexis caused me to sway slightly in my knee-high boots.

"Oh."

A few of the so-called Periphery Girls pandered for Karen's attention, and before she turned to talk to them, she said, "I didn't realize you were that young, Elizabeth."

Either she was saying I looked like shit, or she was jealous. "No one has ever asked me."

"Let's get drinks," Karen said to Veronica even though her wine glass was nearly full. The two disappeared into the crowd, and Alexis started talking to some random woman I'd never seen before which left me standing all alone in the middle of a crowd. Again.

Spiders of anxiety crept and crawled across every nerve in my body. They must have heard. That must have been why no one spoke to me. I had a giant sign around my neck that said, "Mental Case."

No. Sarah wouldn't have said anything. I trusted her completely. So why did it feel like everyone was talking about me? Was it the Pete stuff from the blog? Did they all believe it?

I had to leave. Staying was going to push me over the edge, and I didn't want a public breakdown, and I didn't need Karen and all knowing about me, too. They wouldn't be as forgiving as Sarah.

As I wound my way toward the door, Sarah called out, "Elizabeth, where are you going? You just got here, and we haven't even gotten to the jewelry part."

"I..." I wanted to lie and say I received a frantic text from Jason, but my leaden feet carried me back toward the kitchen and Sarah. Part of me wanted to attach myself to her side, but the other part wanted to run, run, run.

But if I did, everyone would know something was wrong with me.

Next to the counter, Veronica held the bottle of wine I brought.

"It's good," I said.

"I think this is the exact brand Pete likes. How funny." Her chilly, flat voice sounded robotic and the complete opposite of amused.

"Pete and Jason must have great taste," Karen said, but she avoided my gaze.

Karen believed Pete was cheating. In fact, she had told me several times, and each time she grew more adamant about it. But this comment, and the way they were talking, sparked a thought. Did they believe the blog? Did they think *I was* the one he was having an affair with? Were they blaming *me*? Is that why Veronica had turned so chilly towards me?

Fuck it. I'd had enough. I was too old for this game-playing bull-shit. "What did I do?" I blurted. "Seriously, what did I do?"

Karen blinked innocently. "Nothing."

Veronica poured a glass for herself, but didn't say anything. She placed the bottle of Pete's favorite Malbec on the counter and looked at me for a brief moment before walking away.

Sarah stood behind Karen's shoulder with her brows scrunched up. Okay, so wasn't just me. They *were* being weird. "C'mon, Eliza-beth. Let's find Melissa and browse the jewelry. There's such cute stuff!"

Could shopping cure possibly, maybe being accused of having an affair with Veronica White's husband? Could it cure that? Because that's where my mind was, and I couldn't get off it. "I'd really like to go. I'm not feeling well."

Sarah eyed me carefully. "If you go now, you'll just give the more reason to doubt you."

"What do you mean?"

She sighed. "Elizabeth, everyone is talking about it. Maybe they're not saying it to your face, but you kind of seem suspicious." When I didn't respond, she added, "About the Pete thing."

This was bad. Bad. Bad. Bad. Maybe not me having bipolar disorder bad, but bad. "What should I do?"

Sarah linked her arm around mine. "Keep your head up and don't act dodgy." She swished through the groups of women gathered around Karen's living room and pulled Melissa away from her friends without a word. Looking back, it was weird how Melissa just rolled along with whatever Sarah wanted.

"Do you think you can last just a bit longer?" Sarah asked. "Because you need to."

"I'll try." We stopped next a table lined with trinkets I'd never wear. Waterford stuff. Big, gaudy necklaces ruled the table followed by ugly earrings and impractical bracelets.

"Ohhh. This is pretty." Sarah held up an enameled, floral neck-

lace in turquoise and coral. It was hideous. "I'm going to try it on."
She placed her glass down and swooped up the necklace like a bird of
prey. After she arranged it, she peered into a hand-held mirror. "I love
it! What do you think, Melissa?"

Melissa nodded. "It looks great with your coloring. I can see you
wearing it a lot."

"Elizabeth?"

I searched for something to say, but nothing came to me. I
shrugged my shoulders. "Is it a good price?"

Sarah laughed. "You're so practical!"

"I guess." I fondled a pair of dangly, hot pink earrings. They
looked like something I wore as a teen in the nineties. "These are
more my style." I meant it as a joke, but Melissa and Sarah fawned
over them.

"So pretty!"

"I love them. They'll look great on you!"

Wonderful. Now I had to buy ugly earrings I didn't want. I flipped
the price tag over. Fifty-four dollars. That couldn't possibly be right.

"You ladies have any questions?" A smartly dressed woman in her
mid-forties stood across the table from us. "Oh," she said, noticing
the earrings in my hand. "Aren't those divine?"

"Lovely, but I think they're a bit too much for me. I go for a
simpler style."

She wasn't deterred. "What about these?" She held up a pair of
drop pearl earrings. "Simply, classy, and can even be worn with
jeans."

They were just as ugly.

"Elizabeth isn't really a jeans girl, are you?" Sarah said. "She's
more of a dress and tights person."

Funny how well she knew me after just a few months. However,
the problem was, I needed to buy something or risk Karen's wrath,
and the pearl earrings weren't all that bad. "Okay. I'll take those."

The woman beamed. "Wonderful. I'll wrap them up for you. Are
you paying cash or credit?"

"Cash." It's all I carried because Jason didn't trust me — and I didn't trust myself – to have access to large amounts of money. Once I had a diagnosis, I received an allowance for groceries and whatnot, but not because Jason was controlling. It was just safer and better for our family budget.

"It's eighty-three dollars." The woman smiled at me like spending that kind of money on a pair of faux earrings was sane.

Reluctantly, I counted out twenty-dollar bills and handed them to her. There goes my haircut this month.

"Do you always carry so much cash?" Melissa asked. "It would make me nervous."

I shrugged. "I'm used to it. Jason and I are on an all cash system."

"But you have credit cards?"

"Nope. Well, at least I don't. Jason does for emergencies." Talking finances made me uncomfortable. "What are you getting?"

Melissa dangled a chain link bracelet from her fingertip. "It's a bit of a David Yurman rip-off, but I like it."

"Cool."

And that's the thing, wasn't it? We were all imposters in some way, whether it was with our fake jewelry, our fake bodies, or our fake friendships.

Nothing, I'd learned, was real in Waterford.

1 8

I'M MY OWN WORST ENEMY

L et's talk Melissa Foster, shall we? I see her everywhere, but I've never met her husband. It's like she keeps him hidden away. All I know about him is that they used to swing, something that she seems perfectly okay with the world knowing.

Anyway, I saw her cozying up to Pete the other night at the Club. She kept touching his arm, laughing at his jokes, and generally acting too friendly. And Pete? Well, he seemed to revel in the attention. Encouraged it even. Hate to say it, but his reputation is becoming more and more earned in my eyes.

They were totally taking advantage of the fact that Veronica was out of town on a Girls' Ski Weekend with Alexis and Karen. The Bitch Brigade's pictures on Instagram and Facebook are perfect, of course, and they seem to be having the best time ever. In fact, all three of them keep posting, "Having the BEST time ever. Love these girls!" all over the place.

My take? When you have to try that hard to convince others, surely, you're trying to convince yourself, too.

So back to Pete and Melissa. They didn't even try to hide their flirting. In fact, Melissa got up from the table, and Pete followed a few minutes later. Like they thought that would go unnoticed — especially when they slinked back in, separately, thirty minutes later.

If Veronica doesn't hear about it, I'll be surprised. But the question is, what will she do? Will she continue to ignore the rumors, or kick him out?

Oh, and then there's Elizabeth, left out of the ski festivities and sitting alone at a table, looking miserable...or was that jealousy. It's hard to tell with her bitchy resting face.

I shouldn't have been surprised. I mean, why would Karen invite me on her mid-week ski trip when my relationship with Veronica was tense at best? And even if I had been invited, I probably couldn't have gone because there was no one to watch the boys.

Still, I would have liked to at least been invited. Sarah and I both agreed on that. We had pulled up Alexis's Facebook pictures and broke them down into different categories: trying too hard, trying too too hard, and down-right pathetic.

I slammed my laptop shut and sunk into my pillows. Music blasted through the headphones and into my ears, and I closed my eyes. I needed to pull myself together. I wasn't jealous of Melissa and Pete – if there even was a Melissa and Pete. I was, however concerned. Pete was acting exactly like a man who had possibly, maybe, probably been cheating on Ashley Madison. And my association with him had cast a shadow over my reputation.

"Elizabeth, it's time to go." Jason stood at the end of the bed and pulled on my toes. Here was a man who was committed to me. To our family. And I doubted him daily for no reason other than past history. "Hey, you look panicked."

"Just thinking about how big Will is getting. He's going to be gone in three years, and I'm having a hard time wrapping my brain around that."

"Sentimental?" Jason pushed my legs over and sat on the edge of the bed.

"Something like that."

"Well, we don't have time for that. We have to get over to the Jones' so we can get the requisite pictures." My husband wore a faded green t-shirt that clung to his athletic body and dark jeans with Vans. If it weren't for the gray in his scruff, he could have passed for five years younger.

"Should I change?" I asked. This was a social event, and we needed to look presentable.

Jason shrugged. "I'm wearing this, but you might want to. You look a little rough."

If Jason thought I looked rough, I no doubt looked terrible. I slid off the bed and marched into my closet. "This?" I asked, holding out a cream sweater dress. "It's casual, and I won't look like I'm trying too hard."

"Wear the navy one instead. I like it better."

Since my stay at the hospital, Jason had been overly attentive, catering to my every need and making sure I never left the house looking less than perfect. I had an image to maintain, even if it was a fake one.

Admittedly, sometimes it grew tiring.

I had bipolar disorder not cancer. I wasn't going to die. At least, not unless I hurt myself. And in that moment, I had no plans on ever doing that again.

"We're going to be late," Jason said, pointing to my messy top knot. "You look cute, but you sure you want to go like that? People may talk."

I had on the navy print dress he'd selected and tights, and my messy top knot bobbed when I shook my head. "Why not? It is about the kids after all. Just let me put some lipstick on."

"If you think you look good, then it's on you when people wonder why you look like you just woke up."

The thought of anyone in Waterford seeing me with less than perfect make-up and hair made me nervous. I didn't want to look like a crazy woman.

Jason watched me from the doorway. "Meet me at the car in five minutes. That should be enough time for you to fix yourself."

I rushed to the bathroom, found my favorite plum lipstick and blotted it with my fingertip after applying it. Jason was wrong. I looked cute in a messy, but in that effortless European way I tried to perfect when we lived in London. At least I hoped I did.

Will and Jason waited in the SUV for me. My son bounced his knee in the backseat and clutched the plastic corsage box.

"You nervous?" I asked.

"No." He avoided my eyes. I knew Will well enough to know that he was in fact nervous, but I wasn't going to push.

"Let's go over details one more time. The dance starts at eight, but you and your friends are going to dinner first, and the Jones' have arranged for the limo." A limo that had cost me a hundred dollars.

"It's more of a party bus."

"How many of you are there?" I asked. I thought he was going with a small group.

"Twenty. Maybe thirty. I don't know."

"Why am I not surprised," I muttered. Jason shot me a side-eye glance that told me to shut my mouth. "So, it's a big group, and you're all going to Rocky's for dinner?"

"Yeah."

"After the dance, you're going back to the Jones' for an after party?"

"Right." Bounce, bounce, bounce.

"We'll pick you up at one."

"Okay."

Jason pulled in front of the Jones' house. Girls in barely-there dresses and boys wearing suit jackets sprinted toward the house to escape the cold, and a gigantic bus was parked along the curb in front of us.

"Is that the party bus?" I asked, spinning around in my seat. It was sleek and looked like something a band would use on tour.

"I guess so." Will leaped out of the car and jogged up the driveway in his dress shoes. I wanted to yell after him to be careful. To not slip. But I kept my words sucked in.

"I know having a schedule helps you, but he's nervous," Jason said. "Let him be."

"Innocent questions that we need to know as his parents."

"Maybe so, but take it easy. No need for an inquisition."

Point taken.

As we walked up the driveway, Jason took my hand. His skin warmed mine against the frigid night air. It was moments like this when I realized most how much we almost lost, and how much we could still lose.

"Did you take your medicine today?" Jason asked.

I paused. Was I acting like I hadn't? Should I be worried? "I did. Not the night-time stuff yet, but I got my morning pills off the table where you left them."

"Good. Then you should be fine." My husband held the front door open. Other parents milled about inside, some taking pictures, some chatting in small groups. It was pretty calm despite the chaotic frenzy of thirty plus kids running all over the place, and yet, I didn't feel calm. Jason's comment has left me frazzled, and I tightened my grip on his hand.

We were half way into the living room when I spied them: Pete and Veronica. Their backs were to me, but it was them. They didn't touch or really act like a couple. He was talking to some guy I didn't recognize, and she was laughing with a woman named Luanne something. My stomach vaulted, and I froze. I should have expected them. They had a daughter the same age as Will, and Waterford's acceptable social circle was pretty small.

"Not now, Elizabeth," Jason said, tugging at me. "You can't do this now. It's just a small crowd."

"I know, but Pete and Veronica are here." My shallow breath and trembling hands betrayed my calm voice. "What should we do?"

"Act normal and pretend they're not here." Jason leaned close to my ear. "Pull yourself together. Are you sure you took all your pills?"

"Yes." It was so unfair. Why did everything always come back to whether I took my meds or not? Why not mention how uncomfortable things were because of Jason and Pete's falling out?

"Elizabeth."

"What?"

"Where's your camera?" Jason hissed. "Everyone's ready for

pictures." The kids had lined up on the dual sweeping staircases in pairs and smiled down at us parents below.

I fished inside my handbag for my phone. "This is all I have. I forgot the camera."

"Then I guess we're using our phones." He didn't sound angry, but he didn't sound pleased either. More like annoyed. Which worried me. I hated when Jason got snippy with me. He placed his hand on my back and guided me toward the center of the room near Pete and Veronica.

Don't panic. Don't panic. Don't panic.

When we were just a few feet away, Pete turned his head. Something in his eyes wasn't right. He looked away. Where was the smile? The sense of superiority? Did he read the blog post about us? Did it even matter?

I thrust my phone at Jason's chest. "Can you take the pictures? I need air."

"No. You're going to stand here and do it yourself. You're not going to surrender."

Surrender? All I did all day, every day was fight with everything I had to appear normal. There was no surrender in that.

Around us, parents jockeyed for a prime group picture taking position. It was impossible to get everyone in one shot, so I knelt down in the front and aimed my phone at Will and Bella. They looked adorable standing together, but no matter how much I cajoled him, Will wouldn't flash any teeth.

"You ask him," I said to Jason. "He's going to look toothless in every picture if he doesn't give a real smile."

"Buddy," Jason said. "Teeth. Now."

Will's lips pulled apart, and Jason snapped a photo. "Better?"

I threw my hand up. "I hope Bella's parents got a better picture."

Someone tapped my shoulder. A brunette with a sharp smile stared down at me. "Are you Will's parents?"

"We are."

"Oh, it's so nice to meet you! We're the Joneses. Steve and Michelle."

"Jason and Elizabeth." My hands shook slightly, and I shoved them into my dress pockets before glancing back at the kids. "Bella looks gorgeous."

"You know, we had such a fight over that dress," Michelle said. "I wanted it shorter, but she said no."

I hid my surprise. Bella's dress covered next to nothing. "Really? It looks great to me."

"Well, it all works out, doesn't it?" Michelle's face lit up. "Will did such an amazing job on Bella's Ask Box. He did the one I'd hope he'd do."

I bit my tongue and smiled tightly. This woman. I swear. She'd sent me a list of suitable Ask Boxes, and Will just went with one. "I'm happy Bella liked it."

The kids thundered down the stairs in a wave of black and swarmed the front door. "Well, it was nice talking to you," Michelle said. "I want to get some pictures of the kids getting on the bus."

The kids pushed and prodded their way out the door. Once they were all inside the bus, a mom with a huge camera lens climbed aboard.

"What is she doing?" I whispered to Jason.

He screwed up his face. "I heard she's a professional photographer and is going to take photos at the restaurant."

Good Lord.

And then it happened. Pete and Veronica walked toward us and, just to see what would happen, I gave a little wave. Not my best decision, I know, but Pete waved back, and I immediately felt better. Maybe he and Veronica didn't hate me after all. Maybe it was just a Jason and Pete thing.

"Don't you dare talk to him," Jason said as he squeezed my forearm.

"But you want me to be friends with Veronica," I challenged. "I'm just trying to be social."

"Elizabeth, don't. You know exactly what I'm talking about."

And there it was. Again. Elizabeth, don't.

19

WHEN THE LADDER FALLS

Drama. Drama. Everywhere drama. And I didn't even have to work hard to find it.

Last night was the Winter Dance, and after the kids packed themselves into the party bus (complete with stripper pole), the adults lingered and had cocktails. The Joneses know how to throw a party. The drinks kept coming, and the more everyone drank, the more people let loose.

Like Veronica.

She, true to her reputation as a party girl, climbed up on the Jones' kitchen table and performed what can only be described as a burlesque show. Off came her belt, then her stilettos. Then a shimmy in a black lace bra, before Pete reached up, grabbed her by the knees, and threw half-clothed Veronica over his shoulder.

This would be normal for Waterford. Acceptable even. But Veronica took it even farther. She hurled insults at everyone. Except Jason and Elizabeth. She went right past them and clammed up. For a moment. Then she went back to screaming about who was a bitch, and who was sleeping with whom, and that someone was transgender (and didn't we all know it?).

She single-handedly destroyed the evening. Women were in tears. Guys were shouting and posturing like gorillas. It was a total shit-show. And of *course, it was all caught on tape. Which means it's making its way around Waterford today.*

I've heard the gossip and seen the video, and it isn't pretty. I think Veronica alienated most of Waterford. Not that she cares. The Periphery Girls will be back to kissing her ass tomorrow, because in this messed up place, being outed or embarrassed by a member of the Bitch Brigade means you've made it. Your business matters to them, and that moves you up a little higher on the social ladder.

People forget ladders can topple. And they can do so quickly.

"Just so we're clear, we're not talking to the Staffords anymore." Karen's bossy voice boomed out of my phone. "Or Julie Argles. She's too questionable."

I shifted on the couch and switched ears. For nearly an hour, Karen had delighted in telling me about the fallout from the Jones' party. Apparently, everyone in my neighborhood was a swinger, a cheater, or a closeted gay person.

Honestly, I didn't care. It felt very high school to me.

"Karen? How do you know all this? You weren't there."

"Where have you been, Elizabeth? It's all anyone is talking about. I saw the video which means I didn't need to be there to connect the dots."

"And gossip."

She blew into the phone. "Hardly gossip if it's true." She paused and let out a little laugh. "Key West should be a blast."

"Or a total disaster."

"Don't be such a pessimist. Even under the worst circumstances, we'll have fun. Haven't you learned anything yet? We *always* have fun."

My phone beeped, and I pulled it away from my ear. It was Sarah. "Karen, can I call you back? My mom is calling." She'd be livid at me for choosing Sarah over her.

"Okay, Sweetie. Love ya!"

"Love you, too." Have I said how much I hated this phrase? After a while it lost all meaning, if it had any to begin with.

I clicked over. "Hey, Sarah. What's up?"

A low moan.

"Sarah?"

"I'm here. I'm just..." Her voice faded in and out. Something was wrong. Very wrong.

"I'm coming over."

"Hurry."

"I'll be right there."

Her words were barely above a whisper. "I need to tell you--"

"Sarah?" I screamed, but there was no response. Just dead air. "Sarah?"

I had run over to my Uggs and yanked my bag from the counter top and my keys from the holder. Once in my car, I flew through the round-about and skidded into Sarah's driveway. The garage door was open, and I let myself in. An eerie silence hung over the house.

"Sarah?"

There was no answer. "Sarah?" I yelled. "Are you upstairs?" I was standing in the middle of the kitchen, and Sarah's phone laid on the counter. It was covered in blood.

"Sarah!"

An oversized u-shaped couch dominated the living room.

There was no evidence of Sarah being in there, and yet I skirted around the couch. I tripped around the couch. I stumbled around the couch.

Screams, my screams, pierced the air.

Sarah laid lifelessly on the floor, her face hidden in a swirl of long, ash blond hair.

"Sarah!" I lunged at her and grabbed her by the elbow. Warm, sticky blood covered my hands. It was all over the rug and running down her arms. Her dripping wrists were slit length-wise. Not in horizontal slits, but straight up the arm.

"9-1-1 What's your emergency?" The man's voice was calm. Too calm.

"My friend. She's bleeding everywhere. I think she slit her wrists."

"Address?"

"I don't know. She lives on Rosecreek Court in Waterford. The house with the American Flag in front and open garage door."

"Is she responsive?"

I roughly flipped Sarah over, and her head lopped side-to-side. "No, but she's breathing."

"That's good. That's very good. Do you have anything to stop the bleeding?"

"Like a Band-Aid?" My mind swirled. Where would I find a Band-Aid? In Sarah's bedroom bathroom cabinet? Would she keep them where I do?

"No. You need to stop the bleeding. Are there any sheets or towels you can easily tear up?"

I sprinted into the kitchen and ripped open the drawers. "There's nothing," I shouted into the phone. "What am I going to do? I can't let her die!"

"How is she now?"

I raced back to Sarah and placed my hand over her faintly beating heart. "She's still not moving. I think she's getting worse."

"You need to apply pressure just above her elbows. Can you do that?"

"I...Yes. Yes, I can." I looked down at my t-shirt. The ratty, over-sized one I've owned since ninth grade. It had paint specks on it from painting Ollie's nursery. Years of memories, but I ripped it off and shredded it into long strips. "I'm going to use my t-shirt as a tourniquet."

The man on the phone instructed me where to place the strips of cloth and just as I was finishing, the paramedics arrived.

I stood back, in just my yoga pants and bra while they worked on Sarah. Adrenaline pumped hard through my system, and I wore a path in the rug.

Sarah was completely unresponsive. They were taking too long. Moving in slow motion. Didn't they know how hurt she is?

"Can you hurry? She needs medical care."

"Let us do our job, Ma'am." A male paramedic stepped around me. I was in the way. I shouldn't have been there. And yet, Sarah called me. Why? Why me?

They lifted her onto the gurney and pushed her out toward the ambulance. A light blanket covered her body and hid her wrists, but dried blood was all over her neck and chin.

The crowd on the street buzzed.

"What's going on?" some woman I don't know asked. "Where is your shirt? Why do you have blood all over you?"

"Sarah had an accident. That's all." I folded my arms over my half-naked body.

The woman pointed at the gurney. "Looks serious."

Go away, I wanted to scream. *Just go away. There's nothing to see here.* The woman scurried back to a small group near the mailbox, and I walked toward a paramedic.

"Can I ride with her?"

"No."

"But she'll need someone when she wakes up," I pleaded.

"I'm sorry, but we have rules."

Fuck the rules. Fuck the whole situation.

"Where are you going?" I asked the female paramedic. "I need to tell her husband."

"General."

"But County is closer. Take her to County."

"Suicides go to General."

The word ground against my brain.

Suicide.

Why, Sarah? Why?

The first person I called wasn't Kyle, Sarah's husband, but Jason. Through my sobs, he put together what I was saying.

"Go to the hospital. Just go. I've got the kids covered." He sounded frantic. "Or should I meet you there? Do you need me there?"

"No. I can do this."

"I love you, Elizabeth."

"I love you, too." The words flew from my mouth before I could trap them. I hadn't told Jason I loved him in over a year. But now, now I really meant it.

Sarah's bloody phone laid on the counter. It was unlocked, like she wanted me to find it. I wiped the blood onto my pants before dialing Kyle.

It went to voicemail.

"Damn it, Kyle. Pick up your phone." I punched his number into my contact list and tossed Sarah's phone back on the counter.

My puffer jacket was crumpled on the floor near where I found Sarah. It, too, was covered in blood. Since I couldn't show up to the hospital in just a bra, I ran up to Sarah's bedroom and grabbed a shirt from her closet. I didn't care what I looked like. All I cared about was that she was okay.

The drive to General took twenty minutes. County was five blocks away. Literally in our backyard. It was ridiculous the paramedics had to take her so far away.

"Shit."

I needed to make arrangements for Sarah's kids. Who could do it? Who would be discreet?

Meredith.

"Call Meredith," I said aloud to my phone.

The phone rang and rang and rang. Finally, "This is Meredith."

I gasped for air and held in my tears in while shifting into Woman-In-Charge mode. "Meredith, it's Elizabeth Mavery. I need a huge favor. Sarah Cole's had an accident, and I'm on the way to the hospital. I left her garage door open, but there's not going to be anyone there for the kids. I need you to grab them at the bus stop and not let them inside. Take them to your house or something, but don't let them inside. And I don't know where the nanny is. Probably with the baby somewhere. Don't let her in, either. No one can go inside except you. Do you understand?"

"Yes, but what's going on?"

"I can't say right now. Not until I get ahold of Kyle."

"Okay. I'll go over right now." She paused. "Is there any cleaning up I should do?"

I made a left and followed a stream of cars into the emergency room parking lot. "There's blood on the living room rug, in the kitchen, and on the foyer floor. Can you clean it up?"

"Jesus. Is she hurt?"

"Something like that."

"I'll go over right now. Let me know if you need anything else. I'll keep the kids as long as needed."

"Thanks, Meredith."

"I'm praying for her."

"Thank you."

White streaks blemished the brilliant blue sky. Such a beautiful day. Did Sarah look outside before she cut herself? Did she think it was a lovely day to die? Are blue skies better than gray, drizzly ones?

I wish I knew.

I slammed the SUV door shut and sprinted to the emergency room. The line of people waiting to register was five deep, so I frantically tried Kyle again. When he didn't answer, I left another voicemail.

My desperate mind searched for a way to reach Kyle. Jason didn't socialize with him, so he wouldn't be any help, and Karen would be anything but discrete. So, who could I call? Who would Kyle pick up for?

Pete.

I scrolled through my list of contacts until I found the one I wanted and waited while the phone rang. Once. Twice.

"Elizabeth? How are you?" His carefree voice caused tears to break free of their barricade and run down my face.

"Pete, I need you." My words were little more than choked sounds. "Sarah hurt herself, and Kyle isn't taking my calls."

Nothing.

"Pete?"

"I'll take care of it."

"Tell him she's at General. I'm here, waiting."

"I'll have him there within the next half hour."

Relief filled my frantic brain, because I knew he would.

Unlike Jason, Pete had never let me down.

20

THICKER THAN WATER

Kyle didn't race into the emergency room like a worried man. No, he strolled in, calm as could be, and demanded to know where his wife was. There was confusion because Sarah had been admitted under an alias — common practice until they verified her identity. I guess picking her up from her home wasn't enough.

I moved through a tunnel of noise toward him. One step. Then two. Until, finally, I stood next to him, my hand hovering near his arm. "Kyle?"

He glanced over his shoulder at me. "Why are you here?"

I pulled my hand back into my side. "I'm here for Sarah. Have you heard anything?"

"Mr. Cole, we'll see you back now." A nurse waited by the admit doors. Her demeanor gave no hint as to what Sarah's condition was. Just a blank face and even voice. What did it mean? Surely, if Sarah were dead, the nurse would be softer, more compassionate looking, wouldn't she? She'd have that I'm-so-sorry look people get when they don't know what to say.

But she had none of that, just blankness and a cool demeanor, and I wanted to lunge at her, shake her, demand to know what was happening. Instead, I said to Kyle, "Do you want me to come with you?"

Kyle side-eyed me. "No. Go. I'll call you with an update." He disappeared through the swinging doors.

"Would you like to sit?" An elderly woman said to me. "You look like you need to sit." I let her guide me toward a bank of orange seats. "Would you like some water? I can ask the nurse."

"No, I'm fine thank you."

"Is there someone I can call to come get you? You're trembling."

I held out my hand, and it shook. "It's my medicine," I said even though I knew otherwise. "It makes me shaky."

The elderly woman sat next to me and rested her hand on my back. She didn't say anything else. Just sat with me.

For a few minutes, maybe more, I sat on that uncomfortable, plastic chair, waiting to see what would happen, but when Kyle didn't reappear, I dug past the balled-up tissues in my bag and found my car keys. If Kyle didn't need me there, maybe it was best I go help Meredith. At least I'd be doing something more than just waiting.

"How is she?" Meredith carried a large pot of water across the room. Her hands were red and raw.

I pressed my lips tightly together until I knew I wouldn't start crying. "I don't know. I never saw Kyle after he went back to be with her."

Meredith knelt and began trying to get blood out of the gray and white throw rug. It was smeared down the front of the couch, too, but most of the blood was on the rug. It was no longer bright red, but rather a dull rust color. Dried. A reminder that time had passed.

"Let me help," I said. "Please."

"There are new dishtowels in the drawer next to the sink. The tags are still on, but it's all I could find."

They were bright yellow cloths. Happy cloths. Not the kind a suicidal woman would buy. At least, I wouldn't.

Meredith and I scrubbed and scrubbed and scrubbed the rug, but the blood smeared and made more of a mess. After a few minutes that seemed like hours, I said. "I don't know why Kyle hasn't called me."

"I'm sure he will. He's probably busy dealing with the hospital. You know how they can be."

She was right. He probably had to fill out a thousand forms and calling me wasn't a priority. Still, I wanted — no needed – to know Sarah's status.

"Should I call?"

Meredith dropped her towel. "No, Elizabeth. I think Kyle has enough on his plate right now. This, right here, needs your attention." She picked up the bowl of red water. "Go dump this and refill it. We have a lot to do before we can let their girls back into the house."

It was strange how Meredith hadn't asked what had happened. She walked into a house with blood all over the place, and her first thought wasn't to find out what had transpired, but rather how to clean the evidence so Sarah's girls could come home.

I placed the clean bowl of water between us, and Meredith soaked her rag before attacking a new patch of blood. "It would be easier to throw this out."

"Probably." I didn't want to make a decision like that without consulting Sarah even though the rug was beyond repair. "What should we do?"

Meredith sat back on her heels. "Let's roll it up and place it in the corner by the TV. That way, if the girls ask, we can say Sarah is redecorating."

Her idea made perfect sense at the time.

As we moved the couch, Meredith got a funny look on her face.

"What?" I asked.

We place the couch down, just off the rug. "I don't want to pry, but what the hell happened here? Is Sarah going to be okay?"

My legs gave out, and I tumbled to the ground with my hands over my face. "I don't know. She cut herself. Badly." The tears I'd been fighting spilled out. "I think she tried to kill herself."

A long sigh rolled out of Meredith, and her arms were around me. "Oh, Elizabeth. I'm so sorry you had to see all that. The aftermath is bad enough, but to actually have found her...I'm...I'm so sorry."

"She was — is - always so damn happy. I don't understand."

Meredith rested her chin on my head. "I don't think things like this ever make sense."

And there it is. The logical response to the illogical. We would never know why Sarah decided to hurt herself unless she told us. My own experience had taught me that, but still, being on the other side of it, well, that made things so much more difficult because at least when it was me, I was in control. I was making the decisions. But with Sarah, nothing made sense.

"Do you think she left a letter?" Meredith asked. "Something for the girls, maybe?"

Of course she would. Sarah wouldn't leave without saying good-bye. It was bad manners, and she was all about having perfect manners. I pulled myself together and straightened up. "I'll look in the kitchen."

"I'll look in her bedroom." Meredith was already to the stairs. "Elizabeth?"

"Yes?"

"I can't say everything is going to be okay, but I promise we'll get through this, okay?"

I closed my eyes and nodded, but my mind was miles away. If I were Sarah, where would I leave a note? The kitchen counter was bare except for her phone. It had been meticulously wiped down by Meredith. I spun around. If not on the counter, where?

I walked over to the built-in desk. Mail and bills littered the surface, and I pushed them around. No note there either.

Meredith stood by the foot of the stairs. "Nothing upstairs. Did you find anything?"

"No."

She tilted her head and pursed her lips. "Do you think it could have been a tragic accident? Like she was a cutter or something, and it went too far?"

Sarah often wore short sleeves and tanks. She never hid her arms. Plus, she sliced vertically up her arms, not across. "No," I said. "It was intentional. There has to be a letter. I would have left one."

Horror flitted across Meredith's face before turning into pity. It was a look I feared, one that told me how Meredith truly felt about the situation. That strong, happy Sarah woke up one day and decided to off herself.

But it never happened like that. It built, slowly, until you felt there is no other way out of your misery.

The thing is, every suicide attempt is different. Different reasons, different methods, different outcomes. But Sarah, she just didn't seem like the type.

Then again, most people would probably say, neither did I.

I guess, that's one thing all the Women of Waterford had in common — we were all good at hiding our pain.

NOW

2 1

THE TRAGEDY HUNTER

Maybe you don't have one in your life, but Waterford has a resident Tragedy Hunter named Naomi. She's the woman who is first to organize meals, keeps everyone up-to-date on the latest happenings (even though she herself may not be privy to that information), and makes treats for first responders because they deserve it for being put in stressful situations.

Basically, Naomi's a pain in everyone's ass, and I hate her.

I don't want to be on a prayer chain or a meal list. I want to sit quietly and reflect.

This post can't be snarky because there's nothing to joke about at the moment.

I'm waiting for my spouse to finish showering. Then we're off to Waterford's latest group gathering: Sarah Cole's funeral.

She died in a freak accident. A fall through a glass table. A slit artery.

And Elizabeth Mavery found her. I can only imagine the hell she must be going through. To lose a friend and to be the one who couldn't save her.

I wouldn't wish that on anyone.

My fingers wrap around Jason's, and I rub his wedding band. So far, between Meredith, Pete, Jason, Kyle, and myself, we've been able to position Sarah's death as an accident. She fell, so the story goes, and crashed through a glass table, cutting her artery.

Because it was printed in the blog, people are buying it.

None of us want Sarah remembered as the woman who killed herself.

Jesus.

She killed herself.

How lonely was she behind her smile and perky attitude? Why couldn't she confide in me? In anyone? What drove her to do something so drastic?

"You look nice," Jason says.

I pause. "I don't think we're supposed to look nice at a funeral."

"Point taken." He brushes his free hand over my arm, and I shiver. Since Sarah's death, Jason has been touching me. Too much. It's like he needs a physical reminder that I'm still here.

"I have to see about the food." Sitting around the church, waiting, is driving me crazy. I need to move, to keep my mind preoccupied. "I want to make sure it's ready for the reception."

Jason spins me around so that I face him. "Let Naomi do it. She seems to get off on it."

"Naomi didn't even know Sarah. Leaving it all to her doesn't seem right."

"You don't need to do any more. You've done enough." My husband embraces me and strokes my hair. "It's not your fault, Babe. It's not. What Sarah did by calling you was unfair. She shouldn't have done it. She was being selfish."

*I need to tell you...*what did you need to say, Sarah? What?

"Elizabeth?" Jason peers into my eyes.

"She wasn't selfish, she was hurting. If anyone should understand, it's us." Numbness tingles down my arms and legs. Life's taken on a hazy, twilight quality for the past three days, and the fact that Sarah is truly gone seems unfathomable. Weren't we joking around just the other day? Wasn't she trying to cheer me up? Was I so self-absorbed that I couldn't see what was going on with her?

"It's not your fault," Jason repeats.

"I know."

"Then don't do this to yourself."

Jason doesn't say it, but he's worried about me sinking into depression. It's in the way he holds me. Gently. Timidly. Like he's worried I'll turn into the next Sarah, and that her suicide is contagious.

And who's to say I won't? I can never admit that out loud unless I want another stay at the psych ward.

"The food," I say.

Jason kisses my forehead. "Go, if you insist."

I slip out of his grasp and through the side door. The reception is in the church's hall across the courtyard, and drizzle lightly dampens me as I dart between buildings.

The kitchen is a blur of activity and sure enough, Naomi is there directing everyone.

"Elizabeth! Hi! Do you need something?" Naomi looks happy, like she is, in fact, getting off on being needed. Which she is not. She just wormed her way into our lives and took over like a nasty parasite. A parasite I want to squash.

A large bowl of salad sits on the counter. It's full of tomatoes and carrots and cucumbers — all things Sarah hated. "Are we having burgers?"

Naomi laughs. "Don't be silly. Why would we do that?"

"Because that's what Sarah loved. And French fries. And Diet Coke."

A tight grimace forms on Naomi's lips. "Well, that's not appropriate, is it? I mean, this is a funeral. People bring casseroles. We don't cater from Five Guys."

"Maybe we should." I don't disguise the testiness in my voice. How dare this random woman tell me what's appropriate? "I think honoring the deceased with their favorite things is a great idea.

146

Maybe if you had asked one of us that knew her, you would know that Sarah hated salads."

Naomi keeps on smiling while she gathers up serving spoons. "I'm sure Sarah would have loved the reception we've put together."

I shake my head. "How would you know? The two of you had never met."

"Because everyone loves pasta and salad. It's a universal law. Now, do you have something more to say, or are we done?"

"You know she was my best friend." When I hear the words spoken, I have to wonder: was she? If she was, wouldn't I have known?

"I understand." Naomi speaks slowly, like I'm a toddler having a tantrum. "That's why I'm not angry with you. You're hurt."

Leave, now, Elizabeth. Don't say anything more. Just leave.

"At least buy some Diet Coke."

Before she can answer, I exit the kitchen. The reception hall is just across the way. It's a multi-purpose room, really, with a stage and built-in benches along the walls. There are basketball hoops, too, pinned back against the ceiling. Folding tables covered in white cloths dot the room. White. Sarah's favorite color was green. Jesus. Did no one know anything about her?

I rest my hand on the cool, cinderblock wall and try not to let the emptiness of the room overwhelm me. Image after image of Sarah lying on the ground hits me, and my heart races as my breath becomes shallow. Did she envision her death the way I do mine? Did she ever get to this part, or like me, did she stop at the funeral? Did she think at all about her kids, and the hell they are going through?

Kyle told me none of the girls will sleep alone, so he has them all in bed with him. But soon, he's going to have to go back to work, and the girls will be forced back into their own beds.

Thankfully, Sarah's mom is moving in and he has the nanny, because Kyle is going to need all the help he can get. Raising three, motherless little girls is going to be time-consuming and difficult.

Oh, Sarah. Why? Why did you not think this far out? Why did

you stop at the funeral? If you had known the suffering of your family and friends, you wouldn't have done this. I know you wouldn't have.

But is this what death would be like for me? Would someone be thinking these same thoughts? Would my boys be able to persevere and move forward? What about Jason? Would he be able to keep the family together?

The impossible burden of existing pushes me to the ground, and I sink with my head in hands.

None of this is right. None of it. White cloths. Salads. Naomi.

A warm hand presses against my shoulder, and my fingers clasp around it.

"She'd hate this, wouldn't she?"

"Yes."

Pete kneels next to me. "Not many people appreciated Sarah the way you did."

I suppress a sniff while trying to hide my tears.

He folds me into his arms, and long-held sobs erupt from the bottom of my heart. "Why?" I cry. "Why?"

Pete nestles my head under his chin and rubs my back. "We'll never know."

I push away from this man who is holding me. I push away and come to my senses. I push away and look at him in the face. "Leave me alone."

"Elizabeth-"

"You don't know anything! This could have been me. Do you know that? Do you know anything about me other than what I choose to show you? Like everyone else here in this town, I'm a façade. Sarah was a façade. She wouldn't have killed herself if she wasn't." I'm on my feet. "Leave me alone."

"If that's what you want."

I'm shaking and trying not to let my legs give way. "It's what I need. Let me be."

"What's going on?" Jason barks from the doorway. His dark eyes flash, and his body is tense, puffed out, ready to spring.

"Sarah would have hated all this," I sob. "It's all wrong."

"And Pete is here, why?"

Pete steps away from me. "I saw her on the floor and came to make sure she's okay."

"Are you okay, Elizabeth?" My husband walks with authority to my side. He encircles my waist and pulls me into him. Unlike before, it's rough and aggressive. Gone is his sweet side.

"I will be."

"I guess that means you can go, Pete." Jason spits out Pete's name. It's obvious there's no love lost between the two of them.

Pete's blue eyes pause on my face before he turns to leave. When he's gone, Jason leans into me. "If I ever see you alone with him again, I'll leave you. Do you understand?"

I tap my head against his broad chest. "He was only trying to help."

"I told you to stay away from him. I meant it."

"Jason, this isn't the time for your grudge match. I have more important things to worry about than whether you do or don't care for Pete today."

My husband takes me by the shoulders and peers down at me. "Pull yourself together. People are starting to leave the church." Jason roughly wipes his hands over my cheeks. "Go reapply your make-up. It's streaky."

"This is a funeral. I think it's okay."

"You can't be seen like this. You're a fucking mess."

I recoil. "Why are you being so nasty? What did I do wrong?"

Jason's jaw sets. "One word: Pete."

"Really? That interaction warrants this behavior?" I step back. "You're making something that wasn't into a big deal. What you saw was nothing."

"So, the other times were?"

I draw a deep breath. Like all of us, Jason has been rattled by Sarah's suicide, and it's bringing out his dark side, but right now isn't the time or place to argue. "I'm going to go fix my make-up. I'll meet you back here in a few minutes. Why don't you find us a table?"

Jason's rigid posture relaxes. "I love you, Elizabeth. I do. I know I didn't act like it during...during my affair. But losing you — especially like this - would destroy me."

I'm so tired of what does Elizabeth need today? What crazy thing can I help Elizabeth with? But mostly, since Sarah died, what can I do to make sure my wife doesn't off herself?

The scary part is that we both know I've tried before. That time in Nice when I downed a whole bottle of Lorazepam and chased it with champagne. And in London, when I slashed my wrists so badly, I had to go to the hospital where I learned that you must cut along the artery to actually die — something Sarah already knew. And here, when I took too many drugs and ended up in the psych ward. Every day I fight to push suicidal thoughts from my mind.

Jason told me this battle makes me strong, but I wonder what he'd say if he knew I was jealous of Sarah. That despite being mad about how she left her family, I understand the need to go. The want. The seeing no other options.

If Jason could see into my mind, he'd have me committed immediately.

I pat my face with one of those crummy brown paper towels you find in church bathrooms and reapply my foundation. Next, I fix my eye make-up, blush, and lipstick. Jason should find me presentable enough. I don't look crazy. Bipolar depression hasn't won today. That is until I step out of the bathroom, and Sarah's three, beautiful girls file into the hall holding flowers. The youngest is just two. She probably has no understanding of what happened. None of them really do.

Mommy hurt herself on a table and died.

Meredith told me Kyle smashed it to make the story more plausible. Naomi, or course, arranged for a cleaning service because we couldn't get all the glass up, but Meredith and I convinced Kyle to throw the rug away.

Erase all evidence of what happened.

Hopefully, we won't erase Sarah as easily.

22

LIFE RESUMES

I t was Karen who insisted we get "back to normal." That Sarah would have wanted us to keep living.

I call bullshit. She has no idea what Sarah would have wanted since she barely ever spoke more than two words to her at a time. And then, they were often backhanded compliments or outright cruel.

And yet, I woke at 4:30am and took a taxi to the airport so Jason and I could sit at another airport for two hours before boarding our flight to Key West. I couldn't help but think about how badly Sarah wanted to do this trip. How it meant everything to her just to be invited.

How by going, I was somehow honoring her wishes.

The prevailing attitude is that the party must continue whether Sarah is gone or not. Actually, Karen implied Sarah's death was over-shadowing Alexis's big day. Well, of course it is! How could it not?

Am I the only one who cares that she's gone?

Jason says I need to let go. Karen says it's time to move forward. But I'm not ready. It's only been thirteen days. I need to grieve. And right now, I'm sad, angry, hurt.

Oh, Sarah. Why? Why? Why?

And what did you need to say?

The first thing we saw upon arriving in Key West: middle-aged people doing keg stands, and Alexis wearing a barely-there string bikini with a tiara. And oops! Right when we walked by her bottoms fell off exposing her smooth, lasered nether region to the world. She didn't even seem to care because she just giggled and ran off, leaving the bottoms on the ground and her toned ass seared into my mind.

The next thing I spied: Karen in the hot tub with a few of the husbands, drinking some sort of pink, fruity drink. She had her arm wrapped around a guy's leg as he sat on the ledge. Actually, she was more or less caressing it. And licking it. Slowly and methodically.

I think she was trying to explain her blow job technique.

Jason gawked for a second, but once he understood what we were witnessing, he hurried us to our room and locked the door. His eyes grew wide, and he shook his head.

The whole thing is like a bad episode of Waterford Gone Wild.

Maybe it was out of necessity, but Jason did five shots of Fireball tonight and is now passed out on our bed with the covers balled at his feet. I want to snuggle into his side and hide from everyone, but my roaming mind won't shut off. Despite everyone else seeming to have moved on, I'm stuck on losing Sarah and the huge hole her absence is causing in my heart.

Our last conversation, the one where she called me a good friend, will always be burned in my memory. How was I a good friend? If I was, wouldn't I have known something was wrong before it led to her killing herself?

I should have noticed the signs.

No. I wasn't a friend to Sarah. I was simply a person passing through her life. Like she was in mine. Hell, I only confided Jason had an affair after getting sloppy drunk. I didn't trust her enough.

And yet she called me. Out of all the women in Waterford, she called *me*. Her lunch-time acquaintance and new friend of a few months. She should have called Melissa – it makes more sense. But me? I don't understand.

Was she really that alone? Or did she really trust me that much?

Where are my answers?

It scares me how I understand her decision. I don't want to, but I do. Sometimes, the pain of staying is greater than the pain of letting go.

There are those who say suicide is selfish. I disagree. Suicide is hard. No one wants to do it. No one wants to be pushed into that position, and by the time you find yourself there, it's often too late to pull yourself out.

Is that why she called me? Because she thought I could pull her out?

I slip out the door of our poolside room, and salty air from the nearby ocean washes over me. A few random people I somewhat recognize still gather around the hot tub, but it's three in the morning, and nearly everyone else has either surrendered to booze or sleep.

But not me. I've taken my pills — even the extra doses of Abilify and Klonopin Dr. Carter prescribed after Sarah's death — and I'm still going strong.

No, I've done everything I'm supposed to, and still, the threat of hypomania haunts me.

Not depression like Jason and I worried about, but hypomania.

My body buzzes. Not sleeping is just one of my symptoms. I'm also not eating and trying to do too much at once. Jason has hidden all my cash so I can't go on a spending bender, and he's indulged my insatiable sexual appetite.

I need more of everything. To calm my brain. To ease my heart. To forgive myself, if only for a moment.

Hypomania is the best place to exist. Tonight, after Jason was too shit-faced to reprimand me, everyone laughed at my bawdy jokes, and Karen complimented me on my tabletop dancing. She said she didn't think I had that kind of thing in me, because I'm normally so reserved and shy — but get me out of Waterford and watch out!

Sarah would have liked me like this. She would have called me 'honey' and joined me in doing cannonballs into the pool. We could have had such a great time.

But she's dead, and nothing makes sense. She was so vibrant. So funny. So full of life.

An intricate metal gate separates me from the empty sidewalk, and I fumble with the lock. Key West in the early morning is a ghost town, and I probably shouldn't be walking around alone, but then again, I don't care.

Tonight, I didn't drink. For the first time in ages, I didn't want to — even though the hypomania craves it. I was able to beat back the beast and instead, I sipped water from a solo cup and pretended it was vodka. I didn't numb or self-medicate. I want, no need, to allow myself to feel, and that means not hiding in a bottle of booze.

Behind me, the gate creaks, and I wearily turn my head.

"Where are you going?" Pete asks. His hair is a rumpled, blond mess, and there's just enough moonlight to make out the scruff on his jawline. He's handsome in that strong, manly way that I love. Dangerous even.

Yes, Pete White is a dangerous man.

I smile. Despite Jason's threat, I enjoy Pete's company. "To the waterfront. Want to join me?"

Pete nods, and for a few blocks, we walk in silence.

"Does Veronica know? About us? Does she know that we used to...well, you know?" Maybe that's why Veronica is cool toward me? Pete told her what happened between us all those years ago.

"No. She knows we were good friends, and she believes I may have had something going on with Amanda. She's commented on how you're not my type — you're not blond enough and are too quiet."

I laugh. "I'm not, am I? Or was I, and I'm not now?" Pete stops walking, and I face him. "What?"

"You've changed." Pete reaches out and tucks a piece of hair behind my ear. It's intimate, and something deep inside me stirs. Like a thawing. "You don't smile like you used to."

What do I say to that? "Life has a way of changing people. You're different, too, you know."

"But it's more than that. It's like the Elizabeth I knew died." He stops. "I'm sorry. I shouldn't— "

"It's okay. Sarah is dead. We all know it." No one wants to talk about her, and it's as if her name is a dirty word. Sarah Cole is dead, I want to shout at everyone. Dead. My knees feel weak, and I grab onto Pete's arm. "Why does this hurt so much?"

"Because you cared about her. She was your friend." No one, not even Jason, has wanted to talk about her. And I need to talk, to get it all out. Pete clasps his hand over mine. "No one expects you to just turn off your feelings."

It seems that way. With all this talk of getting back to normal and Sarah ruining Alexis's party and the whispers of how selfish she was, I may be the only one — other than her family – who cares.

"But this is about more than Sarah, isn't it?" Pete says. "There's a sadness to you that weighs you down. I don't think these new people notice it, but I do. I know you too well."

"Knew me," I correct. "You knew me."

We walk the next block without saying a word.

Finally, "Is Jason asleep?"

"Passed out. I'll be playing nurse in the morning. Five shots of Fireball will bring down even the strongest of men."

"Veronica's in Karen's suite. She's not talking to me again."

I raise my eyebrows even though he can't see them. "I'm sorry. What did you do now?" A tropical breeze picks up, and my hair flies around my head. Above us, the wind whistles through the palm fronds.

Pete reaches for my hand, and when our fingers intertwine, my heartbeat speeds up. Electricity trills along my nerves. For the first time in years, I'm not numb. "I don't know. She's always mad at me lately."

"I would be too. You were on the Ashley Madison list." I hold up my other hand and lift three fingers. "Three times. Everyone knows it, and her image of being perfect kinda got shattered. Oh, and then there was those blog posts about us. And the other about you and Melissa." I pause for effect. "You, Pete White, get around."

He rubs the back of my hand with his thumb, and I crave more. I need more.

Hand-in-hand, we reach the beach where I strip off my shoes and allow the cool sand to move between my toes. My dress billows around me as I sink to the ground, and the crisp ocean air carries the smell of salt and sea to my nose. Being out here is good for my mind, and I already feel clearer. Calmer.

But I tingle in anticipation, wanting whatever it is I can't have.

"Elizabeth," Pete says while stretching out his long, tan legs. "Things are complicated, you know that."

His head is on my shoulder, and the breeze carries his whiskey-scented breath to my nose. I don't move away because I enjoy the closeness. I love when Pete pays attention to me like this. In this moment, there's only us. No Jason. No Veronica. Just the two of us, and I can see our past and future. It would be so easy to leave Jason for Pete.

But I won't. I won't. I won't.

"How are things complicated?" I ask while trying to hold on to all the racing thoughts in my brain.

Pete's words rush out of him. "First there's the kids. I barely saw them last year because I work too much."

"Then work less. That's easy to fix." I drag my free hand back-and-forth in the sand like I'm making a snow angel. I don't dare touch him. Not when I'm like this. It's too easy to make poor decisions when I'm hypomanic. Decisions I always regret after I crash.

"I am," he says. "I'm working from home on Fridays now."

"That's a great start."

"I guess. But Veronica and I are more like roommates. We haven't had sex in months, and all she does is talk about the kids. Plus, she has this perfect image of us to protect."

My laughter can't be contained. "No one thinks the two of you are perfect or happy anymore."

Pete hangs his head and stares at me with hound dog eyes. "I suppose you're right."

"You know I am." I nudge him a little with my shoulder. Once, this would have led to something more, but not now. Not anymore. I'm aware of what I'm capable of, and I'm not going to cross any lines. Especially not with Pete.

"How many women did you meet?" I don't want to know. I don't. But I can't stop myself from asking.

"A few."

"A few?" Anger twinges my words, and I push him away from me. "A few? And you wonder why she's so upset? Poor Veronica. You're not capable of being faithful."

"And Jason is?" When I start to protest, Pete adds, "Don't cover for him. I know about his affair."

"How?"

Pete shakes his head. "Don't worry about it. I'm not going to tell anyone."

My tongue smarts from biting it. "Jason has changed, and we've moved past it."

"Are you positive?"

"Yes."

"So, what are you doing with me? Right now. Why are you here, if you're not a little bit upset with him still?"

I'm here because for Pete gives me feelings — something I forgot how to have. All the walls and ice I've collected over the past two years fall away when I'm with him, and I want nothing more than to feel his arms around me. His lips on mine. His whispered promises in my ear.

"First, *you* followed me." I scoot farther away from him, as if the distance between us can prevent whatever it is Pete's hoping will happen. Whatever it is I'm looking for. "Second, I'm not about to have a revenge affair to punish Jason."

The moon casts ghostly shadows around Pete's head. "That's not what I'm asking."

"Then tell me what you're saying, because right now, it seems like you want me to be your hook-up buddy, again."

Pete snorts. "Would that be so horrible? We had an awesome connection, and it's still there. Tell me it isn't."

My heart is flitting all over the place. Being with Pete would be so easy, and Jason would get a taste of his own medicine, and yet...I can't. I just can't.

"How long has Veronica known about your affairs?" I ask, ignoring his demands.

"She saw the Marriott reward points a few months ago and put it all together. I didn't admit or deny anything — not even when the Ashley Madison stuff came out."

That is such a Pete thing to say. Didn't admit or deny. Jesus. No wonder Veronica tossed him out tonight.

"Does she think it's me?" I ask. Bile lodges in my throat. "Is that why she suddenly started treating me so oddly?"

"Not you. Sarah. She thinks it was Sarah, and that's why she killed herself. But she believes you knew."

"She knows Sarah committed suicide?"

"Everyone suspects."

I push up to standing and loom over him. "You've let Sarah's memory be tarnished by a tawdry affair she had no part in? You did that?"

"Elizabeth, don't."

"Don't what? Defend my friend who isn't here to defend herself?"

Pete exhales. "Trust me, it's better for everyone like this. You need to let it be and not ask questions."

"Why?" A swirling pit opens in my stomach. "Why? You cheated — several times – and cast blame on an innocent woman. What is Veronica going to do to me if I expose the truth? How will she hurt Sarah more than you already have?"

"Veronica's vindictive. She'll destroy you." He stands. "Just let it go."

As I fight the voices stampeding through my mind, Pete reaches out and hugs me closely, and I offer no resistance. "I'm sorry, Elizabeth. I am, but it's for the best."

Despite everything, I melt into Pete. With him, I'm just Elizabeth. I'm not a sick woman who needs tending. I'm not a basket case who tries to kill herself. I'm just me, and it feels good.

Normal.

For the first time in years, I feel normal.

23

THAT TYPE OF WOMAN

I've been told that Key West was a shit show of epic proportions. *Too much alcohol and too many unhappy marriages makes for too much drama. But it wouldn't be a Waterford party unless there was drama.*

My source tells me Karen and Alexis had a total breakdown. Karen called Alexis a 'money-hungry whore,' and Alexis screamed that Karen wishes she had the kind of money Alexis does.

Something tells me there's more to the story than I've been made privy to.

I'm not entirely sure what happened between Pete and Veronica White, but Pete left suddenly Saturday morning and Veronica stayed on as if nothing had happened. I was told it was weird, and she threw herself completely into partying and playing the drunk.

Surprisingly, Elizabeth made herself scarce. After the first night, she and her husband didn't seem as if they were having much fun, and they kept mainly to themselves. He drank, and she sipped water out of a Solo cup. She was trying to pass it off as vodka, but everyone knew.

Maybe it all has to do with how Pete and Elizabeth sneaked back into the compound around five in the morning? I mean, if my spouse did that, I'd get hammered and not speak to him, too.

"Remind me to never agree to go on a birthday trip or couples' vacation with any of those people ever again." Jason flicks off the TV and tosses the remote onto the coffee table. "What the fuck? What the actual fuck? We're not in high school anymore."

"I know." I ball up the tissue in my hand. Since coming home, I've had the worst cold. Probably something I picked up on the plane. "They're all ridiculous."

"The only good thing is that I didn't have to deal with Pete and his superiority complex all weekend," Jason says.

I sniff, and Jason passes me the tissue box. "Poor Veronica. I think she got wasted to avoid answering Pete questions."

Jason locks his gaze on mine. "Do you have any idea why he left?"

Yes. I do. "No."

"Not a clue? Veronica didn't tell Karen who told Alexis who told you?"

"Jason, it doesn't work like that."

"Well, whatever. Do you know?"

I blow my nose loudly before answering. Unlike the rest of Waterford, Jason has forgotten about the blog. How long until he hears the rumors at the Club? The thought causes a chill to run down my spine. I'm dreading that day. "All I know is that she kicked him out of their room and then she went to sleep in Karen's suite because Pete had nowhere to go."

"Veronica told you that?"

"Ummm...no. Karen did." Actually, Pete did, but I can't say that. Jason would murder me if he knew I'd left the compound with Pete and stayed out until five in the morning. He'd divorce me if he knew about how touchy-feely we were.

Yeah. Better not go there.

"Jason?" I stretch out on the couch and place my feet in his lap. "Have you heard anything about Sarah and Pete maybe having had an affair?"

My husband inhales sharply, but doesn't say anything. His eyes focus on something across the room, and he aggressively massages my foot. "Why are you asking?"

"Some of the girls think it may have happened, but I can't see Sarah doing anything like that." I'm testing out how far Pete's lies have traveled. "Sure, she didn't like Kyle much, but she loved her girls, and I can't see her hurting her family like that."

Jason drops my left foot and picks up the right one. His knuckles pound at the bottom of my foot, and I yank it away. "Ow."

"Sorry."

I roll onto my back and stare at the sixteen-foot ceiling. There's a cobweb in a corner that I never noticed before. "So? Have you heard any rumblings about Pete and Sarah?"

"I haven't heard anything about the two of them, but I wouldn't put it past Pete to try. Look at how he is with you."

"And how is that?" My insides flop which is ridiculous because if Jason knew about Pete and me in Key West, he would have said something by now. He's not one to sit on information.

"You know. Like at Sarah's funeral. There was no reason for him to hug you like that. None. Not even because you were crying. But he did, and it was completely inappropriate."

"He did what anyone else would do."

Jason drops my foot and pulls at my toes. "No. He tried to take advantage of your fragile state."

"Why do you think that?" Is that what Pete's been doing all along? Does he know I'm emotionally unstable? Has he played me?

"Like I've said, he isn't a good guy."

I blow my nose again. "You keep saying that, but you never back it up with evidence."

Jason shrugs. "Call it a gut feeling."

We're not going to get anywhere with this conversation except angry at each other. I have to let it go. "I still don't understand what made Sarah do it. She seemed so happy."

Jason pushes my legs off his lap and stands up. "You know, something about the whole situation bothers me. Did you tell her about your suicide attempt in London? About how you cut yourself wrong, because most people make that mistake, but she didn't."

"What are you saying?"

My husband scowls. "How much about your life did you share with Sarah?"

A warm heat creeps up my neck and into my face. "Nothing. She didn't know about that."

"You sure?"

"Positive." Or was I? That day I got drunk and told Sarah everything, did I tell her about my suicide attempts? Did she learn from my mistakes? Vomit sits in my mouth. Oh, God. Did I contribute to her death?

Jason looks down at me. "You look upset. Do you need a pill? Or a glass of wine?"

"No. I'm fine," I answer after swallowing the sour bile in my throat. "Stuffy and miserable, but fine."

My husband shakes his dark head. "I'm getting you a Klonopin. You look like you may jump out of your skin."

I press my lips together and huff. "No. I don't need one. I'll be okay. Just let me focus on my breathing."

Jason disappears through the door, and my spinning mind kicks in. Did Sarah die because of me? Was this all my fault?

And Pete isn't denying he had an affair with Sarah, only that it's better that everyone thinks he did. Which makes zero sense. Why does he want people to think that? Or, I guess more accurately, why is he not willing to deny it?

Then there's Jason, insisting Pete's a bad guy - I don't understand that either. How do they suddenly not like each other?

My brain churns with ideas and theories, but nothing makes sense.

Jason stands in the doorway with a glass of red wine and a bottle of pills. "Hey, are you okay?"

"I feel miserable, but I'll be fine."

I shuffle toward the him, and Jason catches me loosely around the waist. "Hey," he says. "You know I love you, right? I'm not trying to upset you, but you have to see it from my perspective. It's a little odd."

"I know."

He releases me and places the wine glass in my empty hand. "I'll draw you a bath. It'll help you feel better."

———

The longer I sit in the water, the more upset I become with myself. I may not be directly responsible for Sarah's death, but I am responsible for my actions in Key West. When Pete touched me, it was all there — the butterflies, the what-ifs, the desire to feel his lips on mine.

I've been lying to myself. Pete has an effect on my that isn't appropriate, and the only thing holding me back from surrendering to Pete is my desire to be better than Jason. I like holding my moral superiority over him. I haven't broken my vows. I haven't betrayed his trust. I've been a good, loyal wife and stayed with him when it would have been so much easier to leave. Maybe, at first, it was because I didn't want to lose the boys, but now, it's because Jason and I, we are getting back on track. We're trying.

But each time I interact with Pete, the more I want him. His smile, his touch, all of it. Of him. I want all of him.

Jesus. How can I even think such things? Veronica doesn't deserve to be treated like this. She may be chilly toward me, but she has every right to be. Especially, if she can see what I've failed to acknowledge.

Is it possible to fall for someone you never truly got over?

One thing I'm certain of is that I'm definitely not in love with Jason. Or at least not the way I was before I discovered his affair, and with each day that passes, I worry I will never be again. But I have to keep trying. I owe that to the boys. Plus, how many other men would put up with my ups and downs like Jason? No, I'm better off if I stay and try to make this work.

I sink deeper into the water and hit the jet function with my big toe. The water swirls around me as I close my eyes. Jason was right, the steam is making me feel better.

This is my life. I live in the middle of nowhere and am contemplating a possible affair with a guy I fell for twenty years ago. Isn't that enough time for false feelings to disappear? What we had was immature and silly, and I've built a life with Jason – and it includes amazing kids, a mortgage, and one huge broken heart.

I need to stay away from Pete because Key West was just a warning. Who knows what will happen next time — especially if I'm hypomanic.

The problem is, if I'm honest with myself, I want Pete to pick me.

Really, I just want someone, anyone, to choose me.

Because Jason certainly didn't.

And I deserve to be chosen.

24

I'M A FOUR, NOT A TWO

*P*eriphery Girls. They need to know their place. Normally, I don't bother with them much, but damn it if today one of them didn't get to me. Her name is Stacey McLeod, and she thinks she's joined the ranks of the Bitch Brigade because she's lost fifty pounds, got eyelash and hair extensions, and plumped up her breasts with silicon. Oh, and Karen, Alexis, and Veronica all kinda talk to her now. You know, in their talking at you when they're not talking about you kind of way.

Anyway, at my yoga class she waltzed in and unrolled her mat next to Elizabeth. She's never been in one of my classes before. I kinda eavesdropped on her and Elizabeth's conversation, because neither of them noticed me. Actually, I don't think either of them knew who I was. Which is fine, I don't need the recognition, but seriously, what is it with these women?

Enough wallowing. Back to my story. Apparently, Stacey's been practicing yoga for a whole two weeks which makes her an expert. As we moved through class, the room grew hotter, I got sweatier, and I lost myself in the focus of my practice.

Guess class was too much for Stacey, because afterward, she accused Elizabeth, in a snarky way, of being a show-off because Elizabeth did more intermediate moves like a headstand and firefly pose. I'm sorry, but from *what I know, Elizabeth has been practicing for two years compared to Stacey's two weeks. What did she expect? We dedicated yogis have core muscles she can only dream of.*

And then she said she's surprised someone Elizabeth's size could move her body the way she did. Her size? She's maybe size four. A four. I shudder to know what Stacey thinks of me.

Why am I letting fucking Stacey get to me? I have no idea. Maybe it's her ridiculous eyelash extensions that curl up to her brows. Or her spray tan and Lululemon yoga pants. Oh, and the Louis Vuitton handbag slung perfectly over her arm that she uses as a gym bag.

Yup, all those things about Stacey McLeod bother me. Too bad she'll always be a Periphery Girl no matter whose ass she kisses.

And trust me, she kisses a lot of skinny, white, bitchy ass.

"Who was in your class today, Elizabeth?" Karen leans across the table and nearly knocks over her water. No more Diet Coke for her, she's cutting out sugar and carbs and fruit. Sounds wonderful.

"Stacey and a few other people. It wasn't my normal class, so I didn't talk to anyone other than Stacey. I didn't recognize anyone except one girl, but she doesn't live in Waterford." Alexis and Karen have been drilling me for twenty minutes. Question after question about the mysterious blogger.

"Why don't you ask Stacey?" I ask. "She wants into the group badly, according to the blog. You'd make her life if you spoke to her."

"Already have. She doesn't seem to remember anyone familiar, either." Karen blinks. She blinks again. "But whatever. We'll catch the bitch and when we do, they're in for it."

"It's probably Stacey," I say. "She's a total social climber."

"You think?" Alexis says.

"It could be." Karen says between bites of salad. "I'm really not sure who the hell she suddenly thinks she is." She waves her hand. "But seriously. Stacey McLeod actually told you you're fat? I know it was on the blog, but she really said that?"

"Yes," I say with a wounded ego. "I'm a four."

Alexis stabs at her salad like she's trying to kill it. "A four still isn't a two or a zero."

I press my tongue against the top of my mouth. What world do these women live in? "I was a zero when I moved here."

"What happened?" Alexis asks. She shoves a forkful of lettuce into her mouth. I imagine a cow is only slightly more graceful.

"Oh, I don't know. I moved here. I met Sarah. I started walking less and eating more. Oh, and all the booze doesn't help." Antidepressants...

Karen wags her finger. "Excuses. You could go to CrossFit with us, but you won't. Instead you run and do yoga. And what does Sarah have to do with anything. Other than she was a bigger girl?"

My inner fight reflex kicks in, and I tap my foot nervously. This is where I draw the line. This is where I stand up for myself.

"I guess I could do more." I drop my voice. "I've been having burgers and shakes. Stress eating."

Alexis rolls her eyes. "Well, no wonder you've packed on the pounds, but have no worries, we'll get you on the straight and narrow. You'll be svelte again in no time."

I surrender. I don't push back. I don't defend my body. I simply give in, and let the two of them continue to discuss the best way to work off my weight.

"Have either of you two spoken with Kyle?" I ask, breaking into their fantastic plan to re-do my physique.

A hush falls over the table, and two sets of eyes blink back at me.

"I ask because I'm wondering if he needs anything. It's been six weeks, and people probably aren't brining food by or offering to help out anymore."

Karen shifts in her seat, and her eyes dart over my shoulder, back to salad, and back over my shoulder. "Hmmm. That's an interesting thought, but don't you think he has enough help with his mother-in-law and the nanny? I mean, what else could we do?"

"Talk with him? I don't know."

Alexis leans forward and whispers, "Do you think he'll ever admit it was a suicide?" She glances at me. "You were there. Did she really fall through the glass table?"

My hands tremble at what will be another lie spilling from my lips. "It was broken when I arrived, and she wasn't conscious. That's all I know."

"Imagine, though, if it was a suicide. Wouldn't she leave a note behind?" Karen rests her head on her fist. "I wonder what it says."

A letter would give Waterford a whole new thing to gossip about. Pete's right, maybe some things are better left alone. But still...a letter. A way to know...Meredith and I had to have overlooked something.

"There is no note, because there was no suicide," I say sharply. Both woman stare at me. "I was there. I know what I saw. She fell through the table."

Alexis shrugs. "I guess it's possible. She wasn't exactly dainty, was she?"

"No, she wasn't." Karen pushes her half-eaten salad aside. "She had to have been a size ten, minimum."

"What does that matter?" I ask.

"Well, if it had been one of us, I doubt the table would have even have had the slightest crack." Alexis copies Karen and shoves her plate away. I'm the only one left with a salad that I have no appetite to eat.

Karen studies me, and it feels like a challenge of sorts. "Do you think she and Kyle were having problems? I heard he was very controlling and didn't approve of her going out at night. You would know, wouldn't you, Elizabeth? I mean, you're the one she called. You. Not 911. Not Kyle, but you. Why is that? I didn't think you were *that* close. Friends, but not besties or anything."

I swallow hard. "I've asked myself the same question a hundred times. I don't know why she called me. If she'd only have called 911, she might still be here, and we wouldn't have to speculate on the whys and hows of her death."

Alexis bats her eyes. "What did she say when she called?"

My insides tremble. For as long as I breathe, I'll never forget her voice. "She said, 'I need to tell you.'"

"That's it?" Alexis asks. "And you don't know what it was?"

I shake my head and bite down harder to prevent myself from saying anything else.

"I just find the whole thing odd," Karen says. "It doesn't add up."

"Sometimes things don't," I say, repeating the words Jason has said to me a thousand times since Sarah's death. "Sometimes we have to accept that there are no answers."

"Excuse me ladies. Are you finished?" Our waiter stands next to our table. I don't bother to look up at him. I can't. I'm too busy focusing on not crying.

"We're all finished," Karen says.

My plate is whisked away, and I keep my head down.

"What are you hiding, Elizabeth?" Karen says. There's no emotion or accusation in her voice. It's level. Like she wants to know, but doesn't want to at the same time. Which is very unlike Karen. Maybe this is her caring voice?

I close my eyes briefly before looking up at the other two women. "Nothing. I'm just...thinking about Sarah and her precious girls makes me sad. I'm still trying to make sense of it."

Alexis – Alexis of all people – reaches across the table and takes my hand. "I'm sorry. I didn't realize you were as close as you apparently were. Honestly, I thought Melissa Foster was her only friend."

"Me, too." Karen pulls out her credit card and rests it on the edge of the table, and the waiter immediately takes it away. "I'll cover today. Alexis, you can pick up the next one."

"We were friends. I guess I'm sentimental," I say.

"Nothing wrong with that." Karen signs for the meal. "It's just that it really is time to move on. Wallowing won't do anyone any good. Trust me."

A tear slides down my cheek, and I dab it away. "You're right. I know I need to move on, but if you saw what I saw..."

"Maybe you need a good therapist that deals with trauma," Karen says. "She put you into an unfair position when you called you, and obviously, you're not handling it well."

I don't tell them I have a mental health team. I don't confess that Sarah did kill herself. I don't push back on anything.

It's more important to preserve Sarah's memory.

"C'mon," Alexis says. "There's nothing more uplifting than a surprise shopping spree. Why don't we hit the outlets and do some damage?" She throws an arm around me. "It'll make you feel better. I swear."

I have exactly sixty-one dollars in my wallet. I have no credit, just a debit card. I have no money other than what Jason gives me as an allowance because I'm not to be trusted with money. Too many self-soothing spending sprees have caused Jason to cut me off.

"I don't know. Henry gets home in an hour-and-a-half. I don't think I have the time."

Karen whips out her phone. "I'll have Dora pick him up. He'll recognize her, won't he?"

"Maybe. He has seen her a few times playing at the pool with Mathew." Like Sarah, Karen has a live-in nanny for her children — one of whom is in eleventh grade. I can't say I understand, but it is common in Waterford. "I'd have to call the school and let him know."

"Then do it!" Alexis nudges me toward the exit. "It's not that hard, and really, what is Jason going to say? He's the most indulgent husband I've ever met."

In public. He's indulgent when it suits him. More so since Sarah died.

Sixty-one dollars won't get me anything, but if I don't shop, they're going to find it weird. "Speaking of Jason, I need to call him."

"Call the school first. That way they have time to get the message to Henry." Karen spins her keys around her finger.

I find the school's number and speak to the secretary. Once I'm done, I dial Jason. He picks up on the third ring.

"Hey. Is everything okay?" The persistent worry in his voice annoys me. Like I can't call just for an ordinary conversation.

"Everything is great. I'm with Karen and Alexis, and they want to go to the outlet mall. Dora, Karen's nanny, is going to pick up Henry from the bus stop."

"You need money." Thank God, he understands my code.

"I do."

In the background, Jason's keyboard keys clack. "I transferred five hundred to your debit account. That should be enough, right?"

"I believe so."

"All right. Have fun. I can take care of dinner, just let me know if you're going to be late."

I lift my mouth away from the phone. "How long do you think we'll be?"

Karen shrugs. "A few hours."

"Don't count on me for dinner."

"Okay. Have fun." He's always so happy when I get invited to things like this. When it comes to social outings, indulgent is the right word for Jason.

"Thanks." I hang up. "Looks like I'm free all day."

Alexis jumps up and down. "Then we're definitely stopping by Wish for champagne."

A smile creeps across my face. Champagne. That's exactly what I need.

25

LOVE YOU, LOVE YOU NOT

Tongues are a waggin'. Veronica has suddenly left town to 'tend to an ailing family member.' Nothing more specific. Just an unnamed family member and a quick exit out of Waterford in the dead of night.

Oh, and she took the kids with her. If that's not a sign of doom, I don't know what is.

As usual, Pete's hanging out at the Club, drinking until all hours, and hitting on anything female that walks past. He really needs to get control of himself. He's embarrassing himself and Veronica even more than usual. In fact, the rumor of the day is he went back to one of the hotel guest's room. Oh, hell. It's not a rumor. He did. He totally did, and no one here has a problem with it. Well, not the guys. They don't have a problem. Karen and all are frantically trying to prevent Veronica from hearing.

But that's the thing. The wife always finds out. She always knows, maybe not consciously, but she knows. It's the lingering scent of perfume on his clothes; the extra showers; the obsession and secrecy with his phone.

We know.

But Pete, Pete, Pete. Someone needs to stop him before his ruins his marriage, and Veronica stays gone. You'd think he'd learn after their last go-around, but clearly, he hasn't.

Jason rolls onto his side and locks his hand over mine. He gently pulls me into him, and I yield. He's warm and safe, and smells slightly musty in a sexy man way.

"Good morning."

I groan. "Morning is not a good thing."

"It is when you wake up next to a beautiful woman." He nibbles my neck, and I giggle. So often, Jason feels like a caretaker and not a husband that I welcome this change.

"Morning breath is hot," I say. "I know you just want my dragon breath."

He grins. His dark hair is mussed and his cheeks and jaw are scruffy with day old stubble. In moments like this, I know exactly why I fell in love with him. He made me laugh and feel beautiful and smart and he cared about things. Deeply. Jason was everything I wanted.

Too bad what I wanted at twenty-two is different than what I want at nearly forty.

Mental illness and an affair make all the difference.

"Slip into the shower with me?" Jason whispers. "After we brush our teeth?"

I can't say no. I can't, or I risk disappointing Jason. I throw back the covers and immediately regret it. My naked body is on display. Let me correct that. My *size four* body is on display.

Before Jason can get a good look at me in the filtered, morning light, I roll off the bed in a decidedly ungraceful way and land hands and knees on the floor. "I'll get the water started."

"What was that?" Jason laughs. "Did your legs give out?"

"No. I didn't want you to smack my ass."

Jason smirks. "But it's such a cute, tiny ass."

"According to the Women of Waterford, it's meaty, and I need to lose weight."

"They're crazy. It's a perfectly sized ass, and I love it."

When he says things like this, I want to believe him. After a year of trying to get back on track, I suppose I should. But so much has happened: his affair, the move, my bipolar diagnosis. It all piled up until I stopped trying to swim upstream in a flood and landed myself in a psychiatrist's office.

And now there's Pete.

If he had come around in the thick of everything, would I have made the sensible, sane decision, or would I have thrown away my life for a chance at something exciting? Would Jason and I be standing here today? Would I have allowed myself to become *that woman*?

"Hey," Jason says. "What are you thinking about?"

"Do you know Stacey McLeod?" I ask as I crank on the water and duck back out of the shower.

"Kevin's wife?"

"Yeah. Her. She's hanging out with Karen, Alexis, and Veronica now. Or at least she thinks she is."

"I thought Veronica went out of town?"

"She did, but that's not the point."

Jason kisses my forehead before sliding the glass door open. Steam spirals around our naked bodies. "Tell me why I should care about this?"

"Because it's my life."

"No, your life is here, at home, with the kids and me. What those women do is of no concern of yours."

"You know Veronica has basically left Pete, right?"

"Really? That's what you want to talk about? Pete's an ass, we all know it, and Veronica's better off without him."

"Maybe she'll start speaking to me again if he's out of the picture." I doubt it, but I want to judge Jason's reaction to assess whether he believes Pete is a threat or not.

"Why would you want that?"

"Because she's friends with all my friends, and it makes things awkward when we're avoiding each other."

He tosses two towels over the top of the shower stall. "I want you to have friends, but I think your priorities are messed up sometimes. You don't need to be Miss Popular."

He motions me into the shower. "Jason, if I didn't sell my soul to Karen and the rest of her crew, we'd never get invited anywhere. Plus, you love going out on the weekends. You're the popularity chaser, not me."

We stand sideways so that the water can run over both our bodies. Next to Jason, I'm a dwarf, and he takes up most of the water stream. My back presses against the chilly, tiled wall.

"Turn around." He holds a white bar of soap and lathers up the washcloth. I spin and lay my cheek and hands against the tile. Slowly, he rubs down my shoulders and back, and I relax into the gentle massage. "What I love is spending time with you."

I'm so tired of Jason's constant reinforcement of his love of spending time with me. It's as if he's realized that he could lose everything at any moment, so he needs to say it as much as possible.

I can't imagine the hell of being married to a sometimes-suicidal woman with bipolar disorder. Why he hasn't left me is a mystery. I'm certainly more work than I'm worth these days.

"So, you'd give up a night out with the guys to watch trashy TV with me?"

Jason finishes soaping my back and steps aside so water can run over me. Bubbles float over my feet and escape down the drain. "For you, I'd watch all the Housewives of Whatever on marathon."

"Really?"

"Really."

"This Saturday, after the boys are in bed, you, me, and Bravo?" I grin.

Something odd flickers across his face. "Ummm...let me see if I can rearrange some things."

"Drinks with the guys?" I snap. I don't mean to sound bitchy, but that's how it comes out. After telling me he'd spend time with me no matter what, he's back peddling.

Jason rinses his hair without saying anything. He selfishly lets the water run over him while goosebumps form across my skin.

"What do you have that's more important than me?" I place my hand on his bare chest. "What?"

He cranks the faucet off and hands me a towel before grabbing his own. "Elizabeth, don't start. I said I'd rearrange, okay?"

"I'm not starting anything." I step out into the bathroom, and the plush white towel wrapped around my middle drops to the floor. Water drips from the tips of my hair to the ground, and I hug my arms around myself to fight off some of the cold.

"You're making a puddle." Jason points at the floor. "Make sure you wipe that up."

"Yes, Father."

He rolls his eyes. "Stop it. Did you take your meds?"

"My meds? That's what this comes back to? Am I unbalanced?"

"You're acting like it."

I drag my towel along the ground with my foot. "Better? Am I sane now?"

Jason sets his jaw and walks past me into the bedroom. No words, just angry actions. Just frustration with me. Again. Always with something I didn't do. Or at least I don't think I did.

All I wanted was one night of having him to myself, but he doesn't get it. He puts his social life first — the one he criticizes while simultaneously encouraging me to have. I don't understand.

Jason hates me. He must. Why would he do the things he does if he didn't?

My legs give out, and I sprawl on the hard, cold ground, naked, shivering, and miserable.

"What are you doing?"

"Nothing." I sniff and ball the towel under my head.

"Don't do this today, Elizabeth. Don't. I have to get to work. I can't stay home and babysit you." He's wound tightly, ready to pounce which means I need to stay out of his way.

"I'm fine. I have lunch with Alexis and Stacey today."

That elicits a smile from my husband. "Good. That's what I want to hear. That you're making an effort. Just no shopping today, okay? Last time you did some damage."

"With money you gave me."

"No, you begged for it." My husband frowns and turns his back. "Regardless, I want you to be happy and have friends, Elizabeth. Since Sarah died, you haven't put in much effort. Hell, you don't get out of your yoga clothes most days. What happened to my nicely dressed wife? The one I was always so proud of?"

I'm not going to remind him of our earlier conversation about Stacey and how fat I am. He clearly doesn't care enough to remember. Honestly, I don't know why I talk to him. Everything I say floats in one ear and out the other.

He adjusts his tie in the mirror. "I'm leaving. Stand up and let me kiss you."

Like a puppy, I do as I'm told. Three kisses to the forehead. Always three. One for each of the boys I've blessed him with. It's a sweet tradition, but today, the touch of his lips makes my skin crawl.

"Have a good day." Jason squeezes my hand.

"You too."

26

PAPER TRAIL

*L*et's get this out of the way.

A little birdie told me Elizabeth has committed social suicide.

Seems she had lunch with Alexis and Stacey. Can we all just say D-I-S-A-S-T-E-R? I mean, seriously, what did they expect when no one actually eats and instead has a liquid diet of rosé, white, and red? Nibbled edges of salad don't really hold up next to a glass or two or three of wine.

Apparently, Alexis complained the whole time about how not enough of the men are telling her she's hot. She blames turning forty and a small, barely noticeable line next to her right eye. It must be horrible having your entire self-worth tied up in how you look. I'd hate to live my life living in fear of growing old, having a hair in the wrong spot, or a line too close to the corner of my eye.

Her bitching was par for the course until she started in on random people. Namely, Meredith.

Stacey, obviously, agreed with everything Alexis said. Including how Meredith was a frigid bitch who thought she was too good for them.

This is where the wine comes in. They had to all be buzzed, not that that's an excuse, but they were. And Meredith is a good person. She may not run with the "right" crowd, but she's a decent woman, so I kinda get what happened next.

According to my source, Elizabeth stood up and told them to knock it off. That she wasn't going to sit there and let them disparage Meredith. Alexis called Meredith a boring cow, and Elizabeth lost her mind. She actually yelled in the middle of the restaurant that Alexis was self-centered, fake as shit, and a brat. Then she turned on Stacey and said the only reason she was even there was to validate Alexis's self-worth.

Haven't seen Elizabeth with them since.

Brisk spring air strikes my face when I step out onto the Club's veranda, and I snuggle deeper into my knit scarf. I've been here all day, hiding from my problems and eating my weight in chocolate pudding. This time of year, when the golf course is too wet for play, the Club is empty except for the wait staff. Although I normally come here to be around other people, today I appreciate that I'm unlikely to run into anyone I know.

I walk the length of the veranda until reaching the corner. From here, the Potomac River stretches before me and glistens in the low light of mid-afternoon. A few birds skitter through the newly budding trees, but mostly there's a hushed silence.

Like a spider that can't be shooed away, anxiety trills across my skin and spins a web in my mind.

I'm a desperate woman. Over the course of the past two days, I've put in several calls to Karen, one to Alexis to apologize, and groveled with Stacey at the grocery store. Jason's reaction when I told him about my faux pas was to stare blankly at me before saying, "Are you fucking serious? *What* is wrong with you?"

Basically, in his world, I've just destroyed our social life as opposed to having stood up for a friend.

What can I possibly do to make things right?

My bag vibrates, and I fish out my phone. It's Meredith of all people. Meredith who I've been avoiding. Even though she had no direct hand in my blow up, I haven't wanted to talk to her, but this is the third time she's called today. I don't want her to think I'm avoiding her. Which I am. But I don't want her to know.

Sigh.

I send it to voicemail, and a tiny bit of guilt nibbles at me. What am I doing? The one person, other than Sarah, who's been a true friend to me, is Meredith. Shutting her out now would guarantee the end of my Waterford social life.

Still, I can't do it. I can't call her back.

I pace along the veranda, letting my footsteps match my heartbeat. Back and forth. Back and forth. I wish I could do it over, only this time, when Alexis laid into Meredith, I'd sip my wine and listen without comment. Maybe I'd laugh a little, but that's it.

Jesus, what am I saying? Would I really betray someone who's been so good to me?

There's a line of damp, wooden rocking chairs just outside the entrance, and I wipe one off with my sleeve. In the summer, you can barely walk there are so many people, but today, there's not even a stray smoker.

My phone rings again, and with a ball of anxiety in my gut, I answer it.

"Hello?"

"Hey, Elizabeth! It's Meredith."

"Hi."

"I thought maybe you could come over today and have a mid-day drink before the kids get home? We could watch Housewives and catch-up. I haven't seen you in ages."

I stand up and work my way off the veranda and toward the Club's main door. The gray, near-empty parking lot greets me.

"Elizabeth?"

"Sorry. I'm here." A dreary heaviness drives my heart into my stomach. Right now, there's still a chance I may be forgiven, but if I go to Meredith's, and Karen or one of the others finds out, I've taken my stand and will have effectively kicked Jason and myself out of the inner group. Our social lives in Waterford will be over. Forget being a Periphery Girl, I'd be an Outer Circle of Hell Girl.

I like Meredith. She's plucky and funny and discrete. She's not into social climbing, unlike the rest of them. Now that Sarah is gone, Meredith's the person I trust and feel most comfortable around.

"I'm afraid I'm busy today."

"Oh."

A long, awkward pause follows. Finally, "I read the blog," Meredith says. "I know what you did, and I thank you for that."

"It was the right thing to do," I answer even though I'm doubting myself. Alexis and Stacey caught me in a weak moment, if I had been less emotional, I probably wouldn't have exploded. I'd still be in their good graces and not lapping around the edges waiting for forgiveness and an invitation back into the group.

"Well, I appreciate it. I know I can be tough, and that alienates some people, but thank you for having my back."

Storm clouds collide into one another, sending sparks of electricity through the air. "I have to go."

"Is everything okay, Elizabeth? You've not been yourself since Sarah died. You hardly come by any more, and I miss you."

A light rain falls, and the dampness seeps through my jacket. I better get back under the veranda before I'm soaked through. "I'm fine."

"You say you're fine. In fact, that's all I ever hear you say. It's like the Elizabeth I knew vanished when Sarah died."

"I'm busy. Between the boys and Jason and life, I don't have much time for anything else."

"I appreciate that, but you experienced a traumatic event. You can't possibly be fine. Hell, I only saw the aftermath, and I'm not fine."

No one, not even Jason, has asked me how I am. That's not true. Dr. Carter has, but her solution is to pop me up on more pills. Pills I hate.

Until now I've been expected to march on, to put my emotions aside and go on living.

"Have you talked to a psychiatrist?" Meredith asks. "It might be good for you. I can give you the name of my practice, if you want. They're fabulous."

My body tenses. "I...I already have a psychiatrist."

"Oh, you do? Well that's great! I won't pry, but I hope she helps you make sense of what happened."

I tilt my head back and stare at the still ceiling fans and sigh. "I'm not sure she's helping."

"What do you mean?"

What do I mean? That I doubt my doctor's professional opinion? That I think everything Jason and Dr. Carter believe is false? What exactly do I mean?

"It's just, I don't know." I pause. "Since Sarah died, nothing feels right. It's the lies and the cover up, you know? I'm just waiting for someone to call me out on that."

There's silence on the other end. The kind that tells me Meredith is thinking. Or doesn't want to say the wrong thing. Either way, there's silence.

"Meredith? Are you still there?"

"I am. I was just wondering..." More silence. "Since Sarah died, I keep asking myself why. She had everything. And it seems weird that she'd kill herself with no note. No anything that gives insight into the whys. No last word for her girls."

My brain latches on to her thoughts. She's right. Sarah had to have left a letter. Especially if she needed to tell me something. But neither of us found anything when we searched the house. Still, I wrack my mind. "If she left a note, where do you think she would have put it?"

Thoughts speed through my mind. If there is a note, a farewell even, I need to see it. I need it for closure.

"Maybe she mailed it to him. Or put it somewhere only Kyle would find it." Meredith says. She has no idea she's feeding my obsession. "Somewhere we didn't search."

"Like his underwear drawer?"

"Elizabeth, I have to say though, if Kyle isn't sharing it, it's probably for personal reasons. Maybe you shouldn't ask him about it. After all, sometimes it's best to let secrets die with the dead."

Secrets. We all have them. Some worse than others. Mine weigh on me, reminding me daily that I am inauthentic, a fraud.

"Meredith, I need to tell you something." My heart pounds, and my mouth grows dry. I shouldn't worry, Meredith is discreet. She won't judge. At least I hope she won't. "I have bipolar disorder. But that doesn't mean I'm crazy or anything," I add. "It's just that I need drugs to keep myself balanced."

Silence. And then a sigh. "Oh, Elizabeth. I wish you would have told me sooner, but I understand why you didn't. Are you okay? Has Sarah's death pushed you too much?"

I don't know what Meredith knows about bipolar disorder, but she seems to be more concerned about me than about what I may do. "I'm doing better, but it's been tough."

It feels so good to be honest. So good to let it out. One less secret to hide. One less person to pretend for.

But the problem is, I'm a mess, and now someone other than Jason knows it.

27

A SHEEP NEVER STRAYS TOO FAR

If we needed any more proof that Karen wields immense influence over the Bitch Brigade, let me show you exhibit one: Elizabeth Mavery has been forgiven. Sure, they made her squirm for a few days, but once she groveled enough, Karen let her back into the fold. And Elizabeth, like a good little lackey, ran right back to them.

My sources say that the Bitch Brigade is keeping her super close now. In fact, they're even attending yoga class with her on Tuesdays – which they never did before. I only know because I showed up for class, saw Karen's car with the "VA GIRL" license plate and bee lined out of there. No need to out myself.

The whole thing pisses me off, to be honest. I had slightly high hopes for Elizabeth after she stood up for Meredith, but seriously, I shouldn't have. Of course, she'd become one of them. I probably would too if given the chance.

And that's the irony, isn't? I still want to be one of them, even knowing what I know.

Pretty fucked up, no?

"Kyle came by while you were at yoga." Jason says this slowly, then pauses, watches me, and continues. "He said he had something for you."

Jason left work early to spend the day with me, but all we've done since I've come home is fill out the Social Services paperwork my caseworker left on her last home visit. Things that needed to be done to prove I am still capable of parenting my children and not a risk to them.

"Did he say what it was?" I don't bother to ask Jason why he was just now telling me, I'd probably get some lame answer like he forgot. Or that he told me, and I forgot — which is more likely.

Jason shakes his head. "No. He wouldn't leave it either. He said he wanted to give it directly to you. That's weird, right? That he'd have something for you?"

I placed the social services papers on the coffee table and wrap a throw blanket tightly around me. Jason insists on keeping the house at sixty-eight degrees, which I find freezing. "Maybe it's for trying to save Sarah. For helping out?"

"Yeah," he says, nodding his head. "That must be it. After all, you weren't super close or anything."

"We were friends. Good friends."

"How good?" Jason asks. "I know she called you after hurting herself, but how good of friends were you really? She seemed like a hanger-on, if you ask me. Always popping in unannounced and stuff."

I lift my eyebrows. "Well, she told me stuff about her marriage. Like how her marriage with Kyle was complicated, you know?"

Jason recoils. "How would I know? I barely ever spoke more than two words to the woman." He paces the length of the living room. "Life here isn't like it was in Portland. You know that. The men and women don't socialize together, and I don't like Kyle, so why, Elizabeth, why would she have ever confided anything like that to me?"

"What are you talking about?" His words make no sense. None at all. "It was a rhetorical question. Not something for you to get upset over."

Jason sits down. The vein in his neck bulges. "I'm not upset. I'm concerned. Kyle has something for you, and I want to know what he felt he couldn't leave with me. What's so important, Elizabeth?" He reaches out and touches my hand. "What would she have left you?"

"Nothing. She wouldn't have left me anything." I stroke his hand with my free one, trying to calm him but my insides are going crazy. It's the note. It has to be. "It's probably a thank you card or something."

"That he couldn't leave with me?"

My shoulders touch my ears. "I told you, I have no idea what it is."

Jason's breath whooshes out of him. "I'm sorry. I'm tired, Babe. These few weeks have been tough. Between you and the boys...well, it's been a lot."

He doesn't mention his fear that I may be inspired by Sarah, but it's in his words. In the way he holds his body. Out of all my attempts, the one right before Sarah's death had been the most serious. I'd never been hospitalized before. To Jason, it must look like I'm progressing, but really, he couldn't be more wrong. For the first time in ages, the desire to leave this world has lessened. Seeing Sarah's girls at her funeral put everything into perspective for me.

"Here," I say, turning him so his back is to me. "Let me rub your shoulders." I knead the spot between his shoulder blades. "God, you *are* tense." I dig down harder. "How does that feel? Is it too hard?"

"No. That's perfect."

I press around the edge of his left shoulder blade until I find a knot, and Jason grunts. "So knotty. We should get you a real massage. I can call the Club and see if they have anything for today."

Jason turns back towards me. "No, it's okay. I'll be fine." He strokes my cheek with his fingertips. "If you see Kyle, you'll tell me immediately, won't you?"

"Of course." I tilt my head. "Why does this have you so worried?"

"Oh, I don't know? Triggers? Flashbacks? Hospital stays? I don't want him giving you anything without me around. I'm worried it may set you off. And we can't have that. Not when Social Services is trying to decide if you are fit to parent."

Unfortunately, it's a valid concern. Seeing Kyle may trigger me. And if the boys are home...

"Can you call him and tell him I don't want to see him? That I'm not ready? Explain that when I can, I'll reach out to him. Make up something like you did with the seizures."

"Are you sure?"

I nod. "I think it's for the best. At least for now. Until we finish dealing with Social Services."

Jason stands. "Why don't you rest until the Henry gets home? I'll call Kyle, and you take a nap."

"That sounds nice." I close my eyes. "You always take such good care of me."

"Because I love you."

"I know."

28

NO GOING BACK

By now, you may be asking yourself, why do I care about the Bitch Brigade so much? Why blog about a bunch of women who can't partake in a family activity without 1. Drinking themselves into a stupor; and 2. Inviting all their friends along so they don't have to spend time with their family? The answer: I find them fascinating in a train wreck sense.

The only one who was somewhat palatable was Elizabeth Mavery. However, like I said before, something isn't right with her. I can't put my finger on it, but she and her husband seem too happy and her kids too perfect. Plus, she's suddenly everywhere — even after telling Alexis off. She's unexplainably at every party and girl's night. If you ask me, she's trying too hard. Or Karen and the Bitch Brigade are really afraid to let her out of their sight.

But I guess the thing that really nibbles at me is her seizure problem. That little issue has never been resolved. Why was no one given her room number? No one allowed to visit? And no one, according to my source, has a record of her actually being a patient.

She and her husband are covering something up, but what is it? He hasn't thrown her out, so my suspicion of it being Pete related isn't panning out, even though relations between Pete and Jason are still icy Siberian cold.

No, there's something major the Maverys are hiding. A dirty, little secret that's just between the two of them.

With a little help from my friends, I intend to find out exactly what it is.

Panera buzzes with people, but I feel invisible. Like Meredith and I are in a bubble that no one can see into. "Thanks for meeting me."

"Of course! I love grabbing coffee — or tea — with you." Meredith is her chipper self, and it relaxes me.

I swirl my green tea. It's supposedly great for losing weight, and I'm still struggling with my last five pounds - pounds I'm reminded of every time I look into the mirror. "I need you to promise you'll never tell anyone about my condition. I don't think many people will take it like you."

Meredith settles into the dark red bench. "I swear I won't tell anyone. It's no one's business but yours." She blows into her tea. She doesn't drink soda or coffee or alcohol; she doesn't gossip about people; and, she'll never wear yoga pants out of the house. Which makes her the antithesis of a perfect Waterford woman.

I'd been dreading this meet up, but I had nothing to worry about. Meredith will do what Meredith always does, hold moral superiority of those of us who like to gossip. Like Karen. Like me. "Thanks."

She nods. "I want you to know, I worry about you. Maybe you should rethink your relationships with Karen Newbold and her group."

"Why?" I'm genuinely curious. Does Meredith know something I don't?

"I did some reading to better understand bipolar disorder, and one of the things that stood out to me is that you should absolutely never drink alcohol. But every weekend, I know you're drinking with them. I've seen the pictures on Facebook, and there's always a half-empty wine glass in your hand."

"Drinking helps me relax."

Meredith furrows her brow. "That right there should tell you something. You shouldn't have to drink to be relaxed enough to hangout with friends."

She's right. I know she is, but hearing it laid out like this stings. "So, you're worried I have a drinking problem? Because Jason isn't, and he's my husband."

Meredith purses her lips. A heavy silence hangs between us. "I thought of that, and I wonder if Jason should be doing more to keep you from harming yourself. From what I've seen, he encourages your destructive behavior."

"That's overstepping, Meredith. Jason does the best he can while allowing me to be my own person."

"So, letting you get bombed while being hopped up on various medicines is a wise decision because he doesn't want to crush your individuality?" She dips her tea bag. "Makes complete sense to me."

"Don't do this." I can't handle a full Meredith press right now.

"Then when should we have this conversation? When you accidentally OD from mixing booze and pills? Or when you do it intentionally?"

Suddenly, that bubble I thought we were in bursts, and I'm keenly aware of every person in our vicinity. "Keep your voice down," I hiss. "I don't need all of Waterford knowing about me."

Meredith huffs. "Fair enough, but you have to admit that my concern is valid."

"I do." No one, not even Jason, has had a frank conversation with me about my drinking. Dr. Carter kind of does, but not like this. Not with the urgency and disappointment Meredith exhibits. "Can we talk about something else? Like Karen Newbold? I heard she traded in her Range Rover for Jeep. That's weird, right?"

"I'm not going to sit here and gossip with you. If that's what you want to do, call Alexis or Stacey or Veronica, but I'm not your girl."

I know this. Meredith is the morality police, but she isn't a gossip. "Facts are hardly gossip."

Meredith smiles tightly. "Nice try, but no. I'm not going there." She taps her finger on the table. "Besides, we're here to discuss you. What can I do to help you?"

My lip quivers. "I need a reference for my social worker to prove I'm capable of parenting the boys."

"Do you feel you are? Even with all the drinking?" Her gaze pierces me like she's searching inside my brain.

"Yes."

She adds a little cream to her tea. "Then I'll do it."

Meredith has done so much already between helping with the Sarah stuff to helping hide my illness, but I need to ask her one more favor. "Please don't mention this to anyone. I know you haven't, but I need to be sure you won't."

"Elizabeth, don't you know me? Hell, I won't gossip about Karen Newbold – a woman I find questionable — why would I share your secret with Waterford?"

She's so unlike the others. With them, I'm always on high-alert. If I make one misstep, I'm cast out of the group. And if they ever find out I have bipolar disorder or overdosed, I can forget about my social life.

"You know, your worry over those women says more about your place in the hierarchy than it does about them."

I shove my half-eaten chocolate chip muffin aside. "What do you mean?"

"They don't need you, even though you're still shiny and interesting. You, however, seem to think you need them. It's an imbalance of power. Once you realize that there's a whole world outside of the Club, Waterford won't seem as constraining."

I consider her words. "I'm not sure I understand."

"Karen and all aren't the only people in Waterford. You can have non-Club friends. Like me. I don't understand why you spend so much time trying to be what they want you to be when it's clearly making you miserable."

My breath deepens. "This has nothing to do with my condition."

She shakes her head. "I spoke with Jason. He explained to me what happened. How you were diagnosed."

"He what?" My heart launches into a frantic tap dance. Why would he do that?

"Jason told me about his affair." She lowers her voice and leans forward. "He told me how it sent you into a deep depression that you've been trying to claw out of for the past two years."

He told her, and he didn't share that with me. How could he do that?

I push away from the table and nearly topple my chair over. "I have to go." I shove my arms into my jacket. "I need to talk to Jason."

"Elizabeth, don't go. I swear I'll never tell anyone, but it does help me understand you better."

If Jason did tell her, and I believe he did, he must have a good reason. I just can't see what that would be. We agreed to keep it between us, and him telling Meredith – my friend – without my knowledge, feels like another betrayal.

"How does it help you understand me?"

"There's a sense of sadness around you. It's not as bad as when you first moved here, but it's there. And you're trying so hard to make your life seem perfect. I understand the overcompensating now and why you never have friends from Portland visit. Everything makes sense. You're embarrassed and depressed."

"What if I don't want to make sense?" This analyzing of me pisses me off. I am who I am because of Jason. Shouldn't we be critiquing him? "You're probably going to say I'm stupid for staying with Jason. I saw what you did to that Bentley guy at your party. You humiliated him and his wife."

"That was different. Everyone knew he cheated — or tried to cheat. It wasn't a secret, and they were pretending that it didn't happen." She stands and faces me. "You and Jason are fighting so many battles, but I don't doubt for a moment that you love each other."

Love. Just the thought of loving Jason makes my eyes sting. "You don't understand anything. I'll never love him again. He ruined that."

Meredith grabs my arm. "Come on. Let's get out of here and go to my house. We can discuss things more privately there."

I'm stuck because Meredith picked me up. "Why don't we go to my place since you drove? That way you don't need to drive me home again."

"Whatever you want. I just think it's best if we have this conversation privately so that you don't have to worry about someone over-hearing."

"Okay." She's trying to be a friend which is more than anyone, other than Sarah, in Waterford has done. Besides, I need a ride home.

The drive to my house is a short five minutes, but it feels like an eternity. Neither Meredith nor I speak, and she keeps changing the radio station. I don't know why she can't listen to the commercials, but her constant channel hopping is making me a little crazy.

When we pull into my driveway, I jump out of the car before Meredith kills the engine. Part of me wants to run into my house, lock the door, and not let her in. But I know I can't. At some point, every-thing was going to come out and who better to test my story on than Meredith?

I shouldn't be nervous because Jason has already told her, but I am. Maybe because I have no idea what his story was. Did he tell her the truth or just the highlights? What am I supposed to say? It really isn't any of Meredith's business, but the idea of unloading on her — someone who already knows – feels good. Like I wouldn't be hiding a piece of myself any longer.

And maybe, just maybe, she'll still like me despite the affair and my bipolar diagnosis.

"Come on in," I say stepping aside so Meredith can enter my house. It feels empty and cold in here, and piles of dishes sit on the counter. "I'm sorry it's such a disaster," I say, ushering her past the mess. "The boys don't do their chores until after school. But at least the family room is livable."

Meredith snorts. "My house is a wreck. No one does anything until the night before the cleaners come. Then it's a mad dash to straighten up."

"Yeah. That's how we roll over here, too."

I don't offer tea or anything to snack on, that way, if things get too rough, Meredith can leave without feeling like she needs to finish her drink. We both sink into the club chairs facing each other.

"So," I say. "What exactly did Jason tell you?"

Meredith folds her hands. "That he had an affair for nine months with a co-worker, and when you found out you broke."

I nod. "That's right. I was fine until he did that. I was Superwoman and had never experienced any sort of depression."

"Jason said the doctors think you were high-functioning and lean toward hypomanic episodes."

"Yes," I say. "Do you want to hear about it?"

"I do." Her gaze locks on mine. "And Elizabeth, no matter what, I am your friend. I'm here to support you, not tear you down."

"Okay," I say. "But it's a brutal story."

"I'm all ears."

29

SLAMMING DOORS SHUT

Scandal and gossip never die in Waterford, so let's get to it, shall we?

Alexis's husband has filed for divorce. The reason? He fell in love with the pro-shop girl from the golf course. I kid you not. The girl, Kelly, is about twenty-two and knows how to play the pretty girl act that Alexis once had the market on. All tits and ass, long ash blond hair, and pouty lips. Must suck to be upped at your own game.

And there I go being catty again. I really shouldn't make fun of Alexis. I shouldn't take glee in her divorce, and the truth is, part of me does feel bad for her. But there's something about a smug, stuck-up woman getting knocked down a notch that does it for me.

Word on the street is that Alexis has thrown all of her husband's shit out on the front lawn and moving trucks are being loaded up. I've heard Karen has yet to stop by because...well, what is she supposed to say? Sorry your husband left you for a younger version of yourself?

Ah, no. Not even I would say that.

Karen has, however, publicly stated that she's worried Alexis won't be able to find another man since she's forty and has kids. Personally, I'd be more worried about her drinking habit. It's sure to skyrocket now that she's going through this. Really, if Karen were her friend, she'd be making sure Alexis stayed sober, or at least nudge her in that direction.

THE SECRETS WE KEEP

But no, we're supposed to worry about Alexis finding another man to support her lavish lifestyle of Tory Burch, Louis Vuitton, and Jimmy Choo. We're supposed to ignore that she's over forty, with two kids, and her husband's run off with the pro-shop girl. None of those things are important, just whether or not she can maintain her lifestyle.

I'm sure Karen and Veronica (who returned from her "emergency trip" a week after she left) have already drawn up a list of suitable guys and are just waiting to give it to Alexis.

But then again, they may want to steer clear. After all, in Waterford, if you can't keep your own husband, you may go after someone else's

---

Since my conversation with Meredith, I've been more confused than ever. When I confronted Jason over his telling Meredith about our secrets, he said that she already knew and approached him with the gossip she'd heard. Which makes no sense. Why would Meredith, who never gossips, not just come directly to me? Why seek Jason out? And if she didn't hear it from Jason, who told her, and why would she lie?

Still, despite all that, a sense of peace has permeated my life. I'm not sure if it's not having to pretend around Meredith anymore, or the fact that I finally said some things out loud that I've even kept from Dr. Carter. Either way, a glimmer of my former self is emerging.

Too bad it's only taken two years.

Two long years where I jumped at my shadow, doubted my husband's love, and hated myself for every little thing.

But those days are past now, and I'm excitedly moving forward. No more hospital visits; no more going off my meds without Dr. Carter knowing; no more living in the shadows waiting for life to happen. I'm in control, and if feels good. Plus, Karen has forgiven my faux pas which means Jason has, too. We're back to being part of Waterford's elite crowd.

"Elizabeth," Karen says in a hushed voice. When I don't turn toward her, she calls my name again. Seriously, since she, Veronica, and Stacey started coming to my class on the regular, it's been anything but peaceful.

"What?" I stare at her under my left armpit. I'm hanging out in Downward Facing Dog. My breath is even, and a calmness fills my heart. Music pumps around me as I wait for the next cue from the teacher.

"We need to do something about Alexis," Karen whispers.

I shake my head and try to find my zen again. I hate when Karen is here. She's always distracting me, and when Melissa Foster comes too, Karen makes a point to ignore her.

Not awkward at all.

Anyway, Karen has a point. Alexis hasn't been anywhere for the past few days — not since word got out that Dave was leaving her for a younger woman. My heart should go out to her as a woman *and* as someone who's experienced infidelity, but I just can't find it within me. Besides, I don't want her to know about Jason's cheating. Meredith knowing is enough for me. And honestly, Alexis is most likely mortified right now. And hurt. And in shock. She doesn't need me around offering platitudes and sympathy.

Something like this was bound to happen. The neighborhood is a tinderbox of bad behavior just waiting to explode, and it was just a matter of who and when. Unfortunately for Alexis, it was her.

I release into child's pose and snuggle my chest to the floor, stretching my entire back. Sweat slides down my forehead and onto the tip of my nose so I rub my face on my mat towel.

"When you are ready, make your way into Savasana," the teacher instructs.

I sit up and roll onto my back. My limbs lay heavily on the floor, and I keep my eyes closed, but as hard as I try, I can't slow my brain and let myself relax because I know as soon as class is over, Karen, Veronica, and Stacey are going to be all over me, and I so don't want to deal with them. I'm not in the mood for a full-on assault.

For a good five minutes my brain flashes with different scenarios and conversations we may have, and all of them end with me agreeing to whatever it is Karen wants.

I press my eyes tightly together to force out the never-ending thoughts, but it does no good. I'm in obsessive mode with the same thoughts on repeat. The only thing to break the cycle is to have a real conversation with Karen instead of imagining things.

The teacher rings the finger gongs, and my eyes flutter open as I move into a seated position. After our final Om, we bow and exchange namaste. I turn toward Karen and dip my head, but she's already standing and moving toward me. Veronica and Stacey aren't far behind.

"Are you even worried about Alexis, Elizabeth? Because you're not acting like it." Karen holds her folded mat under her arm. Sweat clings her Lululemon shirt, and a towel is slung over her shoulder. "You should go talk to her."

"Maybe you should?" I say.

Karen narrows her eyes. "Do you think I haven't tried? She isn't listening to any of us."

"And she'll listen to me because..."

"Because you're," Karen pauses. "Well, you're you."

I have no idea what that means.

I squat on the ground and slowly roll up my mat. "I feel terrible for her, but I don't know her like you do. Plus, we had that fight, so I'm not sure me showing up at her house is a good idea. I don't want her to feel like I'm trying to pry into a private situation."

Veronica laughs. "It's hardly private. Dave is running all over the place with the little whore."

"We need to stick up for Alexis," Stacey says. Not that this is a private class, but who said she could join us? When did she breach the inner circle? When did I?

"So, what are you going to do, Elizabeth?" Karen asks. "She likes you. You need to do something."

My mat slips from my hands and unrolls slightly. "She likes me? She barely talks to me, and I humiliated her at the restaurant."

"Of course, she likes you! We all like you." Karen's voice raises a little. "In fact, she's wondered why you don't call her more."

I try remembering the last time she's called me instead of sending a text. I can't because it's never happened.

The three women form a tight semi-circle in front of me and sway in unison. We're all covered in sweat and look like hot messes that need showers desperately, but somehow this is the best time to discuss my non-friendship friendship with Alexis. I'm beyond confused.

"I'll call her, and see if she wants to meet at Starbucks." I don't offer Panera because I know just the thought of gluten will send Alexis shrieking.

Karen pats my arm. "Good girl. I knew we could depend on you."

They just punted the responsibility of soothing Alexis to me, and I agreed to it.

Awesome.

There's no connection between Alexis and me.

Even before that disastrous lunch, we didn't really gel. And now? Well, I can't tell you three non-physical things about her, and yet out of some strange sense of duty, I persist with the painful conversation. We've exhausted the weather as a topic, and now stare at each other.

"How's your skinny latte?" Not that I really care. I hate coffee, and I hate this coffee date more.

Alexis blows into her cup. "It tastes like it always does."

"Oh, right."

She sips loudly. "I'm guessing that's not what you really wanted to ask, is it?"

My jaw clenches despite my forced smile. "You know, Alexis, I'm always here to listen if you want to talk."

"That's nice of you." Her head bobbles a little. Side-to-side, up-and-down. Like it's too big for her ultra-thin body. "Thanks for calling me. No one else has."

The sadness in her voice breaks my heart. How could they not call her? Aren't they her friends? Her best friends? Jesus. That's why I'm here, isn't it? To report back to Karen and Veronica.

Of course, it is. How could I be so stupid? Alexis doesn't like me, it's that they're too afraid to catch whatever affair disease Alexis may have.

Wonderful.

Alexis leans forward, and her low-cut top shows off her perky, fake boobs. Her face relaxes. "It's been going on for ages, only I was too stupid to realize it."

"You're not stupid. Trusting, but not stupid."

She glances down at the table. "They met last summer, and he took her to our beach house. The one I begged him to buy, and he only did after he met her."

I fight back images of Jason and his mistress as my jaw goes slack. Now is not the time to have flashbacks. I've got to hold myself together. "You're kidding, right?"

"No. He pranced her around and even got her an apartment of her own in the Town Center for convenience. I should have suspected something when he started volunteering to do two-hour long grocery store runs."

This is bad. Worse than I expected, but I keep my supportive-friend look plastered to my face. Jason at least kept his whore out of town where I would never run into her, and no one would catch them together.

Alexis looks up at me with tears in her eye. "How did I not know?"

Because sometimes we don't. Because sometimes, we just don't want to see it.

"Sounds like he was good at hiding it."

The tears break free and roll down her cheeks leaving a mascara trail behind. "No, all the guys at the Club knew. Some of the wives had to of known too." She buries her face in her hands. "I'm a laughing stock. A total idiot and laughing stock."

"No," I say as I pull a pack of tissues from my bag. "You're a woman with a trusting heart who was taken advantage of. You did nothing wrong."

"I'm positive Veronica knew."

I slide the tissues across the table to her. "What makes you think that?"

"Because Pete and Dave play golf every Tuesday, and Pete's been down to the Beach House a few times with Dave for a 'guys weekend.' That's when the whore was there from what I can gather."

I suck on the inside of my cheek so I don't say anything that can be used against me later. If Veronica hears that I bad mouthed Pete, she'll come after me. "That doesn't mean he told her. Maybe he's more discreet than you're giving him credit for."

"He knew, I'm positive."

"Veronica acted surprised when she spoke with me."

Alexis wipes her tears before blowing into her latte. "That's because Pete was probably there cheating on her with some bimbo off Ashley Madison. All these guys, all of them, are bad influences on each other. Do yourself a favor and don't let Jason socialize. You'll be happier for it." She smirks. "Or are you convinced he's above it all?"

She's strikes a paralyzing blow and doesn't even realize it. Once, I believed Jason would never do such a thing. Now, I know he's perfectly capable. "I'm not delusional."

"Good for you. I'm happy you have such a wonderful, perfect marriage."

Now would be the time to tell her the truth, to offer her some comfort, but my lips become barricades

Alexis tosses the tissue packet back to me. "You can tell those bitches thanks for sending in the b-team. No offense or anything."

This time, I stare with my mouth agape. "Really? This is what I get for trying to have compassion for you?"

Alexis throws her head back and laughs. "How about this: tell Karen she can go screw and tell Veronica that when she figures out who Pete is fucking, I'll be the first in line to bring up what a shitty wife she is. Okay? You got that? Or should I repeat it since you're the JV team and all."

How dare she? "I'll tell them." I grab my bag and stand. "Nice talking to you."

"Whatever."

3 0

PHOTOGRAPHIC EVIDENCE

The other day, I had too much time on my hands, so you know what that means, don't you?

It's time to scroll through the Bitch Brigade's social media accounts.

First up: Karen Newbold. Her latest picture is of her laughing with a bunch of her groupies around a fire pit. Yup, they're all there – Alexis, Veronica, Stacey, and Elizabeth, and of course, the Periphery Girls. Lots of hearts and 'I love these girls' flying around. She looks like she doesn't have a care in the world even though I've heard rumblings that all is not well in her financial life.

Next up: Alexis Frond. She's more subdue in her latest Facebook profile picture. In it, she's wearing a hat and staring off into the distance. It's a black and white, which gives it a slight emo-effect, but we'll let her off because, you know, she's going through a nasty divorce. She's made all her other accounts private. I'm guessing it's so that her husband's girlfriend can't stalk her, which is a totally valid reason.

And then there's Veronica White. Oh, Veronica. Someone's trying too hard. On Facebook, she has the ubiquitous photo of her and Pete wearing their finest and smiling broadly, but on her Instagram account, the only picture she's posted in two weeks is a bathroom mirror shot where her hair looks fabulous, but her expression is one of devastation. Not the picture I *would post if I were trying to convince the world that all is right in my marriage.*

Finally, we have Elizabeth Mavery. I know, she's not truly part of the Bitch Brigade, but she's like their official mascot or something. Her accounts are scrubbed — or at least they seem to be. There's nothing posted before she moved to Waterford except for a few pictures of her boys on vacation. I went through her Instagram, Facebook, Twitter, and Pinterest accounts, and nothing. Just a random post here and there about her kids.

Out of the four, my wager is on Elizabeth having the biggest secret because everyone in Waterford knows, if it's not documented on Facebook, it never happened.

And I'm positive there's something Elizabeth is trying to forget.

"How have you really been doing?" Dr. Carter sits in the office chair across from the plush one I'm situated in. We've danced around a plethora of topics like how Jason and I are doing, but I've kept everything very surface level. I don't feel like getting into specifics today.

"I'm good."

Dr. Carter stares over the top of her glasses at me. Her salt-and-pepper hair is in a sleek bob and she wears a long, flowy skirt. She reminds me a little of a hippy. "Did you finish the Social Services paperwork?"

Argh. That stupid paperwork. Jason and I have been scrambling to show that I'm fit to mother my boys. The process involves lots of paperwork, home visits, and Jason using up vacation time to "supervise" my interactions with the boys.

Basically, it's a clusterfuck, but a suicide attempt triggers the system, and now we have to deal with it.

"We finished."

"Is this all I'm going to get from you today? Simple answers?" Dr. Carter balances her notepad on her knee and folds her hands.

I shrug. "Not much has changed from the other day."

"When you were here last, you mentioned you were having obsessive thoughts. Are you still struggling?" Dr. Carter has a soft but firm voice that reminds me vaguely of my father. I never wanted to disappoint him just like I don't want to disappoint Dr. Carter. I have to show her I'm making progress.

"Not so much."

"But a little?"

I hang my head and cast my eyes up. "I don't know. Sometimes, I get stuck on an idea, but if I sleep, it passes."

"Can you give me an example?"

I study my wedding band and engagement ring. They hold so little value for me now. In fact, I wouldn't wear the tainted metal at all if Jason didn't insist. "Sarah."

Dr. Carter nods. "She's still on your mind. Are you having flashbacks?"

"It's not that," I say. "I'm...I'm stuck on what she said to me. What she had to tell me. And her husband has something for me, but I'm afraid of finding out what it is."

"Elizabeth, I have to tell you, I agree with Jason. I think, for the time being, avoiding Kyle is best for you. In fact, I told Jason as much when he called the other day. We need to do everything we can to prevent you being triggered."

I recoil. "Jason called you?"

"Did he not tell you?" Dr. Carter studies me. "He was very concerned, and said you were acting erratically and refusing to take your medicine again. It's why I'm hesitant to sign off on your Social Services papers."

"No." I furrow my brow. "That didn't happen. I've been good lately — both with my mood and my meds. You must have misunderstood him."

"I'm sure I didn't."

My breath catches. "So, you're not going to sign my papers?" Tears sting my eyes. "I've done everything right. I've been so good. And I take my medicine religiously."

Dr. Carter clasps her hands. "Jason is concerned. He wants what's best for you." She scribble, scribble, scribbles on the yellow legal pad again. "How's your memory?"

"It's fine." I bite the inside of my cheek. "You know, Jason told my friend Meredith about the affair and what happened to me after. But he claims she approached him about it."

Dr. Carter waits as if wanting me to say more. "Do you not remember telling Meredith about your condition?"

"I do."

"Is it possible you mentioned the affair, too?"

I close my eyes and subtly shake my head. "No...I don't believe I did, but I don't know who I believe – Jason or Meredith."

"Why would Jason lie when he's trying to get you healthy?" Dr. Carter asks. "He has no reason to out himself. And if Meredith is a moral as you claim, would it be out of character for her to confront him?"

She has a point. Meredith would confront him.

"You're confused, aren't you? Jason said as much when he and I spoke."

"No," I say. "That's why I don't understand where this is coming from. I've done nothing concerning lately. I know I haven't. It's just this one little thing about Meredith and Jason."

Dr. Carter gives me her patient smile. The one that tells me she's going to speak to me gently. I brace myself against the angry words percolating inside me. "Sometimes, what we present externally is different than how we feel internally. Jason witnessed something that gave him pause, and he called me. You can appreciate that, can't you?"

"I don't..."

"Yes."

I close my eyes and exhale. Is she right? Did I do something to worry Jason? Something he couldn't tell me about?

"You know, Elizabeth, your file is open to Jason because of the waiver you signed. You can revoke it at any time."

I shake my head. "No, it's fine. I just don't know why he didn't say anything to me."

"That's for the two of you to discuss." Dr. Carter has a way of walking away from disagreements between Jason and me. Probably because she's not a marriage therapist or something.

"Now, tell me, do you think Sarah mentioned you in her suicide letter?"

I shrug. "I don't know."

"What do you think?"

That's such a loaded question. "I think, despite what you and Jason believe, I need to talk to Kyle. There is a letter. Maybe she hid it somewhere where only Kyle would find it — like his underwear drawer. Or maybe she mailed it to him. But I know she wrote one. And I know she needed to tell me something."

"I see."

Dr. Carter never tells me what to do. Instead, she guides me toward a conclusion.

"And if I don't talk to Kyle, I'll keep envisioning a hundred different scenarios and drive myself crazy."

"Then you know what you need to do." Dr. Carter writes some more before discretely checking the clock. "How are things with your friends?"

She means Karen and all. "They're not really my friends. Not like Sarah was," I say. "But I did try to talk to Alexis this week over coffee. Her husband left her for the pro-shop girl, and I thought maybe I could do some good."

"Your idea or someone else's?"

I hate the way she can see through me. "Karen, Veronica, and Stacey's. They backed me into it."

Dr. Carter stares at me, and I swear she can see straight into my brain. "Or you set yourself up."

"Ummm, probably that." The hands of the clock tick away slowly, and it's as if time moves at half-speed when I'm here.

"What are you doing for self-care? We've discussed several times that the environment you live in is toxic."

"I know, but Jason loves Waterford's social life, and the boys are so happy. Asking them to give up their happiness for mine seems unfair." The clock hits ten forty-five. Time to wrap up. "I see we're done. Are you going to okay my paperwork?"

Dr. Carter's eyes flick over to the clock. She sets her notepad on the desk. "I want to see you next Friday. I feel that you still need intensive counseling." She spins the chair around and types on the keyboard. "Same time on the ninth?"

I scroll through my phone. "Yes, that works."

"Ten A.M.?"

"Yes."

"Good. We'll discuss the Social Services paperwork then." Dr. Carter stands and opens the door for me.

My heart drops. Another week of uncertainty. Another week where Jason needs to come home early to watch me with the boys — only he doesn't. He still rolls in after eight and goes out for drinks with the guys most nights after I'm in bed.

If Social Services found out, what would they do? I hurry outside to my car. I don't really want to know the answer to that question.

Before I pull out of the parking lot, I check my phone. There are three texts from Karen that I scan, but don't respond to; a few Facebook posts from Karen that I've been tagged in; and an Instagram photo of Karen showing off her new hair color which looks exactly like her normal color.

Basically, it's Karen showing the world how much validation she needs.

Right now, the last thing I need is a reminder of how fake my life is, and being around Karen - in virtual or real life - always drives that point home. So much so that sometimes I forget what's reality and what's a carefully crafted mirage. Like this confusion over Meredith and Jason. Maybe Dr. Carter and my husband are right. Maybe my outsides aren't matching my insides. Maybe I did tell Meredith, and she confronted Jason.

Does it matter? In the end, the result is the same: Meredith knows.

I stuff my phone into the cup holder and guide my car out of the parking lot, but I don't turn towards home. Instead, I get on the Greenway and head toward DC. Waterford is a toxic environment, and I need out. Life is keeping me down, and being around woman like Karen and the Bitch Brigade depresses me. I need a change of scenery and a day away from the stifling suburbs.

A Taylor Swift song comes on the radio, and I crank up the volume. As the music surrounds me, I belt out the lyrics. Some of the tension I'd been holding in dissipates. I slow down long enough to pass through the toll gate before gunning the engine and flying toward the District.

"Call Jason," I say to my Bluetooth. The music dies down and is replaced with a ringtone.

He picks up on the third ring. "Hey."

"Hey, back at you." I decide to hold off on confronting him about what Dr. Carter said until I can talk to him face-to-face. "I'm coming into the District today and thought we could grab lunch."

Jason clacks away on his keyboard. "Why?"

"Ummm...I don't know." I lie. "Because I miss you. You've been working like crazy to make up for your days off."

"Days I missed because of you."

Ouch.

"Jason, c'mon. Just meet me for lunch."

The click-clacking stops. "Seriously, Elizabeth. I can't just take time off whenever I want. I have an actual job. One that requires me to be in an office. Don't you have a friend you can go to lunch with?"

A fireball lodges itself in my heart. I'm about ready to snap, but I have to show Jason I'm pulled together. If I don't, he may believe I'm not safe to be around the kids. And then what? We haven't discussed it because we're both pretending this isn't our life.

"Okay. I'll call Karen or Meredith. I'm sure one of them will be around."

"That's my girl. They'll be better company than me."

What I don't say is that I want to question what he told Dr. Carter, and why he hid it from me. Maybe it's for the best, though. Especially after our disagreement over Meredith the other night. "Well, have a good rest of your day."

"I'll try. I have meetings back-to-back until 4:30." He pauses. "I'll see you when I get home. I may be a little late."

"So 7:30?" He used to get home at seven, but the time keeps getting pushed back later and later.

"More like eight-thirty."

So much for Social Services. I force myself to sound upbeat. "Okay, see you then."

I click off before I can say anything damaging. I don't want lunch with Meredith or Karen. I wanted to see my husband who's been MIA most nights for the past two weeks. Between coaching Ollie's basketball team and his late nights at work, I'm feeling a bit ignored. Not that I'm jealous of the time he spends with Ollie. No, never that. He needs to spend that time with our son to rebuild their relationship, and I understand. Still, I wish he'd carve out a little more time for me. Most nights, he gets home, says 'hi,' gives me my meds and goes out. And that's not even getting into all the time he spends golfing on the weekends. We never talk or catch-up unless it's about my mental health.

At the next off ramp, I exit and turn so that I'm headed in the opposite direction, back toward my home. Maybe I should take myself to the movies. I'm not sure what's playing, but it would be a nice distraction.

Or I could eat lunch by myself at the Club. They do have amazing, high-calorie crab mac-n-cheese after all. Like a Pavlov dog, my mouth waters at the thought of it, and my decision is made. I'll eat at the Club. I haven't been there in a while — not since before Sarah died – and maybe after lunch, I'll treat myself to a massage at the spa.

I push the speedometer up to eighty even though the limit is fifty-five.

For trying to get out of the Waterford bubble, I've decided to plant myself right back in it.

Will I ever escape?

3 1

I'M NOT YOU

W*ell, that didn't take long. I guess pretty, popular girls know things I don't.*

It's only been a month since Alexis was devastated by her soon-to-be ex-husband's affair, and she already has a new piece of Man Candy: Jack Perry, a self-made millionaire who owns a limo rental company. He dumped his slightly older wife last year, so ironically, Alexis is a newer, shinier model with longer legs and a flatter stomach.

Seriously, though. These people. You can't make this shit up. You can't.

Picture this: It's Thursday, which means all the guys are out playing golf while the women wait at the clubhouse and sip wine (or something stronger depending on how much they hate their husband). Alexis rolls in dripping, like literally dripping, in a new diamond necklace. Okay, maybe not literally dripping, but there was some serious bling that skimmed the top of her cleavage.

Oh! I didn't even mention the HUGE diamond studs in each of her earlobes. Someone must be pretty damn good in bed to be getting gifts like that after a few weeks of dating. Or someone else is having fun dressing up his latest conquest.

The confusion, then anger, then rage that crossed Karen's face was priceless. Alexis simply glided past and over to some Periphery Girls without even a hello. Completely froze Karen and Veronica out. They stood there, without their groupies, holding chilled chardonnay and trying to remain composed.

Stacey McLeod glanced at Karen then at Alexis and the Periphery Girls. She took two steps in Alexis's direction before Karen snagged her by the elbow and yanked her back. Stacey stood there, dazed and clearly confused.

I guess we all were.

But not anymore.

Ladies and Gentleman, things are changing, and Karen doesn't like it one bit.

"Something needs to be done. Alexis is making an ass of herself," Karen says while refilling our wine glasses with healthy pours of rosé. "The question is, what do we do?"

I hate these pow-wows. Ever since Alexis showed up at the Club with her diamonds and new boyfriend, all we've discussed is how to bring her back into the fold. It's been an especially tiring week for Karen who has lost her grip on the Periphery Girls. It's like once Alexis went rogue, they all did too. Except Stacey. She's still faithfully hanging on. Even if it's not by choice.

The whole thing kind of cracks me up.

With a flick of my wrist, I check my Fitbit. "I have to go. I promised Jason I'd make a lavish dinner tonight."

"Why?" Stacey says. "It's not like it's your anniversary or anything."

Because I need him to trust me. "Because sometimes I like to do nice things for him."

Veronica, Stacey, and Karen look at me as if I'd just announced I'm an alien out to infiltrate their group.

"Well, that's weird," Stacey says. "If it were me, we'd just go out to dinner. To a steak house or something."

Thankfully, I'm not her.

Karen waves me away with the back of her hand, dismissing me

THE SECRETS WE KEEP

as if I'm a bothersome child. "Go. We're probably just going to drink anyway, and you have barely touched the rosé. Don't you like it?"

"It's fine. I'm just not in a drinking mood, that's all." I'm never in a drinking mood anymore and normally can hide it in larger groups. It's harder when it's just four of us.

"That's something I'll never understand," Veronica says while laughing. "You'll have to pry my wine glass from my cold, dead hands."

Sad thing is, she really means it.

As I leave someone whispers my name, but I'm in too much of a hurry to go back. If they want to talk about me, they will, and besides, I have to get a hot dinner on the table at least once this week, or I'll be a total failure.

Success on the home front is important to me — especially since Jason seems to think I'm still falling apart. He needs to see I'm capable of running our home, and I owe it to him for taking care of everything while I work through my up-and-down emotions. Plus, I need him to tell Dr. Carter that I've got my shit together.

Jason's car isn't in the driveway when I arrive which is a good thing. I still have time to whip up something. What that something is, is a mystery to me at the moment. But it's the effort, right?

My keys clink against the crystal bowl on the side counter when I drop them in, and I toss my shoes into the newly purchased shoe basket and leave my bag on coat rack.

I pause beside the oven. The house is eerily silent.

Oh, God. What if Jason's already been home and has taken the boys out because, once again, I didn't make dinner? He'll hold that over me forever.

"Boys?"

Nothing.

The door to the basement is cracked open, and I yell down. "Boys, I'm home."

The sound of TV gunfire answers me. Jesus, they listen to that loudly. I'm too lazy to walk down the short flight of stairs, so I text Ollie.

. . .

Me: I'm home.
Ollie: I'm in my room.
Me: Who's in the basement?
Ollie: I don't know.
Me: You're supposed to be in charge
Ollie: sorry

I tap out a message to Will telling him to find Henry. Within seconds, the two boys thunder up the stairs.

"Hey, Mom!" Will pats my head. He's nearly ten inches taller than me now, which I still don't understand how that happened. I mean, I know kids grow and all, but he sprouted so quickly he has stretch marks across his back. Ollie and Henry, thankfully, are taking their time. They're still my little guys. Well, Henry is. Ollie and I see eye-to-eye these days. He'll be taller than me by the Fall.

"Can you two help with dinner? Henry, you wash the salad and do the spinner; Will, you chop up the onions in the food processor."

Will huffs. "What about Ollie? What's he doing?"

"Setting and clearing the table."

My oldest pulls an ugly face.

"Stop it," I say. "I'm making your favorite. Be grateful."

"Onion quiche?" Will's a vegetarian — the only one in the family which proves interesting and difficult at times, but after eleven years, I'm getting the hang of it. That or I've tired of making two meals every night and now cook primarily vegetarian. Either way, it's gotten easier.

"Quiche? Ugh." Ollie stands in the doorway. "Why do we always eat what Will wants?"

I close my eyes and shake my head. Just once, I'd like to have a meal where no one complains. "We had steaks last night. It's Will's turn tonight. If you don't like it, you can eat fish sticks."

"Can I have fish sticks, too?" Henry asks. "I like your cooking, but-"

"No, you don't. No one does apparently." I unroll the pre-made dough and drape it over the pie plate. "I have yet to make a meal that everyone agrees on this month."

Henry presents me with the dried lettuce. "Thank you," I say. "Can you make the dressing? Just red wine vinegar and olive oil."

He nods and gathers the ingredients. Say what you will about my boys, but at least they know their way around the kitchen.

"How's Bella?" I ask Will. Since the Spring Dance, they've been inseparable.

"Good."

"Which means?"

Will blushes. Like me, he's fair and turns red easily. A lock of floppy, dark blond hair covers his eye. "She's fine. We're chill."

And that's all I'm getting out of him, so I turn to Ollie.

"How's the game going?" Ollie is an avid gamer and constantly talks about online teams he's part of. I understand none of it, but he's passionate about it, so I try to engage.

"I made senior level, and once I turn sixteen, I can turn pro."

"You're eleven."

"I'm planning ahead."

I chuckle. "Okay. I like that you have a plan. Now set the table."

And so it goes.

"I had drinks with Karen and Veronica today." I wipe off my mascara and eye Jason in the mirror. We've barely talked since the weekend. In fact, we've barely seen each other. Something Jason probably prefers since he became defensive when I eventually confronted him about calling Dr. Carter. He claimed I'd been forgetful, but I pushed back. It ended with us on separate sides of the bed with our backs to one another.

Jason stands at the sink next to mine brushing his teeth. "Veronica, huh? I thought you two weren't talking."

"We only hang-out when Karen's around." I drop the dirty cotton pad into the garbage. "Today's topic was Alexis. Or, more specifically, how to get Alexis under control."

With my fingertips, I rub night cream onto my cheeks. Jason slides behind me and kisses the top of my head. "She has all the guys talking."

"Oh?" Maybe there is something to Karen and Veronica's concerns after all.

Jason strips off his shirt, exposing his broad chest. "Nothing major. Just that she's hot."

I purse my lips. I'm sure there's more to it than that, but I'm not going to press. What the guys say about the women of Waterford worries me sometimes. If Jason is to be believed, they're almost as gossipy as the women. Plus, they're a bunch of cheaters.

Jason smacks my butt.

"Ow!"

"See you in a minute." He laughs and walks out of the bathroom.

Jason has left my nightly pills on the counter. I pick them up one-by-one. They sit heavy in my hand, an unwelcome reminder of how messed up I am. Before I can back out of taking them, I unscrew the top of my water bottle and toss the pills into my mouth. Contrary to what Jason believes, I've been religious about taking my medicine.

Our bedroom is empty, but the light is on in Jason's closet. "Jason?"

He charges through the room and sprawls across our bed in black boxer briefs and nothing else. He's always been so comfortable in his skin. A naked person. That's what he is. A person who is completely okay walking around naked in front of others.

I am not a naked person.

"What are you staring at?" he asks. He knows exactly what I'm staring at. At forty, he's in the best shape of his life. He runs, lifts, and generally eats well. His body is his temple.

"You."

"And? Do you like what you see?" He's teasing me, but it feels like a test. Like if I don't say the words exactly right, he'll become upset.

I brush my hands down my thighs. "Jason, look at me. I'm in yoga pants and a tank top. You look like Adonis. I look like middle-age run amok."

My husband laughs and grabs for me, but I jump away. "I want to shower before bed."

"Why? You never shower at night."

"I just want to rinse off. Not wash my hair or anything." I smile and shake my head. "I really need to wash away the yuck factor I suffered through at Karen's."

"I know I sometimes push you toward her, but maybe it's time to ease up on your friendship with Karen? Look at Alexis. She dumped Karen and Veronica, and now she's Miss Popular."

"I don't want to be popular. I like having my tight group of friends and a lot of acquaintances."

My husband catches me this time and pulls me onto the bed. "That would be great if you had a tight group of friends. You don't. You have a bunch of random people who don't hang out together."

"I like it like that."

He nuzzles my wrist. "What's that smell?"

"What smell?"

"On you. You smell weird. Like a guy. Are you wearing cologne?" Jason pushes up onto his elbows and glares at me. "Are you?"

"No. I..." Damn him for not letting me shower first. "I did some shopping today and tested out colognes for you."

Jason's eyes narrow. "Let me guess, you didn't buy anything, did you? There's no proof of you testing cologne. No one was with you. No cologne. No receipt."

What he's implying makes me want to vomit. I pull away from him. "As a matter of fact, asshole, I was with Karen and there is a new bottle of cologne in my closet. But thanks for ruining it."

"Go get it."

This lack of trust, it has to end.

I'm not him. I'm not, and I've done nothing. Nothing.

3 2

KEEPING UP APPEARANCES

Here's a mind-bender for you: The Maverys invited the Newbolds to dinner and...the Newbolds declined. Told some BS story about needing down time because the kids had non-stop sports this weekend. Plus, they were looking forward to ordering in Chinese and watching a movie.

So not believable. Karen and her husband never do anything alone together. Never. In fact, after a glass or two of chardonnay, Karen's been known to bitch about how she has to have sex with her husband because she's out drinking. Seems the two of them only do the deed when she's plowed.

Lovely, right?

If I had to force myself to have sex with my husband, I'd leave him. I mean, what's the point? Oh, right. Money. The one language both sexes speak in Waterford. No one wants to divide up the mutual assets, so they stay together...and apparently cheat until one gets caught and they're more or less forced to separate.

I guess if everyone is on board, it's a fine arrangement. Unless you end up like Alexis and your husband simply replaces you. But if you're like Veronica, you stick your fingers in your ears and go on with life.

Enough of that, let's gossip, shall we? Karen doesn't have a nanny anymore. It seems she let Dora go because the kids "out grew' her. Appar-

ently, leaving your eleventh, eighth, and fifth graders alone after school while you shop is now perfectly acceptable.

She's also downgraded her white Range Rover for a smaller Highlander – which means her sixteen-year-old son now has a nicer car than her (the Suburban that was once Dora's). She says the Range Rover was no longer practical for her lifestyle, but if that's the case, wouldn't she get an Audi sedan or something similar?

Anyway, they denied the Maverys, dropped their nanny, and got rid of the expensive car. Maybe we should keep an eye on the Newbold situation.

I sense Pete before seeing him and turn my head a little to the right. We haven't talked, or really seen each other since Key West, and I have so many unanswered questions. Like was it just the alcohol talking that night on the beach? Is he interested in me? Why is he so insistent that I let Sarah's memory be tarnished? And more importantly, why is he allowing his to be?

Our eyes lock, and my heart goes into overdrive. "Hey, Elizabeth!"

There are three tables between us, and he could have easily waved, but he chose to shout and draw attention to me.

The passage of time hasn't done anything to erase the butterflies in my stomach which is a sign that I should stay far, far away from Pete. But after my fight with Jason last night, I'm itching to do something reckless. Something like flirt with Pete.

I flash him a pretty smile, and in a moment, he's around the other tables and standing across from me.

"What are you working on?" Pete points at my iPad.

"Nothing really. Just surfing Facebook and doing some reading."

"You looked concerned."

Why does he care? I wag my finger. "You're being nosey."

"That response makes me curious." His perfect smile lights up his face. Looks wise, he couldn't be more different than Jason. Fair where Jason is dark; smiling while Jason is more brooding.

"Okay, so I was reading that blog. The Surviving the Suburbs one."

Pete grins. "I thought you were above that."

I give a half-shrug as the waiter appears at my elbow with a salad chock full of strawberries, blueberries, and apples. Dressing on the side, of course.

"Rabbit food?" Pete says. "I thought you were a burger and beer girl."

"Is there something you want to discuss with me, Pete, or are you just here to harass me?" I want to talk about what happened between us in Key West, but I'm playing coy, and he knows it. We're both pretending that something else entirely is going on — like a conversation about salad.

"Where's Jason?" Pete's teal golf shirt brings out the blue in his eyes. He looks like he belongs on a sailboat in Martha's Vineyard, not stuck out here in mind-numbing suburbia. I once asked Veronica, before Jason warned me off of the Whites, how she tolerated being locked up in Waterford when she's lived in cities all over the world. Drinking, she said. Lots and lots of drinking. Looks like Pete subscribes to the same mindset.

"He's at work. Like most normal guys who don't live adjacent to a golf course." I point at him. "I see you're dressed for work."

"Fridays are work from home days, remember?"

I shake my head. "So, my taxes are paying for you to golf?"

"Something like that." Pete laughs, and the sound fills me with excitement. If Jason wants to believe I'm like all the other women in Waterford, eager to dismiss my husband and take up with someone else's, then maybe I should stop being so damn loyal. He doesn't deserve it.

"Wanna hit some balls with me? I find it's therapeutic."

I bristle. "Who said I need therapy?"

"Me. You look on edge."

"That's because I'm trying to eat, and you're bothering me." I let the playfulness of my mood flow through my words.

"You. Me. And a bucket of balls." He's grinning because he knows the game we're playing, and he's confident he's going to win.

"I don't know how to golf."

"You mean you've never golfed with Jason? Even Veronica's been out with me and that meant she had to wear ugly shoes." He laughs. "Her words, not mine."

"Jason's not exactly a patient teacher." That's an understatement. "My boys don't even play."

"You're kidding, right? He never taught them how to golf? That's a Waterford cardinal sin."

I shake my head. "They play tennis with me instead."

Pete rocks back on his heels. "Isn't your oldest a lacrosse ace or something."

"I don't know about being an ace, but he's pretty good. He made varsity as a freshman."

Pete places his hands on the table and leans forward. "C'mon. Hit some balls with me. It'll be fun."

"I'm eating."

Pete juts out his chin. "Then I'll wait. I have nothing else to do."

"That's what worries me."

He pulls out a club chair and sits down. "Are you happy, Elizabeth. I mean, are you truly, really happy?"

I guess it would be a strange thing to ask if we hadn't shared that time on the beach. If I admit that I'm confused about my relationship with Jason, does that mean I'm unhappy? Is that giving Pete an invitation to pursue me? "Are you?"

"I asked first."

I dig into my berry and chicken salad and shove a very unlady-like forkful into my mouth. A few guys near the bar glance over at us, and I vaguely recognize one of them as a guy Jason was hanging out with at the Member Party. When they catch me staring back, all three turn away. Awesome. I can only imagine what they're saying about Pete and me. And if it gets back to Jason that we were not only talking, but sitting together, he'll lose his mind.

What I need is a decoy subject. Something I can report back to

Jason. "Pete," I say. "What's going on with the Newbolds? Karen hasn't been herself lately."

Pete's eyebrows shoot up. "Gossiping, Elizabeth? That doesn't seem like you."

"I'm curious. I'd ask Veronica, but we're not exactly friends on that level."

"And we are?" His smile nearly swallows his face.

"Stop. You know what I mean." I push my salad away. There's no way I can eat when my heart is going this fast. "So, golf?"

"We'll have to get you clubs at the pro shop, but it shouldn't be a problem." He pushes away from the table. "Do you need to sign?"

"Yeah. Let me get the waiter." I walk up to the bar where the waiter is refilling beers for Jason's acquaintances.

"Hi, Mrs. Mavery. Do you need the check?" the bartender asks.

"I do. Thanks." I push closer to the bar and away from the men. Their gazes burn through me. Part of me wants to confront them, but the other part of me wants to run. I drum my fingers on the bar top.

"Here you go," the bartender says. "Have a nice day."

"Thanks." I write in the tip and sign. When I turn around, Pete's talking to the three men and has a plastic cup in his hand.

"Elizabeth, do you want one to go?" He lifts the drink in my direction.

"No, I gave up beer years ago."

"A wine then?"

"I'm just fine, thank you."

With a deep breath, I walk up to the group. One of the guys immediately shifts his gaze to the TV over the bar. The other two stare at me like I'm on display. I do a mental check of my clothes and hair. My tennis skirt isn't too short, and I'm sure my ponytail and make-up are okay.

I look, like I always do, like a perfectly acceptable woman. Not too edgy. Not too dowdy. Just somewhere in the middle.

"Do y'all know Elizabeth Mavery?" Pete asks. "She's an old college friend of mine."

A balding man sticks out his hand. "You're Jason's wife, right?"

"I am," I say as we shake hands. "I think we saw each other at the Members' Party."

He frowns. "Sorry. I had a lot to drink that night and don't really remember." Something about the way he avoids my eyes tells me he's lying. But why? Why would a stranger lie about remembering me?

"You ready, Elizabeth?" Pete asks as he sets his cup on the counter. His hand presses against the small of my back, and I make no effort to pull away.

"Yes."

I march out the door toward the pro shop. Those men give me an odd vibe. I mean, it's probably weird to see me with Pete, but can't a man and woman be friends?

"Hey, wait up." Pete takes long strides to catch up to me. "Is everything okay?"

"It's fine."

Pete grabs my hand and spins me around. The hallway is empty, but it's the only one leading from the pro shop to the bar. Someone could come along at any moment. "Pete, I don't--"

His warm, salty lips are on mine, and he presses me up against the wall. The smell of beer pricks at my nose. I should tell him to stop. That this isn't appropriate. That someone will see us. Oh, God, what if someone sees us?

I wedge my hands between us and push lightly on his chest. "Don't."

Pete steps back. "I'm sorry. I...I...Oh, God, Elizabeth. I'm sorry. It's the beer."

I nod my head. "It was bound to happen. This thing between us has been simmering for a while."

"Still, it was wrong of me. Flirting is one thing, acting on it is wrong."

This is where I should tell him to leave. That I'm a respectable, married woman. That I can't hurt Veronica the way I've been hurt by Jason.

This is absolute madness, but that kiss has left me completely ravenous. "Kiss me again."

"What?"

Before he can protest, I grab the back of his head and kiss Pete deeply. Our bodies press against one another, and I tingle from head-to-toe. There's nothing in the world but Pete, his lips, and his hands gently skimming along the waistband of my tennis skirt.

What the hell am I doing?

I break away and put distance between us. "There. Now it's out of our system. Let's go hit some balls."

Confusion fills Pete's eyes. "What are we doing?"

"We're two friends going to hit golf balls. That's it."

"Elizabeth, you can't pretend there isn't something between us." Pete runs his hand through his hair, messing it up in an adorable way.

I toss my head back and laugh. "One thing I'm very good at Pete, is pretending. And lying."

He watches me for a moment before shrugging. "If you say so."

"This," I say, motioning to the space between us. "Is done. No more."

"So, you're ready to hit balls?" he asks.

"I've never been more ready."

33

IMPOSTER SYNDROME

Elizabeth Mavery is one cool cat. Nothing seems to rattle her. Not the Bitch Brigade. Not her hot-cold husband. And certainly not other people's judgment — at least until now.

She's hiding secrets, things that could ruin her image and her position with Waterford's haughtiest bitches.

What are her secrets? Well, let's start with her unfaithful husband. He had an affair, and they had to move here because he lost his job over it. She'll tell you a completely different story about taking a chance and trying something new, but really, she's a humiliated wife batting clean-up.

Then there was that kiss with Pete White in the Club hallway. Did they really think their little tryst would go unnoticed? Did they not realize there are windows everywhere and spying on them wasn't too difficult?

However, the thing Elizabeth doesn't want anyone to know, more than her blooming relationship with Pete, is that her trip to the hospital for a seizure was actually a stay in the mental hospital. Elizabeth, it seems, is bipolar. A secret she doesn't want out.

But it's too late for that, isn't it Elizabeth? You've confided in one too many people.

"Are you serious, Elizabeth? Are you fucking serious?" Karen waves her phone in my face.

"What is it?" I can't read her phone when she's tossing it around like cocktail shaker. Veronica, Karen, and I stand outside Panera where I unexpectedly ran into them. I hadn't been prepared to see them, so I'm a little off kilter.

Veronica shoves her hands into her dress pockets. "You haven't heard? You and my husband are apparently having an affair."

I gape at her. "What?"

Karen taps her finger on her phone's screen and begins reading to me. Heat rushes over me, but I keep my face blank. "Guys, that didn't happen. You can ask Pete. We hit balls, that's all. No kissing, I swear."

I'm lying, lying, lying. I need to save my ass. I knew kissing Pete was a bad idea, but I did it. Jesus, if Jason hears, I'm dead. Why didn't I think before acting? I knew people would find out. I knew it, and I did it anyway.

What the hell is wrong with me?

I want to get caught. That's the only logical answer. I want Jason to hurt the way I've hurt, and I want him to know what it feels like to be tossed aside.

Just thinking that makes me feel woozy.

Jesus. I want to get caught. Not by Veronica, though. No. I don't want to hurt her.

Veronica glances away before staring back at me. Her steel blue eyes bore into me. "I almost believe you, but there are too many things that the blog has been right about." She takes her fists out of her pocket. There's a slight shrillness to her voice, like she's trying to keep it all together. "And what about the other stuff? Did Jason have an affair? Are you bipolar? Have you been lying all this time?"

"I *have* bipolar disorder," I correct. "And yes, Jason had an affair that forced us to move here."

Karen's mouth falls open, but Veronica purses her lips.

"Elizabeth? What?" Karen blinks rapidly. "You have what?"

"Bipolar disorder." Funny how Jason's affair doesn't even register.

"But you're so...normal. You don't seem crazy."

I laugh dryly. "I take a lot of drugs."

Karen nods her head. "Who knows about you? Who? Because she — and it's a she – knows too much about us. The question is, who is it, and why do they feel the need to bring us down?"

"I don't know," I answer. I scroll through the blog posts, and my heartbeat thunders in my ears. "I mean..." I shake my head. Meredith. Meredith would be the logical answer, but I can't do it. "I really don't know."

Karen tilts her head and studies me. "You don't know? Well, it's someone in your yoga class because they wrote a detailed account of your Stacey McLeod conversation — the one you told us about when she called you fat." Karen pauses dramatically. "And it is someone who was at Will's Spring Dance pre-party. And they were at the Member Party. So, who was there on those days with you?"

Oh, God. She's been thinking about this for a while. My mind scurries, trying to find the best answer. "I...I don't know. There were, like, twenty people at yoga. I wasn't really paying attention. And at the dance thing, I really didn't know anyone."

Karen crosses her arms. "Think, Elizabeth."

"Melisa Foster may have been at yoga," I sputter. "She's been coming lately."

"If Melissa were there, Elizabeth, she would have spoken to you. Plus, I didn't see her on the video of the party."

"She wasn't at the party," Veronica says.

My mind races. "But everyone's seen the video. And people were talking, so maybe she just pulled from that?"

Veronica presses her fingertips to her lips. "She was close to Sarah, wasn't she? Did Sarah know about your condition and Jason's affair?"

"Yes," I say. "But why would Sarah share that with her, and why would Melissa do this? What's the point?"

Karen huffs. "She wants to be us. She always has. And you were taking Sarah's attention away. It makes perfect sense." Karen reaches out and touches the back of my hand. "I've read through every one of those fucking posts, and we'll get to the bottom of this.

Someone is going to learn a lesson about messing with the 'Bitch Brigade.'"

Oh, Melissa. I'm sorry, but I really don't know what to do.

"Whatcha doing?" Jason stands at the end of the chaise lounge. His hand darts out, and he grabs my freezing toes. "You look worried."

I sigh loudly.

"What's wrong?"

Jason's going to hear about it soon. It's all over the Women of Waterford Facebook page, and I'm sure the husbands are going to get an earful over dinner tonight. Still, I don't want to tell him because I'm sure once he reads it, he's going to kill me. Despite what I said to Veronica and Karen, the stuff between Pete and me really did happen, and unlike the women, Jason will automatically assume it's true.

And part of me wants him to know that it's true.

Better to tell him now, then wait to get outed, right? At least I can control the issue this way.

"Okay, so you know about that blog, right? The Surviving the Suburbs one?"

"Yeah. What about it?" He side-eyes me. "Are you on it?"

I inhale. "Karen, Veronica, Alexis. Sarah, and sometimes Stacey McLeod. And me."

His face drains of color. "What did it say about you?"

I fold my hands. "Ummm...a bunch of stuff."

Fire flashes in Jason's eyes, and his body tenses. When he's like this, it's hard to predict what he'll do. "Like what? Don't play around. What did it say?"

If I tell him, he's going to lose it. But if I don't, he'll just google the site. Despite my need of self-preservation, I have to be honest. With a big breath, I let it all rush out of me. "It says that I have bipolar disorder, and that you cheated on me and lost your job because of it." I pause. "And that Pete and I may be having an affair."

Jason kicks the chaise. "Damn it, Elizabeth. Is it Meredith?

Because she's the only one who knows you have bipolar disorder." He doesn't touch the Pete stuff. Interesting.

"No. Meredith would never do such a thing. She's discreet and very loyal."

"Then who?"

"I told Sarah, remember?"

Disbelief rolls across Jason's face. "But she's dead. She can't possibly be writing a blog from the grave. So, who?"

"Veronica and Karen thinks it's Melissa Foster."

"So, no one knows shit except that you're crazy and having a fling with Pete, and I'm a cheating asshole. Awesome." He narrows his eyes. "This was supposed to be our do-over. Our fresh start, and you ran your mouth to someone who clearly told other people. Way to go."

I try to speak, but no words come out.

"And what's this shit about you and Pete? Why would they write that if it's not true?"

Breath returns to my body, and I pounce. "How about you try being a bit more supportive? You cheated on me. That has destroyed me, but that's same old, same old by Waterford standards. You're just like the rest of the cheating husbands. But me? I'm now the crazy one going after the gorgeous Veronica White's husband. I'm the one everybody is going to stare at and gossip about, not you. Do you think I want that?"

Jason sits on the edge of the chaise, his body turned half-toward me. "I'm sorry, Babe. I know that your privacy is a big deal to you." He runs his hand up my bare leg. "When we figure out who this is, we'll sue for damages, okay?"

"You...you can do that?"

"It depends, but possibly."

His words are supposed to calm me, but instead, they send me into panic mode. "I don't want to sue people. I want this to go away. I don't want anyone staring at me funny or whispering behind my back. Just make it go away."

"It'll blow over. The Women of Waterford have a two-day attention span."

He's right. I know he is, and yet I can't help the queasy feeling in my stomach.

"You look like you're going to puke," Jason says.

"I think I might." I tip over and rest my head on the arm of the chaise. "The whole thing is turning my stomach."

Jason rubs my back. "We need to figure out how to tell the boys about your condition. If they hear this from someone other than us, they may get confused or hurt."

Oh, God. I didn't even think of the boys. My body trembles. No doubt Karen and Veronica and every other woman in Waterford is pouring over the blog right now. I'm either going to be a hussy or a crazy lady. Or better yet, the uncontrollable crazy woman who tries to steal husbands.

Awesome.

"Elizabeth, we have to tell the kids."

I nod slowly. "Okay. Tomorrow. You'll come home early, and we'll tell them over dinner."

"Are you sure?"

"They need to hear it from us. I just hope they're not mad we hid it from them."

Jason creeps up the chaise until he's sitting next to me. "Don't worry what other people say. You're going to find out who your real friends are, and the rest of them can go screw." He rests his head on my shoulder, and my fingers drift to his hair. "How sure are you that this is about Waterford?"

"Very. Whoever writes the blog, uses our real names and actually mentions Waterford."

"And no one knows who the traitor is?"

"Just suspicions."

Jason plants a kiss on my cheek. "We'll figure this out, but right now, I want you to focus on the boys. It's important we protect them from whatever people are going to say about you, me, and us."

"I agree. Do you think this will impact my Social Services case?"

"No. Not unless you're screwing Pete. Then we have a problem that you and I will have to work out in court." His lips move from my cheek to my neck, and I shudder. "Come to bed? It's late, and we have a lot to do tomorrow."

Something's not right. Jason is being too calm. Too collected. Almost like he knew something like this would happen. I expected him to at least blow up over Pete, but this is barely a whimper.

I stare into Jason's deep brown eyes, and one phrase loops through my brain: What are you thinking? What are you thinking? What are you thinking?

The fact is, I'll never know.

And that scares the hell out of me.

34

CALL ME MAYBE

M y guess is that the ladies who lunch are going to be pissed about today's post. You see, Pete is in trouble again. This time there are multiple calls to an unlisted number he can't explain. A number Veronica can't trace to anyone — not Elizabeth or anyone else — and instead of believing her husband, she's thrown him out.

Finally.

Can't say I blame her, but her theatrics are beginning to draw more attention to the situation than I would want. After all, she stayed after the Ashley Madison debacle. She stayed after the blow-up in Key West. And she stayed despite rumblings of his affair with Sarah and possibly Elizabeth.

Basically, Veronica has proven she's never going anywhere because she likes her lifestyle too much. I mean, who wouldn't? Pete works for the State Department (Or so he says. I have my suspicions.), and they cycle in-and-out of Waterford every two to three years for stays all over Europe. She always has the latest designer clothes, he pays for her plastic surgery, and she's Little Miss Popular at the Club.

Personally, I'd love to know where the money comes from because Pete's a lowly civil servant, and it's not like guys in his field make a ton of money. At least not Waterford kind of money.

Anyway, yeah. Veronica's not giving up her lifestyle anytime soon even *though her carefully crafted family image has been shattered. Nope. A Louis Vuitton bag is worth more to her than a happy, healthy marriage.*

Yesterday, she was overheard ranting to Karen while in Starbucks about how much she hates living in Waterford. She hates the people, the fakeness, the need to perfectly curate your life on Facebook. She hates the men, her husband, and that her kids spend more time online than off.

And yet, to Karen's horror, Veronica wants to take him back.

So, what does that mean? Only that Pete is so getting away with his indiscretions. Again.

"Who the hell is writing this crap?" Veronica shouts into the phone. "And how the hell do they know about the phone calls? I only told a few people."

"Obviously, people are talking and sharing info. We can't trust anyone," I say as I swirl my teacup. This whole thing is a disaster, and Veronica is reeling. Guess she knows how it feels now.

"One thing is clear," Karen says. We're on speaker with Veronica, and Karen holds the phone between us. "We need to stop them before they do any more damage."

"Oh my God, Karen," Veronica screeches. "People are reading this shit! I don't have the luxury of waiting around to catch someone. This person is directly fucking with my life."

I lean forward, closer to the phone. "Can we somehow make a public statement? Cut it off by ending the speculation?"

"Are you serious?" Karen huffs and shakes her head. "You want to do what exactly? Tape fliers to the light posts telling the world that Pete's possible cheating, your mental illness, and my financial troubles are make-believe?"

"I thought you weren't having financial problems," I say.

"I'm not," Karen snaps. "And if I were, it's not anyone's business."

"And my personal life is?" Veronica cries. "Why is that?"

"Maybe we should just let it die away," I say. "After all, the Ashley Madison thing only lasted a week or so."

"It's not going to die away if this jackass keeps posting. Fuel for the fire and all that." Karen stares at me. "Aren't you a little mad they exposed your condition?" She won't say bipolar. In fact, both she and Veronica act like the word has never been mentioned. Calling it a 'condition' is about as close as she's come which is fine by me.

"You know, not everything on there is true," Karen says slowly, like she was carefully considering her words. "My trip to Brazil was all about yoga. I've never had plastic surgery." I bite my lip as I try not to laugh. Everyone knows about Karen's various surgeries. She can deny it as much as she wants, her tummy tuck in Brazil happened. "There's so much that just doesn't match up. I mean, they alluded to the fact I'm having financial troubles which totally isn't true. I mean, think about it. How could I afford plastic surgery in Brazil *and* be having financial troubles?"

"Someone is making things up and dousing it in truth. Someone who knows just enough about us, but not everything," Veronica says. "You're very quiet, Elizabeth. Aren't you upset? Look what this person is doing to your reputation."

"Of course, I'm upset, but it's out there, and I need to manage it now. I need to show it doesn't bother me, and I need to protect my kids." Jason and I had sat the boys down the other night and explained my condition to them. Will looked relieved, Ollie confused, and Henry indifferent. Their main concern was that I would die, and once we assured them that that wasn't going to happen, they seemed okay.

Karen flips her hair over her shoulder and laughs. "But Janet Tildy in the wheelbarrow totally happened. That's a true fact."

I stand up. "I need to use the bathroom."

Karen takes the phone off speaker and presses it to her ear. Everything about Karen screams nouveau riche from her clothes to her home. Gilded mirrors, overstuffed arm chairs, and couches. Persian rugs. Tiffany lamps. Oil paintings.

It doesn't look lived in at all, and I'm not sure where she hides her kids' mess.

Black and white damask wall paper covers the bathroom walls.

It's dark and somewhat gothic compared to the rest of the house, yet it doesn't feel out of place.

A large, gold mirror hangs over the sink, and I pause, studying the woman in the reflection. She isn't me. Yes, she looks like me, but it isn't me. There's something off. Something I can't define. A sadness, maybe, but how is that any different from when I'm depressed? Is it mingling with my anger and creating this strange, new expression?

The woman in the mirrors says, "What are you hiding, Elizabeth? What?"

I have no solid answer because I've been hiding everything for so long. It's like all the little pieces that make up my façade have been held together by the pressure of keeping secrets. Now that those secrets are out, I'm crumbling around the edges, and it's only a matter of time before I completely crack again.

My phone chimes with a text alert.

It's Melissa Foster, who I've literally only hung out with once when we were with Sarah. She wants to have drinks — probably because people are blaming her for the blog. I don't want to, but what can I say that doesn't sound bitchy? I've already postponed twice, doing so a third time is a total blow-off.

Maybe, if I keep avoiding her, she'll see it as me believing the rumors that she's behind the blog. Rumors I've helped fuel, and everyone is talking about.

God, when did I become this person?

After I use the bathroom, I slip back into the living room where Karen has a piece of paper and her phone on the table. She doesn't look up when I enter the room.

"What did I miss?" I ask.

Karen points at the paper. "We're making a list of fact-versus-fiction on that blog. So far, there's a lot of fiction."

"That's what I thought." I sit down next to her to better see her list.

"Too bad people are believing it. We look shallow and stupid," Karen says.

I frown. "And I look crazy."

"It *is* weird," Veronica says from the phone. "So many of the things about you are true, Elizabeth. Except the part about you seducing my husband in Key West and at the Club." There's an accusatory note in her voice that I don't like.

"I didn't seduce Pete. We're just old friends. That's all." Of course, I don't say I flirted, it went too far, and I stopped it — which is a very different situation. I stare at the paper. Karen's filled it with names and has been placing notes listed as 'facts' under each one. Mine is suspiciously large compared to the other women. "I wonder why there's so much focus on me?"

Karen tilts her head. "Maybe they were jealous of you and dumped everything they had on you at once? I mean, you have had it easy since you moved here. You're friends with us, after all, and we don't give that honor to many women."

Great. Lucky me was tapped to be in the Mean Girls' club, and that makes me a super, shiny star.

"Here," I say, extending my hand. "Let me look at that."

Karen gives the paper to me. Melissa Foster is the prime suspect as is Sarah. "Why both of them?" I ask. "Sarah can't be doing this from the grave."

"No, but she could have started it, and passed it on to Melissa."

"How? Wouldn't that mean Sarah had to have given Melissa the blog before she decided to kill herself?"

"I thought it wasn't suicide?" Veronica says through the phone. "That's what you've been drilling into us. Sarah didn't commit suicide, she fell through a table. Isn't that right, Karen?"

"Right. So, what is it, Elizabeth, did she have an accident, or did she kill herself?"

All these weeks of hiding the truth, and I go brainless and let it slip. Damn it. Damn it all. I have no choice. If I try to cover it up, I'll look deceitful — and that doesn't look good when Karen and Veronica are engaged in a witch hunt. "It...The table wasn't broken when I got there. I think Kyle did that later."

"What are you saying, Elizabeth?" Karen raises her eyebrows.

"Sarah slit her wrists before calling me. She was unconscious when I got there."

"Jesus," Veronica whispers. "I'm so sorry, Elizabeth."

Karen's in full detective mode. She stands up and paces before the flat screen. "What haven't you told us? What did she say?"

I cast my gaze downward. I've been protecting Sarah, but now I need to protect myself. "Just, 'I need to tell you,' nothing else."

"She wanted you to see what she'd done." Veronica says. "That's the only reason she called you and not Melissa. She wanted you."

Karen nods. "I think Veronica is right."

"I am," Veronica says. "She was better friends with Melissa, so that makes more sense, but she called you. And now, Kyle has something for you. Why you?"

How did I never think of any of this before? Or, of how suddenly Sarah dropped into my life. It was like one day we were Facebook acquaintances, and the next we were night time friends getting drunk together. "I don't know."

"Think about it," Karen says. "Out of all the women in Waterford, what did she have on you, Elizabeth? Or better yet, what did you have on her?"

"I...It...It is all written in the blog. I knew she wanted to leave Kyle, but someone else — someone like Melissa – had to have known too. Maybe she'd planned her death for a while, and part of it was passing off secrets? I read somewhere that suicidal people do that — give away their belongings. Maybe this blog was her gift to Melissa?"

Veronica blows air into the phone. "There's only one way to find out. One of us needs to have drinks with Melissa. She can't control her mouth when she's drunk."

"Well," I say. "She's been asking me to meet up for a while now, but I keep making excuses."

Karen gapes at me. "What? Are you serious? What if she wants to confess or apologize to you? You have to go to lunch with her."

And so it is declared, and so it shall be. And right now, I feel sick as hell.

35

GIVE YOURSELF UP

*B*y now I'm sure you've formed a few theories on who I could possibly be, but I'm not going to dwell on that. I trade in gossip, not self-confession.

For example, those mysterious phone calls on Pete's cellphone bill. If they weren't to Elizabeth and they weren't to Sarah, just who is Pete messing around with? And if he's not messing around, what exactly is he doing?

But let's not forgot this important thread: Kyle Cole has something for Elizabeth. We still haven't found out what that is, but at this point, I'm banking on it having to do with Pete. Like blackmail or something — maybe a note Sarah left behind giving the details about Pete and Elizabeth's relationship.

Oh, you don't know? Seems the love birds dated in college.

That's news to you and their spouses.

The restaurant has a weird Godfather-esque vibe. Even though it's eleven-thirty in the morning, the lights are dimmed, and there's a veil of smokiness that hints at a bygone era. No one else is here except

Melissa who waits in a circular booth near the back. Like Sarah once said, she's tiny, cute, blond, and perky. All the things a Waterford wife should be.

"Elizabeth!" Melissa scoots around the curved, black and gold seat and jumps up to greet me. Two kisses, one for each cheek. "I love your dress! Who is it?"

The fitted gray t-shirt dress hangs lifelessly from my narrow shoulders. Once, I filled it out, but since Sarah's death, I've shed pounds quickly. I don't need two-and-a-half-hour workouts when I have the grief diet.

"It's nothing fancy, just Banana Republic."

"Really? I would have guessed Michael Kors. It has that look, you know?"

Actually, I don't. Other than Louis Vuitton, I'm not up on all my designer labels. "I never thought of it like that." I slide onto the pleather bench, making sure my dress doesn't bunch above my upper thighs. "Why the big booth?"

"Oh, someone else is joining us." Melissa casts her eyes downward and shrugs her shoulders.

Uneasiness builds inside me, and I curl toward the table. "Who?"

"Kyle."

That was not the name I expected to hear. Not at all. "What?"

"He knew you wouldn't meet with him alone, so he asked if I'd set it up."

My brain whirls. What if he's only meeting with me now because he wants a witness to whatever he's about to throw down? But why Melissa? My memory may be hazy sometimes, but I'm pretty sure Sarah said Kyle despised Melissa.

So why are the two of them meeting me for drinks?

I wipe my clammy palms on my dress. This really is like the Godfather. I'm just sitting here, slowly getting a clearer picture of what's about to happen, and fighting the panic growing inside me.

Screw that.

Before I can inform Melissa that I'm leaving, the outside door swings open, and Kyle storms past the red velvet curtain and into the restaurant. His eyes dart around the dimly light room until he sees us, and without a wave or anything, he stomps toward Melissa and me.

My stomach is down near my ankles.

Kyle's an oversized man with a shiny bald head and every ounce of him screams, "Don't fuck with me." I'm unsure what kind of law he practices, but I'd be terrified if he showed up as my opponent's representation. Hell, I'm scared now.

"Ladies." He picks the seat opposite me, next to Melissa. She turns her head slightly to the left, away from Kyle. It's as if she doesn't want to be seen by him. Like his gaze strikes her face, and it physically pains her to be here.

So why did she agree to set this meeting up? What's her angle?

"I don't have a lot of time, so let's get to it." He doesn't wait for our responses. "I've asked you both here because of this." Kyle pulls an envelope from inside his suit jacket. "Do either of you know what this is?"

Bile snakes up into my throat. Sarah's letter. It has to be. All these weeks of wondering have come down to this moment, and I clench my stomach to hold myself together.

Kyle throws the envelope on to the table. "It's Sarah's phone bill. There are 719 texts to an unlisted number without a voicemail. Multiple calls to the same number. I counted each one. Literally sat at my kitchen table and counted."

Sarah's phone bill? This is what he wanted to show us? "Is this what you've been wanting to show me?"

His lips tug upward, but the result is a hard, cruel look. "What did you think I had, Elizabeth? A thank-you card?"

Heat spreads to my cheeks. "I thought, maybe, Sarah..."

"Left something for you." He laughs. "Right, because she was so thoughtful. She didn't even care about her kids, so why would she give you a second thought?"

I mull over his words as tears burn my eyes. "There's no letter?" I whisper. "How could she not leave a letter? Are you sure she didn't mail you something or leave it in your underwear drawer?"

"Are you crying?" Kyle says as I sniff. "Are you kidding me?"

Melissa rubs my arm. "Leave her alone, Kyle. This is stressful for her."

"She's fucking upset that my lying wife didn't leave her a special note. Are you serious?" His cruel laugh echoes around the empty restaurant. "She didn't even leave one for me, but for some reason, Elizabeth gets to cry about it."

There's no air. No way to breathe. I double over and lie my head on the table while trying to catch my breath. How could she not say goodbye? Was it true that she hadn't really wanted to die?

"Are you okay?" Melissa says.

I rub my head back and forth on the table before sitting up. "I'm... I'm fine. I'm just surprised."

"Nice dramatics. I almost believe you care." Kyle picks up the phone bill and glowers. "There are dozens of calls to the two of you the day before and the day that she died. I want to know two things: who are all the other calls to, and what did she say to you?"

Could the calls be the same ones Pete had on his bill? Did Pete lie, and he really was involved with Sarah? Heat builds along the base of my neck and beads of sweat dot my hairline.

Kyle notices and zeros in on me. His bald head glows even in the dim light. "Elizabeth, you look uncomfortable. What do you know?"

"She called and told me I was a good friend. That was the day she died. Just before I found her."

Kyle shakes his finger at me. "You're avoiding the real question. Who were the calls to?"

Melissa folds her hands on the table. "You should be asking me. I know."

Kyle and I both turn our heads toward her.

"Who?" he demands. "Who was my wife writing hundreds of texts to?"

"Me."

That wasn't what I expected, and I screw up my face while staring at her.

"Why isn't the number listed like your other one?"

Melissa tucks a piece of butter blond hair behind her ear. "I had a burner phone. I didn't want Jake doing exactly what you're doing right now."

"And what's that?" Kyle squares his body to hers. "What secrets were you and my wife keeping?"

"That's private." Melissa crosses her arms. "It's between me and Sarah and God. You have no part of it."

The vein in Kyle's neck bulges. "She was my wife. I deserve to know how she spent her final days." He bashes his balled-up hand on the table top. "I didn't come here to meet with two idiotic women. I want answers, and I'm going to get them."

I shake my head. "Not from us you're not."

Secrets. Everyone has them. I do. Sarah still does. Even Melissa, apparently. And Kyle is dying to know what they are.

"I'll go to Jason and Jake if you two won't cooperate. Then we'll see what happens." His threat means nothing to me because Kyle fails to understand not all marriages are dictatorships.

I give a weak smile. "Try. My money is on Jason telling you to piss off."

"Jake, too." Melissa has moved closer to me, away from Kyle, so that the two of us sit shoulder-to-shoulder. "Do whatever you feel you need to do, but I'm having no part in it."

"Me neither."

Kyle grabs the phone bill from the table. "Some friends you two are. Don't you want her name cleared? People are already talking about her affair with Pete White." He shoves the bill inside his inner coat pocket. "People are talking, and I want to clear my wife's name. Why can't you help me?"

Despite his plea, it seems like what he really wants is to save face. He doesn't want people thinking Sarah cheated on him. He doesn't want to look like a buffoon. I get it. I do. But I'm still not helping him.

"Why don't you talk to Pete?" I say. "He's been staying at the resort since Veronica threw him out."

"She threw him out? For what now?"

Melissa chuckles. "It's not a secret. She's been hysterical about it for the past week. Plus, it's all over Surviving the Suburbs."

I need to redirect Kyle. If he matches the info about Pete's mysterious calls to Sarah's without checking the dates or time, just going off this information, he's going to go after Pete.

And Sarah and Pete had nothing to do with each other. I'm sure of it.

"What's that?" Kyle says leaning towards me. "And what did the bastard do this time?"

"It's nothing. Just some Women of Waterford thing." I drum my fingertips against the table. "As for Pete and Veronica, ask them. It's their marriage, not mine."

"Nothing?" Melissa says. I kick her under the table to shut her up, but she keeps going. "Surviving the Suburbs airs all our dirty laundry. You should read it, it's highly entertaining."

"I'm not reading a gossipy woman's blog." Kyle stands and looms over Melissa and me. His meaty hands grip the edge of the table as he stares down at me. "You're an interesting woman Elizabeth Mavery. I've asked around about you, but no one seems to really know you. Why is that?"

I keep my face blank. "I keep a close circle of friends and don't feel the need to be Miss Popular."

"Ah, but you were in Portland, weren't you?" The color must drain from my face because I feel faint as Kyle nods his head. "I know what you're hiding, Elizabeth. What you and Jason are hiding. I know everything."

He really must not have heard about the blog because if he had, he would know this isn't a threat. At least the Jason and me stuff.

"If you ask me," he says. "Your secrets are far more interesting than my dead wife."

Melissa's head swivels between the two of us. "Wait a minute. Are you trying to blackmail Elizabeth? Is that what you're doing? She has to give up what info she has on Sarah, or you're going to expose some big secret of hers that hasn't already been exposed on Surviving the Suburbs? Really? That's all you've got?"

"I don't know what blog the two of you are blathering about, but I'm sure it's ridiculous like everything else that comes out of your mouth." Kyle grinds his teeth and points his finger at Melissa. "You need to tell me why you had a burner phone. What were you hiding?"

"Jesus, Kyle. Haven't you lived in Waterford long enough to know we all have dirty laundry. I mean, I know yours." She smiles and bats her eyes. "I know all about how important it is to you that the world see you as a ferocious litigator, but in the bedroom, you're a passive kitten. In fact, you have impotence problems unless you're being dominated, don't you?"

I choke on my spit. "That's a secret I wouldn't want getting around and definitely not blogged about."

Kyle's crimson face wears a look of fury and embarrassment. "You don't know anything. You're just making shit up."

"Really," I goad. "I believe Melissa. It's a very plausible story."

"I'm out of here." Kyle bangs on the side of the booth. "I don't know why I bother to reason with women."

"Because we're as sweet as can be?" Melissa says.

Kyle storms off. When he's out of earshot, I turn to Melissa. "Were the calls really to you?"

"No."

"Do you know who they were to?"

Melissa shrugs. "Does it matter? She's gone. There's no point in disparaging her any more than that blog has."

"People are talking. They're saying she and Pete were involved." Just saying those words makes me ill.

"I've heard the same about you, only difference is that you and Pete are up on the blog together and Sarah isn't. I wonder why that is?"

"I'm not involved with Pete," I say. At least, not exactly.

Melissa gives me a strange look that I can't decipher. "Sarah wasn't involved with Pete, either. I've heard the stories and theories, but I knew Sarah, and she wouldn't cheat. She couldn't do that to her family." She studies me carefully before proceeding. "How are you doing with all the blog stuff?"

"I..." Does she mean my involvement with Pete or the other stuff written about me? "I'm good. It's kind of nice to not have to pretend anymore, you know?" I choose my words carefully. I don't want Melissa to have any ammunition against me later on. "And you? You know they all think you're the one behind it."

Melissa laughs. "I'll survive. I've been through worse."

"I guess I will, too." Only I don't know how she does it — her not giving a fuck. I wish I could be so brave.

"And the Bitch Brigade? How are they holding up?" She laughs. "That's a brilliant name, by the way. I wish I'd thought of it."

I take a sip from the glass of water in front of me and study the beads of water colliding and condensing on the outside of the glass. They drip onto the table, leaving a small puddle and I dance my fingers through it. "Karen and Veronica are dealing. Karen better than Veronica. I don't know how Alexis is. She doesn't really talk to me — or any of us - anymore."

Melissa takes a baggie of pills from her bag and studies the contents before selecting two pills. "Adderall," she says. "And Excedrin. I have a killer headache from all that, and my attention span is, like, zero. And before you say anything, I take this because I have ADHD not to stay thin. It's a nice side effect, though" She places the pills in her mouth and swigs from her water glass. "Do you want my opinion?"

Did I? Melissa confused me. I wasn't sure if I liked her or trusted her, but she had Sarah's best interests at heart, so I felt something like kinship. "Sure."

"If I were you, I'd stay far away from all of them for a while. They're toxic, and it sounds like you have a lot going on."

I nod slowly. "Probably. But according to Karen and Veronica, we need to look united."

"Your call." Melissa says. "I'll never understand the pull of those three. Sarah wanted so badly to be their friend when she had two loyal ones right here. I mean, look at us, still protecting her after she's gone."

"Speaking of that, what are we going to do about Kyle?"

"He's going to flip out if he sees the blog posts about Sarah. The

Bitch Brigade's efforts to piece it all together will look juvenile next to the war Kyle will rage. I mean, seriously, all he has to do is get an IP address, and the person will be exposed. Unless, he wants that info for blackmail."

I hadn't thought of that. "Can he do that? Can he look up an IP address?"

Melissa widens her eyes and nods. "It's what I would do if I had the means. And unfortunately for whoever is writing it, Kyle has the means — and apparently, the time - to go after that kind of information."

I'm faint and woozy. "I'm going to be sick. This whole thing is awful."

Melissa slides my water closer to me. "Drink. It will help."

After I have a sip, I lean my spinning head against the back of the booth. "He's up to something."

"You're right, but a good attorney doesn't play his hand before it's necessary, and I've heard he's one of the best."

Damn it. Damn. Damn. Damn. "He's coming for me, isn't he?"

"Seems like it."

I hate the thought of ever having to interact with that man again, but I don't think for a minute that he's gone away quietly, and Melissa agrees with me.

No, Kyle Cole has something else planned for me. I'm sure of it.

36

THE BAND'S GETTING BACK TOGETHER

*I*t was bound to happen, wasn't it? I mean the Bitch Brigade can only survive so long without each other. Seriously, without someone constantly telling them how hot they are or how amazing their new extensions are or that they lust for the very Chloe bag you just bought, what do they do?

I guess hanging out with a group of Periphery Girls didn't do it for Alexis. Plus, she got dumped.

Poor thing. Found out through social media along with everyone else when her boyfriend changed his status to 'single.' And her soon-to-be-ex-husband? He's already proposed to the pro shop girl. Obviously, Alexis isn't handling it well and has taken her drinking to a new level of perpetual drunk.

Lucky for her, she has a tight group of loyal and supportive girlfriends by her side (insert sarcasm).

And then there's Veronica. Kyle publicly accosted her with Sarah's phone bill and demanded to see Pete's. He'd heard through social buzz that Pete's was full of mysterious numbers too, and wanted to see if Pete and Sarah had been communicating. Actually, he wanted to know if Pete was sleeping with his wife, but he didn't come out and say it. But we all know.

Everyone knows. No matter what Kyle and Veronica do there will always be this accusation hanging over Sarah.

But here's the shocking discovery: the calls on both bills are to the same number. Which means the mystery person is someone both Pete and Sarah knew. The problem is that they both knew pretty much everyone at the Club, so there are suspects everywhere.

So, who among the usual suspects were they calling and why?

"Oh no, take that off. You have too short of a torso to wear it." Karen tosses a hot pink bikini with a palm tree print at me. My insides jitter. Just being with Karen and Veronica has me on edge — especially after my lunch with Melissa. "Try this one. It'll look cuter."

The pale blue one-piece I wear has a plunging neckline and crocheted body. It's tasteful but still sexy. I love it. I spin in front the mirror and check out my butt. "You really think this is unflattering?"

Veronica nods her blond head. She's recently chopped off her bra strap-grazing hair into a wavy, above-the-shoulder bob. It looks...odd. Why do women going through crisis feel the need to change their hair? "Karen's right. It's awful. Matronly."

"Fine." I clench the skimpy bikini to my chest. If I have to try on a million inappropriate suits to keep the conversation off Melissa, I will. "I'll try this on."

Pool season starts next week on Memorial Day, and all the women of Waterford are frantically trying to find a bathing suit no one else has and drop ten pounds by either starving or juicing. I've been doing a little of both and have cut out all alcohol, and still my stomach bumps out in an unflattering way.

The suit Karen selected for me is a string bikini and triangle top. It barely covers anything. How the hell am I supposed to wear this in front of other people when I can't even leave the fitting room?

"How does it look?"

"Okay?" I say from my side of the heavy curtain.

Karen lets out a loud, exasperated sigh. "Let me see." She peeks around the curtain. "Oh."

I have no clothes on. Just naked me, standing in a badly lit room. "I just took it off." God, I hope Karen doesn't think I look terrible.

"Well put it back on. I want to see." Karen drops the curtain and disappears. If she knew about my meet-up with Kyle, she and Veronica would lose their collective minds. As far as they know, it was just me and Melissa, and I've already filled them in on the basic fact of our conversation: she doesn't know who's writing the blog.

"Did you see Alexis?" Veronica asks. "She's looks anorexic. I think she's given up eating."

From the safety of my changing room, I roll my eyes. "Stressful situations can cause extreme weight loss. Plus, she never ate much anyway."

"I'm telling you, it's the Adderall," Karen says while I finish tying the bikini top behind my back. "It's amazing. It keeps us all thin and energized."

My jaw drops open. "She's on it, too? Where do you even get it?"

"There's a mom who sells it," Veronica answers. "Come out. Let us see."

After checking my bikini line, I fling back the curtain. Both of them are dressed in...string bikinis that sit so low on their hips that there's no way they have any pubic hair, but is still high enough to cover tummy tuck scars. They look amazing. Toned bodies. Flat stomachs. No stretch marks. And then there's me with my normal, albeit thin, mommy body. At least my boobs are naturally perky, unlike theirs which needed implants to get a nice, full look.

"I'm not going anywhere near a pool dressed in this. Especially not with the two of you."

Karen tsks her tongue. "Don't be ridiculous. You look fab. Doesn't she, Veronica?"

"Absolutely. And we can take care of those stretch marks with some tanner. Don't worry about them."

"I'm not worried about them. I'm worried about what Jason will say when he sees me like this."

Karen slings her arm around my shoulder. "He'll think he has a hot, confident wife."

I'm going to have to buy this bikini. If I don't, and I go for the one-piece, I'll never hear the end of it. "Does my ass at least look nice?"

Veronica backs up and checks out my butt. "How do you not have cellulite? What procedure did you do? Cool Sculpting?"

"Nothing. I'm lucky, I guess."

"Well," she says with a hint of envy. "Isn't that nice?"

She doesn't think it's nice at all, and the conversation must be redirected, or I'm going to be torn to shreds. "Any new leads on the blog writer?"

Karen flips her dark brown hair over her shoulder in her haughty-cool-girl way. "No. And there was a new post today. All about me and Adderall, ironically, and Pete and Veronica. I'm so suing once we figure out who's doing this."

"I hate this," Veronica says. "It's making me so sick. Seriously. I can barely get a few nuts and water down." And she was the one talking about Alexis. Pot meet kettle.

"At least it's good for bathing suit season." I joke, but neither of them laughs. Time to do a conversation pivot. "How come Alexis didn't come today? I thought she was back in our good graces."

Veronica blows a stray hair out of her eyes. I still can't fathom what possessed her to cut off hair. She has the delicate features for a short cut, but her hair before was so much prettier. "She is, but she claimed she was 'busy.' I don't have any clue what could be more pressing than making up with your best friends and doing some retail therapy."

"Have either of you actually seen her? Other than from a distance?" I ask.

"I've been a little bit crazy. Especially with the Kyle-Sarah-phone bill thing," Veronica says. Thank God, they don't know that Kyle was at my meeting with Melissa. The last thing I need is for them to think I somehow pointed him in Veronica's direction. "I mean, I really, really can't think of anything else."

And yet she can shop. "Yeah, it's odd they both had so many calls to the same number." I raise my eyebrows. "Pete won't say who it is?"

"No. And until he does, he can't come home."

I swallow my laugh, and it comes out as a choking noise. I bet if he turned up on the doorstep with a new Louis Vuitton, he'd be welcomed in. "So, he's still at the Club?"

"For now. I think it's for the best, don't you? I mean, he's covering something up and until he comes clean, how am I supposed to trust him? Plus, he let Kyle scream at me in a parking lot without defending me. Or clearing his own name. I don't get it. I really don't."

Karen nods in agreement. "The whole thing is so weird. Like, what's more important to Pete than protecting his own image?" She glances at me. "Do you know, Elizabeth? I mean, you did have lunch with Melissa after all. Did she have any insights? Do *you* think she's writing it?"

Damn it. I thought I'd dodged that one, but I should know better. Karen never forgets anything, and right now, she's hard to read so I have no idea what exactly she knows about the lunch. "She didn't say much about the blog, but I got the sense that she's not writing it."

"And why is that?"

What can I say that won't give away that Kyle was there? "She didn't have any info beyond what the blog had. She's as clueless as us."

That seems to be good enough for now because Karen goes back to eyeing herself in the mirror. "Well, whoever Pete and Sarah were calling knows why Sarah killed herself — and yes, Elizabeth, she killed herself so don't go into defense mode." Reflection Karen glares at me. "I'm sure Pete knows too, and I really don't get why he's protecting them."

I suck on the inside of my cheek and wait for Veronica to chime in, but she just browses the clothes hanging on a rack near us. Since Alexis left the fold, Veronica's been less chilly — all right, maybe even friendly – toward me. In return, I feel bad for her. She's caught up in the middle of something that's making her look bad, but she keeps sucking it up and putting on a brave face.

It takes guts to do that.

"Okay, let's get out of these and head over to Tory Burch," Karen says. "I need a few new pieces before anyone else gets them."

Don't groan. Don't groan. Don't groan. Our entire community dresses in Tory Burch or Lily Pulitzer. There's such little creativity it's numbing. "Who would steal your look?"

"Stacey, for starters. She thinks she's one of us, but she's not." Karen turns toward me. "She's not like you. She's annoying and always around. I want to tell her to scurry away, but she seems to think she belongs in our group." Karen yanks her curtain shut.

"Do you think it could be her?" I need to control the conversation, and I don't want Karen and Veronica to suspect Melissa anymore. "The one writing the blog? She's a 'Periphery Girl' to use the blog's terminology which means she's close enough to us to get some dirt, and she knows you guys better than Melissa. Plus, that would help explain the blogger's infatuation with me."

Karen pops her head out of the dressing room and points at me. "I bet you're right. It all makes sense."

"It does!" Veronica says. "Elizabeth, you're a genius."

"I could be wrong," I say, shrugging. "But think about how she pushed her way into your lives. No one does that unless they're up to something."

"We're going to get proof." Karen smirks. "In the meantime, I swear, if she shows up in anything I own, I'm going to send her semi-small ass back to the store."

Veronica laughs. "You're such a bitch."

"I know," Karen says blowing a kiss. "And you love it."

"Jason, you don't understand, it's like two wisps of fabric held together by a string." I shake my new bathing suit at him. "Look at it."

"Put it on." He grins. "And I'll have fun taking it off."

I shove him playfully on the chest. "I'm serious. They want me to wear this to the pool. Where our children are. I have lingerie that covers more."

"Then you should get that out, too. I'm particularly fond of the bondage one."

With closed eyes, I shake my head. "Listen to me. This," I hold up the small pieces of fabric, "is embarrassing."

"Not if that's what everyone else is wearing. Plus, I bet you look hot. You have a killer body." His eyes roam over me. "Put it on. I want to see."

He doesn't understand. How could he? Jason is a guy, and guys don't worry about what they look like in swimwear, or at least they pretend not to. He doesn't understand that women dress for other women, not for men. We wake up each day knowing we'll be judged by the other women around us.

Sarah once told me that she dreamed about living somewhere else. Somewhere drama free. I bet she hated swimsuit season with its tiny bikinis and Adderall and salads. I bet she ate her kids' chicken nuggets and didn't feel any shame about it.

God, I miss her.

"How long does it take to put on something so small?" Jason calls from the bedroom. I turn side-to-side, checking my reflection in the mirror. The extra skin around my stomach has always bothered me, but does more so now. How could Veronica and Karen let me buy this? What were they thinking?

A nasty realization settles into my mind. Oh, God. They coerced me into buying it so that they look better standing next to me.

"Damn it," I exclaim. "I'm not wearing this. I'm going back and getting the one piece."

Jason stands in the doorway of my closet. "What's wrong? I think you look amazing."

"You're paid to say that."

"Am not. And you do." He sneaks in behind me and cups my breasts. "Take these for example. Look how yummy they are." He playfully taps my ass. "And this has just the right amount of fullness." His hands run over my stomach, and I pull away.

"There's nothing you can say about that area to cheer me up."

"You're too hard on yourself. But you're right. I can't let you wear this out. Too many guys will be ogling you." He strokes his closely cropped beard. "Yup. I'm going to have to get you a muumuu-type thing, or maybe board shorts and a t-shirt. Something to hide my wife's banging body."

I laugh. A genuine, belly laugh. "Okay. I get the point. You think I look good, and this is appropriate pool wear."

"I do."

"Jason?"

My husband's hands knead my shoulders. "What?"

"You know they're all on Adderall, don't you?" I turn around and look up at him. "That's how they stay thin and energized."

"Elizabeth, don't go there. Don't. I struggle enough with watching you obsessively count calories and exercise. I know your doctor told you to watch your weight with all the drugs you're on, but you've gone past what's healthy."

"Just since Sarah died." I wrap my arms around his neck. "Running and yoga give me a sense of peace. Plus, Dr. Carter says exercise is good for my mental well-being."

"You haven't been sleeping. And don't lie to me. I've heard roaming around in middle of the night. I know you've been awake awhile when I roll over, and your side is cold."

"What are you saying?"

"I think your hypomanic, Sweetheart, and we should call Dr. Carter." Jason pulls me in tightly. His arms, once so comforting, remind me of the fact he cheated. When I don't wrap my arms around him, he huffs. "One day, you'll love me again."

"One day," I repeat, but I don't know if it's ever going to happen. I keep hoping, and I know Jason does too. But one day keeps moving farther and farther into the distance, and I'm losing sight of it. I don't trust Jason, and he doesn't trust me out of his own guilt. We're at a love impasse.

I pull away and strip the bikini from my body. It doesn't take long, just three little tugs. Jason grins and scoops me up.

"The boys," I protest.

"Are downstairs playing X-Box, and I locked the door."

Of course, he did. This was probably his plan all along. "Jason," I say before planting a kiss on his neck. "Did you love me during your affair?"

He drops me onto the bed and straddles me. He's fully clothed, and I am vulnerable beneath him. "I didn't love anyone. Not myself, or you, or the boys. I've told you this."

"But her. Did you love her?"

There's a long pause. Nothing annoyed or angry. Just silence. "She made me feel normal, and that's all I wanted." He brushes the hair off my face. "But right now, in this moment, I love you more than anything."

I close my eyes as his kisses cover my body.

This should be enough. Having a repentant husband and amazing kids, should be enough.

So, why isn't it?

37

CATCH ME IF YOU CAN

M y days as a blogger are numbered. Not that I want to quit – I don't — but every day that passes is one day closer to my identity being discovered. I can't risk it.

And yet, I can't keep my fingers away from the keyboard.

Sigh

Anyway, this is where we are in the story (and I'm going to summarize so things are easier for you, Karen).

1.Someone is writing a blog about the Women of Waterford, and no one — at least no one in Waterford - likes it.

2.Pete White and Sarah Cole made a hell of a lot of calls to a mysterious number.

3.Karen Newbold is hooked on Adderall and may be having financial trouble.

4.Alexis Frond is still an alcoholic and going through a nasty divorce.

5.Elizabeth Mavery thought she could keep her mental illness and husband's infidelity secret.

6.Veronica White has kicked Pete out, but is willing to let him come home — for a price.

7.Elizabeth and Pete may have a side thing going, but who knows with the two of them.

See, it's an easy story, really. One that's not hard to follow, but the Bitch Brigade is having a difficult time understanding it. All they're focused on is their small part of the larger picture. None of them comprehend that what I write is scathing because it's true. They may lie to themselves, but I know, and you know, that those who protest too much usually have something to hide.

And the Bitch Brigade is protesting. Loudly. They've mentioned lawsuits, but none of that scares me.

So, to them I say, "Bring it on."

But first you have to catch me.

Today, I'm going to face my fear and do a trail run. I mapped it out last night after getting a recommendation from a woman in my yoga class. She said it's an intermediate level run with some gently rolling hills.

I'm going to do it.

All I have to do is get out of the car. I have my clothes and shoes on, my music and headphones are ready, and I made it here and that's the tough part, right?

I can do this.

One, two. I swing the car door open and slide off the seat. When both feet are planted on the ground, I reach back inside and grab my stuff. After I take out my phone and earbuds, my purse gets locked in the trunk.

Slightly humid air surrounds me, but it isn't oppressively sticky and hot yet. Today is supposed to top out at ninety which is why a run now, in the early morning, is crucial.

The gravel parking lot gives way to a dirt path that runs along the Potomac River and under a leafy canopy of trees. No one else is out, which is fine with me. If I have to stop, I don't want anyone to witness it.

But then again, if I get hurt or lost, no one will be around to help me. And if no one can help me, how will I get home in time to get Henry? What will he do if I'm not home?

I'm falling right back into my paralyzing habits. Everything will be fine. It will be. It's just a pretty run, and if I get tired, I can turn around and walk back. A 5K is nothing. I'll be done in twenty-seven minutes max.

Plus, I have my phone. I can always call for help.

The water sparkles and small rapids form around river rocks creating the sense of peace my brain needs.

After double knotting my shoelaces, I roll back-and-forth to stretch out my calves while inhaling deeply. On the exhale, I launch forward into a jog. Slowly at first, then quicker until the tamp, tamp, tamp of my feet and the patter of my heartbeat are in rhythm. Every once-in-awhile, I jump over a stray tree root, but other than that, the trail is well-worn and smooth.

Despite the endorphins pumping through my body, the stress of the past few days doesn't melt away. The blog. Sarah and Pete. Jason. It all rolls together into one messy ball of anxiety. And Kyle. Can't forget Kyle.

My shoelaces slap against my ankles leaving a stinging sensation. I check my Fitbit. Only a few minutes left, and I should be done with the loop. I did it. I was afraid, but I got myself here and actually did the run. Nothing bad happened.

I could do this every day and give up the treadmill.

Maybe.

The parking lot appears up ahead, and I speed up to better my time. When I land on the gravel, I tap my Fitbit. Not too bad. A 5K in twenty-four five. One of my better times, lately.

Sweat drips off my forehead and runs down the length of my nose. With the bottom of my shirt, I wipe it all away. There are a few other cars in the lot, but not a soul around. I pop the trunk of my SUV and retrieve a bottle of water. It's warm, but I don't care. I need to hydrate.

The sun sits higher in the sky than when I got here, but doesn't hit me because I'm in the shade of my car's tailgate.

A new-ish Audi pulls into the lot. A man in running gear exits and leans against his car. He glances toward the road and then at his watch like he's waiting for someone. When he spies me, he runs his gaze over me before looking away.

A few minutes pass, and a white Camry parks next to the man's car. He walks over to the driver's door, and a woman jumps out. Like the man, she's dressed in running clothes, but from the way she throws her arms around him, I'm guessing she's not there for the running as much as she is for him.

Am I witnessing an illicit affair?

The man bends down and kisses the woman before taking her hand and leading her off toward the trail.

Anger percolates inside me. I should follow them. Make them know they're being watched. Would that make any difference? Do cheaters even care?

Probably not.

Last night, Jason insisted he didn't love his mistress. That he didn't love anyone, and mostly not himself. It's all so difficult to believe. How do you stay with someone for nine months and not develop feelings for them? Especially, after you've promised to leave your wife and children for them? How do you just walk away and never look back?

You don't.

My raging brain needs to blow off steam. I should have followed that couple. I should have been like Meredith and confronted them.

Then what? Would they laugh at me? Would they lie?

I guide my SUV down one-lane roads and through hairpin turns. Back here, in what remains of the old plantations and farms, it's like DC's encroaching suburbia doesn't exist on just the other side of the trees. There are wineries and horse farms, and occasionally, a real farm. When I agreed to move here, I had images of us spending leisurely weekends in the country, taking hikes, and enjoying the outdoors. Unfortunately, we were swallowed up by the Waterford development and rarely get out unless it's to go to a winery.

The anger gives way to a familiar sinking feeling of depression. Did Jason and that woman do things like that? I know about some of them — like the hike they did in Hong Kong and the stroll through Rome they took while eating gelato.

Yes, I'm positive they did, and those two people, they weren't a couple. They were cheaters.

My breath burns in my lungs. What if I could have stopped someone else from suffering heartbreak? I had the chance, and I looked away.

What kind of person am I?

There's a sharp right curve around a tree, and my brain spins. I need to be careful. I could run my car into it if I took the turn too fast.

Images of Jason and *Her* loop through my mind. Them laughing. Holding hands. Tangled up in sweaty sheets with wine stained lips. Over-and-over again.

Oh, God. I could end this heartache, and it would seem like a plausible accident if I took the turn too fast. No one would have to know I did it on purpose, and Jason and the boys would still get my life insurance money.

It would be an easy out.

Stop it. Thinking like this is crazy. I know it is…and yet…

I turn my car around and head back toward the tree. When I see it, I speed up enough to make my heart race, but not enough for me to lose control. It's a giant oak tree, and when I pass under its ropey branches for the third time, I gun the engine and take my hands off the wheel.

Ring.

I slam on the brakes and fishtail despite having anti-lock brakes. My car spins around, and I end up sideways on the road, just inches from the tree.

Ring.

Ring.

My jagged breath echoes in my ears. I glance at the dashboard of my car. It's Ollie.

"Hi, Baby." I sound awful.

"You okay, Mom?"

"I'm fine. Just finished a run, so I'm out of breath."

"Oh. I left my math homework at home. Can you drop it off for me?"

Hearing Ollie's voice ask for something so mundane brings tears to my eyes. I sniff. "Sure. I'll head home now and grab it for you."

"Thanks, Mom!"

"You're welcome." I pause. "Hey, why did you call instead of text me?"

"I don't know. Guess I just wanted to talk to you?"

My body shakes with silent tears. "Love you."

When I click off, I right my car, pull over to the side of the road, and sob. How could I even consider taking myself from my kids? Jason, yes. The boys, no. What kind of selfish woman am I?

What am I doing with my life? I'm not unhappy in my marriage, but I'm not happy either. Not the way I once was. More like I'm on friend auto-pilot with Jason, and we have sex twice a week. There's no romance, no trust, no deep love. Not like there once was.

I don't want a divorce. I want to keep my family together, because if I don't have them, I have nothing. Plus, Jason would destroy me in a divorce. I'd have no money and more importantly, would probably lose custody of my kids.

I have to make things work.

But then there's Pete. Why did I kiss him? And why do I entertain thoughts of leaving Jason for him. Pete's a proven player who's given me no indication he'd even do such a thing with me, so why am I fantasizing about it? What is wrong with me? I like Veronica. She's perfectly harmless and generally nice to me when she isn't ignoring me, so how could I even consider hurting her the way I've been hurt?

Didn't I once say that on the scale of infidelity, cheating with a friend is the second greatest betrayal? I know we're not best friends, but we are hanging out more, even if our conversations center around the blog, Alexis, and who's hotter than whom. Cheating with Pete would be something I'm not sure I could bounce back from — emotionally or socially.

I glance at the dashboard clock, and sigh. Enough wallowing. I need to get Ollie's math homework to him.

It seemed like a good day to die.

But it also seems like a good day to live.

38

MEMORIES OF THINGS PAST

Nothing is worse than waking up with an emotional hangover. It lingers all day, makes your insides jittery, and threatens to bring forth tears at any moment. That's me, right now. Emotionally hungover because Jason didn't come home last night and didn't bother to call until 5:30 am. 5:30. I spent hours worrying about him. Envisioning him dead in a ditch. In jail.

With *Her*.

I couldn't fight the images of Jason with *Her*. What if she was in town, and they decided to start their affair again?

What if...

His excuse is garbage. He had a work dinner that he insisted he told me about. "Elizabeth," he said. "We talked about this before I left for work. You knew I was working late and needed to stay over. You knew."

I didn't. He never said a word. I absolutely know he never told me.

When I started crying, Jason grew angry. "I'm talking to you now, aren't I? I'm safe, aren't I? Jesus, we need to up your meds or something. This forgetfulness is really becoming a problem."

And so it went, until I hung up on him and curled into a ball on the couch. I've been laying here all morning, waiting for motivation to get up, but none's coming. The boys are at school, and I'm lonely, but I don't think I can handle Karen or Veronica right now. Melissa and I aren't really friends. Not yet anyway. And Meredith, well, I don't want to lean on her any more than I already have.

Alone. God, I hate that word. Alone.

That's all I've been since Sarah died.

I replay the conversation with Jason and envision different outcomes. What if I'd been more forceful and demanded to see receipts? What would Jason have done then? If he'd hesitated, I'd have my answer. I'd know.

And I'd leave.

Surely, a judge wouldn't award custody to a man who is a philandering asshole. At least not under normal circumstances. I, however, have bipolar disorder and a history of suicide attempts. Nothing but huge, black stains on my Social Services record.

I'm not fit to parent.

Plus, I have no money of my own. Jason, changed all the passwords and took my debit card. My credit cards have all been closed, too. I have literally no money or credit other than the allowance he gives me twice a month.

I couldn't go anywhere if I tried.

Trapped.

In my brain. In my marriage. In my life.

I flip my iPhone over and punch Dr. Carter's contact info. The phone rings and rings and rings until hitting voice mail. I leave a message, and go back to being a ball on the couch.

A few minutes later, my phone vibrates and Dr. Carter's name flashes on the screen. "Hello?"

"Hi, Elizabeth. It's Dr. Carter calling you back. You said you had a question."

"Hi, Dr. Carter. I did. Is it normal for my memory to still be spotty? Jason keeps insisting we've had conversations that I have no memory of."

"Well...He and I have discussed this, and I told him that it could be a side effect of your medication, but it's very unlikely you'd have zero recollection. Are you taking your medicine as prescribed?"

"Yes," I answer angrily. "Jason gives it to me every night." They've been talking again and not telling me. Since when have I become a bystander in my mental health recovery? "If I'm taking my meds, I should remember things. Is that what you're telling me?"

"Yes, I believe so."

"How about inventing conversations? Like remembering things that didn't happen?"

"I'm not sure I follow."

"Before Sarah died, I had those few instances of having conversations that Jason said never happened."

"Yes, I remember." I can hear the scratch, scratch, scratch of pen on paper. "Has anyone else mentioned this to you?"

"Sarah. There was one time where I swore we went shopping together for paint, but she claimed I passed out on the couch after drinking too much. I had the cans of paint, but no other explanation on how they got there." I pause, while I try to pull up more details. "Jason insisted I hadn't taken my pills, so I promised to take them and go to bed."

"Did you remember taking your pills before Jason gave you more?"

"I don't know. It was so long ago."

"Was there anything else?" Dr. Carter asks. She doesn't ask why I never told her. She must know that if she did, I wouldn't have a good answer.

I push the fuzzy blanket off my legs and wiggle my legs around. "I did drink a lot. I always did with Sarah, but I'm positive I didn't drink as much as she and Jason said I did."

"Mixing your medication with alcohol could be deadly, Elizabeth. We've been over this, so I'm not going to lecture you about that." More scratching. "What I *am* going to say is that based on the amount you supposedly drank combined with possibly two doses of medicine could possibly create a memory loss situation, but I've never heard of it creating new memories."

"What are you saying?" My heart races, and a slightly sick feeling sits in my stomach. "Is Jason making things up? Like with the conversation with Meredith?" Before I said it, I hadn't fully committed to that position, but now, I knew in my heart, he was lying.

"That's for you to determine."

But I don't want to decide. I don't want to go down that road again. But I needed to do something. However, if I revoked his access to my files, Jason may get suspicious of me.

"Is there anything else, Elizabeth?"

I drag my hand up and down my thigh. "That's all."

"Then take care."

"You, too."

I fall back onto my couch. Is it possible that Jason has orchestrated everything to make me think I'm crazy? And why? To make me more dependent on him than I already am? Is he that insecure that he's willing to drive me to madness so that I won't leave?

Stop. I'm getting away from the pressing issue. Did Jason lie about telling me about his late night? Did he lie to cover his ass, and it was convenient to blame it on me because of my past episodes?

I don't know, but when he gets home, I'm not going to let this go.

"What are you talking about?" Jason says as he strips off his shirt. Since he's arrived home, I've done nothing but played the nice, sweet wife, getting him a beer and making sure he had a hot dinner. I kept the boys busy while he ate and then put them to bed without asking Jason for help. I've done everything, everything that I know he wishes I did on a daily basis. All for this moment.

"Today, when I called, you said you told me that I knew you were staying in the District."

Jason's mouth twitches, but he stares straight at me. "I didn't say that."

"Oh? What did you say?"

"That I was sorry I didn't tell you. That time got away from me and by the time I realized it, it was so late that I didn't want to call and wake you up." He strides across the room and takes my shoulders in both his hands. "Jesus, Elizabeth. What's going on in your brain?"

That's a good question. A better one is, what's going on in his?

"Are you sure? I remember fighting with you. I remember that clearly."

Jason nods. "Right. You were upset. I tried to calm you down, but you hung up on me."

That part I know is true. It led me to the fetal position on the couch for hours. "Yes, I recall."

"But I'm home now, and I want to put it behind us. Can we do that?"

I nod my head slowly so I don't give away my true thoughts. "That's probably for the best. I don't want to fight."

Jason nuzzles my hair. "That's my girl." He kisses my head. "I'll be right back. I need to pee."

When he disappears into the bathroom, I quickly lift my phone from my nightstand table and flip it over. The voice recording is still going, so I turn it off and place the phone back onto the table.

From now on, I'll make sure my memories with Jason are recorded.

39

NOTHING'S MORE DANGEROUS THAN A
MAN SCORNED

K yle is still on the hunt for the mysterious phone call person, and Pete White isn't talking. Veronica did allow him home after he proved he wasn't calling Sarah, but he had to come bearing gifts — this time a new bracelet from David Yurman. Did I call that one or what?

Meanwhile, Alexis had a little ménage-a-trois with Melissa Foster and her husband. It all started at the pool, aka Middle-Aged Spring Break. People go effing nuts at the Club pool. They drink heavily and ignore their kids. A kid could drown, and the parents wouldn't even know it because they're drowning themselves in buckets of Long Island Ice Tea.

But that isn't the good stuff. This is: Melissa's husband Jake was all over Alexis, rubbing her down with lotion, making sure her drink was always full, and telling her how great she looked in her barely-there bikini. He kept it up at the after-party at Karen's. And while everyone else was outside on the deck eating (or in the women's case pretend eating) pizza, the three of them slipped upstairs to the guest bedroom.

No one would have been wiser if Karen hadn't followed them and immediately ran downstairs to tell everyone. That began a stampede upstairs because, of course, everyone had to see.

I'll admit it. I watched the video. Curiosity got the better of me. And you know what, not one of them seemed to care that people were pushing into *the room, watching and recording them. In fact, I think it turned up their performance even more.*

Now Melissa and Jake are in high-demand at parties, and Alexis has a string of suitors.

It was like a real-life sex tape, and they've all just become Kardashians.

Melissa is no longer a "Periphery Girl." Not that she ever really was, but she floated out there. Not quite in, not quite out. More in than Sarah, but less so than Stacey. I don't know. The politics of it all makes my head swim.

Now she's in a league of her own.

Meanwhile, since my accusation while bathing suit shopping, Karen has kept Stacey very close. In fact, she's never far from Karen's side — a position Stacey likes very, very much.

Too bad it's going to end poorly for her.

"So?" Karen leans into me, and Stacey copies. "Would you?"

"Would I what?"

Karen huffs. "Have you been sleeping with your eyes open?" She reaches across the table and peels one of my eyelids back. I yank my head away. "Have a threesome. Would you?"

I've already shared enough of my husband with others, but I don't say that. Instead, I shrug. "Would you?"

She laughs in her nasally way. "If it was anything like what Alexis and Melissa put on, sign me up."

This is all anyone has talked about for days. We've moved on from Ashley Madison. Moved on from Sarah's phone calls. Moved on from Pete and me. This last "scandal" has me vexed and frankly, I'm sick of it. They had sex? So, what? Consenting adults and no cheating. What's wrong with that?

Stacey motions us to lean in. "Did you hear? Veronica and Pete are going out to dinner with Melissa and Jake." She winks. "I wonder if that means, you know, after dinner desserts?"

The world around me grows fuzzy. "Excuse me? They're doing what?"

She blinks her big bug eyes. "It's true, Veronica told me."

The urge to run floods my body. I don't want to hear this. I don't. This has to be a misunderstanding. It has to be.

The thought of Pete with someone else...

"Elizabeth, is everything okay?" Karen stares at me. I don't want her prying into the deepest recesses of my mind. I just need to get out of here.

My metal chair topples over when I stand. "I'm late," I say. "I promised Jason I'd be home by seven and completely forgot."

I ramble on, making no sense, before clumsily grabbing my bag and charging toward the exit.

If I can make it to my car, I'll be safe. I'll be able to do the breathing exercises Dr. Carter gave me and calm myself down. Veronica and Melissa, Pete and Jake. Their faces swirl before me, over-and-over again. Would they?

Does it matter?

A loud thump on my window causes me to bang my knee on the steering wheel. Kyle stands outside my door with a look of pure fury.

"Jesus, Kyle," I say, rolling down the window. "What's wrong with you?"

The vein in his neck bulges, and his dark eyes flash. Kyle holds up a thumb drive. "Do you know what's on here?"

"I don't know." I answer, but my brain whirls with possibilities: phone records, Internet logs...Sarah's letter.

He smirks. "But you want to know, don't you?" He leans in closer to me. "What will you do to get it?"

"What? Tell me what it is first." Being this close to Kyle frightens me, but I keep myself composed.

"How about you tell me the identity of that blogger? If you do, you get this." He held up his hand, exposing the thumb drive.

"Why would I know?" I tilt my head and study him. "I'm not sure I understand."

Kyle tosses the thumb drive in the air and catches it. "I think you know more about it than everyone else."

"Look," I say as I fight to keep my voice steady. "I've read it. Everyone has. Why would I know any more than anyone else?"

He drops his hand to his side. "It's interesting, isn't it? The insider information this person has on so many people."

"Wrong information. Half-truths and made-up stories. Hardly damning."

"But there's still enough truth, isn't there, for it to be someone close to Karen and her friends."

"Your point?" The anxiety from earlier has dissipated. I'm ready to go twenty rounds with Kyle.

"When did you start hanging out with the Bitch Brigade?"

"You know, I'm not sure."

Kyle rolls his shoulders back. "I do. It was in Sarah's diary." The shock I feel must register on my face, because Kyle laughs. "That's right. Sarah kept a diary, and she had some choice things to say about you."

I can't let him rattle me. I can't. "Really," I say with an air of disbelief. "What did she write? That we drank too much?"

"You could read about it here." Kyle shows me the drive again and smirks. I want to steal it from him, hit reverse, and peel out of the parking lot. The answers I've been searching for are so close. I'm sure of it.

"Just tell me."

"If you insist." Kyle licks the corner of his lip. "She wrote that you'd been taken into Karen's flock, and she was jealous. Oh, God was my wife jealous. You didn't know that, did you? The way she detailed everything the two of you discussed and how much she hated pretending to be your friend."

My insides roll, but I keep my breathing even and my body language neutral. "You're lying."

"She said she'd spent years trying to get an in, and you didn't have to do anything but show up fresh-faced from London. And if that didn't piss her off, I'm not sure what did." He studies me carefully. "It's all here."

My gut bottoms out. Did she really say those things? "What's your point?"

"If someone hated me that much, I'd try to make their life miserable too. Like maybe spread rumors about them." He glares at me, and my heart rate quickens.

"Sarah didn't hate me, and I don't know who's writing the blog," I answer. "Anyone could be behind it. In fact, Karen and Veronica have some strong leads. Like Stacey McLeod."

Kyle's bald head glistens. It must be ninety degrees in the relentless sun. I know I'm melting in the air conditioning with the window down. "Things don't add up, Elizabeth. They don't add up at all. Especially not your friendship with my wife."

"No, they don't. And that's because the blogger wants it that way, don't you think? Cast doubt on everyone so that no one can be found guilty. As for my friendship with Sarah, it was what it was." I'm lying again. His revelations — lies - hurt, but I can't let it show. I need to press on.

"You know, I'd buy that, except for one thing. The blogger, whoever it is, has a fascination with you."

I swallow a laugh. "Hardly. They've spilled all of our secrets. I haven't been singled out. In fact, there's over thirty people mentioned. I know because Karen, Veronica, and I counted."

"But you only shared your secrets with Sarah, right? At least, that's what she says in her diary. That you were crazy and had a cheating husband, and didn't want anyone to know."

Meredith knew. And I think Melissa did, too, but I keep my face a mask. "So? Would you want anyone knowing that?"

Kyle chuckles. "You're good, you know that? I'd love to be able to lie like you." He fiddles with his phone before flashing it at me. It's a picture of a brunette woman with high cheekbones and a too-wide smile. "Look familiar?"

It's *Her*. The woman Jason had an affair with. I've spent so much time stalking her on the internet, that even though we've never met, I could find her in a room of strangers. Why is he bringing her up?

"No. I have no idea who that is."

Kyle shoves the phone in his pocket. "Damn, you're good. Nothing rattles you. No wonder Sarah liked you. You kept all her secrets, didn't you? And she, supposedly, kept yours."

For the first time, I'm nervous. "What's in her letter, Kyle?"

He smirks. "I told you, there is no letter. She was a selfish cunt who abandoned her family and devastated her kids." His words cut through me. "But the diary, now there's some tasty gossip. All about alcoholic Elizabeth. And neglectful mother Elizabeth. And suicidal Elizabeth. The kind of stuff you wouldn't want Social Services – or that blog — finding out."

"You can't bully me."

"Is that what I'm doing? Bullying you? I thought I was trying to get to the bottom of the great Waterford mystery and protect you before even more gossip is spread about you." I look away for a moment, just to gather myself, but it's long enough for Kyle strike. "Sarah was sick. You should know, shouldn't you? Only the mentally disturbed do the crap you two did."

"You know what?" I shout. "Sarah was not mentally disturbed. She was hurt, depressed probably, and wanted out of your marriage, but she wasn't mentally disturbed."

The smirk fades from Kyle's face. "What do you know about my marriage? I treated Sarah like a fucking princess. She had everything, and she was an ungrateful bitch."

His lies overwhelm me, and I snap. "She wasn't a princess, you asshole. She was a queen *you* didn't appreciate. And ungrateful? Have you considered maybe she couldn't take being around you anymore? That the only way she saw to get out was to kill herself? Have you ever stopped to consider maybe you're the reason she's dead?"

"My wife did not kill herself because of me." Kyle leans into the car. The smell of coffee hits me hard, and I pull back so that our faces don't touch.

"You're so full of yourself," I counter. "You think you can scare me. Try again."

"Do you want to know what I know? Fact: there were hundreds of texts between my wife and an unlisted number that routed through an internet service. Fact: Pete made calls to the same number. I'm in the process of subpoenaing the records from the internet phone company, and I'm going to find out who it belongs to. My money is it's you – Sarah's best friend who wasn't."

I purse my lips. Now is my time to bargain. "Kyle, you're not going to find anything connecting me to the phone number. However, if you let me see the files, I may be able to help you figure out what you need to know."

His beady eyes study me before laughing. "Nice try. Not going to happen."

"Why?"

"Because if Sarah wanted you to see her journal, she would have left it for you. Plus, it's none of your business."

"And yet you keep trying to drag me in. Why is that Kyle?" The sun's sunk lower, and I shield my eyes to better see him.

He drops his gaze. "You were the last person she called, and the last person to see her alive. She called you. Out of everyone, she called you, Elizabeth Mavery, a woman she supposedly barely knew and talked trash about in her diary. It doesn't make any sense — unless you had something on her. Like who she called all those times."

Kyle's attempt to upset me so he can get the upper-hand is almost working. Almost.

"Are we done here?" I ask. "Jason is waiting for me."

"I've said all I need to, but if I were you, I'd tell Jason about this. After all, you wouldn't want it getting around that you have something to do with the phone calls. It'll make your affair with Pete look even more plausible."

I don't blink. I don't move. I simply don't respond. And Kyle hates it.

"Go. I'm done with you." He steps away from the car.

"And I am with you." I shift into reverse and roll up my window. I glance into the side view mirror before speeding off, leaving Kyle standing with his arms crossed.

He wants to hurt me, but why?

4 0

BOOM CRASH

*L*adies and Gentlemen, all is not well in the land of Waterford. In fact, things are blowing up. Like majorly.

First, we have Kyle Cole, Sarah's husband, running around accusing everyone of having something to do with her death. I heard he attacked Elizabeth Mavery in a parking lot and accused her of having something to do with this blog. Right. Like a mental case could pull off anything like this. He thinks he's closing in on me, but he isn't. And that gives me the one-up.

Oh, and Kyle still isn't convinced Pete White knows nothing about Sarah's death. To tell you the truth, neither am I. But Veronica is, and really, that's all that matters, right?

As for Alexis Frond, well, aside from being dubbed 'The Hottest Woman in Waterford' by a bunch of horny, middle-aged men, she's moved a much younger guy into her house. She claims he's the new manny, but we all know the truth. She's totally doing him. Plus, no one has ever seen him with the kids AND he's been going to all co-ed events with her. Has she gone from wanting a sugar daddy to being the sugar mommy?

Finally, there's poor Karen Newbold. And when I say poor, I mean literally poor. A few of her husband's investments fell through, and it looks like they're going to file for bankruptcy and possibly sell their seven-thousand-

square-foot house. I heard they're thinking of asking a cool 1.2 million for it. It's a lot, but it is on one of the most desirable streets in Waterford.

So how is Karen dealing with all of it? By shopping and pretending none of it is happening. The other day, she dropped a ridiculous two grand on a new bag that she later flaunted at the club. It's like her head is so deep in the sand, she can't figure which way is up. In fact, she's hosting another party this Friday. A pool party, of course.

I'll make sure to tell you all about it.

Jason paces the length of our bedroom. Since arriving home from work, he's been at it. "Tell me again, exactly what did Kyle say?"

I cover my tear-swollen eyes with my hand. "I can't tell you exactly. I don't have that kind of brain, remember, but basically he implied I'm behind the blog and that Sarah hated me, and then he showed me a picture of *Her*."

"What picture?" Jason glares down at me. When I don't answer, he repeats himself.

"It looked like a picture he grabbed off her firm's website."

Jason blows out a loud rush of air. "He's digging up the past."

"Probably, but I don't see why this is a problem. Everyone in Waterford knows we moved here because of your affair."

"What else did he say?"

I wring my hands. "I told you, I don't know. I was trying to stay calm and not let Kyle see how rattled I was." I stare up at the ceiling and sniff. I'm all out of tears, and my face is puffy and red. "Do you think it's true? That Sarah hated me?"

Jason shrugs. "I don't know. It didn't seem like it."

"But Kyle said--"

"That's great, but I need you to focus. What can you tell other than the fact that Sarah may have hated you?"

I scrunch my scratchy eyes shut. "He said we're going to have to do damage control because of the phone calls. That people will think that I know something about them." Just the thought of Kyle's words causes my stomach to churn. I can't go through this again. I can't. Our life is finally back on track, and I'm doing better mentally. If Kyle digs everything up again, I may never bounce back.

"I've read the blog," Jason says, slowly like he's over-enunciating each word. "It's very damning. You look guilty."

For the past several days, I've prepared myself for a confrontation over Pete, but when it's here, Jason just lets it float into the conversation like it's no big deal. "It's not true."

My husband stops pacing. "If it's not true, tell me why is Kyle going after you? It's like he's picked you out for a bigger reason."

"And that would be?"

Jason leans against the edge of the bed. "He's never liked me. Or you, really. What if he really has — oh, I don't know – something on you and Pete. Something more than an accused kiss in the club hallway. Something Sarah wrote in her diary that you wouldn't want people to know."

Wham. It was bound to happen, but I didn't expect it to be so harsh. "There's nothing on Pete and me because there is no Pete and me."

"Right. I forgot, he's too good of a guy to sleep with my wife. Even though making out with you in a hallway is apparently okay."

I'm like a fly bumbling along, looking for an open window. "There is nothing between Pete and me."

The walls push in on me, and my field of vision narrows. All I can see is Jason seething. This has been bubbling between us for some time, but I wanted to ignore it. I wanted to pretend everything was normal because it was easier.

But it hasn't been normal. Not since he had his affair.

"If there isn't anything between you, why did you sneak away from Alexis's party with him? Why did the two of you disappear at the Members' Party? Why were you kissing in the hallway?" Jason clenches his jaw. "Give me a good answer, Elizabeth, because right now, you look guilty as hell."

I am guilty of all those things. I did them, and he knows it. To deny would be futile, and will probably lead to a bigger fight. So, I inhale sharply and begin to count backwards from five in my head. When I get to 'one,' I say, "Okay. Yes. Those things happened. Pete and I have a history, but it's over now. That kiss was a one-time thing, and I'm sorry it happened."

"History?" Jason uncrosses and re-crosses his arms. He looks like a bouncer ready to throw me out, and for the first time, I'm scared, because I'm on the other side of cheating. I did wrong. Me. And now I have to face the consequences.

"We dated in college." The words hang in the air, heavy and tense, just waiting for Jason to acknowledge it.

My husband presses his tongue against the inside of his cheek and rocks back and forth. "I knew it." He points his finger at me. "I fucking knew it. All this holier than thou shit you've been spewing was just an act. You're no better than me."

I reach for Jason but he steps away. "You're overreacting. What happened between Pete and me happened twenty years ago. It's the past. The long ago past."

"Am I supposed to be okay that he kissed you? Jesus." Jason runs his hand through his hair and frowns. "I told you he wasn't a good guy, didn't I? And you defended him. Now I know why."

Panic wells inside me. "It wasn't like that. I swear."

But it's too late. Jason is in his closet, pulling a gym bag from the top shelf. Filling it with things from his closet. Filling it with things to leave.

"Jason, please, let's talk about this. You're not being rational." Pressure builds in my chest until everything inside me threatens to explode. "What are you doing?"

"Leaving. I need to clear my head."

"When are you coming back? What should I tell the boys?" Frantic. That's me. Completely frantic. He can't leave. Not over this. He can't.

Jason finishes shoving neatly folded shirts into the bag. "I'll come back when I'm ready."

"Stay," I beg. "Please. I'm sorry. I'll stay away from Pete, I promise."

My husband scowls and pushes past me. He flicks off the closet light. "How can I stay when everyone is laughing at me? Poor, stupid Jason. His wife is all over that damn blog, and everyone knows she's fooled around with Pete. Guy doesn't have a backbone."

"No one is saying that. No one. People think the blog is full of half-truth and lies." I'm desperate now, I need to save my marriage. After everything we've been through, I can't let this misunderstanding be the thing that destroys us.

"I stayed," I cry as I throw myself around his legs. "I stayed even though you treated me like crap. Hell, you slept with someone else and told her you loved her, and I stayed. What does that say about me?"

Jason shakes me off. "You didn't stay. You came back," he corrects. "Staying wouldn't have been abandoning your kids for a life in London. And you stay now because you know you would never see our boys again if we divorced." He sneers. "You're a shit mother, and you know it."

His words sting, but I can't let Jason walk all over me. Not again. I need to stand up for myself. "It wasn't like that." We're downstairs now, his hand is on the door and his other hand has his keys. The gym bag is hanging from his shoulder. "Jason, please don't do this. Don't."

He yanks the door open, and warm air strikes me. "Like you, I'll do whatever I damn well please."

And then he's gone

What the hell just happened? And why is my indiscretion so much worse than Jason's cheating? Is it because Pete was a friend?

I close my eyes and sink to the ground. What have I done?

41

PUZZLE PIECES

*I*t's a sad, sad story when I know more than anyone else. I have most of the pieces of the puzzle while others are running around trying to jam squares into circles. I can almost make out the full picture, but there are a few things I need to sort out.

Let's start with Jason Mavery, shall we? Until this point, he's been a background player, someone who escorts Elizabeth around, pays her tab, and makes sure she doesn't make too big of an ass of herself. He's also a cheater. Let's not forget that part.

When Elizabeth turned up at Karen's party without her brooding shadow, people noticed. Elizabeth's reason for Jason not coming: he didn't feel like it. That went over about as well as you can guess. Whispers all over the place about the state of the Mavery's marriage.

Maybe that's why Elizabeth left early?

Anyway, I'm pretty sure there will be big news coming out of Karen Newbold's camp in the near-ish future. Her party last weekend wasn't her normal display of new money trashiness. And if my source can be trusted, Karen locked herself in her room for a good hour. When she came out, it was obvious, she'd been crying.

Is she that sad about moving, or is there something else going on?

I'm in the gleaming white bathroom taking off my eye makeup when Jason slips in. He looks sheepish, with big eyes, and a fistful of roses.

"Hey," he says. "I got you these."

It's been two days. Two days of Jason not taking my calls and me not having any idea where he was. I've had to lie to the boys and everyone else about where Jason was, and part of me wondered if he was ever going to come home.

"Hi," I take the orange roses and lift them to my nose. "They smell nice."

"I know you love orange the best, and when I saw these, I knew I had to get them for you."

It's not going to be that easy, Jason. It's not. "Thank you." I set the roses on the counter and go back to removing my makeup. "Where were you?"

"D.C. near my office." He keeps his distance. "I hope you weren't too worried."

Worried? I thought he was consulting a divorce attorney. I imagined him plotting to steal the boys from me because now, in addition to having bipolar disorder and being a suicide risk, I'm also a cheater. One more nail in my coffin.

"I knew you'd come home when you were ready." I drop the dirty cotton pad in the trash, tighten my robe, and walk past Jason without touching him. The flowers stay on the counter.

Jason follows me into our bedroom and watches me climb into bed. "Are we good?"

I'm already tired of this conversation. "Did we have a fight?" I snap. "Because my brain has a hard time remembering things."

My husband shakes his head. "Look, I needed a few days to think. My mind is clearer now, and I'm not pissed anymore."

It's always all about him. Always.

When I don't acknowledge him, Jason says. "Those blog posts. How true are they? I know you admitted to the stuff with Pete, but what about the rest of them? Are they true?"

I give a quick nod. "As far as I can tell. Why?"

"Is the Pete stuff the only thing Kyle has on you? Is there anything else I need to know?" His voice is level, even, but something is off.

"Nothing that I can think of." Uneasiness builds inside me. This whole conversation feels calculated. I reach for my phone and tap on the voice recorder.

"What are you doing?" Jason asks.

"Looking at Facebook."

"We're talking. Can you put that thing down for once?"

I lay the phone face down on the table. I don't know why, but this seems like a conversation I need recorded. I can't leave it up to my foggy memory.

"What do you know about the phone calls. The ones from Sarah to an unlisted number?"

I shrug. "Only what Veronica and that blog have said."

Jason's gaze fixes on something in the distance. "Do you think Sarah said anything about me in her journal?"

That never crossed my mind. Never. So why would Jason go there? "What do you mean? Kyle's blaming Pete. He's never mentioned you. Never with Sarah. Never."

There's a paleness to Jason's naturally olive skin. Like someone drained him of all his blood. There's something he's not saying. His tense body is ready to pounce, and panic fills the deepest corners of his eyes.

I know my husband. I know him well, and this...this reminds me of...

Chaotic images and memories assault me. The way Jason would flinch at Sarah's name. Sarah telling me I'd had too much to drink and had passed out. Jason telling me to make new friends.

The memories that may or may not be real.

Blood whoosh, whoosh, whooshes in my ears and heat consumes me.

I haven't been losing my mind, but I've been blind as to what's been right in front of me.

"Did you..." I choke the words out. "Did you and Sarah have something? Is that why you're here acting remorseful?"

Jason collapses onto the end of the bed. "What? No. Of course not."

The world grows distant and fuzzy. These words, I've heard them said before in the same tone when I first confronted him about his affair. He denied, denied, denied until proof showed up in the form of emails.

"Just tell me." The words and my body no longer belong to one another. It's as if my skin's been turned inside out, and I'm floating above us, watching, listening, waiting for my life to end. Again. "Who is she?"

"There's no one."

Stillness envelops me. *Run, Elizabeth, run. Don't sit here. Get up and go.* My body remains motionless, but the tiny, knitted fissures of my heart crack again. He's lying. I know he is.

"I don't believe you," I say. My voice is surprisingly calm which conflicts with the woozy feeling I have.

Jason scowls at me and sits up. "Are you seriously accusing me of being unfaithful when you're the one running around with Pete White? What is this? A deflection game?"

Something isn't right. Jason isn't worried about me, he's worried about himself. He's spinning the story around on me. I see that now. "No," I say. "I'm just trying to understand your fascination with Sarah's journal. Did she know something I don't?"

"You know what?" Jason leaps to his feet. "If I go down, so do you." It's not said in a threatening way, but there's no doubt in my mind that is how Jason meant it.

I stare at him. "What are you talking about?"

Jason crosses his arms. "You know exactly what I'm talking about: Pete. You'll never recover from something like that, and you'll never see the boys. Especially not with your condition. I'll make sure of it."

I jut out my chin and steady my breath. "Let me get this straight, you want the boys growing up thinking their father was a philandering asshole that drove their mother to madness. Because that's how it's going to look." I climb off the bed and stop in front of Jason. Despite towering over me, he doesn't scare me. "I'm going to be the poor, suffering wife who was driven to madness."

"Hardly. Not when people find out about you and Pete."

I shove him in the chest. "You're an asshole. You've made me wholly dependent upon you. You control every aspect of my life. I have no money, no credit, no way to leave and you know it! Was that your plan? Keep me dependent on you so I can't leave?"

Jason's face shows no emotion. Nothing. He's just standing next to the bed looking at me like I'm crazy. And maybe I am. Maybe I'm imagining what's happening, which maybe, possibly would be better than it actually happening.

But no. I have a recording. I'll be able to listen to this over-and-over again.

His silence infuriates me. "Get out. Just go," I snap. "I don't care where. I don't want to look at you anymore. I'm done playing your games."

"Do you know how difficult it is to be married to you when you're always locked away in your head?" Jason says as he jams clothes into a gym bag. "You ignore me. You ignore the kids. You don't do shit around the house. Can't you appreciate what I've been through with you?"

"With me? Are you serious? I wouldn't be this way – Dr. Carter has said as much — if your affair hadn't triggered me."

"Don't blame me for your faulty wiring." His words strike mini-blows, and I brace for the full wind-up. "You know what? Jocelyn made me happy. That's a lot more than you've done in ages."

I give a shallow laugh. "Then maybe you should have stayed with her. I hear she's doing really well for herself. Made director. Travels the world. It's funny how fast she moved on from you."

"Fuck you." Jason throws the bedroom door open. "When you come to your senses, and you will, I'll be staying at the resort."

"Mom? Dad? Are you guys okay?" Oliver sticks his head in through the doorway. "It sounds like you're fighting."

I sigh. Of course, Jason had to do this. Of course, I'm going to be left picking up the pieces of myself and my children again. "We're fine, baby. Dad is just home picking up a few things before leaving on another business trip."

"Where?"

Jason glares at me. "New York. I'll be back in three days." He's testing me, trying to get me to fight in front of Ollie, but I won't.

"We'll see. Sometimes Dad's trips run long. Go back to bed, buddy."

"Okay."

Jason pats Ollie on the head. "I'll see you in a few days."

"Okay." My sweet, middle son disappears through the door.

"Feel better now?" Jason says. "You've gotten rid of me for at least three days."

"You tried to get rid of me forever."

He glares at me. "Elizabeth, I don't want this. I don't. We've been good lately. You've been stable, and we've been good."

"Because you feel guilty about something. Have you found a new plaything to replace Jocelyn? Is that why you didn't come home and have all the late nights?"

He doesn't answer as he crosses the room to where I stand. He rests his hands on my shoulders. "I love you. I've always loved you, but you can't see it because your brain is so messed up."

"Don't blame your inability to keep your pants zipped on me. Don't you dare."

His lips press against my forehead, and I shrink away. "I'll go," he says. "But I'm coming back. This is my family too, and I want us to all be together."

I shake my head. "I need space away from you. I'm not thinking straight."

"Try to get yourself figured out. I won't tell Social Services about this, but I would be careful if I were you."

My mouth drops open. "Is that a threat? Are you seriously threatening me?"

Jason shrugs and disappears through the door.

I fling myself onto the bed. My brain hurts from all the cruel words we've flung around, and my body can't take much more. I'm emotionally and physically exhausted. But the physical ache of pain can be dealt with more than the never-ending pain of emotion. That pain will always be there waiting for someone to come along and yell, "Enough! You've suffered enough."

But for now, no one is yelling. It's just me, sobbing into my pillow, and Jason leaving me without a good-bye.

42

AFTERMATH

The hazy light of early morning strikes my face. It's too early to get up, but I've never really gone to sleep. I've been up with a spinning mind all night.

I stumble into the bathroom and toss a white washcloth into the sink before blasting cold water over it. If I had cucumber slices, I'd lay them over my eyes, but I don't, so a cold cloth it is.

When I found out about Jason's affair, I ran. I packed my suitcases and left for London that night. Thankfully, I had enough presence of mind to make arrangements for the boys, find an apartment, and buy a plane ticket. Jason claims I abandoned the boys. Would a judge see it that way even though I clearly cared for them?

This. This right here is why I kept the wall between Jason and me solid. I refused to fully let him in for this very reason.

He hurts me over and over again. Picks at my wounds and then expects me to be okay.

I slam my hand on the counter, and my fingers tingle. Jason's bottle of cologne — the one I tried to surprise him with – sits next to the damn orange roses. The night I gave it to him, he accused me of being with someone else. He *accused* me. Did he really think I had it in me to be so damn despicable?

"Fuck you!"

The bottle flies from my hand and smashes into the shower door which shatters. Glass and safety glass mingle on the floor, and the overwhelming scent of Jason permeates the room.

"Mom?" Will stands in the doorway. His hair sticks out at funny angles, and he rubs his eyes. "What are you doing? Where's Dad?"

I bite my tongue. How easy it would be to poison the boys against Jason. They'd never forgive him, because I'm never going to forgive him for manipulating me.

But I can't do that to them. He's their father. I must protect the relationship for the boys' sake.

"Mom?"

"Dad had to go on a work trip to New York. He'll be back in a few days." My son steps into the bathroom. "Careful, honey. You have bare feet."

"So, do you." He skirts the worst of the mess and stops before me. "Why are you so angry?"

Dr. Carter would tell me to send Will away. She'd find my actions understandable, but only if done out-of-sight of the boys. "Dad and I had a fight."

Will puts his hands on both my shoulders. "I heard. Last night. Before Ollie came in."

"What did you hear?" My heart sputters. Please, please, please don't let him say anything about Pete and me.

"Dad was mad at you because you're sick." Will pulls open my drawer of pills. "I know these help you feel better. Why don't you take something?"

This isn't right. I should be comforting him, not the other way around. "If I take anything, I won't be able to get you all ready for school. I'll pass out."

"Maybe that's for the best. You didn't sleep, right?"

I try smiling, but all I can muster is a tight-lipped grimace. "After you're all at school, I'll take something, but right now, I have a job to do."

Will leans forward and kisses the top of my head. "No matter what, Mom, I love you. We all do. Please don't forget that."

I can't. I can't do this. I slide to the floor. A crumpled heap at the feet of my child. I'm falling apart again, but this time, I'm fighting like hell to prevent it.

So why can't I?

———

Once the boys are off to school, and after many reassurances to Will that I'm going to be okay, I call Dr. Carter and leave a message. Then I find the garbage bags under the kitchen sink and begin filling them up with Jason's things.

And I give zero fucks. He can have his philandering ways and pseudo-single life. He's never going to have me again. Never. I'm done being manipulated and hurt and accused. I. Am. Done.

I pitch the first bag into the middle of our bedroom, and yank another bag from the box. When I'm done loading it with dress pants and shirts, it gets tossed next to the first bag. Then, I pull open his dresser drawer full of colorful socks and shove those into a third bag. When I get to his underwear, my hand grasps a piece of paper. I clear away the clothes and come up with an envelope. Postmarked and with Jason's name and work address is scrawled across the front.

Fear rolls through me. It's a feminine script, and nothing like my awful scribble. The day we searched Sarah's house looking for her suicide note, Meredith said Sarah may have hid it in Kyle's underwear drawer – a place where only he would find it.

Jason doesn't let me do his laundry anymore. He said it was to help me out, but...

I'm now holding a letter, clearly not meant for me, found in my husband's underwear drawer that I didn't put there.

I pull back a corner of the envelop and peer inside. The paper is just normal lined notebook paper. I slide it out and hold it between my thumb and index finger for a long moment. Whatever it says was never meant for my eyes.

Or was it?

Why would Jason hold on to it — more importantly, why would he hide it – if it meant nothing to him.

I flip the paper open.

Dear Jason,

I love you. I love sitting on your lap and listening about your day while you play with my hair. I love the way you smell and the roughness of your beard against my neck. I want you, all of you. It's all I asked for, and you promised it all to me. You said we'd be together, and I believed you.

I always believed you. Don't you understand that?

I can't go on like this. Every time I see you, it's a knife is being wrenched in my heart. Do you care at all? I see you laughing with Elizabeth and all I can think is how that's supposed to be me. We're supposed to be together. Not the two of you, but us.

You said you were waiting for her next hospitalization to leave, but that was just talk wasn't it, because who could leave a sick woman? I was foolish for believing you.

There is no reason for me to go on without you. You were my one bright spot. Not my children. You.

I had hoped Elizabeth would leave you. I believed she knew, and I allowed myself to buy the lies you fed me. There will never be an us, I see that now.

I have no choice. Forgive me.

I love you with all my life. I always will.

xoxo

~Sarah

The room sways around me, and I drop to my knees.

Oh. My. God. I didn't read that right. I couldn't have.

Was I right? Sarah and Jason?

With shaking hands, I re-read the letter. There's no question what this is. Sarah's suicide note. She wanted Jason's attention, so she hurt herself. There's little doubt in my mind that her intent wasn't death, rather a cry for attention. My husband's attention.

But did he want me to find it?

The pressure between my ears builds, and I tip over onto the floor. I pull my knees up to my chest and rock back-and-forth. What did the two of them do to me? To themselves?

Does Jason feel the slightest bit guilty? And how the hell does he sleep knowing he not only betrayed me, but Sarah too?

My phone vibrates on the floor next to me. I wipe the snot dripping from my nose with the back of my hand before answering.

"Dr. Carter," I choke out.

"Elizabeth, I got your message. Are you okay? Do you feel safe?"

Safe? No. Everything, I believed has been shredded again. The one person who was supposed to protect me is causing me the most pain. "I'm not going to hurt myself, but I'm a wreck."

"That's understandable. Fights with our spouses are always painful."

"No, it's not that." My gaze lands on the pile of bags in the middle of the room. "I was packing Jason's things and found a letter from Sarah to Jason."

"What kind of letter?"

"I think it's her suicide note."

"Why would Jason have that?" she asks.

I sigh. "They were having an affair." Dr. Carter doesn't say anything, and I pull my phone away from my face to make sure we're still connected. "Hello?"

"I'm here. I'm going to make room for you today. Can you come in at eleven?"

"Yes."

"Until then, I want you to practice mindful breathing. And allow yourself to feel. Don't stuff your emotions down. Feel them, Elizabeth, but don't make rash decisions."

"Okay."

"Bring the letter, too. I want to see it."

"Okay."

"Elizabeth, it's okay to feel confused and hurt. Two people you cared about betrayed you. Getting angry is normal. Don't forget that."

"Thank you, Dr. Carter. I'll see you shortly."

I hang up and drop the phone to the ground. Angry. Yes. I'm angry. But not at them. At myself for being so stupid.

43

WITH FRIENDS LIKE THESE

I spent the day diagraming and time-lining Jason and Sarah's relationship. It ended right before her death, and I was too blinded by pain and mental illness to see what was happening before me.

What a sick game the two of them played. And to think I thought I was the one who needed to change. I did everything I could to make Jason happy. Maybe that's why I overlooked so many signs? But he and Sarah played me for a fool, and I gladly performed the part.

I wonder whose idea it was for Sarah to befriend me? And the lies. Why did they have to make me think I was crazy? Because there's no doubt that's what they did. They jointly made up stories to make me think I was crazy. That my bipolar disorder was ruining my life and that I needed Jason to keep me together.

I see it all so clearly now.

Damn Sarah for calling me. Was it all a ploy to get sympathy from Jason? A stunt, like Meredith once said, gone horribly wrong? Or was she really that distressed by their break-up that she did kill herself? No matter what, she wanted me to know, that's the only conclusion I can draw.

"Why are we here, Elizabeth?" Jason sits across from me. Per Dr.

Carter's instruction, I asked him to meet me in a public place. A hotel lobby bar seemed like the perfect selection given that he is so fond of frequenting them. When I called him to meet up, I didn't give away anything. I didn't want to give him a chance to spin a story even though I'm long past believing anything he says.

"Tell me about Sarah."

My husband takes a sip of his Old Fashioned. "She was your friend, and she died. What is there to say?"

I smile. "I don't know? That you thought she was a hanger-on and socially boring."

"Is that why you asked me here? To speak ill of your dead friend?" Damn, he's good.

I slip my hand into my bag, taking care not to touch my phone. Hopefully, despite being inside my purse, it will pick up our conversation. But that's not what I'm searching for. No, I want the envelope. The one that changes everything.

When I find it, I pull it out and set it on the table. Jason eyes it coolly. "What's that?"

"Why don't you tell me?" I answer.

Jason clinks his ice cube against the glass before slamming the rest of his drink. "Where are the boys? Did you leave them alone again?"

He's not going to do this to me. Not ever again. "Will is babysitting. He's old enough." I keep my hand on the envelope. "Tell me what this is."

"You read it?"

"Yes."

"Then you know." There's no remorse or emotion in Jason's voice. It's like he doesn't care that I just had my world turned upside down again.

I glance around the bar. The only other people here are a few flight attendants sitting across the room. No one can hear us. "How did it happen?"

Jason cracks his neck. "I met her on Ashley Madison."

"Who?"

"Sarah."

I blink. "What? You weren't on the list and neither was she."

He nods. "I used my work credit card and address, so I wasn't included in our zip code round-up. I don't know why Sarah wasn't on there."

"Tell me everything." I keep my voice level. If I show any emotion, Jason wins.

"It's just...you weren't here. I mean, you were here, but you weren't," Jason says. "I needed someone to talk to. Someone who would understand."

"And that was Sarah?"

"Yes."

How am I breathing? How am I sitting here, listening to this confession and still breathing? "How long?"

"A year. We ended things shortly before she died."

I crinkle the envelope in my hand. "Why not a psychiatrist? Why another woman? Why Sarah?"

Jason tries to touch me, but I slap him away. "It started right after we moved here. We didn't know anyone, and you were so damn depressed all the time. I was lonely, and Sarah was a good listener. For what it's worth, it started before the two of you became friends."

"That's even worse! I was miserable because of you!" How could she — how could he - be okay with her befriending me? What planet did the two of them come from?

"Elizabeth, don't." Jason grabs at my hand again, this time catching it, but I yank it away. I can't stand his burning touch. His tainted, burning touch. "It's complicated."

"No, it's not," I say. "You have a hard time keeping your pants zipped. Seems pretty simple to me. But let me ask you this? Why keep me in this marriage? You obviously want out."

Jason shakes his dark head. "No. I love you. I want us to be a family."

"Funny how you show it." I pause. "Here I was, running around, trying to make us a solid family, trying to defend Sarah's good name, and you two had an affair." I press my lips together to keep my chin from quivering. "I actually believed Pete may have had something to do with it. God, I'm fucking stupid. And blind. To fall for this twice. Twice. I can't."

"Like I said, you weren't emotionally available. If you had been, none of this would have happened."

Anger sears my heart. "You're kidding, right? You're not really trying to blame me for your affair."

He shrugs. "If the shoe fits."

Dr. Carter warned me of this. She said he'd try to manipulate the situation so that I felt bad for him. And if this was me of three months ago, hell four weeks ago, it may have worked. But I'm seeing things a lot clearer now.

"Who else knows?" I ask, ignoring his accusation.

Jason hangs his head like he's actually remorseful. Which he isn't. He never was. "Pete saw us, once, while I was dropping her off at her car. He called us out."

"But he didn't...why did he never say anything to me?" There's too many lies, and I'm trying to keep them all sorted in my whirling brain.

Jason spins his empty glass. "I told him it would break you. That you had bipolar disorder. I told him everything about you."

Oh, my God. Here I've been, running around Waterford, believing all this bullshit was behind me, and I didn't know a fourth of what was going on.

"Why?"

"I can't lose you, Elizabeth."

I snort. "Didn't you think I may get pissed about this? Are you that much of a narcissist to believe I'd forgive you again? Well, you are wrong."

"Sarah made me happy."

"Like Jocelyn?"

"Yeah. I guess." He leans away from the table, and for a moment, it looks like he's about to stand, but he just readjusts on the bar stool and glares at me. "Like I said before, you weren't available."

A disgusted laugh spills out of me. "You know what? You obviously didn't make her happy because *she killed herself.* See the common denominator here? In case you don't, I'll fill you in. It's you. *You* drove me to insanity, and you probably did the same to Sarah."

Jason motions to the waiter with his glass, a sign he wants more. Which is good because when he drinks, Jason talks. And I want him talking. I need evidence that he manipulated everything.

"She was never your friend, Elizabeth. Don't you understand that?"

My rational brain knows this. How could Sarah have been my friend when she used me to get closer to my husband? Or was it to help drive me crazy and get me out of the picture? As much as it hurts, Kyle probably isn't lying about her journal.

"I have one favor to ask you." I don't want to hear his requests, his pleads, his requirements. "Elizabeth," he says, snapping his fingers. "Listen. If it gets around that Sarah and I had an affair, life is going to be hard on all of us. You, me, Kyle, Pete and our families, not to mention Sarah's memory. Let's try to keep it between ourselves."

Fuck Sarah's memory, I want to scream. Fuck all of you. But I don't. "I won't tell Kyle, but I am going to talk to Pete."

Jason dips his head. "He tried to convince me to stop, for what it's worth."

"I'm not surprised. Pete's a good guy."

"Yeah. So good, he was on Ashley Madison, too. Don't forget that."

I push back from the table and shove the envelope back in my bag. "We're done. Don't bother coming home. I'll drop your things off at the Club."

Jason gives a lopsided grin. "Sweetheart, you're not getting rid of me that easy. You still have an open Social Services case. Did you forget?"

My heart plummets. I'm trapped. "What do you want?"

"My family."

44

WHEN THE CHICKENS COME HOME TO ROOST

W ell, it's official. Karen Newbold is selling her house. She won't admit to the why, but everyone knows she's broke. She claims they're downsizing, and that she doesn't feel like maintaining a house that large anymore.

But she told her friends, in confidence of course, that she's freaking out. Her credit is trashed, and her husband's job prospects are near zero. All these years of treating people like crap is finally catching up to her. Both Veronica and Alexis are avoiding her, but not for the reason Karen thinks. No. They're jockeying for Head Bitch in Charge status, and falling from that number one spot is like catching one of the big three suburban diseases: divorce, poverty, or cheating.

So far, Veronica is winning. The Periphery Girls have flocked around her. After all, she's the one who's still married. Who still has a fabulous house. And who still pretends her life is perfect while we all look the other way and give her a pass because, hey, she's pretty.

It must be exhausting always pretending your life is Facebook ready. I mean, how much time does Veronica spend taking photos and editing them so they frame the narrative she's promoting?

Think about it. Really, how much time do any of us devote to this? Maybe it's as simple as touching up a photo so we look better, or maybe we *set-up a picture so you can't see what's going on just outside the frame. We're all guilty of it. It's just that some, like Veronica, are better at it than others.*

One last morsel: Alexis has announced her engagement to her "manny." He's twenty-seven and has never held a nine-to-five type job. For the life of me, I can't figure out what the hell she's doing. My understanding is she gives up her alimony if she remarries, so there goes the money that's always been so important to her. Maybe she really does love this kid, but part of me wants to shake her and ask if all the Adderall has made her common sense disappear. He seems like an opportunist, if you ask me.

And there I go, caring about the Bitch Brigade. See what happens when you're here for too long? You start to develop feelings for even the nastiest of people.

"When does Jason get back from New York?" Veronica asks. "He's been gone for a while." She unexpectedly invited me to mid-day drinks, and even though the two of us are "surface only" friends, I needed to get out of the house and away from my wallowing.

It's been a week since I confronted Jason, and it's been a week since we've talked. He's FaceTimed the boys on three occasions, but hasn't once reached out to me. Honestly, I'm imagining every scenario: he's filing for divorce; he's with another woman; he's just making me suffer. My week has consisted of putting one foot in front of the other, popping pills, and trying my hardest to keep it together for my boys. I can't, absolutely can't, let them know what's happened.

"His trip keeps getting extended. I'm not happy about it."

Veronica tilts her head. "Really? Because I drove through the resort parking lot this morning and swear I saw his car. It's a black, convertible BMW, right?"

We're the only ones sitting in the lounge — probably because it's one in the afternoon and most respectable people work - or have private sessions with their trainers.

My large glass is full of Malbec, and Veronica's drinking prosecco.

Doubt nibbles away at me. Veronica doesn't know me well, and she doesn't know Jason, so why ask me out now if not to cause problems?

"Huh," I say. "That is weird. I'm pretty sure he's in New York. Must be a similar car. After all, there are a lot of black, convertible BMWs in Waterford."

Veronica touches my arm. It's a strangely intimate gesture. "You know, I'm here to talk. I have experience with throwing out a cheating husband."

My lungs seize. "I'm not sure I understand."

"I think you do." Her voice is gentle, almost like Dr. Carter's. When I remain silent, she says, "I've known for a while. Since before Sarah died. Pete told me."

This is impossible. Why would he do that? Why would he out us like that? "I have to go."

"Elizabeth, wait. Let me help you." Veronica blocks me from leaving. Her leggy five-foot-ten frame dwarfs my five-foot-two one. "I'm good at keeping secrets. No one else knows. I swear. I would never do that to you."

Of course, she wouldn't. I'm the horrible person here. The one who kissed her husband after lusting after him for months. Meanwhile, she's been hiding a huge secret from me.

Horror and sorrow push-and-pull inside me. "Why didn't either of you tell me? You both let me run around pretending things were great between Jason and me. How could you?"

"We thought we were protecting you." She pushes my half-full glass closer to me as we both sit. "Drink. I find everything goes down easier with a nice, large pour." After I've gulped down a mouthful of red wine, Veronica says, "We were concerned about your mental health. Jason told Pete it was precarious. That you were fragile and would end up in a psych ward if you found out. So, Pete told him to stop things with Sarah, and Jason promised he would."

I force air into my lungs. Pete thought I was a basket case, and yet he flirted with me? Kissed me? Did he think the mentally ill chic would be an easy score?

"Why keep my secrets?" I ask. "We're barely friends. And why would Pete tell you?"

Veronica chuckles. "I'm his wife, remember? He tells me everything."

"Except when he's cheating on you."

She shrugs. "Technically, we were separated. It stung and was embarrassing, but he didn't do anything wrong."

How did I not know that? For the past year, I've been friends with these women. I've passed judgment on them and never thought twice. And here's Veronica White telling me that everything I thought was wrong.

"Veronica, do you know who the phone calls were to? Pete must have told you."

"They were to Jason."

My heart beats faster and faster. "Why would Pete call Jason all those times? Didn't Kyle say there were hundreds of texts and calls?"

"That's right." She holds her breath for a long moment. "Sarah had lost her mind. She was convinced Jason was going to leave you, and Pete wanted Jason to know. The two of them fought about it, and Jason ended their friendship." Veronica sips her drink. "I assume Sarah called for other reasons."

I nod. "Why do you think Kyle wants to destroy me?"

"Does he?"

"He's subpoenaing the internet phone logs. He'll find out it was listed under Jason's name, and everyone will know my husband had an affair with Sarah."

"Do you really think he wants it getting out? It looks bad on him. Don't you know that?"

I scrunch up my brows. "I don't understand. Why are you protecting me? People think Pete had an affair with Sarah when it was really Jason. Don't you want to clear Pete's name?"

"No one thinks that anymore. There's only flimsy evidence of them both making calls to the same number. That's it." She bats her clear blue eyes. "Pete may not be ideal, but I try my best to make the world think he is."

"Why?"

"Elizabeth, don't you get it? This is my life. It may not be perfect, but that doesn't mean anyone else needs to know that. The same goes for you. You control how you react and what others perceive."

I pour more red wine down my throat. My head buzzes from the alcohol and spins from the conversation.

"Tell me what to do. Last time I ran away. I can't do that to my kids again."

Veronica straightens up. "The first thing you do is tell Jason to come home. He can't keep living at the resort because people will notice. Someone will see him, or his car, and put it all together. So, unless you're prepared for the gossip — and having it end up on that awful blog - I'd get him home ASAP.

"Next, you lay out the rules. Does he want to stay in the marriage? If so, what does that look like? If you both want to stay, you need to hit the social circuit hard. Go to every party, every happy hour, every single thing you're invited to. You take pictures and post them all over Facebook. You present an image of an indestructible, happy marriage."

"Is that what you did with Pete?"

"No." She turns slightly in her chair to better face me. Her butter-blond locks frame her face in soft waves. "I just did what I always do — kept up appearances. There wasn't as much at stake in my case."

"Are you and Pete happy like that?"

Veronica shrugs. "We've been married for eighteen years which is something. I mean, you don't throw in the towel because of one bad year. You don't."

"I've had three bad years."

She motions to the bartender. "Can we both have another?"

"Right away." The bartender refills both of our glasses. As the red wine drowns my glass, my heart pumps harder, and my breathing becomes shallower.

"Are you okay?"

After keeping my mental health a secret for so long, it's refreshing to have someone ask how I am. "Just a mild anxiety attack. It's nothing."

"You sure?" I nod, and she drinks liberally before setting her glass down. "Three rough years out of how many?"

"Seventeen."

"Oh."

"Yeah," I say. "It's not really the same, is it?"

"Look," Veronica says. "You need to decide soon what you want. What's more important? Staying mad at Jason, or keeping your family together? What is it you want, Elizabeth?"

I want my boys to grow up in an affair-free family. I want this all to go away. I want to believe Jason is faithful, and Sarah was truly my friend. I want the life I've always pictured. Not this back-stabbing one I've fallen into.

"Normalcy."

"Then you're going to have to put on a show for a while." She taps the counter with her perfectly manicured pale pink nail. "Eventually, it will fade away, and no one will mention Sarah – it's already happening. She's just another woman who used to live here."

A few golfers stand at the far end of the bar, too far away to hear us. "Why are you being so nice to me?"

"Why wouldn't I be? You've done nothing to me." My gut flops. If she only knew the real me, she wouldn't be so kind. And then there's the fact that I kissed her husband. Let's not forget that. "I know you've had more interactions with Pete, but we both really like you, Elizabeth. You're quiet and keep to yourself a lot, but you're not like other women here. You're authentic."

There's that word again. Why does everyone use it in relation to me? "And yet, here I am preparing to pull off the biggest con of my life."

"We all have to do some damage control at some point whether it's for our marriages, or kids, or our sanity. We all do it. Nothing you see in public is real anymore. And definitely not online. We're all walking around wearing façades."

"Veronica?"

"What?"

"How much do you know about my mental illness?" I have to know what I'm working with.

"Jason told Pete you were bipolar and spent time in the mental ward, so I knew before the blog post came out."

"I prefer to say I have bipolar disorder just like you'd say someone has cancer, not that they are cancer."

Veronica hangs her head slightly. "I'm sorry. That was insensitive of me."

"You didn't know. Now you do." I finish my wine. "I have spent time in an in-patient program, but never before discovering Jason's previous affair. That was a tipping point for me. Up until then, I assumed I was Wonder Woman. I always had so much energy, and I always got all the things done. There was no stopping me...until the affair. Then I sunk into a deep depression that I'm still climbing out of."

"I won't pretend to understand, but I do know how it feels to have a spouse who's unfaithful. Or at least, may be unfaithful. I'm not sure with Pete – it's such a gray area with him."

Karen would adamantly offer up that Pete is a known cheater, but I'd counter that no one, other than me, has any evidence other than his name being on the Ashley Madison list. And honestly, given what I know now, about how he and Veronica tried to protect me, I'm more likely to fight to clear his name.

"Thanks for meeting with me," Veronica says. "Pete would have done it, he's tried talking to you in the past, but you've always shot him down. So, you got me instead." She swallows down the end of her prosecco. "Keep your chin up, Elizabeth. And let Jason come home. No one will talk if you two look united."

"And Kyle? What should I do there?"

She raises her eyebrows. "Bring him into the fold so he'll look the other way."

I have a feeling it's not going to be that easy.

LATER

45

IT'S A CHARMED LIFE

S orry, I know, it's been almost six months. So much has changed that we need to play blog wrap-up. I've been at this for over a year, and to be honest, it's wearing on me. Like all good scandals in Waterford, this one has died away too. Maybe because I haven't posted in ages, or maybe because they've all moved on to something else.

Either way, I think it's time to move on.

But before I go, let me tell you how the Bitch Brigade is doing.

First up is Karen Newbold. She was once the HBIC. Now she lives outside Waterford in a much smaller house and doesn't come around anymore. Not since they gave up their Club membership. It's too bad because Karen provided so much of my gossip. She never could keep her mouth shut.

Next is Alexis Frond. She didn't end up marrying her yummy, younger manny. In fact, she came home early from tennis one day and found him hooking-up with another nanny from the neighborhood. And there went that relationship. But she's bounced back. Since her divorce, she's dated more suitable guys and joined a few dating sites.

That leads us to Veronica White. Vapid, silly Veronica White turned out to be more substance than fluff, after all. Sure, she's pretty to look at, but at the end of the day, her compassion wins over her exterior. No one will ever *be sure of what the situation is between her and Pete, but really, is it any of our business? No. No, it's not.*

I haven't forgotten the fourth wheel, Elizabeth Mavery. She's everywhere on social media and in Waterford these days. Every party, every girl's night out, every charitable function. Her life is shiny and perfect and shows no sign of her mental illness. Must be nice.

Anyway, that's it for me. For now, anyway.

"Are you ready?" Light frames Jason like a golden God as he stands in the doorway. His dress shirt hugs his tight physique, and he's scruffy with his five o'clock shadow and dark, messy hair. He looks like a man any woman would want. "Wow," he says. "You are gorgeous."

I spin around, and my scarlet dress flairs around my knees. Over the past several months, I've gotten good at pretending accept Jason's compliments. It helps that there are no more mind games from his end. At least I don't think there are. "Thank you."

"I love when you do your hair like this. It looks like we just crawled out of bed."

"You're incorrigible." I spent an hour curling and tussling my hair, creating the best possible version of myself. I need to be on point tonight. I need to be believable. "We should go. Don't want to be too late."

"When are you ever late?" Jason teases as I slide past him and disappear into my closet.

"Never. And I'm not going to start now." I select my short, faux fur coat and admire myself in the mirror. My cheeks are fuller than a few months ago, and my curves have returned. Guess that happens when you stop running two hours a day and doing yoga like a mad woman.

"Let's go," I say as I emerge from the closet. "I promised Veronica we'd get there no later than seven-fifteen."

Jason steps aside and follows me downstairs and into the great room. Our boys are flopped across the furniture playing a video game. Social Services cleared me two months ago to be their full-time caregiver again, and I've jumped back into the roll whole heartedly. "We're leaving."

Will waves his hand without looking up from the TV. "I'll get Henry into bed."

"Don't drink too much," Ollie says. "I have basketball tomorrow, and you need to coach."

"Oliver, that's not appropriate." Jason gently whacks the back of our son's head.

Henry sits with his legs over the side of a chair. "Night, sweetie." I kiss his dark blond hair. The other boys are too big for that kind of affection — or so they tell me – but at nine, Henry still lets me hug and kiss on him. I hope he never outgrows it.

My old therapist, Dr. Carter, once said to give everything six months before making any decisions about my marriage. Don't do anything rash and all that. So, I've waited. Six months to the day. Six months of planning and plotting. Of secretly building credit and establishing good mental health.

"Elizabeth? Ready?" Jason stands in the mudroom with his hand on the garage door.

"I've been waiting." My shoes click-clack as I prance across the tiled kitchen floor in four-inch heels while making sure I have just the right amount of swing in my hips.

As I reach Jason, I force a pretty smile to my lips. "This is going to be the best night."

Jason interlaces his fingers with mine, and I don't flinch. "I hope so."

When we pull up to Veronica and Pete's house, Jason jumps out of the car and opens my door. An icy gust of wind hits me as I climb out, and I burrow deeper into my coat. It's almost too cold to speak, and we hurry toward the front door.

Music mixes with laughter. Not everyone is here yet, which is fine with me because large parties can be too intimate. Everyone partners off, and you're forced to make small talk until rescued by someone else. Smaller parties allow for more circulating, and more conversation amongst the guests.

"Elizabeth. Jason!" Veronica rushes over with her arms out stretched. We hug and do the requisite "mwah" on each cheek. "Let me take your coats."

I shrug out of mine and hand it to Veronica. She tilts her head. "We need a picture of the two of you. You look amazing. Like a Hollywood couple."

"Can you do it with my phone?" I ask. "I need to be able to post it."

"Sure, but you have to promise to send it to me if it's a framer."

"Just grab it from Facebook."

She laughs. "You've gotten good at this."

Veronica hustles us across the room to where Jason and I pose before the floor-to-ceiling Christmas tree. His hand wraps my waist and pulls me in closer.

"Wait," I say. "That's my bad side." We shuffle places, and when I'm satisfied, I nod at Veronica.

"Smile," Veronica says, and I plaster a gigantic one on my face. My jaw aches, probably from clenching it, but when I see the picture, I look normal. Happy. Alive.

I definitely need to post this one on Facebook.

More guests pour in and soon, the house full of our neighbors. All around me, people pose and snap. Pose and snap. I'm right there too, smiling, holding my glass up to the camera, kissing Jason on the cheek. Making it all look as fun and believable as possible. Framing the best possible life in the best possible way with the best possible filters.

I've learned well over the past six months.

There's a break in the merriment when the DJ stops spinning and everyone leaves the parquet dance floor that's been laid down in the White's great room. As I stand off to the side, I scroll through picture after picture, cropping and filtering as I go. When I'm done, I load several up to Facebook. "Love this girl," I write under a picture of

Veronica and me. "Best husband EVAH!" goes beneath a selfie of Jason kissing me under the mistletoe.

I wait a few minutes with a half-empty glass of champagne. No red wine for me anymore. Jason says it makes me too mean. And he's right. If I stick to two glasses of something sparkling, I can take my meds with no side effects and no hang-overs.

I can function as a person, but more importantly, I can parent.

My new therapist frowns on me drinking at all, but she says she's proud of me for cutting back. Plus, I've been doing so well, that we've weaned me off lithium and cut my other drugs doses. I have methodically checked off every box that's been holding me back from living the life I want. Except one, and that's going to change tonight.

"What are you doing over here? Hiding?" Pete sidles up to me. "That doesn't seem like you. I saw you on the dance floor. You looked like you were having fun." He plucks my glass from my hand. "Refill?"

"I'm only having two tonight, so I have to pace myself." There's still a glint in his blue eyes. One that tells me that things will never really be finished between us, but one that I've also come to realize is dangerous. "I need to go find Jason."

"He's in the kitchen talking to a Kyle and some other guys."

"Oh."

Pete places his hand on my bare arm, and I fight the urge to melt. "It's weird, isn't it? Kyle and Jason."

"A little, but what can I do? I need to keep up appearances." I click my home screen on and open the Facebook app. Seven notifications pop up, and I absent-mindedly scroll through all the 'loves' and 'like' and comments on my party photos. True to form, Veronica has already commented on them. Even some of my Portland friends have chimed in saying they wish they were here. Which makes me wonder, where have they been for the past two years?

"Are you happier, Elizabeth?"

"What?" I blink at Pete.

"Happier. Do you feel happier?" Pete takes a half-step back and surveys me. "You look like it. I mean, you look really good. Not that you didn't before, but there's something different about you. A sense of peace and calm that I haven't seen before."

"Well, I've come to accept that this is my life, and I need to stop waiting for something to happen and take control." I said this to Dr. Carter once, and she agreed it was a healthy mentality. In fact, everyone likes when I say this.

"Funny how quickly things change around here, isn't it? Just last Christmas, Karen was hosting this party, and you were kinda skirting around the perimeter. Now she's gone and look at you. Other than hiding in the corner at the moment, you're the life of the party." He points at my chest. "You're the woman everyone wants to be. You have the amazing husband and kids, a great lifestyle, and endless friends."

I shrug. "And that's my cue to exit toward the dance floor."

"Elizabeth?"

"What?" I turn slightly so that I'm facing Pete directly.

"Is it worth it?" A flash of something unidentifiable runs across his face. He gestures at the room full of holiday décor and party goers. "Pretending. Is it worth it?"

"It will be." The iciness of my voice surprises me. I'm not a cold, snappy person.

Pete narrows his eyes. "Never mind. Have fun tonight."

"I will."

When I enter the kitchen, Jason spies me and waves. Sure enough, Kyle is next to him. He's still annoying as sin, but the only way to throw him off Jason's trail was for Jason to befriend him. So now, we see Kyle all the time, but not his daughters. Kyle's left their raising to his former mother-in-law and nanny.

But life goes on, even when people are missing from it. We all have to wake up, get dressed, and face the world. We all have to make the best of it.

And that's what I'm going to do tonight. Because if I'm not living authentically, then what's the point?

46

ALL GOOD THINGS MUST END

*H*ere's *a fact: When life first dropped us here in the middle of the suburbs, I didn't think I'd survive. In fact, I tried not to. I thought I was better than everyone. More cosmopolitan. More interesting. More everything.*

Another fact: I'm not. Karen, Veronica, Alexis – they all have redeeming qualities. Each one of them surprised me once I got to know them better.

Last fact: Despite falling apart, I did survive here. I've come out stronger and more confident. I can stand on my own two feet now. So maybe I was right in calling this blog "Surviving the Suburbs" because I'm ready for what life throws at me — like the affair my husband had with Sarah Cole. And while it may seem like I've taken him back, I haven't forgiven him. I never will. Instead of being angry though, I've worked hard, waited six months, and sucked it up. I've dressed my life up in prettiness and poses and perfection.

But I've been waiting for this moment. The moment when I am finally free of pretending.

My husband, Jason, cheated on me with Sarah Cole. I'll never know why she called me except to possibly get Jason's attention. But, I now know I can never trust anyone, and that my marriage is over. It's sad the way the people I thought were my friends turned out not to be, and the people I didn't trust actually had my best interests at heart.

Anyway, this is my letter. My apology and confession to those I've hurt. I'm out. Done. Finished. And moving on.

Love Ya!
Elizabeth Mavery

ABOUT THE AUTHOR

Mia lives in Northern Virginia with her husband, children, and cats. When she's not writing, she's practicing yoga, traveling, or drinking ridiculous amounts of green tea.

She's been known to eavesdrop a time or two.

Join her newsletter and keep up on new book releases and more: http://eepurl.com/dsfaTL

facebook.com/miahayesauthor

twitter.com/novahousewife

instagram.com/miahayesauthor

ALSO BY MIA HAYES

ALL THE BROKEN PIECES (Waterford Book 2)

PICTURE PERFECT LIES (Waterford Book 3)

The Has-Beens (September 2020)

Coming September 2020

THE HAS-BEENS

Beauty fades. Marriages change. But best friends are forever.

Diana has the perfectly planned life: boy-girl twins attending Princeton and Brown; a wonderful marriage; and her own successful crisis PR agency. She never saw this coming.

Kristin's affair has left her adrift. With her daughter off at college, she's not adjusting to her empty-nest life well. She wants to feel something again.

Travel writer and free-spirit Steph loves nothing more than to go-go-go. She doesn't have room in her life for a partner, kids, or anything long-term. She's tired of explaining herself.

Their lives couldn't be more different, but after a run-in with a group of younger women, they end up in the same place: needing each other to find their footing in a world that increasingly pushes them aside.

PREVIEW

ALL THE BROKEN PIECES

CHAPTER ONE
Cry It Out

One stray sock and a toothbrush.

That's all that remained of Ellison's ex-husband. The furniture, sheets, and paintings were new. The townhouse, too.

She hadn't wanted the divorce - didn't see it coming - but it was there lurking, waiting for her to let her guard down. And when she felt comfortable in her life, with the comings and goings of her husband, with the money and the children, he declared he no longer loved her and had fallen in love with someone else.

Someone else.

Not her.

The thought still left her breathless, but she no longer curled into a sobbing ball.

The demise of her marriage wasn't a series of mini-announcements the way many of her friends' divorces had been. There was no arguing over housework or finances. There was sex, albeit a bit mundane, but she made an effort to sleep with her husband at least three nights a week. She worked out regularly and kept her weight down. Botox was a close friend. She was attentive and interested in his work. She kept a neat house and made dinner more often than not. All this, and she had been a kick-ass real estate agent in-between raising her kids and caring for her husband.

No. Ellison did everything right, or so she thought.

A sock and a toothbrush.

With a swift movement, Ellison gathered the offensive objects and tossed them in the garbage. Then, she picked up her cell phone and called the first person she thought of, her best friend Andrea.

"Hello?"

Ellison shifted the phone to hear better. "Hey, Andi, it's me."

"Ellison! I was just thinking of you. What's up?" Andi had a way of speaking fast and running her words together, so if you didn't listen closely, she was nearly incomprehensible.

"Drinks tonight? Josh is picking up the kids, and Mom needs a night out." Since the divorce, Ellison had taken to drinking bottles of wine at home alone after the boys went to bed. But even she knew that kind of behavior was pathetic.

"Sure. What time?" Andi was always ready for something. Having never married nor having had kids, it made her the perfect partner in crime - that is, when she was in town.

Ellison tucked a piece of her shoulder length, ash blond hair behind her ear. "Seven-thirty?"

"Perfect. I say we try out the new bar. What's it called?" Andi rattled.

"Whiskey Blu."

"Right. I'll pick you up, okay?"

Ellison nodded before answering. "So I can get sloshed?"

"So you can have fun!"

Fun. What is that anymore? Ellison thought before saying, "Okay, see you at seven-thirty."

After hanging up, she glanced at the time. Five-eighteen. Josh was late picking up the boys. As usual.

"Mom?" Dash yelled up the stairs. At ten years old, he was already as tall as her. But he looked like a mini-Josh: tan skin, brown eyes, brown hair. "When's Dad getting here?"

"Soon," she yelled back, having no idea. When the judge ordered joint custody of the boys, she hadn't understood how hard it would be sharing them. That and the gossip that went with it. In a small town like Waterford, everyone knew everyone else's business. Didn't help that Josh put it up on Facebook the day he left.

Status update: Josh Brooks is single.

Followed shortly by:

Status update: Josh Brooks is in a relationship with Jennifer Cartwright.

The messages and questions began pouring in almost instantly, and her humiliation was complete. Everyone in Waterford knew she'd been cheated on and tossed away. There was nowhere she could hide, except maybe somewhere new. So that day, she started looking for a new house, in another small town not too far away. It distracted her from the reality of what was happening. That Josh had been having an affair with his work subordinate for nine months. That he really was leaving her.

How did she never pick up on it? Well, that was the easy part. His whore traveled with him on business, and Ellison was too trusting. Her Josh would never stray. He was the ideal husband and a great dad, for the most part. They'd been together since college and had basically grown into adulthood together.

But somehow, the judge declared her cheating husband an equally-fit parent even though through their marriage, all he'd done is play the role of "Big Kid" while she handled all the administrative stuff - like homework, dentist appointments, and discipline. The divorce had only been final for a month, and to be honest, Ellison was still spinning.

Cheating on your spouse, it seemed, didn't really matter to the courts. Or anyone else. How many girlfriends told her it was no big deal, everyone does it? How many times did she listen to her mom tell her she didn't try hard enough? That her marriage failure was her fault?

Well, here she was now. Newly divorced, mom to two rambunctious boys, and sexless for months.

Not a good place to be. Even her vibrators remained packed away. She couldn't bring herself to use them, knowing how much Josh used to enjoy the show.

Ellison walked into the bathroom and swiped on some lipstick before running her fingers through her hair. Tousling it in a sexy bedhead way. There was no point in letting Josh see her look frumpy. In fact, she hoped he saw her and wanted her.

When will that go away?

The doorbell sounded with a tinny dong, and the boys were at the door before Ellison made it halfway down the stairs. She paused on the landing, where Josh could see her, knowing the window behind her backlit her nicely.

"Hey, Ellison," her ex-husband said in his slow, drawn-out way. To think she once found his southern accent sexy. He didn't apologize for being late.

"Hi."

He ruffled the boys' heads. "Why don't you two run out to the truck?"

Dash and Alex needed no further instruction. They left without so much as a good-bye.

"Love you!" Ellison called after them and finished her descent down the stairs. *One foot in front of the other. Steady. Don't let Josh see you as weak.*

Josh didn't move from the doorway. "I need to talk to you. About the wedding."

"I don't have time for this now. I need to get ready. I'm going out." Ellison stood with her hands on her hips, trying to seem firm.

"C'mon, Elle." She cringed at the use of her nickname, but Josh either didn't care or notice. "We're going to have to discuss it at some point."

"I have plans, and you're going to make me late." She prayed it sounded like she had a date.

Josh persisted. "The wedding is in two weeks."

Vomit sat in the back of Ellison's throat, wanting to spew out all over her ex-husband. "Your wedding is not my concern. Your love life means nothing to me." It was lies, lies she told herself over-and-over again. Of course, she cared that *her* Josh, the man she'd been married to for fourteen years, chose a woman five years younger. It hurt. Strike that. It burned. At thirty-eight, she felt washed up and discarded.

"I want the boys there, but it's your weekend."

"I know. We can work something out. Just not now."

Josh gave her one of his looks, the kind that she'd grown to know too well over the years. He was going to devastate her again. She held up her hands as if to stop what was coming next.

It didn't work.

"Jenn is pregnant."

Whoosh. Gut kick.

Breathe, Ellison, breathe.

"How nice," she squeaked before turning away and closing the door on Josh.

"Ellison!" Josh hammered the door with his fist. "We have to talk."

No, no we don't. It took all her strength to pull herself to the staircase. Tears rolled down her smooth cheeks as she balled into her defeated position. Why did Josh have to do these things? Why tell her now? Couldn't he at least let her have one night out without ruining it?

No, of course not. He was selfish, as evident from the affair to his wedding requests.

And right now, it seemed like he existed only to make her life hell.

She cried it all out, marveling at how many tears she could still cry over Josh. While drying her eyes on the bottom of her fitted orange t-shirt, Ellison walked to the kitchen. The green glare of the clock stopped her. Six-thirty. She had exactly an hour to pull herself together. Not that she was ever together anymore. The slightest things sent her into either a rage or a quivering mess.

What is my life? she thought as she willed herself back upstairs to her bedroom and stripped off her clothes.

She cranked up the shower, allowing it to get steamy before entering. Her tense muscles relaxed as she massaged her neck and shoulders. Once upon a time Josh would have done this for her, but he--

Stop it, Ellison. Stop giving Josh so much power over you.

Maybe what she needed was a one-night stand. Andi had mentioned it before, but Ellison dismissed it. Partly because she was a mom, and partly because who would want to be with a hot mess like her?

Still, she made sure to shave all the possibly important parts and lotioned her legs. She left the towel wrapped around her head as she stood in her closet naked, not knowing what to wear.

Ellison ran her fingers on the row of dresses before her. She felt like wearing purple - Josh always said it brought out the green in her hazel eyes, and that made her feel pretty.

To think she'll never hear him say it again almost drove Ellison to tears, but she blinked them away. "Fuck Josh," she said reciting her new favorite motto while grabbing skinny jeans and a loose, olive green blouse.

Andi arrived exactly on time, just like she always did. She was never one minute early or late. Always exactly punctual, which to be honest, drove Ellison nuts sometimes.

"Whoa. Have you been crying?" Andi asked when Ellison opened the door.

"Damn it. I thought I'd de-puffed." Ellison had chopped up a cucumber and rested two circles against her eyes before applying her make-up. She'd gone for a dark, smoky eye hoping to hide some of the redness. And Visine. Lots and lots of Visine.

Andi flung her purse down on the kitchen island. "What did dumb ass do this time?"

This is why Andi was her best friend. She got Ellison and didn't judge her. Didn't tell her the affair and divorce were her fault, but she also didn't badmouth Josh unless there was a reason. And clearly there was a reason.

"He knocked up his whore."

Andi let out a low whistle before laughing. "Guess who's going to be all bloated and pukey during her wedding?"

That was exactly what Ellison needed to hear, and she grinned. "And how will she make it through all those nights without alcohol when he's traveling?" Ellison had heard Jenn had quit her job. Presumably because of the work conflict, but most likely because she wanted to be a stay-at-home mom. Ellison had also heard - from her other friend Eve - that Jenn liked her wine.

"May hellish morning sickness rain down on Jennifer Cartwright," Andi said, taking the cap off a bottle of vodka and swigging from it before passing it to Ellison. Ellison declined. "What, no pre-game?"

"I thought you were my driver tonight?"

Andi put the cap back on. "Right. I get to be reliable Andrea tonight. How boring."

Ellison wrapped her arm around her best friend. "Tell me I look hot."

"You look hot. I love the boots," Andi said. Ellison lifted a leg in the air so her friend could get a better look at her olive green, suede boots. Andi whistled. "Definitely hot."

"C'mon," Ellison answered. "Let's go before we end up here all night having a love fest with my vodka bottle."

Buy ALL THE BROKEN PIECES now

.